God's Horse *and* The Atheists' School

god's horse and the atheists' school

wilhelm dichter

Translated from the Polish by Madeline G. Levine

NORTHWESTERN UNIVERSITY PRESS

EVANSTON, ILLINOIS

Northwestern University Press
www.nupress.northwestern.edu

INSTYTUT KSIĄŻKI

© POLAND

This book has been funded by the Book Institute © POLAND Translation Program.

The epigraph to *The Atheists' School* was translated by Stanisław Barańczak and Clare Cavanagh and appears in *Polish Poetry of the Last Two Decades of Communist Rule: Spoiling Cannibals' Fun* (Northwestern University Press, 1991).

Printed in the United States of America

10   9   8   7   6   5   4   3   2   1

Library of Congress Cataloging-in-Publication Data

Dichter, Wilhelm, 1935–
    [Koń Pana Boga. English]
    God's horse ; and, The atheists' school / Wilhelm Dichter ; translated from the Polish by Madeline G. Levine.
        p. cm.
    "God's Horse originally published in Polish by Znak (Krakow) under the title Kon Pana Boga, copyright (c) 1996 by Wilhelm Dichter. The Atheists' School originally published in Polish by Znak (Krakow) under the title Szkoła bezbożników, copyright © 1999 by Wilhelm Dichter."
    ISBN 978-0-8101-2793-7 (pbk. : alk. paper)
    1. Dichter, Wilhelm, 1935– —Fiction. I. Levine, Madeline G. II. Dichter, Wilhelm, 1935– Szkoła bezbożników. III. Title. IV. Title: Szkoła bezbożników.
PG7399.D5K6613 2012
891.8537—dc23

contents

God's Horse

God's Horse

For Olga Toporowska-Dichter

and Antoni Liber

before everything

Polish Times

My grandparents lived with Milo and Nusia in Wolanka, at the northern end of Borysław. The entrance to their house was in the back, through the courtyard. There was a doghouse there and a tree. The dog ran back and forth, tied to a chain that was stretched between the house and the tree. His name was Fox.

Mother would drag me by the hand up a couple of wooden steps to the veranda and open the door to the kitchen. Everything here was in its proper place. Grandmother Antonina was short and somewhat prickly. She was always carefully attired in a black dress. She had black hair and black eyes, like Mother and me. To everyone except me, she spoke in German.

In the living room, in a wicker étagère, there was a multivolume German dictionary bound in green leather. Its smooth, cold pages were covered with Gothic letters. I turned them slowly, looking for photographs and pictures. German airmen in a rope gondola suspended from a zeppelin fired at airplanes with colorful circles on their wings. Squeezing the handgrips of their machine guns, they leaned out precariously. I was afraid they would fall out of the gondola into the dark night sliced by the beams of searchlights.

On the wall beside the étagère hung Grandmother's mandolin and a photograph of Grandfather in his Austrian uniform, with a medal and a saber.

Grandmother grew up in Vienna. I didn't know what she did before she met Grandfather, because they were already singing Strauss waltzes together in her oldest reminiscences. They adored opera; leaning out of the third balcony, they listened to Mozart's arias reaching them from the deep well of the stage. They also went to the Prater amusement park where they rode in a little carriage fastened to the great Riesenrad Ferris wheel and looked down on a city where Jews were happy. "The Danube flowed with milk and honey," Grandmother used to tell us later.

Milo was born right after the wedding. And when Grandmother was pregnant with Andzia, the war broke out and the men were conscripted and sent to the front. Grandfather became a feldsher in the artillery. Grandmother thanked God that cannons are stationed well toward the rear. Soon, however, the Russian offensive overran Galicia. Fearing pogroms, Jews fled to Vienna from their small towns. The Russians sprayed the retreating Austrian artillery with shrapnel. Grandfather was wounded and received a medal. When Grandmother complained in the field hospital that Germans are too delicate to take on "those Russian savages," Grandfather comforted her.

"Culture will triumph over everything," he said.

One day, the Kaiser died. Silent people stood on both sides of an enormous street. Grandmother, holding Milo's hand, managed to squeeze through the crowd to the roadway. Black horses with mourning plumes pulled the gilded hearse. Hussars rode behind it in their parade-uniform armor. Standards waved above their bowed heads. Behind the troops came carriages with dignitaries and ladies dressed in tulle. The procession was heading toward the grotto where the Habsburgs are buried. A grave carved into the stone awaited them there.

After the war a general strike broke out and the empire collapsed. Men without arms and legs sat on the sidewalks, and before them lay military caps turned upside down. No one tossed them any coins. There was no work.

My grandparents moved from Vienna to Borysław where Grandfather's family lived. After a long journey they carried their bundles out onto the platform and placed them under the Polish flag that had been hung there only recently.

Grandfather, who could count perfectly and had beautiful penmanship, became a bookkeeper in a petroleum firm that was owned by French businessmen. He earned a good salary. Grandmother helped his sisters, who could barely make ends meet. She would slip money into their hands, and before holidays she sent Milo and Andzia to them with baskets of food. She altered her own coat for her sister-in-law, whose father had lost everything at cards.

"She is seventeen and has to look nice," she told Andzia, who was crying from jealousy. "You still have time."

At this time a second daughter was born, but she didn't live long. Grandmother couldn't get over her grief. And although soon Nusia came into the world, Grandmother kept thinking about her little dead daughter and crying.

—

Several years passed and Grandfather decided to start his own business. He handed in his resignation and opened a hardware store in Wolanka. Hammers, door locks, oil lamps, and spray devices against cockroaches appeared on the shelves, purchased with money he borrowed from the bank. The final hour struck for the old hardware store across the street. But the Depression came and people stopped buying. The old shopkeeper remained in his usual stupor, and Grandfather went bankrupt. Fortunately, the French took him back. He scrupulously paid off his debts. Right before the outbreak of the new war, he redeemed the last IOU.

—

Grandfather's hair was gray, he clipped his moustache short, and he wore wire-frame eyeglasses. He wore snowy white shirts with stiff collars. Before leaving the house (he enjoyed going to the café) he would pull a flannel rag out of his pocket and wipe his shoes, which gleamed like mirrors. Then he would brush any bits of dust off the lapels of his suit jacket and open the door. The women of the house treated him with respect.

—

Milo took violin lessons. Andzia tagged after him. Grandfather had ordered her to watch over her brother. As they approached the Fotoplastikon, Milo took out of his pocket the coins that were meant for his teacher and ran over to the ticket booth.

"I'll tell Papa," Andzia yelled, racing after him. They rested the violin against a wooden wall with brass eyepieces behind which the photo carousel was located. Every so often a motor would rumble. The carousel would rotate a few degrees and stop with a screech. New, three-dimensional photographs appeared in the eyepieces. At first, Andzia pretended that she wasn't looking, but soon she opened her eyes wide. An asphalt road went right through a gigantic California redwood. A Ford, its driver leaning against it, was parked in the rectangular opening carved in the tree.

—

One day, Grandfather happened to meet the music teacher in a café and Milo got a whipping. The next day, at breakfast, Grandfather pushed aside his coffee cup and addressed his son, who resembled the artillery man with a medal and a saber in one of the photographs.

"In Poland, everything is closed to Jews except business, the law, and medicine," Grandfather said. "You don't have a head for business. The law isn't a profession. You will become a doctor."

—

Milo and his friends—Jews, Poles, and Ukrainians—either fought with each other until they drew blood or banded together and made other people's lives miserable. Once, during a lecture about ancient Rome, they let loose frogs in the classroom.

"Samuel Mandel! You are getting an Unsatisfactory in conduct!" the history teacher shouted.

Grandfather's pleas were to no avail. Milo had to repeat the year. When he finally graduated, Jews were no longer being admitted to medical school. He went abroad to Prague to study. Soon, however, there wasn't enough money and he had to return to Borysław.

Here, unemployment and boredom were rampant.

At the graduation dance the band struck up a waltz. Andzia glanced at the parquet floor and noticed a tall blond man walking toward her. She stopped flirting with her male friends. When he asked her to dance she held out her damp hand. At first she only looked at the yellow tie that hung between the lapels of his jacket, but finally she raised her head and saw his large green eyes.

"I had never met anyone as handsome as your papa," she told me later.

When they returned to Wolanka after the dance snow was falling in large flakes. She was wearing her navy blue Gymnasium uniform coat and he wore a jacket with a beaver collar and a visored cap. He inquired if she would go to the mountains with him someday by sleigh. She answered that she would have to ask her father. They said goodbye in the doorway just like in the movies.

In the house, Grandfather slapped her face. Why was she going out with a goy?

"Bronisław is a Jew!" she shrieked.

Grandfather didn't believe her. After all, he had seen him with his own eyes through the window. Besides which, Jews are not named Bronisław.

"They are, they are," Mother wept.

Bronek Rabinowicz was five years older than Andzia. He worked in the largest petroleum firm in the city, earned three times as much as Grandfather, and was addressed as "Panie Inżynierze," Mr. Engineer. Having checked all this out, Grandfather allowed Andzia to invite him home. The guest was charming. He looked like Gary Cooper. The older Mandel daughter had won the lottery.

They started going out to dances. While waiting for Bronek, Andzia would look at herself in the mirror. Milo made faces and sang, "Miss Andzia has a date; she's all dressed up like a fashion plate."

In February 1935 they went by sleigh to their wedding. After the wedding they settled on Pańska Street in the center of Borysław. Their one-story house was set back in the courtyard. To the left of the entrance hall were the kitchen and a maid's room. To the right was a series of white rooms, one after the other: a dining room, a living room, and a bedroom from which you could see the police station across the street.

I was born nine months later. I would fall asleep sated and secure in the moist warmth of my wet nurse. They would park me in front of the house in my baby carriage. My father's enormous Saint Bernard warmed himself in the sunshine beside me. The wet nurse and the maid kept an eye on us through the window. Mother would lean over me, blocking the sun.

Then the wet nurse disappeared and soon I no longer remembered that she existed.

Mother read me children's books about Andzia who "didn't obey her mother, pricked her finger and cried"; about Hania who didn't eat and was swept away by the wind, along with her balloon; and about Cesia who told lies and whose fingers were snipped off by a "cruelly wicked tailor." She also set out blocks with fragments of pictures glued on them. Cows on a green meadow emerged from them, and houses. Without her, I turned the blocks over but could make no sense of them; I liked them anyway because they were big and heavy.

Before I could walk I used to try to get under my parents' big bed, which was covered with a brocade bedspread. I was curious about what was under there. I would crawl under the bedspread and Mother would pull me out by my legs.

Mother liked to go for strolls, holding her husband's arm. Father pushed the baby carriage with its sparkling chrome and sky-blue oilcloth sides. The white rubber wheels bounced over the paving stones. I sat facing them, my back to the direction of travel. They would laugh and blow me kisses. There were sidewalks on Pańska Street, streetlights and shops. We would stop frequently, because my parents kept running into their friends.

When I was a year old, Father contracted tuberculosis. In short order, he was a dying man. Mother took him to the pulmonary hospital in Lwów. (That was the first time she traveled by the luxury express train.) They injected air into Father's chest cavity, but it didn't help. After the second such treatment he was sent to the mountains, to a sanatorium in Worochta.

I didn't even notice that he had disappeared.

Grandfather came to see us often and would scratch the Saint Bernard behind its ears.

"Is Bronek going to get well?" Mother asked him.

Grandfather was unable to give her an answer.

"God!" she wept. "What have I done to you that you are punishing me so?"

"Sell the apartment," Grandfather advised her.

"I'll give away the dog and let the maid go."

"And then?"

"Bronek will come home."

I was sitting in my high chair and crying. Mother was shoveling heaping teaspoons of food into my mouth and semolina and puréed lamb were running down my bib. I began spitting it out. She slapped me.

"Don't hit the child!" Grandfather shouted.

"He'll get sick if he doesn't eat."

Grandfather picked me up. He placed his dry, warm hand on my face. As I drifted off to sleep, I felt Mother take me into her arms.

Father came back a year later. I didn't know who that thin blond man was whom Mother wouldn't let hold me. But she preferred him to me, because she never yelled at him and she laughed when he wanted something from her.

A new maid appeared.

I watched from my high chair as Father, wearing a vest with a satin back, laid out cards for a game of solitaire. The kings and queens were the most important; the rows began with them. Mother came in from the kitchen, carrying a frying pan with an omelet sprinkled with chives. I didn't want to eat it and I pressed my lips together. She threw the contents of the pan onto my head. I howled. Father flung down the cards and grabbed Mother's hands. The pan fell onto the carpet. Mother wanted to clean the carpet, but he held her firmly.

"Andzia, he's a little boy," he said in a low voice.

She burst into tears. "I want him to be healthy."

On Thursdays, Father's friends came to play poker. At first, Mother turned up her nose at this, but later she learned how to play.

"I'll take three cards. Will there be a war or not?"

"Two for me. The Germans will have their butts kicked."

"I don't want any. The English will bomb Berlin."

"Five złotys and another five. The French will advance to the Ruhr."

"They'll invade us through Romania."

"We have enough soldiers. Ten, and show me what you have."

Father's wealthy uncle, Pan Unter, who was the head of an orphanage for Jewish children, lived in Drohobycz (to which one traveled by horse-drawn coach or by train). They brought me there from the hospital after my tonsils were removed. I cried, because before the operation they had promised me as much ice cream as I wanted, and all I got was a tiny bit on the tip of a teaspoon.

Pan Unter had three children: Julek, Teresa, and blind Maciek, who made brushes. When Teresa fell in love with Milo, Pan Unter sent her and Julek to medical school in Italy.

Russian Times

Before Yom Kippur, while the Lord was inscribing names into the books of life and death, Germans on motorcycles rode into the police station yard. Laughing gaily, they jumped down from their saddles and crawled out of their sidecars to which machine guns with little handgrips were affixed. They washed up at the well pump and brushed their teeth, spitting out white foam.

After their departure we listened intently for the roar of motors to start up again. There was silence for a long time. Finally, on Yom Kippur itself, there was the clatter of hooves on the sidewalks. Cossacks came riding in, avoiding the streets that were paved with cobblestones. They glanced into our courtyard and withdrew to the police station.

After them came soldiers with red stars on their peaked caps, and civilians wearing military-looking uniforms, who gave speeches at public meetings.

In the movie theater, Russia's annexation of Galicia was hailed. People carrying red banners walked through the streets. Loudspeakers broadcast a song about three members of a tank crew and four samurais. The Russians bought up everything that was in the shops. There were lines even for salt and matches.

Pańska Street—the Street of Landlords—became Stalin Street. (But everyone still called it Pańska.) The police station was taken over by the NKVD. People were arrested at night. Truck motors roared in the yard in order to drown out the screams and shots.

Father stood near the window in the dark bedroom, looking at the building across the street.

⸺

The postman brought a *bumaga,* a sheet of paper, from which it emerged that the apartment on Pańska was too large for us. To keep strangers from moving in, my grandparents sold their house and moved into ours. Porters with yarmulkes on their heads moved their bed and chest of drawers from Wolanka into our living room. Grandmother brought her mandolin and the photograph of Grandfather with his medal and sword. My grandparents' furniture was everywhere. Their tall wardrobe with the double doors was in the maid's room. The dictionary was placed on top of it.

The oil companies were nationalized and combined into a single trust. Even the alphabet changed. Grandfather continued to write in the ledgers, however, because numbers had remained the same. He hated the Russian bookkeepers.

"Those thieves! They give you one ruble in exchange for a złoty!"

On Friday evening, when the first star appeared Grandmother closed the window in the dining room and lowered the blinds. After throwing a scarf over her head, she lit the candles in the silver candlesticks and moved her hands over them as though she wished to caress the flames. My parents' wedding china was on the table. The soup plates had gold designs that looked like treble clefs. The serving dish held boiled potatoes. In the wicker basket there was black bread for Father and Milo. We had the impression that someone was walking back and forth outside the window.

"They're supposed to like Jews," Grandfather whispered, "but it's illegal to bake matzoh."

"It's worse on the other side of the Bug under the Germans," said Father.

"Maybe the Germans will come to their senses."

"Papa! How can you say that?"

The dining room smelled of Virginia tobacco. Grandfather took a pinch from a tin can and sniffed it for a long time. Then he sprinkled it into an open brass cylinder, smoothed it with his finger, and closed the cylinder. A box of paper tubes lay next to the can. Grandfather took one out and, holding it by its cardboard mouthpiece, slipped the cylinder into the empty paper tube. He pushed the tobacco out with a little metal plunger and out popped a cigarette onto the table.

At the other end of the table, Father was looking at a red flush. His game of solitaire hadn't worked out. He collected the cards and started shuffling them.

"We're almost out of tobacco," said Grandfather. "What now?"

"Coarse Russian *machorka*," Father laughed.

Nusia slept in the maid's room. She was pretty and had large green eyes. In the morning, while she ate breakfast, boys waited in the courtyard to carry her briefcase to the Gymnasium for her.

Grandfather glanced out the window.

"All goyim!" he said, agitated. "Aren't there any Jews in Borysław?"

"The school is for everyone."

"Illiterates! Now they've invented a ten-year school!"

—

Nusia was rushing to get ready for the assembly. Dressed in an embroidered Ukrainian blouse and long skirt, she pulled on soft red boots. Then she grabbed a white fringed kerchief that Grandmother had just ironed and ran off to school to dance the kozak.

—

Kopcio, who conducted a dance band at night, was in love with Nusia. (He lived in Lower Wolanka, where the poor Jews lived.) Grandfather gave her permission to invite him home. Grandmother served him tea in the dining room. Kopcio fiddled with a packet of Egyptian cigarettes, turning it over in his yellow, nicotine-stained fingers. Out of consideration for Father, however, who was laying out a game of solitaire, he did not smoke.

"How do you support yourself?" Grandfather drummed his fingers on the empty can of Virginia tobacco.

"By playing at dances."

"That is not a profession."

"People dance," said Father.

"Don't interfere," Mother whispered. "He's attached to her like a leech."

—

One day, Mother took me to preschool. It was a world of lost checkers, one-eyed teddy bears, and cars without wheels. The ball was locked up in a closet. They were constantly counting the spoons and forks. When we napped on the floor, tired out from playing, some children had pillows and others had blankets. Portraits of people with peculiar names hung over us. Marx resembled old Pan Bernstein, who had caught a thief once in his younger days and still grew heated when talking about it. ("He thought he'd get away from me! The bastard!") Engels, in a pince-nez, was looking at a bald Lenin. Stalin had a moustache, but he didn't have a beard. We spoke Russian in preschool, even though the teachers didn't know the language. On the first of May I recited:

> Lenin, dear Lenin,
> In the earth you lie forlorn,
> But when I grow up
> Your Party I'll join.

Pan Bernstein's grandson Marek was my friend from our courtyard. Mother said he was a scamp because he played outside all day long and came home only when he got hungry. I ran after him and imitated him in everything. A tall wooden fence separated our courtyard from the other courtyards that opened onto Pańska Street. We would walk the length of the fence back to where the meadows began. There were oil-well pumps out there that looked like peasant girls with large heads, and drilling towers made of three wooden supports pounded into the ground and connected to each other at the top. Marek would stand beside the fence, hitch up one of his shorts legs, and bend over backward. An amber stream of urine would sail across the fence. Wanting to be just like him, I also leaned backward as best I could. My stream would fly upward at too steep an angle, and sometimes it fell back on me like rain.

Milo and Julek Unter did not return to Italy after their vacation in Poland. They completed their medical training in Lwów. Milo married Teresa and brought her to Pańska Street. Romuś was born there. The short little man who circumcised him had a funny smile as he carried a tray with a bottle of alcohol and a piece of bloody cotton.

Through the open doors of the living room I could see the backs of people bending over the cradle. Laughter drowned out the baby's cries. Grandfather appeared from the kitchen. I grabbed him by the trousers. He patted my head and walked past me. I remained alone in the dining room.

In the summer, the Russians mobilized all doctors. Milo came home in a captain's uniform, wearing knee-high soft leather boots. His straps creaked. Teresa cried and her tears fell on Romuś, whom she was cradling in her arms.

"See, Papa," Milo said, "I'm an officer."

"Yes, but under whom!" Grandfather retorted.

I was standing with my father in my parents' bedroom, looking out at the street. The sky was streaked with black smoke from the burning oil wells. Lines of soldiers filed down the street, fleeing into the Russian heartland. Milo and Julek were leaving with them. Suddenly, the sky was torn apart by a brilliant flash, followed by a deafening roar. Father grabbed my arm. We were hurled to the back of the room. That was the Russians blowing up the electric power plant to prevent its falling into the hands of the Germans.

under the bed in Borysław

On Pańska Street

On the day the Germans invaded, soon after Father left for work we heard screaming on Pańska Street. Through the window of my parents' bedroom we could see Jews being beaten with clubs in the courtyard of the police station. People carrying axes ran into our courtyard and started hammering on the door. Grandfather opened the lock with a big iron key. They grabbed him and Mother, too, who was standing behind him. Teresa, with Romuś in her arms, slammed the door shut and pulled down the blinds in the windows.

Mother came back wet and terrified. Piles of corpses had been found in the cellars of the NKVD. They had jammed a bucket onto her head and ordered her to use her blouse as a rag.

A woman spat in her face. "Wash the people you murdered!" she shrieked.

A Ukrainian policeman who had attended Gymnasium with Nusia saw Mother on the stairs leading to the cellar. He escorted her from the basement to the street. She had no information about Grandfather.

Grandmother, Teresa, and Nusia covered their ears with their hands in order to muffle the groans and screams. My puppet, with its key unwound in its back, lay on the floor in the corner of the room, watching the door.

Two days later things began to quiet down. I saw Grandfather in the open door. He was breathing heavily, as if after a long run. Blood from his split forehead had congealed on his filthy, sweaty face. His eyeglass lenses were shattered. He stood there in his stained vest over his naked chest, supporting himself against the door frame with his bare arms. He stank of something unfamiliar and terrifying. Slowly, his knees gave way under him. Mother and Nusia ran to help him. The door was locked. His clothes were removed over a large basin of water placed in the middle of the room. When they pulled down his trousers, which were soaked with carbolic acid, he screamed from the pain. I saw that his buttocks were red.

Father came back after the pogrom. He sat down beside Grandfather, who was lying down with a towel on his backside.

"It's the Ukrainians," Grandfather said. "They would have sliced us into pieces with their knives. The Germans need people to work for them. Summonses have already come from the Arbeitsamt. We only have to convince them that we are loyal and harmless."

I must have fallen asleep, because I didn't notice when Grandfather put on his Austrian uniform with the medal and the saber. He stroked my cheek and said, "Speak German, and no one will recognize you."

"I don't know German!"

"It's easy," he chuckled. "Say first what you ought to say last."

The confiscations began. First radios, watches, and jewelry. Father had a Philips radio with a round face plate; he used to press his ear against its cloth speaker. The radio kept bringing bad news. The Germans were halfway to Moscow. We didn't know what had happened to Milo.

"He's a doctor," Grandfather said. "The Russians protect doctors."

"He'll kill me if something should happen to Romuś," Teresa wept.

Father dumped the radio and the watches into a sack and took them to the Jewish Council. Mother hid the jewelry.

There were marks on the grown-ups' hands from where their rings had been.

Then came furs. Mother's chinchilla coat hung in my parents' bedroom. Whenever she opened the wardrobe I would always stand next to her, ready to touch the fur.

"You can stroke it," she would say. "It's beautiful, isn't it?"

Now Grandfather brought up two suitcases from the cellar. He put the chinchilla coat and his own fur-lined coat into one of them, and the beaver collar that he ripped off Father's jacket into the other, along with a fox with glass eyes who held his own tail in his teeth, warm muffs, and leather gloves. Mother began to cry and to curse the Germans.

"There's nothing to cry about," Grandfather said. "We'll buy it all back someday."

And he walked out with the suitcases while Father watched, too weak to help.

Finally, the furniture. Before the war, Mother had won four thousand złotys in the lottery. She used half the money to take her sister, Milo, and Teresa on a vacation to Truskawiec. (Evenings in Truskawiec were warm. The fragrance of fruit trees drifted in through the windows of the boarding house. Milo told a story about a woman whose head had to be shaved because a bat had gotten entangled in her hair. The women squealed, but

I was happy that I had short hair.) With the rest of the money Mother bought walnut furniture for the bedroom: a bed with a curved headboard, two night tables, and the wardrobe in which the chinchilla coat hung.

The German who came with a member of the Jewish Council liked my parents' bedroom set. Opening the window, he ran his hand over the polished grain of the walnut wood.

"I'll send a cart and horses tomorrow," he said.

And he left with the Jew who accompanied him.

—

At night I was awakened by screams from my parents' bedroom. I pushed open the big white door and peeked inside.

"If I can't have it, they won't have it either."

Mother was brandishing scissors.

"Idiot! They'll kill us!" Grandfather shook his fist at her.

"Calm down, Papa," Father said, and took the scissors away from Mother.

She pressed her face into his sweater and he bent down and kissed her hair. Grandfather and Father spent all night repairing the bed where it had been scored with the scissors. In the morning Jewish porters loaded the furniture onto a cart and drove off.

—

Peasant wagons began circling in Borysław. A married couple would be seated on the coachman's bench. The husband would stop the horses, climb down with his crop in his hand, and knock at a door. If someone answered, he'd call his wife, and if not, he'd climb up again, take the reins, and drive on. First, they said hello. Stroking the children's heads, the woman would say that God would not allow them to be harmed. At that, the formalities ended. It was possible to buy anything for potatoes and bread.

A peasant picked up one of the dictionary volumes from the floor.

"What's this?" He peered at the Gothic letters. "A holy book?"

"German writing," Grandfather said.

"So the Germans are Jews, too!" the wife marveled.

"What will you take for this?" asked the peasant.

"A loaf of bread."

—

Stalin Street became Hitler Street. (But everyone still called it Pańska.) Mounted police moved into the well-scrubbed NKVD building. Pushing back the curtains in my parents' empty bedroom, I could see the soldiers in their green trousers and white undershirts. They brushed their teeth just as the motorcyclists had done before them. Cold water splashed out of the iron pump over the stone well. They dipped their heads into it and jumped back, snorting with laughter. Mother ordered me to get away from the window. She installed black paper shades and pulled them all the way down. It became dark and stuffy.

Soon, soldiers in green uniforms came to see us. They were Austrians and were pleased with our women's Viennese accent. Grandmother showed them the photograph of Grandfather with his medal and saber.

"My husband also fought against the Russians."

They bent over in order to get a better look at the medal. One of them liked Romuś's yellow curls and blue eyes.

"Where is his father?" he asked.

"He's dead," Teresa said.

"*Er ist gestorben,*" Grandmother translated.

The soldier took a piece of chocolate out of his pocket and gave it to Romuś.

"And what would you do if they ordered you to shoot him?" Mother asked.

"*Befehl ist Befehl.* An order's an order."

One day as they were leaving they said, "If something should happen, we'll post a guard outside your door."

The *Aktion* after the pogrom took everyone by surprise. Suddenly, German soldiers in black uniforms appeared in the streets. The exits from the courtyard were blocked by Polish and Ukrainian policemen. Jewish police in old military caps minus the eagle broke into the apartments. They led out the women, children, and old people. They were driven out of the courtyard into Pańska Street. The crowd, surrounded by Germans, walked down the roadway toward the slaughterhouse and the railroad station. Another crowd, on the sidewalks, stood and watched. Children, whose games had been interrupted by the *Aktion,* pointed their fingers at the fleeing Jews.

Hiding in the cellar, we could hear screams and conversations through cracks in the coal chute. Only Grandmother wasn't with us. Seeing how crowded it was in the cellar, she had hidden at our neighbor's house on the other side of the courtyard. A mounted police guard stood outside our door.

Our drunken neighbor, Pan Kruk, came stumbling over.

"Jews! Crawl out!" he shouted.

The Austrians burst out laughing.

On the second night, the bucket we were using as a toilet started over-flowing. There was nothing left to drink. In the morning soldiers' boots rang out, entering our house. They lifted the hatch to the cellar.

"Come out!" they called. "The *Aktion's* over."

When Nusia ran over to the other side of the courtyard, the Austrian who liked Romuś said to Mother, "They took them all away. That Kruk betrayed them."

We were alone. Grandfather sat on a chair, resting his hands on Mother's head as she knelt before him. Nusia was lying on the floor. Father sat down beside her, his long legs folded under him.

"Maybe a letter will come . . . ," he said softly.

"They'll kill her," Nusia wept.

"They'll kill everyone," said Teresa.

—

Marek Bernstein and his grandfather were also taken away. I heard about freight cars stuffed with the living and the dead. I had seen such freight cars already during the Russian times. Cows had looked out at us through open doors. Now it was people riding in those cars, relieving themselves where they stood. Children slipped onto the floor and suffocated under the feet of the grown-ups. Railroad workers told stories about a camp in Bełżec that was as large as a city. The train rode straight into its center. People were undressed and herded into the baths. But there was gas instead of water in the bathhouse. The corpses were burned on iron grates. The freight cars were washed with streams of water.

"Jews leave only by the chimney," the railroad men said.

—

The Jewish orphanage in Drohobycz had its own vocational school. The orphans, unable to count on anything better, acquired a trade there for the rest of their lives. Maciek had learned how to make brushes. Pan Unter, convinced that the Germans would definitely round up the crippled children from the orphanage, hid Maciek in the countryside in order to save him from a selection.

While the *Aktion* was under way in Borysław, in the courtyard of the orphanage, which was enclosed within an iron fence, they herded the children and the teachers together with their families. The Jewish police formed them into a column. An officer leaned out of a truck filled with soldiers in black uniforms that was parked outside the gate and waved his hand.

"Forward!" the policemen shouted.

The column passed the gate and set off in the direction of the railroad station. The truck followed it slowly. They walked silently, carrying the sick and the crippled in their arms. On a spur line in the meadows, at quite a distance from the station, freight cars were waiting, their doors wide open. The children, who were at the head of the procession, came to a halt in front of them, too short to reach the boxcar floors above their heads. The police began yelling and beating people with sticks. The older boys tried to escape, but they were driven back into the crowd with blows. Everyone climbed into the boxcars in a panic. Bigger people threw in smaller people. When the policemen finished their job the Germans jumped out of their truck and shoved the policemen inside, too. Then they slid the doors shut and wound wire around the locks. A locomotive drove up and slammed noisily into the buffers. The railway men attached the chains. Clouds of white steam escaped from under the wheels and the train began to move.

—

The Austrians wept before leaving for the front. The Jewish Council announced that a ghetto had arisen in the vicinity of the street on which Kopcio lived. On Pańska Street, our mattresses and pillows lay on the floor in rooms without furniture, next to cold tile stoves. Empty hooks protruded from the pantry walls.

A peasant brought Maciek to us, concealed under the hay in his wagon. He sat on the floor, his hair as yellow as straw, his hands resting on his knees. When Teresa spoke to him, he smiled, but he didn't lift his head.

Nusia was lying on her pallet, her face to the wall. She was praying that her mother would take her to be with her. She got up only when Kopcio arrived.

"Don't go to the ghetto," he said. "It's a trap! Come with me. I have a place where no one will find us."

"Without Papa and Andzia?"

"I love you."

—

In the evening, a man and woman came to look at Romuś. Grandfather praised his grandson as Teresa held him in her arms. He looks perfect. He'll be invisible among their own six children. Fortunately, he can't talk yet. The man insisted that a girl would be better. But he took the money. Grandfather took an ampule out of his pocket and broke off its cap. Then he stretched out his handkerchief and sprinkled the liquid from the ampule on it. He approached Romuś and placed the handkerchief on his face. I smelled a strange, sweet odor. Romuś stopped babbling. Grandfather took him from Teresa and handed him to the strange woman.

"If we should perish," he said, "my son, Dr. Samuel Mandel, will come for him."

—

Father developed a fever. His eyes were red and he had a rash on his cheeks. He was breathing rapidly through his mouth. When he coughed, he lurched forward and clutched at his shirt. Then he would spit into a jar and rest for a long time, with his head down.

"It's the end, Andzia. It's the same as before the pneumothorax."

"Children," Grandfather said, "in the ghetto they'll feed us."

I wanted to know where they had taken Romuś. I tugged at Mother's sleeves, but she paid no attention to me. I went over to Father.

"Don't get close to Papa!" Mother yelled.

"Step back," said Father.

It was past noon. I was drinking water from a tin cup. Suddenly someone pounded on the door with his fists and shouted, "*Aktion!*"

Mother grabbed me by the hand and dashed out of the house. Nusia followed us. We ran alongside the fence to the end of the courtyard, then across the meadow toward the stream. The ground was soaking wet. The grass sparkled with water. Our feet sank into it softly and made a gurgling sound as we lifted them. Mother's shoe got sucked into the mud. She didn't stop.

"Andzia, your shoe!"

Nusia turned around. "Oh, God! A German!"

A German on horseback was on the hill, shooting at us with his revolver. We sped along the rocks in the stream. My feet flailed in the air as Mother jumped from one rock to another. Our courtyard disappeared; so did the German.

"Mama, I can't go any farther. I don't want to live."

We slowed down only when it began to grow dark. Mother let go of my hand and straightened her fingers with difficulty. Covered in dried mud, we dragged ourselves over to some apartment blocks with rough brick walls. Shivering from the cold, we walked up to the wall in order to make out the number on the stairwell. Nusia knocked on the door.

"Who's there?"

"The Mandel girls. Andzia and Nusia."

A young woman opened the door; there was a man standing behind her.

"My God!" she screamed.

Under the Bed

The people to whom we fled had one room and a kitchen on the ground floor. During the day Mother and Nusia sat in the corner and I lay under the bed. There was a chamber pot next to me. To relieve myself, I turned onto my stomach and slid it under me. Mother and Nusia would crawl over to the bed and take the chamber pot to their corner. At night, the husband brought in a bucket, opened the window, and left us alone for a while. Then he dumped out the bucket in the latrine, which was a communal one for several apartments. We slept on the floor, and the husband and wife slept in the bed.

Soon, a letter arrived from Grandfather. As she read it, Mother whispered to Nusia, "They separated them. They took Papa, Bronek, and Teresa to the ghetto. They took Maciek to the slaughterhouse. Papa has seen Tytus's father. You're to go to them at night."

During the Russian times I had often seen Tytus through the window while we ate breakfast. His father was hiding from the Russians then, and their family had gathered at their house from various places in Poland. Grandfather would reminisce respectfully about how Engineer Tabaczyński used to ride to work on horseback before the war, but he did not allow Tytus into our apartment. Only after the pogrom, when Tytus had come running to check on Nusia, did Grandfather (lying under a towel in the living room) call him over.

"Please give my respects to your father," he said.

Several days after Nusia left, Father came to fetch us. We went out into the street in the middle of the night. We sped along, hugging the walls. After a while, the sidewalk came to an end and trees without leaves appeared. Far back from the street were cottages surrounded by fences. Between them were black-looking meadows. There were no stars, nor was the moon out. Mother held on to his arm and pulled me along behind her.

"What's happened with Nusia?"

"Kopcio took her to stay with him."

Janka Leń lived with her father in a small cottage in a secluded area. Her father worked as an outside laborer for the same firm as Grandfather. He would come home late, pull off his oil-soaked clothing, and wash himself for a long time in the basin. Janka would pour water from a jug over his head and hands. Then he'd put on a fresh shirt and trousers, and on his bare feet slippers without heels. While he ate his dinner he told his daughter what he had seen that day. Then he slowly rolled a cigarette and began smoking. He slept in a little room that was accessed through Janka's bedroom.

Janka was an old maid. She had a sweet face, moist lips, and eyes brimming with sympathy. With every step she took she leaned slightly to the right because one of her legs was shorter than the other; it hadn't grown properly after she contracted tuberculosis of the bones. She had warm hands. She spoke slowly and calmly.

"You have to pray in order to move the good Lord's heart, and who can do that better than a child? Don't cry because you're alone. Your papa is sick and Mommy has to be with him. You're safe here. We have potatoes. My papa knows Pan Mandel and can't praise him enough. You will be a man like that, too, one day."

I listened to Janka from under the bed in her bedroom. When she limped back to the kitchen and carefully locked the door behind her, I saw her feet. I was like a mouse. Invisible myself, I observed everyone who entered the room. I would turn over slowly, from one side to the other, so the floor wouldn't creak. Freshly scrubbed, it smelled like soup. That smell lingered for a long time, especially in the cracks between the boards. Hunger made me press my nose against the floor and inhale.

Any sound could betray me, especially if there was a stranger in the kitchen. I would grow sleepy from boredom, but I was afraid to fall asleep, because Mother had told me that I groaned in my sleep. When my eyelids grew heavy I opened them with my fingers and, turning onto my back, I looked at the boards on top of which lay a straw-stuffed mattress. I thought about the people who had died or were in hiding. I was reminded of a lullaby that Nusia used to sing to me.

> Wonderful legends, miraculous legends
> My gray-haired nurse would tell me.
> About a fierce dragon, a sleeping princess,
> and a host of knights at war.
> And when she stopped, I'd tearfully beg her,
> "Nurse, tell me more, tell me more."

I was most afraid of children. I was convinced that they would recognize me instantly in the street and hand me over to the Germans. Grownups might take pity on me, but not children. I dreamed that I was running away from them. I was running blindly, farther and farther, until I stopped because I didn't know what to do next. In the shadows under the bed I saw my thin legs in white socks. I slowly lost the ability to walk. During the day I heard the sounds of birds outside the window. Their voices didn't mean anything. I was indifferent to them. I was waiting for the voices of the people who would come to get me.

Grandfather, Father, and Teresa were in the ghetto. They were crowded in together on Potok Street in Pan Skiba's room, while he was now living in our place on Pańska Street. Grandfather worked for the Germans as a bookkeeper. But I didn't know what Father and Teresa did. Mother was here and there. She would rush over to the ghetto to be with Father and run away again, out of fear of an *Aktion.* When she was in our hideout she lay next to me on the floor and talked with Janka, who leaned down from her bed. She told her how Father had fallen ill just as I was beginning to walk, and how he'd gotten healthy and ate spinach and eggs.

"I remember him," Janka said. "Such a handsome man!"

"Now the pneumothorax has opened up again from hunger."

Grandfather came to make regular payments. Janka's father welcomed him in the kitchen and, once he'd counted the money, he'd take a bottle and two shot glasses out of the credenza.

"Money is worth shit," he'd complain.

"*L'chaim!* To life!"

Then we sat on the bed. I was most interested in what Grandfather had to say about children. There weren't any left in the ghetto by now. The healthy ones were taken away. A gigantic German came to the hospital to get the sick ones. He ordered a nurse to pick them up and killed them, one after the other, with a shot from his pistol. He shot the nurse last. A mother who was hiding in a garret smothered her infant when he started crying.

I pictured the ghetto as a large square surrounded by small houses. Falling asleep, I walked into that square and a gigantic German picked me up. Playing with his black tie, I could smell the cologne that Grandfather sometimes splashed on his face after shaving. Mother ran out of the little house and stretched out her arms to the German. He put me down. I woke up terrified that Grandfather and Mother would run away and leave me at Janka's.

Father felt worse and Mother was waiting for Grandfather, who was supposed to take him to the ghetto. When the agreed-upon knocks sounded in the middle of the night, she ran to open the door. In the kitchen Grandfather took off his wire glasses and started wiping them with his handkerchief.

"They took Romuś away," he said indistinctly.

Mother burst out crying. How could it be! After all, she'd just been to see him! She was even afraid that he wouldn't recognize her. But he hadn't wanted to climb down from her knees. He had cried as she left.

"They took off his diaper to see if he was circumcised."

"Who betrayed him?"

"The woman next door."

Maybe the gigantic German grabbed Romuś by the legs and smashed his head against the threshold of a railroad car. Are there any Jewish children alive besides me?

"I don't want to be alone," I said.

"Just stop it!" Mother exclaimed. "Bronek is so sick!"

And they left for the ghetto.

In the morning, Mother came running back. She had escaped at the last minute when soldiers were surrounding the ghetto. Two women who were laundering linen in the river started shouting when they caught sight of her.

"Catch her! She's a Jewess!"

They took Teresa away in that *Aktion*. Grandfather had begged her to run after Mother. She could still have caught up with her. Telling us about this, Grandfather mentioned the Unter family from Drohobycz. Only Julek was left; he was with Milo in Russia.

Grandfather also said that he'd run out of money. He had found some Jews, however, who had cash and were looking for a hideout. He arranged everything with Janka's father. Young Szechter, his mother, and his sister, would move into the attic and pay for us.

In the daytime I forgot that they were upstairs. At night, their footsteps and the sounds of washing up could be heard. Szechter would bring down the bucket and collect their food. I didn't see his face because Janka would turn down the carbide lamp to prevent the man's shadow from showing through the paper-covered windows. As time passed, however, the hatch to the garret began to open in the daytime, too. Szechter and Janka would whisper together.

"She's the only person I have in the world," Janka's father told Grandfather. "She's nice-looking, even though she's lopsided. Szechter's come her way. There can't be a marriage. There's no point in waiting. But your grandson is lying under the bed. I am not throwing you out, but find yourself some other place."

In the Garret

Mother and Janka wept as they said goodbye. Janka's father wasn't there because he worked the night shift. The Szechters were up in the attic. Once again, we went out into the night. Mother and Father dragged me along by my hands. My legs kept buckling at the knees. We walked to Tustanowice, uphill all the way, until we were above Borysław, which loomed up out of the darkness. Pańska Street cut the town in two. Trains hauling tank cars were lined up at the railway station. The electric lights on top of the oil wells were on.

In Tustanowice it was still pitch-black. We felt our way to the barn where Turów was waiting for us. He shoved us inside. We climbed up a narrow unsteady ladder to the top of a haystack. Below, animals were standing and lying around. The smell of horses, cows, and manure mixed with the smell of hay. Turów left us a basket of apples and climbed down the ladder. The apples were sweet and sour at the same time. Juice dripped down my chin and fingers.

Father said to Mother, "They're gray rennets. We ate apples like this when we rode in the sleigh."

Mother sighed. "It was so nice under the sheepskin."

"But you were complaining that it stank."

"Because it hadn't been tanned properly."

All around us was silence. The barn, Turów's house, the village with widely scattered farmhouses—everything was in the forest. Suddenly, light flickered on the boards; the sun was rising. A rooster crowed, a horse stirred below us and stamped his hoof on the ground. Through chinks in the wall we saw a young girl come in to milk the cows. She looked up. Did she know about us? Turów led the horse out and dragged a wagon out of the barn. A boy was scattering straw with a pitchfork. I was afraid that Father would start coughing.

All day, we lay there with our eyes open, making sure not to fall asleep. At night, Turów brought us down. We relieved ourselves in the bushes and climbed up again. Sleep overcame us. Three days later news arrived that

Pani Sprysiowa was expecting us. Father accompanied us to her place and then went back to the ghetto.

⸺

Pani Sprysiowa was a Pole who had married a Ukrainian. She told us that he would get drunk and beat her for no reason at all until he disappeared without a trace during the Russian times. Since then, she hadn't had a man "to take care of her." She was living at her mother's house and keeping Jews at her own. (We had been waiting at Turów's for the previous Jews to move out.)

Pani Sprysiowa's house had two stories. It was surrounded by a wooden fence, alongside of which, on the street side, were flower beds (with no flowers at this time of year). Upstairs there was a tiny room with a red floor. It held a bed and a night table. Across from the bed, on the wall with a window, hung a picture of Christ in a white shirt and a crown of thorns. Soft, light-colored stubble framed his face. (Father's face had just the same kind of stubble.) Christ was looking upward with a sickly smile and one tear was falling from his eye. He was holding his hands in front of him, lifted in prayer, and between them was his heart, which had come out of his chest. The door to the garret was in this room. In the garret was a mattress covered with a blanket and on it were red pillows with feathers sticking out of them. Next to it was a bucket covered with a board and a jug of drinking water with a dipper. Pani Sprysiowa emptied the bucket every evening and topped up the jug with water from the well. She also brought us bread. When speaking with Mother, she would lift her eyes to heaven.

"A piece of onion," Mother begged her. "My teeth are getting wobbly."

"Onion?" Our landlady was shocked.

"And a blanket. It's cold."

"A blanket?" She puffed out her lips in a pout and then gave a little laugh. "Didn't you have a Saint Bernard?"

"Yes, we did," Mother said, delighted.

"A dog like that must have eaten a lot of food!"

⸺

It was Grandfather who found Pani Sprysiowa but she was paid by Kopcio, who was in hiding with Nusia. From time to time a letter arrived from her; Mother would read it carefully.

"Kopcio is a simpleton," she said. "Before the war a Mandel sister would not even have looked at him. Now we owe our lives to him."

⸺

She was always freezing, especially her hands and feet. During the day she would give me her hands to rub. The white bones of her fingers would slowly regain their color. At night, I warmed her feet.

"You always have warm hands," she'd say, surprised.

"I don't freeze."

—

The ghetto was closed off. Several hundred Jews were relocated to barracks where the Polish army had once been stationed. The remainder were taken away to a camp. Grandfather and Father survived. They had no illusions about the future, but they thought they would be able to escape before the barracks were liquidated.

—

Mother's teeth ached and she moaned all the time. Her face swelled up and tears flowed from her eyes. Pani Sprysiowa told Janka's father about this and he informed Grandfather. Grandfather came for Mother one night and took her to the barracks.

It was dark in the barracks. Father was waiting in the hallway near the entrance to the large room where the dentist was. They embraced and wept. Grandfather pulled Mother away and pushed her inside. The dentist lit a lantern.

"Please sit on that chair," he said.

The men in the bunks watched her without saying a word.

"Which one hurts?"

"One of these."

She pointed out where it hurt.

"I'll pull out all of them on this side."

"Fine."

"You understand. I have no anesthetic."

He gave the lantern to Grandfather so his hands would be free.

—

We had grown very thin over the last months. There were dark shadows on our skin where it had sunk onto our bones. Our eyes no longer moved. Our hands had grown particularly sensitive and black-looking from hunger and the lack of work and soap. They looked like dark gray spiders, poised to scurry away at any moment.

—

One cold autumn night Grandfather came to us from the barracks, signaling by his way of knocking at the door that it was he. Mother ran downstairs and let him in. We went into the windowless garret where we could safely light a lamp. We were wearing coats and scarves. Grandfather had brought a buttered roll wrapped up in a newspaper, and coffee with milk and sugar in an old vodka bottle. (Mother had said many times that she would like to eat a roll with butter and have a drink of coffee before she died.) He told us that Father was in a bad way. Even if the doctors could perform an operation in the barracks, it was already too late for a pneumothorax to be of any help. Hunger. There was no point in even dreaming about medicine.

Mother started begging Grandfather to bring Father to us. The two of them were sitting in the shadows and all I could see was their knees.

"Please bring him, Papa."

"Get that out of your head."

Mother's face emerged from the darkness.

"We'll go out into the street!" she screamed.

"Are you mad?" Grandfather was terrified. "Pani Sprysiowa won't take him in."

"You'll arrange it with her, Papa."

"And what will you do when he dies?"

Mother withdrew into the shadow. Now Grandfather drew near the lamp. He opened his coat and scarf, unbuttoned his shirt, and took two cloth pouches tied up with tape from around his neck. He gave one to Mother and held the other in his hand. He undid the tape and took out a little bag made of wax paper. He slid it right under the flame. The odor from the burning carbide made my nose tingle. Inside the bag was a fine powder that looked like granulated sugar.

"Morphine. You lose consciousness instantly. You have to swallow all of it in order not to wake up again."

Mother's face brightened. Pushing her hair out of the way, she pulled the tape over her head and tucked the pouch under her blouse. Snuggling up to Grandfather, she kissed the sleeves of his coat.

Grandfather wiped his eyes and lifted my chin with his damp finger.

"You must not sniff this or touch your tongue to it," he said.

"Does it hurt?" I asked.

"No." He hung the pouch around my neck.

From then on I was constantly checking to see if it was there. I couldn't possibly lose it, but I was afraid that it would disappear.

Father came at night. He was exhausted by the trip. Mother helped him upstairs. He lay down on the mattress in the garret; his breathing was labored. She undressed him in stages and washed him with a wet towel, first his arms, then his chest, his belly, his legs. The parts she washed, she wrapped in the blanket. Father was very long and thin. His head, with its light hair, lay tilted backward. His eyes were closed. Mother knelt down and slipping her hand under his head, gently lifted it. He opened his eyes. She slipped a mug of milk between his lips.

"Milk?" Father was amazed.

"Pani Sprysiowa brought us a little."

"What about him?" He indicated me with his eyes.

"He's already had some."

During the day Mother sat near Father and watched him sketch. A horse's head with crazed eyes. A couple of lines with his pencil. The mane, reins, the horse's back, a saddle, a knight's leg in iron plates. Then he started in a different place. A sword, a gloved hand, and an arm. He sketched rapidly. Spears, wings at the shoulders. A galloping hoof.

"A hussar! I couldn't have done that." Mother laughed out loud.

Father turned the notebook around for me to see. I crept up toward the head of the mattress in order to get a better look.

"Don't come close!" he said, and asked Mother to hand me the notebook.

He had changed a great deal since I saw him at Pan Turów's. His face was yellow. His forehead and cheeks were wrinkled. He lay on his back, covered with a blanket and his jacket, his arms flung out at his sides. He kept his right hand on the pillow. When he had a coughing fit he would sit up, take the pillow, and press his face into it. His whole body shook and jerked from side to side. You could see his clenched fingers on the pillow. Damp hair trembled above it. The sound his coughing made seemed to emerge directly from his rib cage and was like the pounding of a hammer. Father choked and made a gurgling sound. Finally, he put down the pillow and spat into a jar. He covered it with a paper lid and set it next to him on the floor. He fell back onto the mattress, with big drops of sweat rolling down his face. When the jar was full, Mother emptied it into the bucket, checking to see if there was any blood.

Once, when Father started coughing, Pani Sprysiowa showed up. She stood motionless in the open door to the garret. Then she crossed herself and brought up a blanket from downstairs.

"Pan Mandel didn't tell me your husband was such a sick man," she whispered to Mother.

Mother's face twisted into a smile.

"He's getting better," she said.

Toward morning I was awakened by the sound of Mother crying. Sunlight was penetrating the room around the edges of the paper window shade. The window looked like a second picture on the wall. I got out of bed and walked on tiptoe to the garret door. Mother was with Father. She was begging him not to go away. She didn't want to be alone. God would be merciful one more time. Father was saying that she had no right to destroy life, not hers nor the child's.

"Accept that I am dying. What will you do with my body? I have to go back to the barracks."

"No, I beg you, no!"

"Forgive me. Papa will help you."

He broke off and rested. Mother stopped crying and lay there quietly with her arm flung across Father's chest. There was a whistling sound every time Father took a breath. Then he started groaning in his sleep. Mother got up, knelt beside the mattress, and began to pray.

Grandfather came that night. The door downstairs opened and closed. Grandfather's boots and Mother's bare feet thudded on the stairs. We were sitting in the dark, because the lamp made Father cough. Voices reached me from several sides.

"Pani Sprysiowa is throwing you out."

"Andzia and the child, too?"

"Yes."

"What's going to happen?"

"Bronek will return to the barracks. You two will go to Pani Richter on Pańska Street for a couple of days. She has a brother who's a *Volksdeutsch*. No one will search her place. In the meantime, I'll arrange something with Pani Hirniakowa. We have to hurry. The moon is growing brighter and brighter."

In the Attic

Toward morning we were awakened by a racket on Pańska Street. Pani Richter went outside to see what was happening and returned in shock. The town was filled with soldiers. Governor-General Hans Frank had arrived and the troops were lined up for parade inspection. The janitor had stopped her in front of the building.

"Do you have company?" he asked. "A Jewess and a little boy?"

Pani Richter's brother immediately fetched Grandfather from the barracks.

"You have to leave," our landlady said.

"They'll catch us."

"You're not staying here."

"You took our money."

"I'll give it back when I have it."

"Out!" her brother snarled, and shoved us out the door.

On Pańska Street a band was playing. Booming drums, bellowing trumpets, clashing cymbals. Commanders' shouts and the measured clatter of soldiers' boots against the cobblestones. A crowd lined the roadway, but farther along the way the sidewalks were empty. We walked quickly behind the wall of people's backs. Grandfather in his coat and hat, Mother behind him in a kerchief, with me bringing up the rear, my head down. All I saw was legs. Cuffed trousers and work pants tucked into clumsy boots with foot wrappings sticking out of them, the bare calves of women standing on tiptoe, and the black, mud-caked feet of children pushing their way to the front of the crowd.

The cracks between the stone slabs of the sidewalk were filled with sand. Pebbles lay abandoned on hopscotch squares drawn in chalk. My knees hurt. It seemed to me that I was falling behind and that the legs I was staring at were not Mother's legs, but someone else's. Grandfather and Mother didn't turn around to look at me. Had someone recognized me and shouted, "Grab the little Jew!" they would have disappeared without turning their heads to look. I fingered the pouch on my chest. The streets were getting smaller and smaller. Not a living soul anywhere. Everyone had gone to Pańska Street. Nonetheless, we still didn't walk any closer to each other until Grandfather disappeared inside the gate of a certain building.

It was a multistory apartment building, old and dirty. Stucco was peeling off its walls; the roof was patched with tar paper and wood. The blackened window frames on the ground floor were fitted with plywood. There had been a butcher shop here at one time; it was closed now, boarded up. But one floor up, white curtains were visible behind the filthy windowpanes. Grandfather was waiting in the dank entry hall. The wooden stairs led to a single apartment.

Pani Hirniakowa opened the door. She wore an overcoat and cotton gloves. A long braid hung down from beneath her colorful kerchief. Her blue eyes opened wide with amazement.

"I was just on the way out. I wasn't expecting guests . . . today."

Grandfather pointed to Mother and me.

"Someone betrayed them," he said.

Pani Hirniakowa took off her gloves and led us through the kitchen into the main room. There, Grandfather said goodbye and returned to the barracks. Pani Hirniakowa lit a candle and handed it to Mother. Then she moved an armchair that was covered with a woolen throw and raised the trapdoor that was concealed in the wall behind it. Mother and I crawled into the attic through the small opening. Beside a straw pallet there was an empty iron bucket with a round wooden lid. The rafter that supported the roof was above the pallet. I bent over so as not to hit my head against it. Pani Hirniakowa lay down on the floor and looked in at us through the opening in the wall.

"I would have liked to have had a little girl," she said, looking at me.

"You will certainly have a daughter," Mother assured her.

Pani Hirniakowa got up, moved the chair back, and left the house.

Mother and I rested on the pallet. The candle burned on the bucket's wooden lid.

"He's alone in the barracks," Mother sighed.

"He's with Grandfather," I said.

"Papa will bring him to us if he's in a bad way."

"And where's Nusia?"

"In a well."

Pani Hirniakowa came home in the evenings, and soon afterward the soldiers dropped by. Some of them she greeted with squeals of delight;

others, she talked with for a long time through the closed door until she opened up for them. Once, she wouldn't let someone come in because he'd arrived with a dog that might have sniffed us out. Both of them howled outside her door. You could hear everything in the attic. The men slapped the bottoms of bottles. The corks flew out and bounced off our wall. Boots and belts with metal buckles fell onto the floor. The bed creaked. Elbows and knees banged against the wall. Pani Hirniakowa laughed and groaned simultaneously. Sometimes she howled wildly and the bed banged the floor, faster and faster. Terrified by the roars of the men, I would look in Mother's direction, but I couldn't make her out in the darkness. The soldiers blew cigarette smoke. Some of them stayed until morning. I knew the voices of the ones who kept coming back and I tried to picture to myself what they looked like. Sometimes they opened the window and listened to the rumbling of a motor up in the sky.

"*Verfluchte Russen!*" they said. "Damned Russians!"

One day Grandfather brought over Father, who crawled in through the opening in the wall and, without getting up off his knees, crept over to the pallet. Letting out his breath with a whistle, he slowly turned over onto his back. Grandfather lay down on the floor and stuck his head in. Mother kissed him on the cheek above his moustache, knocking his wire-rimmed glasses off his nose.

"Papa, you should go into hiding now," she said.

Grandfather retreated into the room. I could still see his hand picking up his glasses from the floor.

"The Germans at work will warn me," he said from behind the wall. "It won't be long now. The Russians are outside Tarnopol."

After Grandfather left, Pani Hirniakowa appeared in the opening. The German civilians were leaving Borysław. The soldiers were urging her to flee with them. But how could she leave her dear mother, who lived near the bridge over the Tyśmienica River? Besides which, the NKVD wouldn't do anything to someone who was hiding Jews.

And then Father started coughing. Softly, but without a break. At first, he lifted his hand as if he wanted to ask our forgiveness, but then he just looked at the rafter above his head. Pani Hirniakowa disappeared from the opening.

Had Grandfather told her that she wouldn't be able to receive any soldiers?

We had thought about everything in great detail, but every solution led to a dead end. Our life was determined by Father's illness. During the day the heated roof made it hot inside and that's when the jar stank the worst. The candle burned on the bucket. Father coughed or rested after coughing, lying flat on his back with his arms stretched out to each side. Mother, curled up into a ball, pressed herself against his side. She would doze off for a few minutes but then her own groaning would wake her up. Father's notebook lay on the floor but he no longer did any drawing.

Once, he told me to stand up. He stared at me attentively and said to Mother, "He resembles Milo. At his age, I was taller."

When he closed his eyes, Mother signaled to me to sit down.

At night it was cold and dark. I slept at the edge of the pallet, touching Father's burning feet. I dreamed that I was in Pani Hirniakowa's attic.

Oh, if only Grandfather could take me away from here!

One night, Pani Hirniakowa looked in on us with a kerosene lamp. It grew light. Her hair from her undone braid trailed on the floor.

"Pan Tabaczyński has come," she said.

Father asked Mother to slip a pillow under his back. Although he was thin, he seemed gigantic to me. An elderly man crawled in through the trapdoor. Still on his knees, he stretched out his hand to Father. But noticing that Father was in no condition to lift his hand, he pressed it on the quilt.

"I am Tytus's father," he whispered. "I have brought the money that Kopcio left for Pan Mandel. They liquidated the barracks yesterday. It seems they took them to a labor camp. Please accept my condolences."

He asked Mother if she wanted to give him a letter for Nusia. Mother picked up the notebook and a pencil. She looked for a blank page, but they all were covered with drawings. Tearing off the cover, she wrote to her:

> Dear Nusia,
>   Pan T. is with us. They liquidated the barracks. It seems they took
> them to a labor camp. Maybe Papa, with his knowledge of German,
> will get an office job. I begged him to go into hiding. He said that
> the Germans at work would warn him. I don't know how we will
> cope. Bronek will not get up again.
>
>   Andzia

I dreamed that I was in the barracks, walking on tiptoe even though the barracks were empty. In the place where Mother's teeth were extracted I saw Grandfather. He was standing there in his Austrian uniform with his medal and sword, having a conversation with God.

"Take care of them," he was pleading. "I can't do it any longer. In exchange, I won't go into hiding."

"Grandpa!" I cried out. "They'll kill you if you don't go into hiding!"
"Be quiet! I can't hear what he's saying because of you."
Terrified, I closed my eyes.
"Button your shirt; the string is showing," Grandfather said.
I opened my eyes. Father was talking to Mother on the pallet.
"Maybe Papa couldn't take it any longer?"
"Papa would not have abandoned us."

I envied those who died before the war. After Father came back from Worochta, his mother, who suffered from diabetes, came to live with us. In her high bed resting on gleaming metal columns with porcelain handles Grandmother Minia read books that Mother brought her from the library. She was going blind. One day, she placed her glasses with their thick lenses on her night table and said that she could no longer see anything. From then on, Father read aloud to her. She died while he was convalescing. I didn't see this because I was with my grandparents in Wolanka at the time, but I imagined that Grandmother Minia, stretching out her hand in farewell, sank slowly back onto her pillows and her soul flew up to heaven. Mother said that Grandmother Minia was lucky, because she died in her own bed.

Now, death was terrifying. Drunk like Pan Kruk, it murdered everyone it caught. It shouted and it beat people. After the war, death will be beautiful again. But not for us! Father will die any day now. (I had never seen a corpse.) Pani Hirniakowa will run away. We will remain by ourselves in the attic. Morphine.

A letter came from Nusia. She wrote that now there are only the two of them left in the world. She doesn't want to live without her sister. She'll kill herself if Mother doesn't visit her. She'll send Moszek, who's hiding with them, to fetch her. Moszek will come on Thursday night.

Mother smoothed her raven-black hair. She'll go to Nusia, spend two days with her at most, and come back on the third day. She wondered what Nusia looked like now. She hadn't seen her in so long. She had no intention of taking me along. I suspected that she wanted to escape by herself. Father kept silent. Maybe he was afraid that he'd start coughing if he said anything?

Moszek arrived on Thursday, but toward dawn.
"Can we go during the daytime?"
Mother put her shoes on her bare feet.
"Go." Father choked out the word.

It occurred to me that I would never see her again. I stood up and grabbed the rafter above the pallet to keep from falling down. My head was spinning.

"I won't stay here!"

"Calm down," said Mother.

"Take him," Father said.

"He won't make it there."

Moszek approached the pallet.

"Don't worry. I'll carry him on my back."

"Thank you," said Father.

Mother knelt down and clasped his hand.

"I'll just see Nusia and come back."

"Andzia, take care of yourself."

"I'll be back on Sunday."

"Yes."

In the Well

I sat on Moszek as if I were riding a horse, holding tight to his forehead. He walked fast and Mother practically ran beside him. People were still asleep. The streets were empty. A huge red sun shone right into our eyes. I could feel it warming my face.

"We just have to get beyond the town," Moszek said.

There were fewer and fewer houses. Mist was rising from dew-covered garden plots. Finally, the town disappeared behind the hills and we emerged onto an open expanse where there was nothing but grass and trees. The road ran alongside a forest where we could hide if need be. Moszek's forehead was slippery with sweat. I wiped my hands on my shirt.

I was afraid that this time they would catch us. How long could our luck last? Even if God had accepted Grandfather's sacrifice. Still, could one leave one's dying father without being punished? Grandmother Minia went to heaven. But where would I go?

We heard the distant buzzing of an airplane.

Moszek craned his neck.

"Russians!"

"Why did they stop outside Tarnopol?" asked Mother.

"They'll be moving soon."

We entered the forest. Moszek set me down on the ground. I didn't take my eyes off them until they sat down.

"What's the news from the well?" asked Mother.

"Kopcio is writing his book."

Mother opened her eyes wide.

"You didn't know that he's writing?"

"About what?"

"About us."

Again there was the rumbling noise. I was lying on my stomach and big blades of grass were nodding in front of my eyes. Suddenly the ground shuddered, as if something heavy had landed on it. A distant roar reached us, like the sound I'd heard when the Russians blew up the electric plant.

"A bomb!" Moszek yelled.

When the rumbling died down, Moszek lifted me onto his back and we set out again along the edge of the forest. It was beginning to grow dark and soon it was black among the trees. No one could see us now. Swaying on Moszek's shoulders, I floated along on high. The forest smelled good and on the grass our steps couldn't be heard. I must have fallen asleep, because I woke up in the middle of an apple orchard. In the distance beyond the trees a candle was burning in the window of a cabin.

"We're here," Moszek said out loud.

"At last!" A woman's voice reached us from under the ground.

"Nusia!" Mother cried out.

"Andzia!" My aunt's voice bounced off the water.

Moszek grabbed me by the wrists, swung me over his head, and began lowering me. I could smell moss. There was water beneath me. Someone grabbed my legs.

"Now!" Kopcio's voice rang out.

Moszek let go of my arms and Kopcio pulled me through a hole in the well casing. I landed on Nusia, whose face was wet. Then Mother came down. Nusia rushed over to her. They hugged and wept.

We were underground.

During the day it was hot. Soaked with sweat, we sat or lay on clay through which water was always seeping. An intense odor of earth and roots permeated everything. Nusia sat propped up against a wall, wearing a bra, a white slip, and panties. I was curious about what she looked like, but I couldn't see her face. Only a few narrow rays of light in which dust was swirling fell through the cracks between the rocks. Other than that, it was pitch black. So I could see only whatever happened to be illuminated by one of those rays. A green eye between fingers covering her brow, or a white tooth between parted lips.

Kopcio, near the stones, was writing in a notebook on which the sunlight was falling. Next to him were tin cans that once had been used to store film and that now protected his manuscript from the dampness. He sharpened the stump of his pencil with a penknife.

"Who is going to read that?" asked Mother.

"Jews."

"There are no more Jews."

"They will come back from Russia."

"A handful."

"There are Jews in Palestine and in America."

"But they don't read Polish."

"Someone will translate it into Hebrew and English. In these note-books," he struck the tin cans, "Romuś will survive. And he will, too," he said, pointing at me.

"You leave him alone!" Mother shouted.

I dreamed that I was a girl. Marek Bernstein didn't want to play with me. I couldn't see his face. So I didn't know if he was really doing this, or just pretending? Then I turned into a balloon. The wind tossed me around in the courtyard where squares for hopscotch were drawn in chalk. Suddenly, I flew off in the direction of the oil fields. Way up high. Until I burst.

Mother's cry woke me up.

"That's a lie!"

The large stone that concealed the entrance had been pushed aside and lay next to the tin cans. Everything was visible in the harsh light. We huddled against each other like moles. Nusia had her hands over Mother's mouth.

"Murderers!" someone was shouting up above. "The police are looking for you! They found him hanging by his tie."

Kopcio stuck his head out, plugging the hole with his body.

"Max, calm down!" he pleaded.

"Who gave you permission to bring the brat? Only her sister was supposed to come."

"Pull me out."

Kopcio started squeezing through the hole. When his bare feet disappeared, Moszek moved the stone back into place.

Kopcio had a stormy altercation with Max, who had returned, terrified, from Borysław. A bomb had landed on Pani Hirniakowa's house, destroying the front wall and exposing the garret. A skinny man, his knees touching the floor, was hanging from the beam, suspended by his yellow tie. It was confirmed that he was a Jew. The police concluded that he had been murdered by other Jews, who had fled. It was too low for him to have hanged himself. The hanged man was taken to the Jewish cemetery. Pani Hirniakowa had vanished.

Kopcio swore that we were innocent. Max said that that wasn't what concerned him. We have our own God for our conscience. He was only afraid that they would come sniffing around, and here he is, with a well full of Jews. He was finally mollified with more money and a promise that Kopcio and Moszek would go find a different hiding place.

"When?" Nusia asked anxiously.

"Soon."

—

Mother couldn't stop crying. She gave me her potato.

"Eat something," Nusia begged her.

"It's too late," said Kopcio. "He's certainly devoured it all by now."

I froze, my mouth full of potato.

"I want to die," Mother replied.

"Not here," said Kopcio.

"How can you!" Nusia burst out crying.

"Enough!" Moszek shouted. "You've all gone mad!"

I gulped down the potato.

—

I lay down on the clay in order to have a talk with Grandfather, but I couldn't fall asleep. I remembered that twice Mother had asked Father what it feels like when someone is dying. First, after Grandma Minia died, and the second time, when they came for Grandma Antonina and Nusia was crying on the floor. Each time, Father replied that in order to find out you have to die. Slipping my finger between my neck and the string that held the little pouch, I tried to imagine how it had happened. All I knew was that Father had a tie. The rest I thought up, supplying details, like the large, heavy blocks from which Mother had once made pictures.

Father made a loop with the narrow end of the tie and passed the wide end through it. That way, there was a large loop for him to fit his head into. Then, he pushed himself up from the pallet and knelt under the beam. (Even I had to stoop under it.) He tossed the wide end of the tie across the beam and pulled on the knot. Now the tie with the loop was hanging from the beam. He raised himself up just a little more and placed his head into the loop. He was deathly tired. His legs collapsed under him and he fell down.

—

It seemed to me that Father was on the other side of the stones. There was no trace left of his tuberculosis. Once again, he was the handsomest man in Borysław. Surrounded by the well casing, he rose above the water. He had a silver tie pin in his tie, but I couldn't see his clothes. "Papa, forgive us for abandoning you," I prayed. "Help Mama, Nusia, Grandfather, and everyone I love. Fix it so I can live, or if you can't, then make it so it doesn't hurt."

If I didn't feel a choking in my throat, I imagined that Father had accepted my prayer. But if something kept sticking in my throat, I believed he was thinking about vengeance. Then I would pray again. When that didn't help either, I started speaking in a half-whisper in order to terrify Father into thinking that I would betray our secret to others.

We came up to the surface at night. First Moszek, with Max's help, then Nusia, me, Mother, and finally Kopcio, who had no one to hold his legs from below. Once, when Moszek was pulling Nusia out, something heavy fell into the water with a loud splash. Mother and I screamed in terror.

"It's a stone," Moszek calmed us.

We walked around in the orchard. The dwarf apple trees with their strangely twisted boughs looked like women who were holding their hands up to their heads. Spiderwebs hung from the branches and stuck to our faces. They ripped apart as we pulled them off our eyelids. The apples were silver in the moonlight. Their pulp yielded softly under our teeth. Their bitter seeds burst open and floated in the juice, just as at Turów's place.

Kopcio and Nusia would share a cigarette, hiding the flame in their cupped hands. Either they'd whisper to each other or stalk off in anger. Later, in the well, you could smell the smoke on them.

Kopcio and Moszek left for a different hiding place.

"Be careful," Nusia whispered to Kopcio.

Moszek laughed. "I'll look after him."

"Moszek! You are so kind," said Nusia.

Mother shook me by the shoulder. "Say goodbye."

Kopcio stopped her. "Don't wake him up. Let him sleep."

After their departure it was completely silent; Mother and Nusia began talking only many hours later. I kept hearing "Do you remember, do you remember. . . ." Nusia spoke about people she loved, and Mother, about people who loved her. They were one and the same. Grandmother, Grandfather, Father, Romuś, Teresa, Maciek, and Pan Unter. The two of them were waiting for Milo so they could tell him everything. Drops of water started falling into the well, until finally it was pouring rain and steam rose up from below.

Max brought a letter from Kopcio. Nusia read it, kneeling next to the stones where there was light. A ray of light also fell on the slip strap over her thin shoulder.

"What does he write?" asked Mother.

"The Russians have begun to move from Tarnopol."

"What else?"

"There's no more money."

———

Mother's teeth were hurting. She took the pouch from my neck, pulled out the little wax paper packet, and held it up to the light. Touching the powder with a saliva-moistened finger, she smeared it on her gum. She sighed with relief and collapsed onto the ground. Nusia placed her ear on Mother's chest.

"She's sleeping," she said.

Feeling for it with my fingers, I found the packet, folded it along its creases, and placed it back in the pouch. Then I rubbed clay over my hands for a long time. Mother slept for two days. When she woke up, she didn't know where she was. She was nauseated. Nusia gave her sips of a tea made from apple peels.

———

The Russians were coming closer. At night, through the chinks between the stones, we could see the sky light up with flashes. The earth roared and trembled so much that we were afraid we'd be buried. ("Papa, fix it so I can live.") Around noon, Max came running.

"Come out!" he shouted. "The Russians are here."

"Ask him where they are," Mother whispered to Nusia.

"Where are they?" asked Nusia.

"Everywhere."

We began pushing away the stones. Max pulled us up. The wet eye of the well, surrounded by the stone casing, stared straight up at the sun.

"The cans," Nusia remembered.

"What's that about?" Max asked.

"The cans with the notebooks."

Grandmother in Vienna

Grandfather after the outbreak
of war

Grandmother with Andzia and Milo

Father at his radio

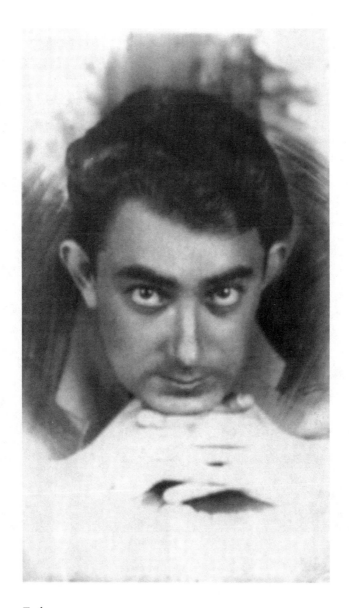

Father

Mother and me

Taking a walk with Mother

The courtyard on Pańska Street, years later (*Photograph by Jerzy Jarzębski*)

Romuś

Milo in medical school

right after the war

On Stalin Street

Nusia went to Borysław to search for Kopcio. Her clothing had rotted in the well, so she wore Mother's dress.

We remained alone in the orchard. Mist was rising from the grass after yesterday's storm. The gray rennets were dropping off the trees. All you had to do to find an apple was to stretch out your hand. But the pears were still green and they had rosy flushes like people who are suffering from tuberculosis. Mother got up from the grass and went to see if someone was coming for us. The farmer's overcoat trailed on the ground behind her. She stopped at the edge of the orchard and shaded her eyes from the sun. There was no one in sight. The hills fell away gently in the direction of the forest. A stone road wound through the stubble fields dotted with sheaves of grain. She dropped her arms and the sleeves concealed her hands.

Could Germans be lying in wait in the forest? I had heard their voices on the other side of the wall at Pani Hirniakowa's, but I had never seen them close up. But I remembered the Austrians in green uniforms who used to visit us on Pańska Street when everyone was still alive.

At noon, Moszek brought Mother's dress. Although the weather was turning bad, Max took us back to town in a wagon.

Soon tall pine trees blocked out the sun. It smelled of resin and birds were whistling. The wooden wheels slipped from stone to stone. The wagon was creaking and Kopcio's tin cans rattled on its floorboards. I sat beside them, my legs dangling outside.

"What will happen now?" Max asked.

"Russia," Moszek said.

"What are you saying?!" Mother shrieked. "Borysław is Polish."

"You'll see that Borysław of yours, ma'am . . ."

There was a gust of wind. The tops of the trees came together and moved apart. There was a smell of something burning. Holding our noses, we tried to figure out what direction the smell was coming from. The stench was getting stronger and stronger. Smoke seeped through the branches and burned our noses and throats. I wiped away tears from my cheeks. It was growing dark. We drove out of the forest onto a barely visible high road.

Ahead of us an oil well was on fire. Its wooden walls were already gone. The fire was consuming the iron tower with its motionless hoist wheel and was spreading down the lines. The smoke was billowing upward, and the wind was carrying it off in clumps. Max whipped the horse and we raced ahead at a trot.

When it became light again I saw other wells. They were standing alongside the high road like hussars without horses. They had gray, wooden cloaks that dragged on the ground. On their heads they wore square helmets constructed out of boards. Iron wheels were visible through their lowered visors. On and on they went, all the way to the horizon, where every so often flashes of light could be seen.

Borysław was becoming increasingly distinct. It lay on both banks of the river, which was channeled through a stone conduit. There was scarcely any water in it. Had it dried up? Pańska Street ran along the bridge across the Tyśmienica River. Long and wide, the street cut the town in two. Among the streetlights and the trees planted on the sidewalks lay long, fenced-in yards. Beyond the courtyards the oil fields began, disappearing in an approaching cloud. Illuminated from behind by flashes of lightning, the cloud gave off a silver glow along its edges. I could see it swallow up the trains at the railroad station and the NKVD building on Pańska Street across from our courtyard.

Moszek said that someone had seen Father being buried near the gate of the Jewish cemetery. It would be easy to find a fresh grave. I started looking around for Pani Hirniakowa's bombed-out house. Where is it? Can the cloud be hiding it? I could sense that it was going to start raining at any moment.

"What is Kopcio doing?" Mother asked.

"Drinking," Moszek said.

"Jews don't drink!" she declared categorically.

As we drove onto Pańska Street it started raining. The water soaked into the dry stones at first and then spilled over the sidewalk and roadway in large puddles. People disappeared into the courtyards, pulling their jackets over their heads. A soldier with a machine gun slung across his chest was standing in front of the NKVD building. Water ran down the gun's black barrel. The soldier's helmet was covered with an oilcloth hood on which drops of rain were dancing. Moszek wrapped Mother in his jacket and said that Pańska Street was again called Stalin Street. Mother didn't respond; her eyes were fixed on our courtyard.

I shut my water-drenched eyes and saw Father standing in the open door, behind which the rain was falling. The downpour had caught him as he was coming home from work. Mother started drying his hair with a towel.

"Do you want to catch a cold?" she yelled at him reproachfully.

Father kissed her and went inside.

The maid brought him his slippers.

We didn't turn in to our courtyard. (Pan Skiba was living there now.) The wagon drove into the next courtyard and stopped in front of a low little house. The horse shook itself, raising a cloud of watery dust. We entered the hallway. Golden light shone into it through the apartment's partly open door and we could hear the rattling of a sewing machine. Moszek gently pushed open the door.

It was a whitewashed kitchen. A table and bench stood in the center of the freshly scrubbed floor. Behind the table, between the stove and a stool with a pink basin on it, there was a window against which the rain was beating. Against the right wall there was a gleaming, white-lacquered credenza; its drawers and little doors with red panes of glass were completely blackened. A book lay on the credenza.

In the left wall there was a door with an iron handle. Next to the door a red-haired woman was sewing on a sewing machine. A kerosene lamp hanging on a nail shone on her braid. It looked like a twist of copper wire, like the wire Father had used to repair our Philips radio.

"Andzia!" Mother shouted from the threshold. "It's me!"

The woman stopped what she was doing and scraps of material fell onto the floor from her lap.

"Andzia!" she cried out to Mother. "You're alive!"

She was as tall as Moszek and Max. She was wearing a skirt made out of a sack that had been dyed brown. She ran over to Mother and hugged her with her freckled arms.

"This is my cousin, Andzia Katz," Mother mumbled, her nose pressed against Andzia's breast.

When we were alone, Mother and Andzia Katz sat down on the bench and I pulled the sewing machine chair over to the table in order to hear them better. I fidgeted on it, because I was skinny and sitting made me ache all over.

"Just think, what baseness!" Mother said. "Kruk—he was our neighbor!—showed the SS the cellar where Mama was hiding. One of the Austrians said that Kruk betrayed everyone."

For me, Grandmother Antonina was already a shadow in a black dress fastened with tiny buttons. I didn't even remember her voice. Did she use German to beg for mercy in Bełżec? Or had she died in the freight car?

That's when they took away Uncle Unter.

"You didn't have such an uncle," Andzia Katz said.

"What do you mean, I didn't?" Mother bristled. "Teresa's maiden name was Unter."

"Milo's wife?"

"Yes. They took her. Maciek, too."

"The blind one who made brushes?"

"Yes."

"And little Romuś?"

"A neighbor woman betrayed him."

Mother dried her eyes with her fists.

Before we'd gotten into the wagon, Max had invited me into the cabin. There was a milk can there, with an enamel ladle attached to it. Max scooped up some milk and gave it to me. I looked up without taking my lips off the ladle. In front of me hung a cracked mirror in a frame with daisies on its corners. My black hair, forehead, and the tips of my ears looked like they'd been lopped off with scissors. (My hair was curly, even though I'd tried flattening it all the time in the well, holding my hands on my head.) Black eyes filled with rage looked at me from under a crack in the mirror. The dry skin on my face was wrinkled. My upper lip was raised, revealing my teeth. Drops of milk were running down my chin. With a face like that I had survived! But Romuś and Maciek, who had blue eyes and hair as light as straw, had perished.

"Janka," Mother went on, "was as poor as a church mouse and lame, to boot. As soon as she saw Szechter, we were done for."

"I once knew a lame Janka," Andzia Katz said. "I sewed a chemise for her before the war."

"That's not her."

"So what was her name?"

"Janka Leń."

"The other woman's was different."

Under the bed I had been most afraid of children. I was convinced that they would betray me to the Germans. Now the Germans were gone, but the children were still here. Riding in the wagon, I hadn't seen them; they were probably hiding from the rain. Tomorrow, however, they would appear in the streets again. I imagined that they would beat me as soon as I came out of the house. Before anyone could notice, it would all be over.

"At Pani Sprysiowa's," Mother continued, "Bronek was already very ill. He was emaciated. We were starving. Once, Sprysiowa brought us some carrots and potatoes. At night I prepared a soup in the kitchen and took it up to the garret. In the morning, the pot was full of bedbugs. Bronek turned his head away. But he!"—she pointed at me—"I couldn't tear him away from the pot. 'Mama, don't pour it out. Just take out the bedbugs.'"

Andzia Katz walked over to the credenza and opened the little doors with the red panes of glass. There was nothing to eat inside it. The shelves held plates, mugs, and a glass. She took out a mug and filled it with water from the barrel.

"Drink." She handed the mug to Mother.

"Me, too," I asked.

Andzia Katz started to move toward the credenza again.

"Sit down, Andzia." Mother grabbed her hand. "He'll drink with me."

I remembered the German dictionary volume that was devoted to medicine. I had looked at it with Grandfather, who was not afraid of medical pictures. I would lift off the celluloid sheets with the red muscles, purple heart, and blue lungs until just the skeleton remained. Once I found a photograph there of two rhesus monkeys: a healthy one and another who had sleeping sickness. The healthy monkey was climbing a tree; the sick one was lying there with his eyes closed. There was no fur left on his dry skin. Grandfather said that monkeys who have sleeping sickness stop drinking, like rabid dogs. They wake up before death and run straight ahead until they die.

"They took Papa away when they liquidated the barracks," Mother was saying. "I begged him to hide, but he didn't want to. The Germans were supposed to warn him. You tell me, how could he have trusted them?"

"There was one good German."

"Who?"

"Beitz. Everyone in the White House survived."

"The children, too?" I asked.

"Rutka Sak is alive. She's the same age as you."

Mother was offended.

"What do you mean? Rutka is a year older."

⸺

Recently, I'd seen Grandfather in his Austrian uniform with the medal and sword. He was asking God to look after us. Could that be why Father hanged himself?

⸺

"At Pani Hirniakowa's," Mother continued, "Bronek didn't have lungs left to breathe with. I notified Nusia that they'd taken Papa. She sent a letter. She said that she'd kill herself if I didn't come. Bronek ordered me to go. Moszek came on a Thursday. While I was putting on my shoes, he"—Mother pointed at me again—"started wailing that he wasn't going to stay there. I didn't know what to do. After all, you can see that he's barely able to walk. Moszek carried him on his shoulders."

⸺

"At night, we arrived at a well."

"Why?" Andzia Katz sounded surprised.

"Nusia was in a hole behind the well casing."

"A wonderful hiding place."

"In the well I learned that a bomb had fallen on Bronek."

"A bomb?" Andzia Katz was amazed.

"On the way to the well we heard the explosion."

"Did they find him?"

"Yes."

"Did they realize he was a Jew?"

"Yes."

"They buried him."

"Near the gate."

"A bomb! Unbelievable!"

"Ask him," Mother said. "He knows everything."

⸺

I had forgotten that it was a Thursday. How could I?! Would Father have forgotten what day I died? I bent over the table. The wood grain looked back at me.

⸺

Late at night we went into the main room through the door with the iron handle. I lay down on the floor between Mother and Andzia Katz's bed. A burning smell from the extinguished lamp seeped in from the kitchen.

⸺

In the morning, Mother went to look for Nusia. I stayed by the window. Maybe she'll bring something to eat? The sun was rising behind the trees, sparkling red and gold. Against the sunlight, the leaves looked black, but lower than the sun they looked golden and green. Near the fence they were mixed in with large burdock plants, which could be cooked like spinach. Behind the burdock there was another courtyard and the house in which I was born. Yesterday's rain had left puddles. Now sparrows were drinking from them. They searched for food, hopping on both legs at the same time. Suddenly, they stopped and flew through the fence. I heard children's voices and withdrew into the far corners of the kitchen.

Andzia Katz was sewing on a machine that looked like a black cat with a yellow zigzag. In the place where its tail should have been a little silver wheel whirled around; she placed her hand on it to slow it down. At the head, a spindle with thread hopped up and down. She kept lowering a foot with a curved lever in order to press down the material as it slipped under the needle. The iron cat lay on a board that had been polished to a shine by wool and percale. The board was supported by iron stalks painted black and connected to each other with gold letters: SINGER. Under the name there was a metal pedal that Andzia Katz pressed with her bare feet. On the right side, between her feet and the stalks, a heavy wheel with spokes in the shape of plants turned around and around. On the floor were large boots with heels pressed up into the shoe parts.

Mother came back, bringing half a loaf of bread that she broke into three parts. I gnawed off my piece so greedily that I couldn't close my mouth.

"You'll choke!" she screamed.

Andzia Katz gave me a mug of water.

"What's happening with Nusia?" she asked.

"They're living with the Tabaczyńskis. Sofas, chairs, wardrobes. I had forgotten that things like that even exist. We are living like beggars."

She sighed.

Andzia Katz looked around her kitchen.

"Here." Mother handed me her bread.

After breakfast, when Andzia Katz went to buy buttons from Salka Krochmal, Pan Rygliński from our courtyard showed up.

"Good day, to you, ma'am. Praise the Lord that you are alive! And he is, too."

"I didn't let him take even a step away from me. I always said that if we're going to die, it should be together."

"A miracle, a miracle!"

"But Romuś is dead."

Mother began to cry.

Pan Rygliński crossed himself.

"I have Pani Teresa's bed at my place," he said. "Only without the mattress."

We went with him immediately to fetch the bed. In the street, out of fear of the children, I looked at the ground. However, seeing only large feet, I slowly raised my head. In the courtyard I recognized a door with the outline of a mezuzah.

"Kruk . . . is he in Borysław?" Mother asked.

"Yes."

We returned with the bed by the same route. Pan Rygliński went first, lifting his legs high. The open clasps on his satin vest jingled softly. He held the head of the bed behind him, and Mother and I lifted it from behind by its lacquered legs. It floated unevenly, like a coffin without a lid. Although we stopped often to rest, my legs were trembling and my knees ached. The hardest part was carrying the bed into Andzia Katz's room. Mother was terrified that it wouldn't go in.

"It will go in," Pan Rygliński soothed her, and started taking the door off its hinges. "If it could fit through my door, it will fit here, too."

In the early afternoon I went to the cemetery with Mother to look for Father's grave. Mother kept smoothing her hair. I had never been in a cemetery and I was afraid that rats were living there in underground labyrinths. When we were in the well I was always touching the damp wall to make sure that a rat wouldn't emerge through it.

We reached a place where broken stones were scattered about. Mother said they were pieces of headstones that had fallen from the trucks when the cemetery was liquidated. The monuments had been smashed with heavy hammers into little granite cubes. Jews had done this, driven here by the Germans.

"The gate used to be here," Mother said, walking between the remains of bricks protruding from the ground.

The paths were overgrown with grass. Moss covered the stumps of trees that had been cut down. Not a trace of digging. Father's grave wasn't anywhere. Mother scraped clay off the stones, looking for Hebrew letters. Alas, either there weren't enough of them, or she didn't know the names. Mainly poor Jews from Lower Wolanka were buried here. Finally, however, she found something familiar and, orienting herself by the destroyed graves, she almost ran straight ahead. I caught up with her only when she stopped.

"Here's where Grandma Minia is lying," she said. "Fortunately, she doesn't have to see her own grave."

I looked around. On a gravestone that looked something like a side-walk, Father was standing. In a dark striped suit, with a white handkerchief in his buttonhole. He had a silver stud in his tie. He bent down and picked up a glittering stone from the ground.

"There are crystals in every stone," he said to Mother, who was stand-ing beside me. "You can smelt them and holes will be left in the stone."

Mother took the handkerchief out of Father's buttonhole and, stretch-ing on her tiptoes, she brushed off the stone dust that had settled on the lapels of his jacket and his shoulders. He nodded, smiling, after which we went to eat cakes at a café.

Birds were hopping over the graves.

From the direction of the town a man and two boys appeared, pulling a small wheeled cart. They entered the cemetery and came to a stop near us. The man took a spade out of the cart and struck it into the ground. He looked closely at us and started walking in our direction.

"Mandel's daughter?" he asked hesitantly.

Mother nodded.

"How good to see someone who's alive!" he said. "I'm Majer."

"I recognize you," Mother replied.

"My wife is in that cart," the man continued. "She died in our hiding place. During an abortion. Now we've brought her here to bury her. Until now she was lying in the forest."

We looked in the direction of the cart. The boys were digging a grave.

"My sons," he explained.

At night, in Teresa's bed, the boards creaked under us and we had to turn over carefully so as not to drive splinters into our bodies. Lying on my left side with my knees tucked under my chin, I imagined that I was a hussar. I was riding on the back of an immense horse with a sword in my hand. The hoofs were pounding. I could hear the sound of wings and the clanking armor of the men who were chasing me. However, I had forgot-ten about the lances, and I had to break off the attack. We moved off again with swords and lances. And the reins? While galloping I bent over the horse's mane and caught the reins between my teeth.

The next morning Pani Hirniakowa arrived. In her overcoat and cot-ton gloves. She embraced Mother with one hand; in the other, she was holding a paper bag.

"What good fortune that you are alive!" she shouted. "And he is, too! My dear mother says it's a true miracle."

"Other mothers abandoned their children, but I didn't."

Pani Hirniakowa turned around and placed the bag on the table. Boxes of matches tumbled out of it.

"They're for you," she said. "I have an entire case of them from the Germans."

Andzia Katz gathered up the matches and put the bag on the credenza next to the book.

"My cousin," Mother introduced her.

The women greeted each other, their braids swaying.

"Did any other children survive?" Pani Hirniakowa asked.

Mother started counting, bending down her fingers.

"Rutka Sak. She's ten. Marianek Krajsberg. Four. He was in a hideout with his mother. Jurek Pordes. Fifteen. Pani Pordesowa's son; her husband was an engineer. She's working as a waitress in the NKVD dining room. Also Tanenbaum's little girl . . . How many does that make?"

"Five," said Andzia Katz.

"My cousin," Mother said, "survived in the Tanenbaums' hiding place."

"Young Weiss is also alive," Andzia Katz remembered. "He was on the Aryan side."

Pani Hirniakowa wiped her eyes on her sleeve and said, "My mother invites you and your son to dinner."

"To dinner?" Mother was stunned. "But your mother doesn't know us."

"She says you're hungry."

"When?" Mother asked.

"Today."

In the afternoon, on Pańska Street, near the bridge over the Tyśmienica, in a little house with white curtains, we sat down to dinner. There were four soup plates on a table covered with a cloth. We each had our own spoon and fork, but there were only two knives (for Pani Hirniakowa's mother and for Mother). Pani Hirniakowa's mother brought out a pot of Ukrainian borscht and a basket of bread from the kitchen. Mother asked for a dishcloth and placed it under my plate.

"To keep him from staining it," she said.

Pani Hirniakowa's mother ladled borscht into the plates. In mine, in the middle of the beets, potatoes, cabbage, and beans, lay a piece of boiled meat.

"Wait," Mother whispered; "don't start before everyone else!"

My jaws began to ache from swallowing my saliva. Pani Hirniakowa's mother crossed herself three times and picked up her spoon.

"Be careful! Lean forward!" Mother whispered again.

At the first bite my jaws went into spasm. I nearly spat out the borscht. Tears dropped into the plate from my eyes. When the cramp let up, I put the next spoonful into my mouth, but my jaws again went into spasm.

"How do you like it?" Pani Hirniakowa asked.

"Very much," Mother answered for me.

I thought it was Father's revenge and I began praying to him: "Papa, forgive me. Don't make me hurt." And the pain disappeared as if it had never happened. I could taste the borscht. Boiled beans, cabbage strips, tongue-scalding potatoes, and large slices of beets. I stuffed spoonful after spoonful into my mouth. I didn't even chew the meat. My cheeks puffed up. But that wasn't enough for me! I wanted to lap it up like a dog that won't tear its muzzle away from a plate! When I could see the bottom, I started stealing anxious glances at the pot.

"Look at your plate," Mother hissed. "You're slopping it over the edge."

The women talked about Father. First Mother cried, and then she said something in an angry voice. But what? I wasn't listening attentively. My eyes and ears opened only when the pot was empty.

On the morning of the third day Salka Krochmal came and brought Mother new underwear. Salka had found out from Andzia Katz, when she was purchasing buttons, that Mother had nothing to wear. Before they handed over their shop with its stock of underpants, brassieres, and stockings to the Germans, they had hidden some of their goods with other people. And now some of them were returning whatever survived. Mother put on the new things and went into town. There she met Witka Astman who gave her fifty rubles.

The afternoon was not as successful. The person to whom Mother had given thirty little boxes of matches to trade brought them back, insisting that he hadn't found a buyer. Then, when we looked inside them, it turned out that each box was missing half its matches.

On the fourth day Mother became a waitress in the NKVD dining room. She was supposed to assist Pani Pordesowa, whose husband had been an engineer. Both of them owed their job to the cook, Pani Baumowa, who remembered them from before the war.

The dining hall was located above the cellars that Mother was familiar with from the first pogrom. Twice a day, at one and at seven, a crowd of Russian officers entered this hall with its large windows. They sat at long tables on which stood baskets of sliced bread. Pani Pordesowa and Mother carried in from the kitchen heavy trays with bowls of soup and immediately ran back for more. When the last officers were served their portions, the men who had already eaten called for seconds. Pani Baumowa's soups were a hit. The plates with the second course were lighter. Usually, they served schnitzel with cabbage and potatoes dressed with lard. They also had beef roulades and pork liver, but not as often. Aside from serving at the table and washing the plates, the waitresses peeled potatoes and carrots and sliced cabbage. They also scoured the pots with sand and took out the garbage. In exchange, Pani Baumowa allowed them to take leftovers home.

I ate them up and crawled into bed with a full belly. Mother, washing up in the basin, complained to Andzia Katz that she hurt all over. Sated, I turned over onto my back and stared at the ceiling until I fell asleep.

At night, the Germans shot at me.

On the fifth day, an officer in a poplin shirt with enormous medals and gold stars on his wide epaulets accosted Mother. She thought he was a general. The Russian had arrived late, after the others had already left. When she set his plate in front of him he placed his hand on hers.

"*Ty, konechno, ne ofitsiantka?*" he addressed her in Russian. "You're not a waitress, of course?"

"My husband was an engineer."

"What do you mean 'was'?"

He continued speaking Russian and she replied in Polish.

"He perished."

"So you're alone?"

"Yes."

"Do you want to be with me?"

"No."

He squeezed her hand.

"I'm a Jew, too."

Mother sat down on the edge of a chair.

"Is that true?"

"I'll take you to Lwów and set you up like a queen," he said, this time in Yiddish.

She leaned toward him.

"You have power now, right?" she whispered in German.

"And how," he answered in Russian, and smiled broadly, giving her a thumbs-up sign.

"There's a man here who betrayed my mother."

The officer took out a leather notebook and wrote down Kruk's name.

On the sixth day the Russian beckoned to Mother.

"Done," he said. "Your little bird is far away." He patted himself on his medals. "So, what do you think? What a man!"

"He thought he had me then," Mother told Andzia Katz. "But what was so special about what he did? Sending Kruk to Siberia? After all, that's his profession."

—

On the seventh day Mother rested. Swinging her bare legs under the table, she ate bread with beet marmalade and complained to Andzia Katz about the work in the dining hall. The heavy trays of soup were breaking her arms. Her hands and knees bled when she scrubbed the floors. She was a servant! And for whom? Papa couldn't stand them! After all she had lived through, didn't she deserve something better?

"And what about him?" She jerked her head in my direction. "He doesn't even listen to me. I have to repeat everything twice, because he doesn't know what's going on. You're heartless," she said, slipping me a piece of bread and marmalade.

That's how the first post-war week passed.

—

Soon, Mother quit her job at the dining hall and became a clerk at UKRGAZ—the Ukrainian Gas Works. She was hired by Professor Stanisław Rosowski, a teacher of descriptive geometry and drawing at the Gymnasium.

"Thank you, Professor."

He put his finger on his lips.

"I'm a *glavbukh* now, a head bookkeeper."

Mother brought news from the Gas Works that Poland would begin west of the Bug River.

"What about Lwów?" Andzia Katz asked.

"They're taking it."

"We'll have to run away before they close the border."

—

Mother earned a pittance minus the sum they deducted for the newspaper, which stank of printers' ink and smeared black all over her hands. Andzia Katz looked at the photos and drawings and then washed her hands so as not to stain her sewing. We didn't read any of the articles because none of us knew the alphabet.

"Their damn letters!" Mother grumbled.

Every day the paper contained photos of Stalin. The photograph on the first page was so large that each of his eyes looked out from a different column. In the middle of the paper Stalin would be smoking his pipe, conversing with Anglo-Saxons who were lounging in armchairs. On the last page, he was surrounded by workers and peasants.

"Why do Russians always stand?" Andzia Katz wondered.

"Because they don't want to sit," said Mother.

In addition to the photographs there were caricatures by the Kukryniks team. A soldier was using his bayonet to stab a snake with Hitler's head. Shoeless peasants were welcoming tanks with red stars on them with bread and salt. Andzia Katz cut out a drawing in which Germans were driving people into a crematorium with whips and she pinned it to her bed. Death was in the group of Germans, wearing a uniform and smiling.

Without the leftovers from the NKVD we were hungry again. In order to add to her earnings, Mother started baking rolls. She took them out of the oven at five A.M. and placed them in a torn oilcloth bag that Andzia Katz had gotten from a client. She covered them with a dishcloth and dropped them off at a tavern on the other side of the river on her way to UKRGAZ.

On Sunday, Mother had the day off. After she returned from the tavern she baked a new batch of rolls.

They were laid out in a rectangle on the table to cool. Eight rows of eleven each. When they were thoroughly cooled and had stopped smelling so good, there was the sound of a harmonica in the entryway and someone started pounding on the door.

"*Otvori!* Open up!"

Mother threw the rolls into the bag and ran into the other room. She dumped them onto Andzia Katz's bed and covered them with a blanket. Two soldiers with red faces came into the kitchen. One of them had a harmonica, and the other a silver can of tinned meat. The one with the harmonica took a look at Andzia Katz's red hair and whistled in astonishment.

"*Germanka?*" he asked in Russian.

"*Evreika.*"

"You're lying." He smiled slyly. "The Germans killed all the Jews."

The one with the can pointed at me.

"The kid's a Jew," he said.

Mother slipped out of the other room and stood behind me. The soldiers looked at us.

"Real Jews," they exclaimed. "*Nastoiashchie Evrei!*"

They walked, lurching, into the other room and sat down on Andzia Katz's bed. They flung the harmonica behind them. The one with the tin opened it with a knife, jabbing it into the fatty, fragrant meat.

"*Pozhaluista.* Help yourselves. It's American potted meat."

We sat down on the edge of Teresa's bed, our knees touching theirs. Each of us took a bite and passed the tin and knife to the next person.

"Don't you have any bread?"

Mother spread her hands wide to indicate we had none.

The Russians stood up with difficulty and pulled out of their pockets bottles that still had some vodka in them.

"Girls! To victory!"

They drank up and sniffed their own hands. It was hard for them to stand like that and they collapsed onto the bed again. The harmonica groaned. The one who had brought it noticed the caricature pinned to the bed.

"Kukryniks? Yes. That's right!" he said appreciatively.

The other soldier stroked my head. He gave me greenish men's socks and, pulling open the top of his tall boot, showed me by gestures that foot wrappers are better.

After they left, we ate the crushed rolls.

The next day, I moved the chair over to the credenza and took down the book. Threads protruded from its binding. A column of Polish letters ran from one page to another. When Mother left with the rolls, I lay down on the floor and started sounding out the words. I kept glancing anxiously at Andzia Katz's back, wondering if she could hear me. Bent over the machine, she didn't turn around even once. Apparently, the rattling drowned out my voice.

From then on, I read every day. Slowly, the alphabet from children's books about Andzia who "pricked her finger and cried," Hania the fussy eater, and lying Cesia came back to me. I read aloud less frequently. When Andzia Katz went out to her clients in the evening, I sat under the lamp near the machine. Mother mixed dough at the table. She complained that it didn't rise because the yeast was old.

"Why am I wasting my energy and health on this?" she sighed.

The first page began with a letter *L* that was half the size of my finger. I liked that page best. But although I had already read it many times I still didn't understand some of the words.

"What does 'sacrificed' mean?" I asked.

"Abraham sacrificed his son to God."

Mother smoothed the ball of dough.

"He was just about to slit his throat when an angel grabbed him by the hand. He commanded him to kill a sheep instead of his child. They taught us that in religion class."

"Who taught?"

"The Jews were taught by a rabbi, and the Catholics by a priest. The priest was so nice! At our math exam he sat down next to me and, fanning himself with his hat, dictated the entire solution. The math teacher was furious, but he didn't dare say a word to the priest."

"What is 'Częstochowa'?"

"A city. Pilgrims used to go there from Borysław."

"Why?"

"There's a miraculous icon there."

She tore off a piece of dough and, rolling it between her hands, started reciting:

Holy Virgin, Thou who defends Bright Częstochowa
And shines in Ostra Brama! Thou, who protects
The Nowogród castle stronghold and its faithful people!
By a miracle Thou returned me to health in my childhood.

"You see!" she said proudly. "They taught us that at the Gymnasium! It's by Mickiewicz."

She stopped setting out the rolls on the table.

"How many?" she asked, covering them with a dishcloth.

"Twelve down and eight across."

"They should be brushed with a feather dipped in egg, but I don't have an egg. For that matter, I don't have a feather, either."

I started going outside. I hung around near the Gymnasium. It was a big, red-brick building. Tall chimneys, a red flag flapping between them, protruded from its roof. Portraits of Marx, Engels, Lenin, and Stalin hung above its door. There was a yard in front of the building, paved with cobblestones overgrown with grass. An iron fence separated it from the road. Across the street, on the other side of the road, a large field began. Men were sitting there, drinking vodka. They were Poles awaiting transport by the State Repatriation Bureau, and Russian soldiers on leave. (The Ukrainians didn't leave their houses.) Squatting behind the vodka-drinking men, I stole glances at a rectangular pond that was surrounded by a tall embankment where children were playing.

One day, two Russian soldiers climbed the embankment. They tucked their forage caps into their belts and took grenades out of their pockets. They waved their arms simultaneously, threw the grenades, and dropped onto the ground. The children who surrounded them also pressed their bodies against the grass. Screwing up my eyes, I saw the grenades fly past me. They fell into the pond and the earth shook—almost like when the bomb fell on Father. I hobbled after the men who started running to the embankment with their bottles. The water was still foaming and fish were swimming to the surface, their white bellies facing the sky.

Mother came back early from UKRGAZ. She told me to put down my book and took me to the Gymnasium. We followed the route that I already knew. The men were sitting in the meadow, but the embankment was empty. I understood that the children were inside the building.

"You're trembling in such heat?" Mother sounded surprised.

"Why are we going? Gymnasium is for older children."

"Yes, in principle. But now they've opened an elementary school there."

The corridor was jammed with mothers and children. I turned away from everyone who looked at me. The door to the classroom kept opening and a lady who was sitting at a desk called for the next in line. Then it was our turn.

"Family name?"

The lady removed her pen from the inkwell.

"Rabinowicz," said Mother.

"First name?"

"Wilhelm."

"Nationality?"

"Polish."

"Age?"

"Nine."

"Education?"

"He hasn't been to school."

The lady put the pen back into the inkwell and showed me a picture in a book.

"Ala has a cat," I read.

"You know the primer?"

"He's already reading *Pan Tadeusz,*" Mother said. "Tell the lady how it begins."

> Lithuania! My fatherland! You are like health;
> How much you should be treasured only he will know
> Who has lost you.

"Enough," the lady interrupted. "What about sums? Nine apple trees and twelve pear trees are growing in an orchard. How many trees are there altogether?"

"Twenty-one."

She admitted me into the third grade.

"It's a good thing she didn't tell you to write," Mother said after we'd left the Gymnasium. "Learn to write or they'll put you back into first grade."

Classes began at eight or ten. Often there weren't any classes at all, because we were celebrating the taking of various towns. I was always the first to arrive. Bottles glittered in the meadow. Semidarkness reigned in the empty Gymnasium corridor. There were no bulbs in the lamps with brass shades that hung from the ceiling. Light filtered in only through the little windows in the classroom doors. On the walls between the doors there were light-colored rectangles where pictures had been removed and remnants of German notices that remained firmly attached to the plaster. Most of the rooms had nothing in them. The surviving benches, teachers' desks, and blackboards had been moved to the few rooms where classes were held.

To avoid meeting anyone, I would lock myself in the toilet and press my ear to the door. At first, the corridor was completely silent. Then the entrance door would open and children's voices could be heard. Whispers and giggles slipped past the toilet. The women teachers' heels made tapping sounds and the male teacher of Russian, who had taken a bullet through the knee at the front, hobbled past. Sometimes the handle moved and someone tried to open the door.

Only when everything had quieted down would I come out and stand behind the children waiting in front of my classroom. The teacher, wearing darned stockings, let us in. In the classroom, too, there were light spots left by pictures. Above the teacher's desk, over traces of the cross, a portrait of Stalin was hanging. The teacher read the same thing from a book several times so we could memorize it. She also wrote on the blackboard, but only occasionally, because there wasn't much chalk. She gave us no homework. No one had notebooks or pencils. (Once, she showed us what a gum eraser looks like.) Then one day she was fired because she had signed up for a Repatriation transport.

"Learn Polish," she told us when she said goodbye. "It is the language of your fathers. If you forget it, you won't know who you are."

—

We were taught arithmetic in Russian by a lame man in a uniform without insignia. He brought along a newspaper which he placed on his desk.

"Children!" he said in Russian. "The best mathematicians in the world are Russians. Lomonosov and Kovalevskaya have no equals. But they are dead. And now, who is the best of all?"

He smiled, seeing us looking at the portrait.

"Yes; just so. Comrade Stalin."

He pulled a piece of paper out of his pocket and asked a boy in the first row, "How much is one times one?"

"*Jeden,*" the boy said in Polish.

"*Odin,*" the teacher corrected him in Russian.

He questioned us each in turn, not skipping a single example from the multiplication table. The numbers kept getting larger and the pupils had to think longer before answering. The Russian yawned and opened his newspaper. The smell of the ink traveled to the back of the class. I screwed up my eyes in order to see the Kukryniks caricature.

"How much is seven times seven?" He turned to me.

"Forty-nine," I replied in Russian.

"Correct," he said, checking the answer on his crib sheet.

That was the biggest number. After forty-nine he began again with one. Soon I was transferred to the fourth grade.

—

Nusia came only rarely. The last time I saw her was when she brought a kilo of flour, thirty grams of yeast, and one egg for the first batch of rolls. I was kneeling over the bucket of water, checking to see how I'd look with a pug nose.

"What is he doing?" Nusia asked, stubbing out her cigarette on a plate.

"What are you up to?" Mother shrieked. "Have you gone mad, or what?"

"A meshuggener," Andzia Katz laughed.

—

At night, I heard a gentle knocking on the windowpane.

"Andzia! Let me in," Nusia was pleading outside the window.

Mother ran on tiptoe to open the door. They whispered so as not to wake Andzia Katz. Every so often a match was scratched and the kitchen grew light.

"Leave him!" Mother said. "You're still young."

"I love him."

Nusia knocked off the ash, tapping her cigarette against the plate.

"Don't be a fool!"

In the morning, the kitchen window was open.

—

Mother decided to visit Nusia.

"You, too," she told me.

She washed my face with gray soap that she had acquired in exchange for matches and ordered me to clean my teeth with the foam from my face. Andzia Katz put the iron on the stove and handed me a warm shirt she had made from a woman's blouse. I had a hard time pulling my shoes over the greenish military socks and I placed my foot on the chair so Mother could tie the laces for me.

On the way I started limping.

"Your knees?" Mother asked.

"No. The socks."

I sat down on the sidewalk, took off the socks, and put them in my pocket.

—

Nusia opened the door for us at the Tabaczyńskis'. They weren't at home. Long tulle curtains hung on the windows. A cat was sleeping on an armchair. Little figurines on the bookshelves watched where we were going. Somewhere inside the apartment a clock was ticking. We climbed the stairs to the main room on the floor above.

A painting in a gilded frame hung on the wall. A wounded uhlan was slumped in the saddle, his reins slipping out of his hands. His shako and saber had fallen onto the snow. Steam rose from the horse's nostrils.

Kopcio was lying on a bed beneath the painting. He had tucked the sheet and blanket up against the wall. His bare feet protruded from his trouser legs. His shirt collar and cuffs were unbuttoned. He was holding a notebook in his delicate hands. His chin and cheeks, covered with a dark blue growth, were trembling convulsively. His eyes were closed and wet.

"Not even graves have remained after us," he bellowed.

"That's true," Mother agreed. "We couldn't find Bronek."

Kopcio opened his eyes.

"But did you peek under the ground?" he giggled.

"Have you gone mad?!"

"He's drunk," Nusia said.

Kopcio threw the notebook at them.

"I spit on it! I am not who I am. You're not, either! Do you think you're alive? Poor fools!"

He glanced at the uhlan and turned his face to the wall.

Nusia covered him with the blanket and picked up the notebook from the floor.

"Maybe he wouldn't drink if someone would print it? But who?"

"Go to the NKVD!" Mother said maliciously. "They print pamphlets and posters."

"Andzia! What are you talking about?!"

"Look at yourself! Skin and bones. You're going to die like a dog."

"I would like to finish it for him. He can't write it himself."

"Leave him!"

"He has lovers."

"What sort?"

"Any at all."

Mother and Michał

Mother came back from work and tossed a rolled-up newspaper onto the table. The paper rolled over to the pot of potato soup that Andzia had placed on the table. Stalin's eyes, the size of Salka Krochmal's buttons, looked at the soup.

"I froze this morning," Mother said.

"Me, too, going to school."

"You?" She sounded surprised. "You never feel cold."

She said that the morning had been awful. The wind had flung dry leaves against her face. To make matters worse, the factory sirens had started wailing. They were howling from the refinery and extraction towers, from the roofs of the electric and gas works, and also from the great pumps positioned above the locomotive depot. She had raced to UKRGAZ, clutching the rubles she'd received for her rolls. She was reminded of the refineries where Papa and Bronek had worked: "Karpaty," "Małopolska," "Galicja," and "Polmin." Such lovely names! What had they done wrong to deserve being changed into these idiotic combinations of Russian letters?

Suddenly she noticed a short man in a black jacket walking toward her. His neck stuck out of his jacket collar, surrounded by a white noose formed by his shirt. His hair was dark blond and he had clear blue eyes. She thought she recognized him. But she didn't know from where. She slowed down and, transferring the rubles to her other hand, wiped her palm on the dishcloth in the roll bag. The man stopped in front of her.

"Don't you recognize me?" he asked.

It was the voice of a boy she'd known in Gymnasium.

"It's you! Where have you come from?"

"From Russia. I went to look for my wife and child. They're dead."

"Bronek died, too."

"I know."

The next day I saw them through the window as they were entering the courtyard. The man did not look like a Jew. They said goodbye outside the door and Mother came into the kitchen.

"Who's that?" I asked.

"Michał."

"A Jew?"

"Yes."

"Jews aren't named Michał."

"They are, they are," Mother laughed.

Soon, Michał paid us a visit. He brought tea in a little jar and a cardboard box with white sugar cubes. Mother placed these presents on the table that she had scoured earlier in order to remove the remains of flour. She took mugs and a glass with a teaspoon out of the credenza. When the water came to a boil, she used a rag to pick up the pot and poured the boiling water into the jar.

"If only it doesn't break!" she said nervously.

"*Kipiatok!*" he said in Russian, rubbing his hands. "Boiling water!"

The tea leaves unfolded and rose to the top. Although they were floating in boiling water, they looked alive. When Grandma Minia drank bitter tea from a glass in a silver holder it smelled just like this. Father would be rocking gently in the rocking chair with the braided wicker seat. He would take white cubes from the sugar bowl next to Grandmother's eyeglasses and suck the strong tea through them.

Mother, Andzia Katz, and I sat squeezed together on the bench. It was so low that the table top came up to my eyes. Mother didn't sit much taller. Only Andzia Katz looked normal. Michał, seated on the sewing machine chair, poured some of the steeped tea from the jar into his glass, added boiling water, and threw in two lumps of sugar. He stirred it carefully and handed the spoon to Mother.

He told us about Siberia and the many months of traveling until he arrived there. When he set out with a group of Russian officials and their families they were bombed by the Germans. Then the war at the rear ended and no one knew where the front was. Displaying his *komandirovka*, his official pass to Orsk, he traveled by trains, trucks, and horse-drawn wagons. Women on kolkhozes wanted him to stay because the men were gone. Finally, he made it to his destination and saw snow-covered cottages in the steppe. That was Orsk.

Soon, trucks arrived and an oil refinery that had been shipped in pieces from America was unloaded onto the frozen ground. The boilers with pipes protruding high above them were immediately covered over with snow. From the snowy distances columns of German POWs crept in, hungry and wrapped in rags. They kept on coming like ants and grew into enormous anthills. They worked as long as they were able to. Then they were thrown into pits that were covered over only when they filled up. Several months later the refinery came on line and tank cars filled with gas and oil set off for the front. They began constructing a pipeline and the anthills dispersed, crawling alongside the lines of pipes as they disappeared underground.

As an engineer, Michał was allotted smoked fish, alcohol, and bread. He lived in a room with a woodstove. An ice-covered window looked out onto a yard where the fish was hanging. He would crawl out, wrapped in his sheepskin coat, and cut off a few slices. He traded the alcohol for potatoes and onions (if there were any). He gave half the bread to his landlady as payment for doing his laundry and cleaning. Whenever he was summoned to the Ministry, he brought back fruit from Moscow.

"Do the Russians take good care of their doctors?" Mother asked.

"Yes," Michał answered.

"I'm worried about Milo."

"If he's alive, he's well-off there."

Mother and Andzia Katz started reciting a list of the dead. Alphabetically, so as not to make a mistake, they called out the names of the students, both girls and boys, from the Gymnasium. They counted up the sisters, brothers, parents, and grandparents for each student they named. And how many cousins, aunts, and uncles there were! Some of the families were so numerous that sometimes they confused the first names or made mistakes as to the dates and types of deaths.

Michał's weak tea grew cold. His neck turned red and his upper lip slipped onto his lower lip. When Mother and Andzia Katz finished, he kissed their hands and paced back and forth in the kitchen for a long time.

At last he said, "I'm not going to stay here. I'll either return to Orsk or leave for Poland."

Outside the window, the trees were swaying in the wind. Their leaves billowed and fell like the skirts of a giant walking around outside the courtyard in the autumn. That was the first time I saw a Jew who had survived somewhere other than Borysław. I wanted to tell him that I had survived by a miracle and I was still afraid. I was holding my mug with what was left of my tea. A sugar cube was dissolving in my mouth. I licked my sweet, sticky lips.

"Sugar destroys tooth enamel," Michał said.

"Don't suck on it," said Mother.

Several days later, rocking on my chair, I was gnawing on a chocolate bar from Michał. Mother came over and knelt on the bench. Licking her finger, she picked up the crumbs from the chocolate and ate them, lost in thought.

"Young Jews are getting married," she said. "Two have already asked me to marry them. They were in love with me even in Gymnasium. But they're beggars. They need help themselves. Yesterday, Michał proposed to me. He's got a job at the petroleum trust. He needs a woman to make a home for him."

I noticed that the burdocks near the fence had disappeared. Apparently, someone ate them. So many leaves had already fallen from the trees that our courtyard could be seen through the black branches. I was suspicious about what Pan Skiba had hung up on the hooks in the pantry.

"Michał was in love with me, too," Mother continued, "but I had no idea. He was living in poverty in Ratoczyn. But he was such a fine student that he didn't pay tuition. After he graduated he got a scholarship to the Lwów Polytechnic even though the *numerus clausus* was already in effect. He graduated at the top of his class with a degree in chemistry."

I slid my tongue over my palate and my teeth in order to dislodge the chocolate that was stuck there. Mother drummed her fingers on the table.

"They took away his mother, sister, and brother," she said. "They burned his wife in the synagogue. They killed his little boy."

"What was his name?" I asked.

"Whose?"

"His boy's."

"I don't know."

I broke off a square of chocolate.

"I told him yesterday that I don't love him. Maybe someday that will change, but now I can't feel anything. Nusia says I shouldn't think about myself, because you need a father."

Michał took me for a walk. We set out along a sandy road that didn't intersect with any others but ran straight ahead, disappearing in its own dust. I dragged along reluctantly because my knees were all swollen. Michał looked at his watch. His colleagues were waiting for him at a meeting at the trust.

"Do your legs hurt?" he asked.

"Yes."

"You ought to have a cane."

I was remembering a dream I'd had. Usually, I slept on my side with my knees tucked up to my chin. But last night I had turned over onto my back and stretched out my arms, like Father on the pallet. Germans carrying rifles showed up in the courtyard. They looked in through the window. They went into the kitchen and opened the door with the iron handle. They leaped out of the Kukryniks drawing that was pinned to the bedstead. Bullets struck my hands and chest.

"You're walking and sleeping."

Michał shook me by the shoulder.

"I'm not sleeping."

—

I sensed that Father was walking behind me. I asked him to agree to Michał. He didn't want to. Repeating my request didn't help. Only when I said in a very low voice, "Papa, help the people I love and Michał, too," did the choking in my throat subside.

"What are you muttering? You're daydreaming."

"I'm not daydreaming."

—

Michał glanced at his watch and took my hand. His fingers were like Grandfather's, short, with carefully trimmed nails.

"Your mommy and I want to get married," he said. "I know how much you loved your father. I won't take his place, but I will take care of you. I will guarantee you an education, because under socialism that is the only property you can own. Your mother also deserves something after everything she lived through. I lost my wife and my two-month-old son. I wanted to take them to Russia, but my father-in-law said that you mustn't travel with an infant."

"What was his name?" I asked.

"Who?"

"Your son."

"Romuś."

—

Is God able to change what he himself wrote in the books of life and death? Maybe so. After all, I saw Grandfather promising God that if He saved us, he could be taken from the barracks. What about Romuś? Teresa had certainly pleaded with God to take her instead of Romuś. But she wasn't eligible for an exchange, because she herself was supposed to perish. But could I have died in place of Romuś?

—

Mother and Michał went to Ratoczyn. I stayed with Andzia Katz, who was sewing at her machine. I read on the floor about the Polish gentry's battle with the Muscovites in *Pan Tadeusz* by Adam Mickiewicz, and I played with a spider that was trying to crawl under the credenza. When I moved my finger close to it, it retreated, and when I took away my hand, it started moving again in the direction of the credenza. Moving its thin legs one after the other, it kept a constant distance from my finger.

That's just how old Maciek walked, parrying Gifrejter's bayonet with his saber. He pushed his glasses onto his nose with his free hand. (Grandfather also used to put on wire-rimmed glasses without interrupting his writing in his account book.) Looking at his opponent, Maciek started backing up. Gifrejter, certain of victory, thrust with his bayonet so forcefully that he lost his balance. Maciek knocked the rifle out of his hand and slashed his hand and face.

Thus fell Gifrejter, first among the Muscovite swordsmen,
A knight of three crosses and four medals.

Leading his men, the gloomy, mysterious count galloped straight ahead at half a battalion of Russian infantry who stood ready to fire. I imagined that he looked like Kopcio, who also was afraid of nothing and always did whatever he wanted to do.

It was dark now. I left the open book on the floor and stood up. The spider had escaped under the credenza. There was nothing to see outside the window. Maybe someone attacked them? They killed Michał and Mother is lying wounded in the courtyard. She's groaning, and I can't hear her because the machine is rattling.

I lifted one foot and froze. My knee hurt. I tried breathing as slowly as possible, but I couldn't stop completely. When the noise in my ears drowned out the rattling of the machine, it seemed that I had stopped time. Mother is not bleeding now. I waited with my foot raised for someone to come to her aid, because I myself was afraid to go out into the courtyard.

"Meshuggener!" Andzia Katz laughed. "Why are you standing like a stork?"

We heard their voices outside the window. Andzia Katz set out plates on the table.

Michał appeared just in his shirtsleeves, carrying a red goose-down quilt. Mother came in after him, his black jacket draped around her shoulders.

"The lights are burning again on the oil wells," she said.

Michał carried the quilt into the other room and on his way back picked up my book from the floor.

"Don't read lying down," he said. "You'll ruin your eyes."

"There's a table for reading," said Mother.

—

Michał ate his soup and left. (In the morning, someone important was supposed to come to the trust from Lwów.) Mother put the dirty plates and spoons on the stove so she could wash them with sand in the morning and started telling about their visit to Ratoczyn.

It was a long journey. They walked from one hill to another, and each time you could see farther and farther. The wind was stripping the remaining leaves from the trees and carrying them over the stubble fields to the oil fields. The wells, which from a distance looked like matchsticks stuck into the ground, reached all the way to the dark forest. Michał pointed out an isolated cottage down below. That was his home. They began walking downhill. The cottage disappeared and reappeared among the hills and trees, as if it were skipping from place to place.

"What did you live on here?" Mother asked.

"Mama had a little shop. Vegetables in the garden. Our own milk."

"A cow?"

"A goat."

A low fence overgrown with grass and nettles surrounded the cottage. Rusty hinges were all that remained of the gate. A scarecrow had no eyes under its hat. A woman and a man holding a kitchen knife in his hand emerged from inside the house. They stopped on the top step. The lower one was broken and propped up with a stone.

"What happened to my mother?" asked Michał.

"They took her away together with your sister's little boy," the woman said.

"And you, have you come back to Ratoczyn?" the peasant asked.

"No."

"We would have hidden her." He hid the knife behind his back. "But not with the child."

"There's a quilt left," the woman said. "I'll bring it right away."

—

Andzia Katz blew out the flame in the lamp above the sewing machine. We went into the other room in the dark. It was as soft on the quilt as on the hay at Pan Turów's.

"During the first war, Michał's father appeared to him in a dream." Mother pulled her dress off over her head. "He was standing in no man's land in his Austrian uniform. A Russian bullet caught him in the head. Michał woke up and ran to the stall so as not to awaken his mother. He spent the night pressed against the goat and crying. Then an official letter arrived from Vienna. His father had actually died that very night."

"You don't say!" Andzia Katz marveled.

"If you had seen that poverty!" Mother sighed, and lay down on the quilt. "I don't know how his mother coped! And he! He must have been incredibly gifted to have gotten an education."

"A lot also depends on luck," Andzia Katz yawned.

Repatriates

On November 15, 1944, we set out for Drohobycz. (Nusia took over the roll business.)

Michał came for us in a truck that had a crank for starting the motor. He and the driver brought out Teresa's bed and placed it on the truck bed. We climbed up steep wooden steps and clambered into the cab. Inside, it smelled of gas and grease. Michał sat in the center of the bench and took me on his knees. Mother, holding the quilt, sat next to the door and spoke with Andzia Katz through the rolled-down window. The driver turned the crank.

"Give it some gas, sir," he called out.

Michał pulled on a brass knob near the steering wheel. The motor growled and the truck began to shudder. The driver came inside, banged his fist on the wooden steering wheel, and then pressed down on a metal rod that stuck up from the floor. There was a grinding noise, the truck lurched, and we drove out of the courtyard. On Pańska Street Mother rolled up the window to keep out the cold.

"What kind of truck is this?" I asked the driver.

"Russian. The devil take it!"

"What's it called?"

"ZIS 5."

"Don't bother the man," Michał said.

We moved into a house near a bakery. There were two rooms and a kitchen. One room was occupied by engineer Tusiek Sejden and his wife, and the other was Michał's. There were three mattresses on Michał's floor. Mother transferred two of them to Teresa's bed and covered them with the quilt. She placed the third one, for me, on a table because on the floor there was a draft from the window.

The next morning Mother told me to get down from the table. I watched as she removed the mattress and set the table for breakfast. When Michał finished rinsing his teeth in the kitchen, she tied my shoelaces and sent me out to wash up. The soap wouldn't dissolve in the cold water. I added some boiling water from the kettle and made foam, splashing my fingers in the basin. I returned to the room after breakfast. Michał put on a dark blue overcoat and ran down the stairs.

"Your turn," Mother said. "With oil?"

"Yes."

She poured a thin, glistening stream out of a bottle onto slices of bread. I gnawed them quickly, because they were soaked and the oil was dripping onto the plate.

"Tea?"

"Yes, but make it strong, please."

She went into the kitchen to prepare the tea. I heard the clang of the stove lid and the voices of Tusiek Sejden and his wife, who were leaving for work. After licking my plate I went over to the window. I blew on the ice-covered pane to see if snow had fallen. There was an uproar near the bakery. I opened the window.

"There's no bread," the baker, wearing an apron, was shouting.

"Then bake some!"

"There's no flour."

Mother came in with a glass of tea. She set it on the table and ran over to slam down the window.

"You're crazy!" she screamed. "The whole apartment is going to be freezing."

The tea was hot and bitter. I stuck a few white cubes into my mouth because the bitterness nauseated me and, drinking in little sips, I blew on it carefully so as not to spit out the sugar.

"Sit straight," Mother said. "Michał says you are bent over like a *melamid.*"

She said she was going out and I was to sit in the house because the weather was terrible and I had to be careful about my lungs. She looked in the mirror and smoothed her eyebrows.

I saw her walk past the long bakery line and disappear around the corner.

—

At Andzia Katz's place I used to read in the middle of the floor. Now, when I was alone, I crept under the bed. I licked my fingers, wiped them on my trousers, and opened the book.

It was the night in *Pan Tadeusz* after the battle with the Muscovites. In the castle, Father Robak, who had shielded the count from the Russian troops' salvo, lay dying. Next to the bed, the old steward stood leaning on his rapier.

"I am Jacek Soplica," the dying man confessed.

The steward reached for his sword.

Long ago, his master, the haughty Horeszko, had refused to grant Soplica his daughter's hand. Jacek had lurked near the Horeszkos' castle, thinking about revenge. Candles were burning in the windows. Music resounded in the halls. They were carousing and drinking, adding insult to injury.

This took place at the time of the Targowica events, when wealthy Polish magnates called upon Russian support for their opposition to the new reform movement. Now the Muscovites were attacking the castle. The gentry mounted a furious defense. Corpses of jaegers were everywhere. Fury overcame Jacek at the sight of their defeat.

"They're cattle; they can't shoot straight!" he thought.

When a triumphant Horeszko came out into the yard, his diamond pin glittering, Jacek snatched up a Russian rifle and killed him. Then he stood there next to the walls. He did not run away, even though the steward was shooting at him.

A traitor! Everyone shunned Jacek. He ran away from his country and became a monk. Like a worm, he penetrated the border. He organized an uprising. He was arrested by the Germans and the Austrians. The Russians beat him with sticks. He was wounded at Jena. Now a bullet had struck him in the same spot. Dying for the count, the last of the Horeszkos, he begged for forgiveness. The steward hesitated.

I imagined that Mickiewicz wrote quickly. He put down a period, then dipped his pen in his inkwell and began a new line. He left a blank line after a paragraph, but he didn't stop. Only after he'd completed a chapter did he cover his inkwell to prevent the ink from drying out and go into the courtyard to breathe some fresh air.

Once, Father and Mother were blowing soap bubbles. I was in the living room at the time, sitting astride Grandfather's knee as if riding a horse. When I saw Grandmother Antonina going into my parents' bedroom I slipped off his knee and ran after her. She opened the big white door and I flew into the room. Trembling colorful balls were revolving in the air. Mother and Father were blowing on long straws with flared ends. A chain of little bubbles was flying out of Father's straw.

"Like children!" Grandmother smiled.

It was dark now and it had started raining. I crawled out from under the bed. There was no one in front of the bakery now. Where is Mother? She hadn't said she would be back so late. I was terrified that something bad had happened to her. Only Father could fix it. Who else was capable of turning things around and erasing everything from the memory of witnesses?

"Papa, make it so that nothing happened to Mama."

They came back in the evening. Soaking wet, but jolly. They brought a bar of chocolate wrapped in wax paper that was part of Michał's rations at the trust.

"Don't touch it!" said Mother. "It's for a winter coat for you."

Michał rubbed his hands and smiled.

"We got married by a rabbi," he said.

"The witnesses were his wife and son," Mother added.

On warmer days, Mother took me along to the market. But even then she made me wear Michał's coarse, itchy sweater. I carried the torn oilcloth roll bag for her. In the bag the jar in which Michał had once brought us tea rocked from side to side. Thanks to its tight screw cap it was possible to use it as a container for milk. Mother sniffed the milk in the big jugs to check that it wasn't sour and shook the eggs, listening for signs that they weren't "flying around inside."

The market was legal, but not the goods that were sold there. Policemen in plain clothes showed up several times a day. They had red armbands and cocked German rifles. At the sight of them, the entire market ran away in a panic. The peasant women would grab their heavy milk containers and drag them toward the exit or run away with their baskets of eggs and butter wrapped up in paper. The women who ran the fastest, however, were the ones who had brought pieces of meat in old schoolbags. The buyers also fled, pressing their purchases to their chests. Soon, only soldiers would be loitering in the square. They didn't fear the police and had come here to sell their greatcoats and caps with earflaps.

Mother bought a shaggy greatcoat for me at the market in exchange for the bar of chocolate. She also found a tailor who agreed to make it into a winter coat. He told her it was his last job in Drohobycz, because he was leaving for Poland on the first repatriation transport.

Walking behind Mother, I avoided the puddles so as not to splash the coat, which I clutched tightly against my chest. We passed two squares. In the first, old trees were growing. They were so big and dense that they blotted out the sky, even though they'd already lost their leaves. The second square was smaller. A sandy path with protruding iron supports for benches ran alongside the bushes. Mother turned right past the church and the Gymnasium on Zielona Street.

The tailor lived in a one-story building at number 12 Floriańska Street. In the entryway, Mother took the greatcoat from me and walked up to the door on which hung a sign:

BON. CHURLUSZ
MASTER TAILOR

"What does 'Bon.' mean?" I whispered.

"Bonifacy," Mother replied. "But his whole name wouldn't fit."

A thin little man in a black suit and a vest with a gold watch chain opened the door. A tape measure dangled from his shoulder and a notebook stuck out of his jacket pocket. Beckoning to us to come inside, he retreated to the main room. It had a peculiar smell.

"Welcome, welcome," he repeated.

He took the greatcoat from Mother, held it up by the shoulder boards, looked carefully at the lining, and sniffed the underarms.

"The cloth is good," he confirmed. "Take it apart. Discard the lapels, collar, and cuffs. Cut from the rest. Change the buttons. It will become a coat."

He threw the greatcoat onto the floor and knelt in front of me, extending the tape measure.

"From the shoulder to the wrist. A loose fit."

He wrote down the measurements in his notebook and put the pencil behind his ear.

"Pan Churlusz," Mother asked, "what smells so wonderful here?"

"Cinnamon. The Jews on the other side of the wall had a spice shop."

"Did you by any chance know Pan Unter from the orphanage?"

"I used to sew for him."

"He was his father's uncle."

"A good-looking man," said the tailor.

The kneeling tailor's head was at the same height as mine. He had blue and red veins around his moist pupils. Did he know Father? Had he, perhaps, sewn something for him? I was terrified that he would ask me something. I shut my eyes so tight that I saw colored circles.

And then the master tailor slowly started to rise up. First, the vest with the gold watch chain passed by, then his hands with the tape measure, and finally his bent legs. Only when he was under the ceiling did he stretch out comfortably and remove the perfectly sharpened pencil from behind his ear.

"My dear lady!" he said to Mother. "Before the war not only did I sew, but I made sketches for fashion magazines. That suit won first prize."

He made a quick sketch in his notebook. He moved the point from top to bottom and, going back to where he'd started, drew a wide lapel with a zigzag mark. He put in buttons with three little flourishes, though there was no jacket as yet. He made a buttonhole with a horizontal line and planted a handkerchief in it with a smudge from the eraser. With parallel lines he sewed in the sleeves, and with wavy lines, trouser legs without cuffs. He went back to the jacket. With the side of the exposed pencil point he shaded in wide bands, leaving thin white stripes between them.

(I saw Father in this suit at the cemetery!)

"That's my husband's suit!" Mother screamed. "Do you remember it?" she asked me.

"Children remember," the master tailor muttered.

"He knows everything."

"And the morphine?" The master smiled bitterly. "It was in a little pouch tied with a tape. Wrapped in wax paper that appeared to come from a bar of chocolate. What happened to it?"

I touched my neck. The pouch was gone.

"Eh, there!" Mother waved her hand dismissively. "He didn't need it anymore."

I opened my eyes. The tailor was still kneeling in front of me. He was holding the pencil between his teeth now. His notebook with the figures written down in it was on the floor.

"Turn around," he said indistinctly. "We'll measure the back. Across the shoulders. From the neck to the calves."

"Not too short," Mother interjected. "Room to grow."

"We'll arrange it. At the hem and in the sleeves."

"Will there be something left over for patches?"

"A little."

"Churlusz . . . What kind of a name is that?" Mother asked.

"Tatar."

"So you're going to Poland even though you're a Tatar . . ."

"A Polish Tatar, my dear lady."

I put on my new coat and fastened the chin strap of the leather flight cap that Michał had brought me a few days before. Mother looked me over, pleased, and warned me not to get dirty.

I went for a walk among the small houses surrounded by wooden fences from which the stakes had been ripped out. Then I walked as far as the gray apartment houses. The shops on the ground floors were padlocked. Sparrows and crows were preening their feathers on the roof. The water in the puddles had turned to ice, but I was warm.

Mother sent me to school. When I saw children I crossed to the other side of the street. But near the school, both sidewalks were occupied. Brushing against other children, I walked down the stairs to the coatroom. No one had a flight cap or a coat cut from a greatcoat. I snatched the cap off my head and stuck it into my pocket, just as I'd done with my armband on the Aryan side. I almost tore off my buttons when I unbuttoned my coat. I hung it on a hook and with my eyes fixed on the floor I ran out into the corridor. I walked into the wrong classroom. I backed out and, glancing at the cards with Roman numerals affixed to the doors, I made it to the right room.

Because I didn't look around, I saw only the children at the front of the class. But I had no idea who was sitting near me. In Russian class, arithmetic, and conversation about Stalin, I thought about the best way to walk out of the school after classes were over.

During recess, I remained at my desk. Students' voices and the shuffling of shoes reached me from the corridor. When someone looked into the classroom, I pretended I was picking something up from the floor. Under the bench I whispered lines of verse that were woven together like Andzia Katz's red braid: "Oh, springtime of war, springtime of harvest!"

Autumn was almost over, and I was still alive.

On my way back from school, I saw Mother standing in front of the house.

"We're waiting here for Michał," she said.

"What happened?" I asked, astonished.

"Tusiek wanted to pull me into bed."

"But he's got the flu."

"That's why he's at home!" she yelled.

We walked around until Michał came home from work. Mother left me then and ran to him. She pressed her face into the lapels of his dark blue overcoat. He kissed her hair. They were standing at a distance. Then they moved toward me.

"Scum!" I heard Michał say.

"He said, 'That puppy won't be enough for you.'"

"I'm going to have a talk with him!" Michał ran into the house.

Soon, he came out and took Mother inside.

"Wait here," he said to me. "Tusiek wants to apologize to Mother."

On the day they changed the film at the theater, I got leather gloves from Michał. I loved putting them on, flexing my fingers, and tugging on the fragrant leather. They looked great. But in front of the theater entrance

I slipped them into my pockets. On the street, I clutched the rubles in my numb hand.

The seats were already filled with a lot of children and soldiers who were stamping their feet and shouting, "Get on with it! Get on with it!" A tall boy squeezed his way through my row and sat down next to me. When the lights went out, I unfastened my cap and pulled on my gloves.

The war on the screen was silent for a while; the sound wasn't working. The field guns fired silently, and people only moved their lips. Suddenly, there was a resounding crash and an officer with a revolver on a leather strap bellowed so terrifyingly, "*Za Stalina! Za rodinu!* For Stalin! For the motherland!" that a shudder practically ran through the audience. But the sound system was immediately adjusted and now the soldiers leaping out of the trenches were howling much more quietly: "*Uraa! Uraa! Uraa!*"

Marshals bedecked with medals were standing around a large table on which maps were laid out. Stalin, wearing a uniform with only a single star, was pointing to something on one of the maps. The marshals leaned over, concentrating intensely, exchanged glances, and began clapping enthusiastically. The soldiers in the auditorium and the boy sitting next to me also started to applaud.

A crowd of people near the Kremlin shouted, shook their fists, and spat on unshaven German generals clothed in rags. Behind them, across the great square, an endless line of prisoners of war dragged themselves along. Stalin, standing on a platform, raised his finger threateningly. The theater seethed with anger.

Waiters with bottles of wine froze in obsequious postures. Diplomats seated against the walls rose from their chairs. Roosevelt and Churchill drank to Stalin's health. Stalin stood up modestly and rapped his finger against his glass, asking for silence. The soldiers howled with joy. The boy gave me a nudge with his elbow.

After the war there was a fairy tale. On a large stove, such as I had never seen, a father was dying. He was surrounded by his children and a cat. Suddenly, Kostiei appeared, his face concealed under his hood. Meowing, the cat ran out of the room. Kostiei promised to heal the father in exchange for the flower of a fern that he needed in order to rule the world. The children went into the forest and tore off the flower at midnight. When they went back, the entire audience, in two languages, advised them what to do. At home, they were greeted by Kostiei. Bony fingers emerged from his sleeves and, from under his hood, a skeleton's skull. The children recognized Death and didn't give him anything. The father died, but immediately came back to life, touched by the flower of the fern.

When the lights came on and the doors were opened in order to air out the auditorium, smoky from cheap Russian tobacco, my neighbor grabbed my hand.

"Where did you get such nice gloves? Why should you have them?" he demanded in Russian. I could feel his breath on my face. "Give them to me!" he barked.

He tore the gloves off my hands and walked out of the theater with them. There was fresh snow in the street. On the way home, I thought up various stories about how I lost the gloves. It turned out the stories were unnecessary. On the table lay a *komandirovka,* an order to proceed to Orsk, and a train ticket filled out in pencil.

"I won't go." Mother was crying from rage. "I'd rather drop dead."

"They saved our lives," Michał said.

"They're boors!"

"Not so loud!"

The next day, Michał discussed the matter with his boss at the trust. His boss thought he should send a petition to the Minister and, at the same time, sign up for the repatriation transport that would be leaving in a week. Before an answer could arrive from Moscow (undoubtedly, a refusal) he would already be in Poland.

"Make a run for it," his boss said in Russian as he and Michał said their good-byes.

"We will be traveling," Michał explained, "through Sambor, Chyrów, and Malhowice. Then Przemyśl, Radymno, Jarosław, Przeworsk, and Rzeszów. Poland begins in Przemyśl, and in Rzeszów there's Winkler, who will help us."

The train station was surrounded by a cordon of soldiers. Red flags and a portrait of Stalin hung on the iron sign that announced DROHOBYCZ. Beside the gate was a desk on which lay notebooks with lists of names. Officers wearing caps with earflaps with stars or eagles on them were seated on chairs taken from the waiting room. Every so often, they went into the building to warm up and then a soldier who carried a rifle with a long bayonet affixed stood guard over the notebooks. There was a line in front of the desk. Her teeth chattering, Mother fastened my coat under my neck with a hook and eye. Michał, shivering in his dark blue overcoat (he'd left his sheepskin in Orsk), strained to see if there were traces of red ink next to his name.

"*Pochemu uezhaete?*" an officer with a star asked.

Michał didn't respond.

"Why are you leaving?" a Polish officer with an eagle interpreted.

"I have family there."

"Aha."

"*Prokhodite!* Go through!" The Russian shut his notebook.

Mother and I were next.

"*Prokhodite!*"

There was a cloud of steam over the locomotive. The engineer, his head out the window, watched the crowd moving along beneath him. The people walked alongside open freight cars. The letters PUR (for State Repatriation Bureau), painted in white, were visible on the open doors. The train was considerably longer than the platform, and the line of these PUR cars stretched somewhere into the distance.

Our car was at the end. Jumping down from the platform, we stepped clumsily over the railway ties of the neighboring track. Michał carried a valise and a briefcase with documents, and Mother a bag of food. My hands were empty. The floor of the car was way over my head. Michał lifted me under the arms and planted me inside. Then he and some other man helped Mother get in.

The inside of the car was filled with wooden benches placed back to back. There was a narrow aisle between them and a wall with little windows under the ceiling. At one end, behind a wooden partition, was a bucket with a lid, and on the other end, a stove with a pipe that went through the roof and a barrel of drinking water.

The bench was narrow and slippery. In my thick coat and flight cap I felt like a hussar in a helmet and armor. I kept sliding off and having to push myself back up. With my legs dangling, I thought about how hussars managed to tie their shoes. Suddenly, it dawned on me: their boots were made of iron.

"Don't swing your legs; you'll kick someone," said Michał.

"Undo the hook," added Mother.

While I was struggling with the hook, the car lurched forward violently. I fell onto the floor. Michał snorted with laughter.

"They've hooked up a second locomotive," he said, wiping his eyes.

"Stand up, or you'll get your coat dirty," Mother said.

Heads kept poking in through the open door. Some people passed by several times, looking for their seats. One boy, who was shorter than the floor, had to jump to see into the car. However, he didn't find the person he was looking for, and walked away. The car was so large that it still seemed empty, even though entire families were climbing into it.

"Christ be praised!" someone said to us.

Mother smiled at the greeting.

"This damn car!" she whispered to us. "They took my mother away in just such a freight car."

By the time the doors were closed late at night, the car was full. People for whom there were no seats lay down on their own and other people's bundles. Members of families who arrived at the last minute were scattered over the whole floor and talked with each other over the heads of other people. In the dim light of the lamps hanging from the ceiling the peasant women's colored kerchiefs stood out, now draped around their shoulders. Coal was burning in the stove, brought in that evening by railway workers. Faces, illuminated by the glow from the ash pit, flickered red and gold.

The rear locomotive whistled. We heard the hiss of steam being released. The banging of the buffers drew closer to us. The car lurched and we were moving. The front locomotive whistled. The wheels began to rumble. The station lights were reflected in the windows and then disappeared.

The family next to the water barrel started singing. Soon, others joined in. Finally, the song spread throughout the car and surrounded us. The thin, high voices of women and boys rang out:

> Kind-hearted Mother, protectress of people,
> may the weeping of orphans move you to pity!
> Exiles from the Garden, we cry out to you:
> have mercy, have mercy, save us from wandering.

A young woman from the Tarnopol area who was sitting on the floor near us broke off praying the rosary as she'd been doing all day and, holding a bead to mark her place, began singing along with the others:

> 'Tis the truth, for our evil, we deserve to be punished
> by God with His scourge of severity;
> But when the Father, angered, wields his lash,
> happy is he who flees to our Mother.

As the train picked up speed the lamps swayed faster and faster, until they finally started spinning on their hooks. Elongated shadows of hands and heads whirled on the walls. A carousel of the most amazing animals and birds went round and round. A large crow appeared on the ceiling and disappeared near the window, outside of which there was darkness.

I was awakened by the noise of doors being locked into position. Before ours were slammed shut, I saw the platform and a sign that read

SAMBOR. We started moving, but then the train stopped immediately and began to back up.

They kept shunting us back and forth all day long, allowing military transports to pass.

At night, we were where we had been in the morning.

The next day, we were stopped on a side track in Chyrów. It was pouring, and the fields all around were covered with mist. We stretched out as best we could. People who left the car to relieve themselves had mud-covered boots afterward and scraped off their soles on the bolts in the floorboards.

From Chyrów we headed south. The train was traveling at breakneck speed. Dark lines of telegraph poles flashed by in the windows. The sky was gray without any rays of sunlight. The travelers grew animated.

"Tomorrow we'll be in Poland."

"And Lwów?"

"It, too, will return."

The woman from near Tarnopol told how a gang of Bandera's men had attacked her village. They came at night. They hurled grenades through the windows. People fled to the church. She didn't make it and hid inside a chimney. After the screams and shots grew quiet she waited a few more hours and, completely black, came out of her hiding place.

"They burned everyone in the church," she said, returning to her rosary.

Again I was looking for Father in the cemetery. I was floundering in dense grass among broken stones. I lifted up a fragment to see if it might have my family name on it.

"Our Father, who art in Heaven," the woman prayed.

"Papa!"

"Thy kingdom come. Thy will be done."

"Here and in Rzeszów."

"And forgive us our sins."

"That we are abandoning you again."

"As we forgive those who trespass against us. Amen."

I had learned to pray from Janka.

"Do you know 'Our Father'?" she'd asked, looking under the bed.

"No."

I slid out just a little.

She bent down with difficulty and touched me on the forehead, heart, and shoulders.

"Cross yourself and repeat after me."

When we finished, she straightened up.

"If they catch you, pray out loud."

—

The train was slowing down. The wheels clattered less frequently. Finally, the brakes squealed and we stopped. The coal in the iron stove was burning down. It was cold. We heard soldiers' voices. Someone climbed on a bench and looked out the window.

"Hey, fellows! Where are we?"

"In a field."

"Why are we stopped again?"

"Who knows?"

The travelers were falling asleep. Mother leaned her head against Michał's shoulder and dozed with her hands on her knees. Michał was snoring.

—

Again, the clatter of doors being pushed open. Cold air blowing in. A soldier was standing in the early morning sunshine and rubbing his hands. Clouds of steam rose from his mouth and nose.

"Whoever wants to can go outside!"

He ran to open other cars.

Yawning, we stepped over the sleeping woman from near Tarnopol. Michał jumped down onto the cinder-strewn embankment and held out his hands to Mother. I slid down slowly. Soldiers were perched on a roof near a telephone box. A long, rotting wire protruded from the box.

"Women to the left! Men to the right!" an officer ordered.

I walked among the peeing men and boys. Only when everyone was behind me did I relieve myself.

Michał was waiting for me next to the car.

"Where were you? Mama is upset."

"I had an upset stomach."

"He had an upset stomach," Michał told Mother inside the car.

—

By the time we were moving again, there had been nothing to drink for many hours. Fortunately, the ride was short. Apparently, we had been stopped the whole time outside of Malhowice. At the station, they brought in buckets of water from a large pump for the steam locomotives.

In the morning we were awakened by the clatter of fast-moving trains. We pushed open the doors. Military transports were passing on the neighboring tracks. Small flags and cloth portraits of Stalin flapped between the locomotives' headlights. Soldiers were lying in the freight cars. On the flatbeds, there were tanks, field guns, and trucks that I couldn't identify.

Every train pulled a platform with machine guns. Next to the gun barrels that were pointed upward sat soldiers on iron saddles.

"That prick wanted a war with Stalin," someone said.

"That's Russia!" Michał whispered to Mother.

In Przemyśl, Michał went to phone Winkler. Unfortunately, he couldn't get a connection at the post office and the stationmaster's telephone was only for railway workers. He returned in a good mood, however. He pointed to the station's roof truss. A cardboard wreath of wheat with a hammer and sickle in the center was hanging from it.

"Do you see that bird?" he asked.

Squinting, I looked at the spikes of wheat, blackened from the damp. "I don't."

"Neither do I!" He snorted with laughter.

"Laugh all you like," said Mother, "but what about Winkler?"

The poles that supported the truss were plastered with proclamations in Polish. The oldest poster, which was almost entirely covered by others, bore the title MANIFESTO. The newest were narrow strips of paper on which was printed in large letters: HOME ARMY—HITLER'S HELPER; HOME ARMY—FILTHY REACTIONARY DWARF!; BEWARE HOME ARMY SPIES. On this one, small cards were pasted: "If you are alive, come to . . . ," "We are alive and are at . . ." Rain and snow were washing away the ink.

Walking along the high platform, I peered into the cars. They looked like apartments with the doors torn off. Women were rocking their infants. Men were tying up small trunks with string. Little girls were showing their dolls the people on the platform. The boys had gone to check out the locomotives.

During the Hitler times I lived on Pańska Street, at Janka's, at Pani Sprysiowa's, at Pani Hirniakowa's, and in the well. I was always losing someone and I had to remember more and more dead people. At Andzia Katz's I started to forget. What did Grandma Antonina look like? I didn't know. In the train, I asked Mother where Teresa's bed was. She shrugged.

If they seal the border, Nusia and Kopcio will remain in Borysław forever. Will I forget them, too?

A black top hat threaded its way among the heads of other people. I thought it belonged to Pan Bonifacy Churlusz, who was supposed to be traveling in this same transport. He was probably wearing a coat with a beaver collar like the one Grandfather ripped off Father's jacket. But the man in the top hat turned out to be a chimney sweep. He had a chain wrapped around him from which hung a black ball and a wire brush.

A black umbrella! That was definitely Pan Churlusz, an eccentric to beat all eccentrics. Under the umbrella, however, on a board covered with cheap felt and mounted on wheels, rode a legless boy. A sign hung around his neck: BLIND, DEAF, MUTE. The man who was pushing him held the umbrella so high that snow was falling on the boy's blond hair. I wanted to give him my flight cap, but I was afraid of Mother and Michał.

Someone called out, "Careful! Please don't step on it!" Perhaps Pan Churlusz had dropped his fashion album? The snow was melting fast and the paper could get soaked through. I ran to help him. But it was an elderly man who had dropped his books. Some boys had already picked them up and were wiping them with their sleeves.

"Well, we made it!" said Michał as we stood in the soup line in front of the PUR shed. "There's still Radymno, Jarosław, Przeworsk, and Rzeszów. Two days at most."

antidote

At Winkler's

We were standing in front of the train station in Rzeszów. The valise and the briefcase with documents were lying next to us in the snow. Mother was stamping her feet, shaking out the empty roll bag. I unfastened my flight cap and scratched my head.

Winkler drove up in a green Willys topped with a tarp with celluloid windows. Under the wiper blade on the windshield an eagle in a gold frame had been pasted; the top of the frame was cut off along with a piece of the eagle's head. First, high-top boots appeared from under the tarp, and then all of Winkler emerged in a leather overcoat with a fur collar.

"This is Winkler," Michał whispered to Mother.

While Winkler kissed her hand, the driver, in a greatcoat without a belt, shoved the valise into the rear seat. Michał squeezed into the center and took me onto his knees. Mother sat down next to him with the briefcase and the bag. During the drive Michał conversed with Winkler, who sat turned around to face him. Outside the celluloid windows hazy, distorted apartment houses were passing by.

That's what the world looked like through the fish bladders that Grandmother Antonina used to carefully remove when she prepared carp in aspic.

We stopped in front of a gray apartment house and walked up wide wooden steps to the second floor. Winkler pressed a black button in the door frame. The bell rang. A beautiful woman with golden hair opened the door.

Winkler introduced her: "Nella."

"*Pozhaluista.* Please enter," she invited us in in Russian.

Hot water was running out of the faucet. Steam formed clouds and settled in droplets on iron pipes that ran from the bathtub to the ceiling. Mother told me to lift my arms and she pulled off my shirt. I unfastened my belt and my trousers dropped to the floor. Finally, I took off my underpants, which Andzia Katz had sewn from the same woman's blouse from which she'd made my shirt. I got into the tub and Mother turned the faucet. When the water stopped foaming, I saw my feet. They were red and seemed to be disconnected from the rest of my legs. Water flowed over my back, chest, and belly as though it were running through pipes.

"There's no flesh on him." Nella spoke in Russian, touching my ribs.

"He's thin as a stick," Mother sighed, speaking in Polish. "He eats and he doesn't gain weight."

Nella looked at my legs.

"His knees are swollen," she observed.

"He limps," Mother confessed, and squeezed my shoulder.

Holding on to the rims of the tub, I slid into the hot water without bending my knees. It poured over my chin and seeped into my mouth. A bar of soap moved over my head. Mother's fingers scratched pleasantly, but my forehead and neck itched even more. I started scratching.

"Don't scratch," said Mother.

"Look at those lice!" Nella exclaimed.

"Lice!" Mother screamed. "He must have picked them up in the train."

Nella brought in a can of kerosene and a basin that she placed in front of me. Mother bent my head down until my forehead touched the basin's tin bottom. The cold, stinking kerosene gurgled. Mother's fingers again began to move around in my hair.

Nella threw my clothes into the stove and telephoned Winkler. She told him that I had lice and was naked. Could he send the Willys? Soon, the driver appeared. Nella and Michał went shopping. Mother laid out my coat on the floor. Wearing Nella's colorful bathrobe, with a towel wrapped around my head, I watched as she cleaned it under the arms with a kerosene-soaked rag.

"The seams are the worst," she said. "They lay their eggs there."

—

Cigarette smoke was everywhere at Winkler's ball. Sausages lay among uncorked vodka bottles and open tins of fish in tomato sauce. Officers in uniforms with the hooks unfastened surrounded two tables that had been placed next to each other.

The Russians had wide epaulets with glittering stars and wore gold, ruby, and green ribbons on their chests. The Poles' shoulder boards were narrower. Stars and bars were embroidered on them in silver thread. Silver, brown, and blue crosses hung on their uniforms. (Among the Russians' medals there was an occasional dark-brown Polish Cross of Valor with its extended arms.)

Among the officers there were officials of the Central Administration of the Oil Industry wearing jackets and sweaters. Some of them wore high-top boots, but the majority wore ankle boots or galoshes. They were all speaking louder and louder, gesturing broadly with their hands while holding glasses and cigarettes. Smoke flowed out of their mouths and noses.

A Russian major with a Cross of Valor stained with tomato sauce was recalling the first days after the liberation of Rzeszów. He was serving at that time in a general's quarters; the general was asleep on the other side of the wall. A soldier came in and reported that partisans with rifles had arrived. The major didn't want to wake the *komandir*.

"I put on my hat and go outside. I ask their commander, 'Who are you?' He says, 'The underground mayor of the city.'"

The major spoke in Russian. He tilted his head back and, moving his lips like a fish, blew out several rings that floated upward. Before they could break up on the ceiling, he forcefully exhaled the rest of the smoke.

"So I say to him, 'And the men standing here?' He answers, 'Government police.' I say, 'What government?' 'Polish,' he answers. 'Who appointed them?' 'The Home Army,' he replies."

He removed a piece of tobacco from his upper lip and brushed it onto the floor.

"'And where did you get the rifles?' He answers, 'We fired them at the Germans when we recaptured Rzeszów along with the Russians.'"

He shook his head at the underground mayor's cunning.

"Just look, what a clever tongue he has! So I say to him in a cultured way, 'Thank you for your assistance, but those little guns of yours are of no use now.'"

A general was seated on the couch in the corner of the room. Smoke filtered through his teeth onto rows of colored ribbons and an Order of Lenin. Flicking his cigarette ash into a crystal ashtray, the general listened to Winkler, who was saying something in Russian from the depths of his armchair.

Behind them, the silent engineers sat on chairs. Michał was fanning himself, driving away the blue smoke. He set his glass under his chair; he had filled it with water before the ball began. When Winkler stopped talking in order to take a breath, Michał glanced in Mother's direction.

She was standing among the women, wearing a dress I'd never seen, near the hot tile stove. She wasn't drinking or smoking. She looked smaller than usual. She looked like a girl with a colorful face. The only one prettier than her was Nella, who took tiny sips of her vodka and rubbed her back against the smooth, violet tiles.

"What kind of ball is this?" she laughed, addressing Mother in Russian. "There's no music."

Curtains, longer than at the Tabaczyńskis' house, hung from the tall windows. I pushed away the tulle and leaned on the windowsill. The street was illuminated by the light from the windows. A light snow was falling on the Willyses parked alongside the sidewalks.

—

Soon after the ball, Winkler sent us to Krosno in a Studebaker. The truck was similar to the ones I had seen on the flatbed cars in Malhowice. The motor whined and we drove so fast that the arrow reached the end of the scale. The windows got covered with frost even though the wipers were working nonstop. There was no one on the highway. Artillery guns were firing at each other from behind snow-covered hills. A boom on the right, the whistle of the shell, and an explosion on the left. Then a boom on the left, a whistle, and a detonation on the right. Squeezed into the cab of the truck, we sped from curve to curve with our heads down. After we drove over the thudding planks of a bridge and entered the forest, the driver slowed down.

"Germans?" Michał asked. "So close?"

"Partisans."

"Ukrainians?"

"Or ours."

—

We moved into the ground floor of a building that belonged to the Central Headquarters of the Petroleum Industry. A glassed-in veranda opened onto the main street. You went left to go to the market; to the right was the end of town. There the street became a highway and led across hills overgrown with snow-covered woods.

There was a wicker chair on the veranda. I sat on it in my coat and flight cap and watched the passersby through the large window.

At noon, Mother opened the door just a crack so as not to let the cold into the apartment, and handed me bread smeared with lard with bits of crackling in it and a slice of damp white cheese.

In the evening, she called me into the kitchen. Steam was rising from a bowl of cabbage soup with a bone in it to suck on. She told me to blow on it so as not to burn my mouth. She didn't eat. She was waiting to have dinner with Michał.

At night she turned out the light and stood near the window. I lay down on the sofa under a blanket. The down pillow smelled of starch. I could hear the footsteps of the engineer who lived in the apartment above ours.

—

Through the window I could see a flagpole with a white-and-red Polish flag.

In the corridor, the janitor pulled on the rope of a brass bell. Rapid footsteps could be heard approaching. A teacher dressed in riding breeches and high-top boots entered the classroom.

"Be seated!"

He threw his day log onto the table.

The talons of the white eagle that hung on the wall almost touched his head. With its outspread wings and legs, the bird looked like the letter *X*. A crown rose above it, not touching its feathers. Just as at Pani Sprysiowa's, where the thorns hanging in the air didn't wound Christ's bloody brow. The eagle's beak stuck out in profile; its upper part was curved over the lower part, like Michał's clenched lips.

The wind lifted the flag.

"Today is the three hundred sixty-third anniversary of the truce with Moscow," said the teacher. "The war was started by Ivan the Terrible, the Grand Prince of Moscow. A criminal with colossal ambitions, stained with the blood of innocents. And yet, Elizabeth the Great offered him her friendship."

The flag was flapping violently.

"Ivan was stopped by Stefan Batory. The Poles laid siege to Pskov. They built a wooden town with streets and a market square around its defensive walls. Two hundred thousand knights and their attendants were encamped there."

The flag drooped and snow began to fall.

"Muscovite envoys came running to Rome. The Orthodox want to unite with Catholicism! The Pope sent the Jesuit, Possevino, to persuade Poland to accept a truce. Ivan lost Inflanty and Polotsk, but he escaped with his life."

The janitor rang the bell. The teacher backed away from beneath the eagle.

"Warsaw is dead," he said, picking up his log book. "Lwów is captured. Targowica, those eighteenth-century puppets of Moscow, have reappeared in Lublin! Thank God, the Germans lost in the Ardennes."

The pupils stood at attention at the benches.

"At ease!" he said, and left the classroom.

⸺

I found out that the last class is religion. Should I get sick? And what will I do next time? I know "Our Father" and "Hail Mary." Father Robak pretended throughout his life. No one is who he is.

The priest made the sign of the cross over us. From his black soutane, which was fastened with buttons, he pulled out a notebook and pencil. Without looking at anyone, he read out the names.

"Were you at mass on Sunday?"

"Yes," a boy slammed the lid of his desk.

"Were you?"

"Yes, Father," a girl curtsied at her desk.

"Were you?"

"I was sick."

"A note from your parents . . ."

"I forgot."

"Don't lie."

He said that there are a lot of atheists now. The devil sent them. Whoever listens to them will go to hell. Then he began asking questions from the catechism. Someone called out that there's a new boy in the class.

"Last name?" asked the priest.

"Dichter," I answered. It sounded better than Rabinowicz.

"First name?"

"Wilhelm."

"A German?" he asked, surprised.

There were giggles and whispers.

"Catholic?"

He lifted his eyes from the notebook.

"You may stay or go home," he said.

After religion we went to the coatroom, which was in the basement. Putting my leather backpack on my shoulders, I tried not to let it creak. The boys held their noses. The coat smelled of kerosene.

"He's little, but he already stinks," one of them said.

"They all stink."

"Of what?"

"Gas."

With my flight cap in my pocket I ran out into the street. But I slowed down right away because my knees hurt. Seeing grown-ups, I calmed down and stopped looking back. I put on my flight cap. Although the sun was shining, my ears were frozen. The ice in the puddles cracked under my boots. The snow was steaming and the air was damp.

Even after the war, childhood was not safe. Anyone could hit me. I wasn't able to run. I ought to just sit at home and wait until I grow up and am strong like Moszek. But would that guarantee safety? There is always someone stronger. I shall become an engineer. The drivers take off their caps when they speak to Winkler and Michał. Education is property.

I knew that we wouldn't be staying here long. Winkler told Michał on the phone that Rzeszów is too small to be an administrative center for petroleum. Kraków will be the new capital. He and Nella are already sitting on their suitcases, but there is so much confusion in Lublin that there's no one to sign a decree about his transfer. In the meantime, other people are occupying the best hotels near St. Mary's Church. As soon as he gets settled in Kraków, he'll bring us to the west. Maybe not to Kraków, but to the west. I didn't pray to my father for a quick departure. I was afraid that everywhere it would be the same as in Krosno.

Immersed in these thoughts, I reached the main street and turned right. When I rounded the corner my heart began pounding. I felt a pain in my chest and my throat.

Germans were descending from the hill! A blue cloud surrounded them. They had already entered the city and passed our house with its dangling icicles. They were marching across the entire breadth of the roadway. The granite stones of the sidewalk disappeared under their boots. Their uneven thudding turned into a roar. They marched in unbuttoned overcoats, in hats with long bills, or bare-headed. Brunets, redheads, and others who had hair like Maciek's, more glittery in the sun than the icicles. (Mother and Janka hadn't succeeded in turning me into a blond, because my hair turned red when it was bleached.)

Not a single green Austrian. Just Germans. They entered the market square and still the end of the column couldn't be seen. I was standing so close to them that I could have touched the holes in their belts. Each of them was twice as big as me. I was terrified that they would pull me along with them. I stepped back abruptly and fell over backward. Propped on my backpack, I lay under a street sign with the words KRAKAU 172, KATOWITZ 249. Wiping off the water that was dripping from the sign onto my face, I wondered why I hadn't run away. And what if they hadn't been prisoners?

A Polish soldier on a horse rode by on the sidewalk.

"Get up, you little shit!" He burst out laughing at the sight of me.

Winkler left for Kraków and summoned Michał to see him. Several days later the telephone rang. Michał had become the director of a refinery in Ligota.

"Ligota?" Mother expressed surprise, pressing the receiver to her ear. "Not Kraków? Aha. Near Katowice. Aha. An apartment house. Upstairs? Aha. A painting in the hall! And a balcony. Aha. A black Smyrna in a floral pattern. Aha. An extendable Chippendale. Aha. A Persian larger than the Smyrna. Aha. Tiles everywhere. The bathroom? Aha. Formerly German. Kisses. 'Bye!"

In a Formerly German Apartment

We arrived in Ligota late at night. Our apartment occupied the entire second floor of an apartment house on Panewnicka Street. As I was falling asleep I heard Michał telling Mother that a Pan Łytek would come for him tomorrow.

In the morning, I was awakened by the sound of the doorbell. I jumped out from under the quilt to see what Michał's driver looked like. A slight man with his thumbs in the pockets of his leather jacket was standing in the stairwell. He said that he would wait for the Director and ran down-stairs. I went into the living room. Through the window a brown DKW with its headlights blacked out could be seen. The paint on its roof was peeling. Pan Łytek opened the passenger-side door. Soon Michał appeared with his hand outstretched. They shook hands. Pan Łytek got in on the driver's side. The DKW set out in the direction of the refinery, growling loudly and emitting a stream of dark blue smoke.

Around noon, the telephone rang. Michał told Mother that the night watchmen had found an enormous black Mercedes in the shed, hidden among the storage tanks. Corrugated silver pipes protruded from its hood, which was attached with straps. Pan Łytek suggested that it might be one of Göring's autos. Michał informed the Russians, who collected the Mercedes and sent over a white Adler with a gear shift next to the steering wheel as a "gift." I asked Mother what would happen to the DKW. She said it was given to young Edward Kubec, who administers the refinery when Michał goes into the field or to meetings in Kraków.

In the afternoon, while I was in the living room looking through issues of the quarterly *Deutsche Bildhauerkunst und Malerei,* Mother, standing near the open window, suddenly cried out. I lifted my head to see what was happening. Pushing back the lace curtain, she called me over and pointed out an old man who was walking past our building at that very moment. From one floor up, we could see his gray head.

"He looks just like Papa!" she whispered. "Go take a look."

I flung the magazine onto a chair and ran down the marble stairs to Panewnicka Street. Soon, however, I had to slow down because of my knees. We were both moving slowly. As I caught up with him I could hear the tapping of his wooden shoes more clearly. When we reached the trees in front of the church, I noticed that his feet were filthy and bare inside his shoes. He was wearing a jacket with a torn-off collar. Without a shirt. There were no silver eyeglass frame wires sticking out behind his ears. Maybe they got broken in the camp?

I started to pass him. I saw his ear and his emaciated cheek covered with white stubble. His eye glittered. The man turned toward me. He had marks from eyeglasses on his nose. Grandfather? I wasn't sure. I held out my hand. He took a step back.

"*Lass mich in Ruhe, bitte. Ich komme nach Hause zurück,*" he said in German. "Leave me alone, please. I'm returning to my home."

I went into the churchyard. I could hear the wooden shoes moving off into the distance. I sat down on a bench and massaged my knees. Red squirrels watched me, shaking their heads. The trunks and trees quickly grew darker. The sun disappeared behind the church and reappeared in its elongated windows, which could be seen through the open doors. A multicolored light fell on the tripartite golden altar. Figures made of colored glass shone on the empty pews. Joseph was helping the Mother of God get down from a donkey. He held out his hands gently in order to take the baby from her.

I was reminded of Grandfather taking Romuś from Teresa's arms after he put him to sleep. I could smell the odor when he broke off the cap on the ampule. But I couldn't remember their faces. I saw only the smiling faces from the stained-glass window. And Milo? I'd forgotten him, too. Maybe he's in Ligota, walking the streets in the uniform of a Russian captain, in soft, knee-high leather boots? But how would I recognize him?

It occurred to me that Mother was waiting by the window, and I got up from the bench. When I came back out onto Panewnicka Street the streetlights were on. The little trees that grew in square cutouts in the sidewalk had turned yellow in their light. I stopped in front of a three-story building surrounded by an iron picket fence. The living room windows were above a crocus bed. Ours were dark.

In the morning, it was pouring rain. Mother came into the nursery to check if it was raining onto the parquet floor.

"April showers bring May flowers . . ."

She shut the window.

She reminded me that I hadn't taken the magazines out of the living room yet even though I had promised many times that I would do so. After she left there was a roaring sound of motors. It intensified quickly and soon the windowpanes began to rattle. My tin soldiers fell off the bed frame. I picked them up and put them back, watching with curiosity as they slid slowly toward the edge.

Hearing the doorbell, I leaped out from under the quilt. Pan Łytek said that the Russians were moving through Ligota. An entire army! He had parked the Adler on the far side of the Katowice highway and would wait there for the Director.

I stepped out gingerly onto the street. The stones in the roadway glittered like ice. Panewnicka Street was empty, but the space between the apartment houses was filled with the roaring of motors. I walked under the balconies to the intersection with the Katowice highway. A girl in a helmet and Russian leather boots was sitting on the hood of an open Willys. Her arms dangling by her sides, she was holding miniature red flags and watching the trucks streaming in from Katowice. They were driving in pairs in the pouring rain, taking up both sides of the roadway. I stepped out from under the balcony in order to see better. Blue-black smoke from burning exhaust rose into the air as far as the distant bend near the soccer field.

At one point, a Studebaker skidded and ran into a Dodge. Wooden boxes fell out from under the tarps and broke apart on the roadway. Silver tins of potted meat rolled under the wheels of approaching vehicles. Before the slowly sliding trucks struck the Willys and crushed it, the girl in the Russian leather boots jumped down and fled, dropping her flags. The drivers got down from their crushed cabs. They yawned and rubbed their eyes. Soon, someone called them over and they rode off with the column, the remaining trucks passing the wrecks on either side.

Returning home, I noticed a group of soldiers shouting. Inside the gate of the apartment house next door to ours a Pole and a Russian were fighting. Bloodied and exhausted, they waved their fists, cursing at each other. Soldiers with stars or eagles were goading them on. An Opel flying a white-and-red flag drove up from the direction of the church. Two Poles with rifles were standing on its bed. A gigantic lieutenant got out of the cab. Shoving the onlookers apart, he grabbed the Pole who was fighting by the neck and threw him onto the truck bed and then jumped up on it, too. The Opel made a U-turn and drove off. The Poles and Russians went their separate ways.

I rang the doorbell. Mother was waiting in the hall with a towel. She undressed me and rubbed me dry before I stepped off the cocoa-fiber doormat. Dry trousers, socks, and a shirt were already hanging on the coat tree. How could I have gone out in such a rain! With my lungs! A wet head! Water in my ears! I will definitely get sick! She dressed me in dry clothes and carried the wet ones to the bathroom.

The hall was rectangular. On the right side was the glass door to the balcony where there was a man's bicycle with a headlamp, dynamo, and brake on the front wheel. A little farther on was the beginning of the hallway that led into the main rooms of the apartment. On the left wall was a large, creamy-white French door. Two pairs of similar doors were also on the front wall. A mirror hung between them, and under it was a little cabinet with a telephone. Mother slipped her black, high-heeled shoes under it.

The first creamy-white door from the hall opened into the living room. On the floor was a black carpet with two concentric embroidered wreaths of pink and red flowers. In the center of the inner wreath stood a round table with a black glass top and two armchairs. The outer wreath, which followed the walls, ran between the legs of the piano and beneath the window, and then it disappeared under a mahogany-veneer bookcase. The light that filtered in through the lace curtains fell onto the piano's black box and a painting in a silver frame that hung above it. Clumps of hardened paint cast shadows on bluish mountains. Among them shone a lake sheathed in ice. I liked the painting on the other side of the bookcase much better. In the corner, wives of fishermen were standing on a pier. Shading their eyes from the sun, they were looking at boats with billowing sails. I couldn't figure out if the boats were arriving or departing.

The mahogany bookcase was made of three parts, like the altar in the church on Panewnicka Street. There had been books in its wings behind thick glass tiles, but Mother threw them out when she noticed the swastikas stamped on their spines. In the central section there was a polished panel that could be pulled down to form a writing surface. In the middle were empty drawers and a long white lightbulb that turned on automatically when the panel was opened. Beneath the lightbulb there was a red, leather-bound stamp album. Above the panel, behind glass, were the issues of the quarterly *Deutsche Bildhauerkunst und Malerei*.

Lounging in an armchair, I leafed through them in chronological order.

Every page had black-and-white photographs of statues and paintings. Sculpted girls, stretching their skin that had been polished to a shine, were tying stone scarves. Painted girls bathed in springs, looking at their own reflections, or rested naked on hay. I touched them with my finger on the slick coated paper. Sometimes they became half-birds or half-fish. Wrapped in their own wings, they knelt on cliffs, looking for victims. They struck the sand furiously with their long, scaly tails.

Naked boys with dogs hunted in the mountains. Rays of sunshine penetrated the boughs of the trees, illuminating the legs and paws of the runners. Water flowed from the cliffs, washing the trees' roots. It foamed over the rocks. Streams flowed together into waterfalls, startling birds. Boys looked proudly at the plains where the exhausted water became a river. Sometimes, however, I turned a page and found them dead. They lay on the shore of a lake with their faces in the water, while waves were breaking on the surface, churned up by the tails of sirens fleeing into the distance.

The men were huge. They wore helmets with horns on their heads. Skins of animals hung from their shoulders. They held axes in their hands. From virgin forests, they stretched their hands out to gods concealed in the clouds. Sometimes they galloped on horses. Behind them sat naked maidens, clinging to their coarse sheepskins.

Suddenly, I noticed a color photograph. It was a photo of Hitler on one of the magazine covers. He was wearing a brown jacket, and on it a red armband with a black swastika in a white circle. Underneath him was a wavy golden ribbon with the inscription 1889—20 APRIL—1939.

In the living room hung a beautiful colorized photograph of Mother on vacation in Truskawiec that had truly survived by a miracle. She had a lovely smile, but aside from her lovely red lips and rosy cheeks, the rest of the photograph was black and white. The colors on the magazine cover were real. But I couldn't look at them and I turned the page.

In earlier issues I had seen buildings in front of which generals in *Pickelhaube* sat astride horses. On the sculpted roofs were green figures of women holding scales and men holding triangles and compasses. In the Hitler issue I found sketches and models of a future colossal Berlin.

In front of Hitler's palace there were statues of two nude men on pedestals. In the roadway, a man who was no bigger than their hands was holding his hat in his hand. Behind the backs of the statues rose a gate that made even them seem like dwarfs. A balcony extended over the gate from a wall. I made out a man the size of a pinhead on it. The pedestrian in the street below had taken off his hat and was holding it in front of his body. A gray eagle holding a circle with the swastika in its talons hung above the balcony. The eagle's wings cast a shadow on the wall. Above the bird there was a frieze inside a stone frame. In it, naked men larger than the ones on the pedestals were fighting both on foot and on horseback. On both sides, to the very edges of the photograph, stretched rows of columns. The thicker ones reached from the ground to the eagle. Thinner columns were on top of them, from the eagle to the frieze.

A triumphal arch, sketched in pen and ink, rose sky-high. On it, horses were pulling chariots. The people in the road looked like specks of ink sprinkled from a pen as it scratched the paper.

Mother came in, stepping soundlessly on the carpet's flowers. She spread out a cloth on the black glass table-top and set a plate on it. It held pieces of bread, with thin slices of kielbasa and hard-boiled eggs.

"Colored pictures?" she asked, surprised, picking up the issue.

"Yes."

"I can't look at him."

She went over to the window and pushed aside the curtain. She said that yesterday someone wearing striped concentration camp clothing had walked past. But he was too old. She let go of the curtain and picked up the empty plate.

"Tea?"

"Yes, but make it strong."

"You drink undiluted essence," she sighed, walking away.

Starting with the Hitler issue there were color photographs in every number. White and pink soldiers bathed in a sky-blue lake. Flaxen-haired or red-haired. They laughed and splashed each other with water, paying no attention to me. I closed and opened my eyes, but they were always in the same place. As long as they were in the water, I had the advantage over them. But only a few steps separated them from the rifles placed on racks beside their backpacks with blankets strapped to them. An officer in a *feldgrau* uniform, with a yellow riding crop under his arm, stood on the bank. His back turned to them, he was talking with a *Feldfebel,* who was pulling on his shirt. If the soldiers in the water were to alert the officer, he would pull his pistol out of its holster and shoot before I could rip out the page and tear it to pieces.

The stained-glass window of the cathedral, like an enormous wagon wheel, kept changing colors. Chimeras looked down from the gallery on the band below. The sun was reflected in the brass trumpets and cymbals. Drummers raised sticks above the drums suspended around their necks on straps. The conductor watched the color guard. A tall blond man with a bandage on his forehead was carrying a flag just like Hitler's armband. He had soldiers with naked swords on either side. Behind them, a column of exhausted boys in helmets was approaching. Between the column and the sidewalk rode officers on horseback, covered with the dust of the road. People were standing up from their tables in front of a café in order to get a better view.

A sky-blue metal tripod was set in the snow. A machine gun with a gunsight like a spiderweb was suspended from it. Its trigger grips touched the face of a soldier who was lying flat on his stomach. Above the scarf that he had wrapped around his nose and ears, his rosy cheeks and frost-covered eyebrows could be seen. His blue eyes scanned the white field, all the way to the enemy's line in the woods. Snow was falling on the wrecks of tanks and corpses in yellow-green greatcoats. With clenched fingers sticking out of gloves from which the finger tips were cut off, the soldier loaded bullets into the belt hanging down from the machine gun.

In another picture, a bright yellow explosion was pictured. The farther away from the explosion, the darker it was. The wind was blowing and a stream of sand was whirling in the air. Shadows of turrets with barrels blazing fire loomed out of the darkness. The picture hung in a museum. In front of it, their backs to me, stood a grandfather and his grandson. I didn't know who they were since I couldn't see their faces, nor if the tanks were German or English. The only tank I knew, after all, was the Russian T-34.

Mother came in with my tea. Setting it down on the table, she went over to the piano and lifted the lid over the keyboard. With a rag that she always had with her, she began cleaning the keys.

"Maybe you'd like to learn to play the piano?"

Suddenly, the glass flew out of my hands and the hot water spilled all over me. Jumping up from the chair, I pulled the burning cloth away from my chest. Mother unfastened my buttons and removed my shirt. She remembered that she had some curdled milk and ran to get it from the kitchen. She sent me off to the bathroom. We met there a moment later.

"Well?" she asked, smearing me with the white jelly.

"It hurts."

"But less . . ."

"Yes."

We sat down on the rim of the green bathtub. The floor, walls, and even the ceiling were covered with matching tiles. The light that entered through a window up near the ceiling diffused in greenness. Only the taps, faucets, and the showerhead on the bottom of the bidet shone silver. Mother turned on the hot water to wash the milk off her hands. Green steam appeared above the porcelain sink.

"It's because you drink lying down, like a pasha," she said. "I've never seen anything like it! Don't say anything to Michał. There's no point in worrying him. And take those magazines into the nursery at last."

The second pair of creamy-white doors in the hall opened into the dining room. I would go in there to look at the chandelier. From the center of the ceiling, on a thin chain, hung a bronze ball with eight curved rods. Electric candles topped with lightbulbs in the shape of flames burned at the end of each rod. A two-headed eagle with crowns on each head was suspended from the ball on a thinner chain. The heads faced opposite ends of the extendable table, which Winkler had said was a Chippendale.

Sometimes, engineers from Kraków who were either on their way west to repossess refineries or were on their way back would sit down to dinner around the table on the soft chairs with tall backs. They traveled to the front in olive-green Willyses. They returned in German trucks covered with tarpaulins securely fastened with ropes.

After dinner the guests drank coffee that Mother ground in a coffee mill and steamed Turkish-style in cups. Adding sugar, they would complain that there wasn't room to stick a pin in Kraków or Łódź.

"So who tells them to stay there?" Mother would ask later, bringing me sandwiches in the living room. She didn't like the engineers. She wondered, which one of them used to beat up Jews at the Polytechnic? Michał trusts everyone, but she knows what she knows. They travel in order to steal! Under the tarps they're transporting furniture and carpets, not machines. There's no repossession. The Russians aren't returning anything. They themselves are "repossessing" watches in the streets.

There was a carpet in the dining room, too—under the table. After we came from Krosno, Mother looked at it carefully for a long time. So small? After all, the Persian rug was supposed to be bigger than the Smyrna.

"That's not ours," Michał laughed.

"Whose is it?"

"Winkler's."

"It's not Persian?"

"It's Persian, but smaller."

"And ours?"

"Winkler took it."

The third pair of creamy-white doors led from the hall into the nursery, where there was a white metal bed. At night, I would slide the tin soldiers around its snow-white, enameled frame. The frame was smooth and shiny, but when I brought my eyes close to it I could see tiny black spots in places where the enamel was chipped.

I lifted the sheet to check out the mattress with its long blue stripes. Mother thought it was stuffed with sea grass. I made a little hole in it with a tin soldier's bayonet, but I didn't find any grass.

I had three pillows from which fine stems of thick down stuck out. I would pull them out and, puffing on them, blow them into the room. They swirled in the air and sometimes sailed into the hall. Two of the pillows were large, and the third was very small.

"What is this?" I asked.

"A throw pillow," Mother said. "You had one just like it once upon a time."

The tin soldiers lay in a box under the bed. I could reach them with my hand. First I would take out the infantry, recognizing them by touch, and line them up in single file on the bed frame. They hurled grenades with long handles or ran with fixed bayonets that looked like flat kitchen knives. (The Russian watchman in the Drohobycz station had a bayonet as slender as Gifrejter's stinger in *Pan Tadeusz*.) They also carried canteens and containers with gas masks. I set up machine guns in the folds of the quilt. Two soldiers were affixed to each one. One took aim and the other loaded the cartridges. (Maybe the gunner in the German magazine had already lost his comrade?) Then I pulled the cavalry out of the box. These fell over easily, because the horses' front legs were raised too high. I wrapped the cavalry in the quilt and treated them as infantry in trenches. Alas, they wore caps instead of helmets. Since I didn't have any tanks, I would take out of the night table a copy of Mickiewicz's *Konrad Wallenrod* that one of the engineers from Kraków had given me, slide it under the sheet, and pretend it was a tank that had been painted white to camouflage it.

I divided the soldiers into Germans, Russians, and Poles. The Germans always lost and their corpses became new Russians. I brought back the dead Russians as reinforcements from Siberia. The Poles didn't die. They were made of soldiers whose flat bayonets I had snapped off, and I cut off the rims of the helmets that covered the backs of their necks. (Mother complained that I had blackened the knife with tin.) The Poles went into battle just as I was about to fall asleep. They broke through the front. I didn't feel like playing at the Russian offensive.

In the morning I would pick up the soldiers that had fallen onto the floor during the night and, after throwing them into the box, sit near the window next to the steam machine. I poured water into its boiler through a glass funnel that Michał had brought me from the refinery and lit a candle under it. When the valve started emitting steam I would carefully position the lever. A whistle would sound and the iron wheel turn slowly. It was propelled by drive shafts, just like the many train wheels I had seen.

When Mother heard the whistle, she'd bring me my breakfast.

One day I was eating bread thickly spread with butter and sprinkled with sugar. Mother said she would be going out soon to buy eggs and would make me an omelet for lunch. Making the bed, she gathered up the soldiers from the quilt and threw them into the box. She told me to pick up the ones that had fallen on the floor.

She complained that she was having a hard time. At night, she walks around to keep from falling asleep because she can't "look at" everything again. During the day, she watches to see if Papa might be walking by. Not a word from Nusia. And I, instead of showing her even a little sympathy, slink around the rooms gloomily. Michał says we have a Hamlet.

"He would move the heavens for you! You don't know how lucky you are. Other children are grateful to their parents even though they have nothing."

When we were alone she referred to him as "Michał." If the phone wasn't working, though, she would send me to the refinery to ask Pan Kubec if "Father" was coming home for dinner.

I hadn't prayed in a long time. Apparently, I didn't need anything. All I wanted was to look at Father's photograph, which had survived along with the snapshot from Truskawiec. But I didn't know how to ask for it without making Mother cry.

I didn't pour the water out of the boiler even though Michał warned me that it would rust. The soldiers remained on the floor; I almost stepped on them when I brought in the magazines and the red album from the living room. Shoving everything under the bed, I noticed a yellow ribbon tied to the bed frame. I tore it off and threw it into the garbage. Then I went to find it, but Mother had already taken out the garbage on her way to get eggs. I lay down on the bed with an issue of *Bildhauerkunst und Malerei* and, yawning, fell asleep.

I dreamed that I was at the intersection of Panewnicka Street and the Katowice highway. There wasn't a living soul around. In the transparent air, houses, doors, and even keyholes were perfectly visible. On the roof were huge dark-green statues that were conversing with each other. I didn't understand what they were talking about because motors were roaring constantly even though the exhaust fumes from the Russians' march-past had long since cleared. I noticed that the statues disappeared when I stopped looking at them. All I had to do was glance over at a different roof and the previous one was already deserted. Soon, only one statue with a fiery crown around its head remained. The rising sun turned its face golden. It shone like a mirror.

Suddenly, the motors grew silent and its voice reached me. But I also heard the clicking of heels near the soccer field and I turned around. From the direction of Katowice my teacher was approaching, the one who had shown us an eraser in Borysław. (Looking at her darned stockings, I remembered that Winkler, when he left for America, had promised to bring back stockings for Nella that didn't run.)

"Good day, ma'am." I bowed to the teacher.

"What is this?" she asked.

With astonishment, I noticed that I was holding the spare key to our apartment in my hand. Instead of a string, it had the yellow ribbon I had been looking for in the garbage. But I had never taken it from the coat tree in the hall where it dangled "just in case," because Mother and Michał had their own keys.

"A key," I answered, surprised.

The teacher pointed to the empty roofs.

"You've forgotten," she said. "Now you will not know who you are."

—

I got sick, even though there was nothing wrong with me the day before. I lay in the nursery under the quilt, which was constantly forming new pleats and making me feel seasick. I smoothed it with my hands and tugged on it with my feet. It seemed to me that it was sliding onto the floor and flowing into the rest of the apartment, like curdled milk. When Mother came in I had the impression that she was splashing through something with her boots.

"My ears hurt," I complained.

"And your throat?" she asked.

I swallowed saliva to check and shook my head, no.

"Because you don't have tonsils," she said with satisfaction. "If I hadn't had them removed, you would not have survived the war. Strep throat would have been the end of you in a hideout. Do you remember how we went to the orphanage from the hospital?"

"No."

"And do you remember Uncle Unter?"

"No."

"You must be joking!" she said indignantly, and touched her lips to my forehead. "Like an oven! It's all because you went out in the rain! I'll phone Michał and tell him to bring a doctor."

I asked Mother to turn the pillow over. She did it deftly, even managing to beat it in the air.

A sweet smell woke me up. A thin little man in a black suit and a vest with a gold watch chain was sitting on my bed. Red rubber hoses hung from his neck and on his knees he had an open leather bag. I recognized him immediately: Pan Churlusz! How good that he's also a doctor! I'll tell him that I'm nauseated all the time from the tea I drink and drinking it in smaller and smaller sips isn't helping at all.

Something strange is happening with my memory, too. At Andzia Katz's I couldn't recall Grandmother Antonina's voice. Then I forgot what she looked like. In Ligota the same thing happened with the Unters. And Milo? I follow every Russian officer with creaking straps. If he's not a Kalmuk, I wonder if he's my uncle. Mother sends me out unnecessarily to follow people in wooden shoes or striped camp clothes. I wouldn't recognize Grandfather! I've even stopped dreaming about him. I can only smell the odor from the ampule.

Pan Churlusz asked for a teaspoon, which Mother handed him immediately. She said she had also prepared a thermometer, because she knows what's needed for an examination.

"His grandfather," she pointed at me, "was a feldsher."

Pan Churlusz told me to open my mouth and say "aaah." He pressed my tongue down with the spoon and looked in my throat.

"His tonsils were removed," Mother whispered.

"When?"

"Before the war."

He slipped the thermometer into my mouth. He placed his hand where I had scalded myself with the tea and tapped with his finger. Then he placed the rubber hoses into his ears and bowed his head. He had a lot of gray hair. Something cold moved over my skin. Pan Churlusz put the tubes away in his bag and extracted a shiny, black tube. He placed it gently into my ear.

"Red," he said to Mother. "Sulfa. Aspirin. A compress on the head. Oil into the ear. A lot of tea."

"Cupping?" she asked.

"Not necessary."

"His lungs?"

"Clear."

"He's so hot!"

"Thirty-seven point seven."

I woke up wet. It was hot in the room. Pan Churlusz was gone. I had forgotten to tell him that I'm forgetting. Who knows when I'll see him again? Suddenly, I realized that I no longer remembered Father's voice. I tried to picture his mouth. In vain. His cheeks. His forehead. Hair. Nothing! . . . Only his eyes.

Mother sent Michał in with the news that semolina would be ready in a moment. Michał sat down beside me and picked up the book from the night table.

"Oh! The count who became an Arab."

He was pleased.

Holding the book in one hand, he placed the other on my forehead. I could feel each of his fingers moving slowly toward my hair. He removed his hand in order to turn a page and then he touched me again. He said that he loved this poem and began to read.

> I smell a corpse's smell, he crowed,
> Stupid rider, stupid steed.
> The uniformed rider seeks the road,
> Seeks a white-legged pasha.
> Rider, horse, your work's in vain,
> The one who was here won't come again.
> Only the wind wanders these roads
> Every last trace erasing,
> This meadow is for vipers alone,
> Not for horses grazing.
> Here only corpses spend the night,
> Here only vultures gather.

I pretended that the quilt was a desert. That was easy, because the setting sun cast yellow and red shadows on the bed. The wind was howling and stirring up clouds of sand. A lone rider in a turban was galloping along the cliffs near my feet and knees. He had wrapped a scarf around his face so the sand wouldn't sting his eyes. His black horse had white legs. (The German cavalrymen were smaller.) The bones of those who hadn't made it were lying on the quilt. Under the ceiling, near the lamp, a vulture was flapping wildly.

Dash on, white-legged glider!
Cliffs, make way!

Vultures, make way! Michał said that the best people always had to flee our country. That was Poland's tragedy. Now the time had come for enlightened, industrious people.

Mother came in with a steaming bowl of semolina. Bits of butter were swimming in it, sinking into the cocoa sprinkled over its top.

Repossession

Engineer Michalik came from Kraków and we set out together in the Adler to repossess a synthetic gas refinery. At first, Mother didn't want to let me go. She had heard that German *Werwolf* commandos were shooting at passing cars in the forests. She agreed, however, when Michał joked that there were more Russians than trees in Silesia.

—

We drove through Bytom, Gliwice, and Opole—cities that bore no resemblance to Rzeszów or Krosno. Blackened trees were higher than the Prussian walls. White sheets and red comforter covers hung from the windows of apartment houses. Women and children stood in front of the gates. Men without arms and legs sat on the sidewalks and watched as our Adler passed by. We drove down the center of the street along the streetcar tracks. The street was empty. The streetcar stops were pasted over with announcements and portraits of Hitler with the face ripped out. Signs with Gothic lettering hung over the intersections. Bumping along on the tracks we descended from Schlesienstrasse onto Am Waldfriedhof. We passed an empty streetcar at a turnaround, its pantograph lowered, and a T-34 tank with a raised barrel and open hatch doors. Russians were sitting under the linden trees and digging tinned meat out of cans with their knives. We drove out of the square near a church on which someone had written in chalk, "Hitler kaput!"

"No one is afraid of the *Werwolf*," Michał laughed.

—

The white Adler climbed uphill. Then, coasting in order to save gas, we rolled along a highway that had not been destroyed by the caterpillar treads of tanks. It was already dark in the valleys, but the asphalt on the hill was still shining. Dark pine trees slid past the side windows. Michał, turned around to face him, was carrying on a conversation with Engineer Michalik, who was sitting next to me.

"History is beginning again," Michał was saying. "A new concept. The end of social injustice. For the time being, nothing can be seen. War. Ruins.

Resistance. Ignorance. Mistakes. But changes will come. Polytechnics and universities for everyone. Houses for workers."

"The Russians won't give them to us."

"They saved us."

"We had two enemies."

"That's just it!" Michał cried. "That's madness! Mickiewicz already understood that. Do you remember what Ryków said after the battle? 'The tsar orders this, but I pity you.' In the 1863 January Uprising they embroidered on their banners: 'For our freedom and yours.' Russians were hated differently than Germans."

"They attacked us just the same."

"So as not to let Hitler advance too far."

"They're keeping Lwów."

"They deserve something, colleague. We have to face forward. Why cry over Borysław oil when we're getting industrial Silesia? Our people will come back from the east. They've deported the Germans."

"They will come back and take it away!"

"You don't know Russia," Michał laughed.

Around a bend a clearing appeared in the forest, plowed up by tanks; traces of their caterpillar treads led from the clearing onto the highway. The Adler began to bounce around. The windows rattled in their frames. There was a loud noise, as of a shot.

"A flat tire!" Pan Łytek cried out, and slammed on the brake.

—

The tire lay next to the iron wheel with spokes. We watched Pan Łytek clean the red inner tube with glazed paper. He smeared glue over the hole, put a black patch over it, and squeezed it with a pair of pliers. (There were already a lot of patches like it on the inner tube.) As he started heating the patch with the blue flame of an alcohol torch, a Studebaker drove up and stopped near us. The cab was crammed full of Russian soldiers.

"*Podkinut'?* Need a lift?"

Michał glanced at his watch and bent down to Engineer Michalik: "You go ahead, colleague. Please tell them to wait."

Soon after Engineer Michalik rode off, the Adler began moving again. We turned onto a side road. The traces of caterpillar treads disappeared. The asphalt was replaced with concrete paving blocks. The tires thudded where the blocks met. Alongside the road a carefully raked strip of sand appeared. Behind it stretched a grass-covered embankment on which wooden poles with white porcelain insulators blinked by. Against the sky, rising and falling, ran wires that were attached to the insulators.

Every few hundred meters we passed a tower with a wooden hut on its peak.

Beyond the bend there was a wide open fence. We drove through to the other side of the wires. In front of an empty guard hut, in the middle of a flower bed, was a flagpole with a rope for lowering the flag. Next to it stood a Willys with a red pennant.

"Where are they?" asked Pan Łytek.

"In the refinery," said Michał.

Pan Łytek looked around.

"There!" Michał pointed at a hill. "Underground."

Enormous steel doors stood open in a stone wall. Railroad tracks extended out into the open from the dark interior. Bumping over them, we passed a row of switches with control heads pointed down, and then we drove inside. Suddenly lights went on. Blinded, Pan Łytek stopped the car.

On iron posts supporting the ceiling, floodlights in metal hoods had been turned on. In the ceiling and on the walls, the crystals embedded in the rocks glittered. Everything gave off a strong odor of earth, roots, and petroleum. The railroad tracks ran along the ground beside wooden walkways. Freight cars were standing around like abandoned toys. They were piled high with lathes, drills, and milling machines. (I had seen similar machines in the refinery workshops.) Here and there were cranes on caterpillar treads. Chains with hooks dangled from their high frames. Between the walkways the foundation was cracked. Bent screws and clumps of shiny copper wire protruded from it. Engineer Michalik was standing with two Russian officers under the nearest floodlight. The younger officer was holding a leather briefcase, and the older had his hands on his shoulders.

"What's happened?" asked Michał, flabbergasted.

"They ripped it right out of the foundation," said Engineer Michalik.

"We're taking German goods," the older officer said in Russian.

"But it's ours!" Michał protested, also in Russian.

"Those are our orders."

The older one took the briefcase from the younger man and took out a paper.

"I won't sign," Michał said.

"The general gave the order."

"Where is he?"

"At the front."

"The machines will rust in transit."

"That's not our business."

"Sign," Engineer Michalik whispered in Polish. "Don't waste your breath."

Mother grieved over the lack of news from Nusia. Ironing Michał's shirts, she said that she didn't even have anyone to cry her heart out to, because Papa had stopped coming to see her. I was terrified. Grandfather didn't appear in my dreams, either. Maybe she was forgetting? I started observing her. I waited for her to touch the iron with a saliva-moistened finger. Would she say that on Pańska Street she'd had a better heater for the iron? And rolling out dough, would she sigh that in Borysław the rolling pin was smoother and nothing stuck to it? Twice, I exhaled with relief.

Formerly, every sight or smell reminded me of something. People from the past would appear. When Mother poured broth over the pasta in our soup plates, I could see Grandfather entering the dining room. He'd take the fourth chair and ask for the salt. I would carefully slide the little porcelain salt and pepper bowls over to him. Once, I spilled the white and black grains onto the tablecloth.

"Blind as a bat!" Michał yelled.

"Bad luck," Mother added.

Today, we were eating alone. Mother didn't have an appetite. She was pushing the round peas around the flat carrot slices with her fork. She's all alone in Ligota. She'd rather live in Kraków, where at least there are some Jews. At least Karola Sznepf is there, who has two diplomas and is an attorney. Michał muttered that while Winkler sits in America, there's nothing to discuss. Anyway, there's no refinery in Kraków. The closest one is in Trzebinia. An hour's drive from Kraków. Suddenly, he beamed and began to tell a story about how his older brother, Julek, had drilled down to oil in Ratoczyn; smeared with black grease, he had come running into the house, crying, "Michał! We're rich!" Ah, so he remembers, too! Until then, preoccupied with the refinery and politics, he hadn't recalled anything. Maybe only children forget? The spoon fell out of my hand into the plate.

"Clumsy!" Michał yelled.

"The tablecloth!" Mother added.

Michał went to Austria with Pan Łytek. They made it all the way to the Danube in the Adler. Behind an underground airplane factory in Gusen they passed a freshly opened grave in which ten thousand corpses were lying. They stopped next to the concentration camp gate. Leaving Pan Łytek and the Adler among the American tanks, Michał entered Mauthausen. Inside, it was jammed with people. Thousands of prisoners whom the Germans had not had time to shoot in the Gusen hangars were walking around among the barracks. Those who were dying from dysentery (after eating chocolate) had been pulled aside, next to the wooden walls.

Michał was looking for his brother. It seems they had brought him here from Auschwitz. He soon met a man wearing prisoners' stripes who knew Julek. Right before the Americans came there had been an aerial bombardment. The prisoners took cover under the freight cars. Suddenly, the train moved. A wheel crushed Julek's toes. After the bombing, they went back to work. They dragged themselves back to the barracks only at night. The next day, Julek could no longer stand up. He was taken to the gas chamber.

The man in the striped clothing accompanied Michał around the camp. He showed him the setup for shooting people in the back of the head; it was modeled after a slaughterhouse and was used for killing Russian prisoners of war. He took him to the Wienergraben stone quarry and showed him the one hundred eighty-six steps that the prisoners had to run up, carrying granite blocks, until they died of a heart attack. There, they encountered a Spaniard who told him that ten thousand Republicans, betrayed to the Germans by the Vichy regime, died in Mauthausen. Michał spoke with him in French. He'd learned that language at the Gymnasium.

In front of the crematorium, the prisoners were speaking in Yiddish with a rabbi wearing an American uniform, telling him that the Dutch had been gassed over a three-day period, but the Jews from Auschwitz and Hungary waited in a line for weeks. The commandant of Mauthausen gave his son fifty Jews as a birthday present so he could learn to shoot.

Michał said goodbye to his guide at the gate. When he got into the car, Pan Łytek told him that the commandant of the camp had been killed just a few moments earlier. He'd been trying to hide among the prisoners.

———

I brought in poultry scissors from the kitchen and climbed onto the dining room table. Rotating the chandelier, I took a close look at both heads of the eagle. I used the blades to cut off the one whose eyes were more protuberant. Squeezing the finger grips, I twisted the scissors around the bird's fat neck. A bright crack appeared on its brown feathers. Golden dust fell onto my shoes and the table. The head started to wobble. Grasping the beak, I broke off the head and climbed down. I gathered up the filings and threw them into the garbage together with the head.

"What happened to the eagle?" Mother asked the next day.

"I cut off its head."

"Why?"

"So it would have just one head, like the Polish eagle."

———

Although Mother cleaned the entire apartment every morning, on Tuesday she dusted the piano a second time in the afternoon. She cleaned the keyboard from above and from the sides. Various sounds rang out. She

blew the dust off the gold arrow of the metronome and polished the winding knob in its back.

When the doorbell rang (not as long as Pan Łytek's ring), she parted
the curtains and, having taken her habitual look at the street, walked out of
the living room. On the threshold she turned around once more to check
whether the painting in the silver frame was hanging straight. In the hall,
she put on her shoes and opened the door to the piano lady.

The lady sat down beside me. She wound up the metronome. She
checked to see if I was straining my muscles while playing scales. I could
see in the open lid of the keyboard that Mother was hovering over us.

"What's happened to the conservatory?" she whispered.

"It's closed," the woman sighed. "A tuner?"

"He ran away," Mother said. "A German, apparently."

One Tuesday, during my lesson, the telephone rang. Mother went out
into the hall. I stopped playing, but her words were still drowned out by
the metronome. Suddenly, the receiver crashed down.

"My husband phoned." Mother ran into the room. "The war is over!"

The woman pushed me aside and, stretching her large white fingers
over the keyboard, began to play the Chopin polonaise with which every
radio broadcast began.

"Ram! Pam! Pam!" she sang.

"They'll open the conservatory!" Mother said.

"A tuner will come from the east."

After the war, drawing lessons began. We were taught by a young, but
bald, man who came from Drohobycz and was awaiting the opening of the
Academy of Painting in Katowice. He placed a water jug on his desk. He
pulled down the shades over two of the windows. The light from the third
window fell on the jug.

"Roundness! Shadows!" he said.

He didn't guarantee that anyone would become a painter. He himself
had been scribbling since he was a little child. But not all scribblers are
equal. He had learned to draw faces only in Gymnasium. They had had
an excellent teacher. A Jew. A German shot him with a lady's pistol. Our
teacher painted his portrait from memory and hid it under his bed. Unfortunately, the Russians had requisitioned the portrait during repatriation.
Do we know any painters? One boy raised his hand.

"I have to go," he said.

"So go," said the teacher.

Drawing the jug, I decided to say nothing about the *Deutsche Bildhauerkunst und Malerei*. Instead, I added hind legs and a tail to the pot-bellied

jug. Because it resembled the trunk of a rearing horse. Short lines around the hooves. Grass. I smudged in a bushy mane with the side of the pencil lead. I inserted an eye with a little flourish and was surprised to see that it looked furious. An iron-shod foot. A wing.

"Do you collect stamps?" The teacher leaned over me.

"No."

"I had a stamp with just such a hussar," he sighed.

Before the war, he had been a stamp collector. He collected painters. Matejko, Grottger, Kossak. In '39 he'd gotten a magnifying glass. He lost the album along with the portrait.

"Does anyone have stamps?"

I raised my hand.

"But you don't collect them."

"But I have them."

In the afternoon I stole out into the street and headed for the school. Dust covered the roadway. Between the apartment houses, fields of wheat could be seen beyond the church. The teacher was waiting for me in the classroom. He bent over the red album, which I had placed on the table, and slowly turned its thick pages. Decorative envelopes and large stamps were stuffed behind transparent strips of wax paper. Hitler, Goering, Goebbels. Twelve field marshals with batons. Messerschmitts firing at airplanes with colorful circles on their wings.

A relief map of Europe was printed on one of the envelopes. The continent as seen by a giant standing on Gibraltar (the bottom of the map), who was looking east (the top of the map). Europe lay in water. Various seas washed its beaches. Along the spines of the Pyrenees, Alps, and Carpathians marched battalions with banners. From under the feet of the giant a phalanx of Spaniards was emerging. Framed in red, a band of yellow waved above their flat helmets. Frenchmen, marching through a vineyard, carried a tricolor flag. Carabinieri were pushing through the forests of the Alps. Their green-white-and-red flag was following the trail of the blue-yellow-and-red Romanians. The Danes were carrying a white cross on a red background. Above the Finnish army, standing in snow, shone a blue cross. Only Germany was empty. A lone red flag with a black swastika in a white circle waved amid plowed fields. *Wehrmacht,* stretched across the map, stopped in Poland, which was deprived of any geographical features.

"A crusade!" the teacher laughed.

"The Danes, too?" I asked.

"Propaganda!"

On two stamps, which were as large as my hand, there were warships. On one, the gray-blue *Bismarck,* covered with camouflage paint, was slicing the waves that flowed away from its bow. Long gun barrels sprayed fire over the water. Behind it sailed a rather small *Prinz Eugen,* whose masts disappeared in a low cloud. On the other stamp, the *Scharnhorst* was leaving a fjord. A band was playing. Women were waving handkerchiefs. A white line of sailors in round caps with ribbons lined the deck. Beyond the rocky walls of the fjord the sea was foaming.

"What happened to it?"

"Glug-glug-glug!"

The teacher thought that my album wasn't worth anything. Who cares about German stamps? Besides which, special issues require an experienced philatelist. Perhaps I will become one someday, but you have to begin with something easier. I said I could give him the album.

"Philatelists trade."

And he handed me an envelope with Russian stamps.

For supper we had smothered dumplings. Mother jabbed a heavy silver fork into the soft dough with browned meat poured over it. I opened my mouth.

"Well?" she asked.

"It's good."

I sat down Turkish-style near the steam machine. She covered my legs with a cloth and placed the hot dish on it. Gulping down the dumplings, I thought about whether I would ever be starving again. While I was licking the plate clean, the doorbell rang. Mother took the cloth and walked out of the nursery into the hall. She put on her shoes. She wiped her hands. I stood up. We didn't usually have guests at that time of day. Through the partly opened door I saw young Pan Edward Kubec, who sometimes brought over documents from the refinery. He was holding a valise tied up with string. Next to him stood a girl in a long-sleeved sweater.

"Pan Edward!" Mother sounded taken aback.

The man stared at her. Mother moved uncomfortably.

"Nusia!" she suddenly screamed.

"You didn't recognize me?"

The girl's lips started to tremble.

"Skin and bones!"

Pan Kubec set the valise down beside the coat tree and left. The girl held her arms out to me. I approached her with my empty plate.

"He's healthy again," she said to Mother.

"I'll bring you back to life, too."

We walked through the living room, dining room, and nursery.

Mother turned on the faucet over the bathtub. A hot stream burst out of the tap. Drops of water appeared on the sisters' faces. They were the same height, but Mother had on high heels. Their reflections disappeared in the mirror, which was coated with green steam.

"I was terrified!" said Mother. "Kubec at this time of day!"

"I went to the refinery from the station," Nusia said.

"Did he drive you here in a DKW?"

"Yes. But his name's not Kubec."

"Then what is it?"

"Karol Horowic."

Although it was summer, Nusia slept under a down comforter. For two days, we kept checking to see if she was breathing. When she got up, Pan Kubec came and took her to dinner in Katowice. She brought me back two volumes of *David Copperfield* in a green binding.

Ligocianka, the city soccer team, played in the soccer field near the Katowice highway. Michał, as refinery director, sponsored the players. He didn't go to their games, however, because he didn't have time. Once, he decided to attend an evening practice and phoned Pan Łytek. Mother allowed me to go with him.

A brick gravel running track encircled a grassy field on which there were two goals. Practice had just ended and the players were walking toward us. Pieces of cardboard protruded from under their socks. Their shoes were tied with string. They surrounded us. Could the refinery pay for the leather and sewing? Michał promised to help. Someone handed me the ball. It was light, yet hard as a rock. I kicked it. It rolled for several meters. They laughed. They applauded. Would I like to be a soccer player? I couldn't answer that question. Michał said he wouldn't detain them any longer. We went back to the Adler.

The next day, I rolled the bicycle out of the balcony and took it downstairs. I walked up and down Panewnicka Street for a long time and then headed over to the soccer field. With my right foot on the pedal and pushing off with my left, I rode it as if it were a scooter. The dynamo, driven by the tire, rumbled. I rang the bell. I squeezed the hand brake. Finally, I placed my left foot on the pedal and, after pushing off with my right, I cautiously slipped my right leg through the frame. Holding on to the handlebars, suspended on the left side of the bicycle, I pressed down on the pedal on the opposite side. Rising and falling, I rode along the red running track.

I came home with a sharp pain in my knees. Mother ordered me to put the bicycle on the balcony and go into the kitchen. As I walked down the hall, Michał observed me from the dining room. I could hear Nusia crying in her room. Sandwiches were waiting in the kitchen. Bread and chopped eggs with onion. Moist slices of sour pickle. A silver teaspoon lay next to an empty glass. Steam was rising from the copper kettle on the stove. A little porcelain teapot holding the brewed essence sat on top of it. Mother put the spoon in the glass and removed the teapot from the kettle.

"Kopcio has arrived," she said. "He's in Ligota."

Nusia told us once how Kopcio, smoking a cigarette, had walked over to an open bottle of ether. There was an explosion! She had even wanted to cancel her departure for Poland, but he already had someone else. I asked Mother if Kopcio has a scar. She shook her head no and went into the dining room.

"It's Kopcio again!" she said to Michał.

"Don't be afraid. Nusia's smart."

My knees swelled up. After breakfast I hobbled over to the back of the building where there were tomato plants tied to stakes. I pulled one of the stakes out of the ground and started using it as a cane. In class, it lay under the bench. At home, it stood in the hall next to the coat tree.

"Old bard Wernyhora!" Michał laughed.

"Watch out for splinters," Mother warned me.

While I was sitting on the bench near the church, a huge German shepherd came up to me and put his head on my knees. Waving his fluffy tail, he warmed them with his breath. I buried my fingers in his thick fur.

I set off with him alongside the wheat fields in the direction of the cow pastures. He ran in zigzags, sniffing the earth. He disappeared in the wheat. I heard him digging up subterranean nests and chasing after mice. I watched the waving ears of grain in order to detect where he was. Every so often he would emerge to touch me with his cold, wet nose.

I sat down in the pasture, laying my stick aside. I unpacked the bread and kielbasa Mother had given me for the road. Breaking off a piece, I pushed it under the dog's nose. He turned his head away, although saliva was dripping from his protruding tongue. Only when I placed his piece on the grass did he devour the whole thing in one bite.

Curled up against the dog, I pulled out Mickiewicz's *Konrad Wallenrod* from under my shirt. Leafing through the book, I stole a glance at the last pages. Had they recognized Wallenrod yet? I was afraid of the Teutonic

Knights' commanders. In order to avoid the death scene, I started fooling around. I closed my eyes in the middle of a line and tried to guess the rhyme. I also read from the bottom up.

The dog turned over on its side. We both were yawning. I fell asleep with my arms around him. When I woke up I no longer felt afraid of the rhyme that the boys in Krosno used to recite, transforming the popular "Catechism of the Polish Child" into anti-Jewish mockery:

> Who are you?
> A little Jew.
> What's your sign?
> A slice of challah.
> Who gave rise to you?
> Bad times.
> What awaits you?
> A strong limb.
> What's beneath it?
> Level ground.
> And upon it?
> Piles of shit.

"I am a Pole," I said to the dog, who was trying to get out from under me. I stood up so as not to be in his way. He shook himself. I brought him home. He settled in on the balcony beside the bicycle. He ate everything. Even the chicken heads that Mother threw out, holding them gingerly by the comb.

We went for walks every day. Soon, I got rid of the stick and stopped being Wernyhora. Once, we went farther than usual. Beyond the pasture, near a small house, a tethered goat was grazing. The dog started growling. His black lip was lifted up, exposing his fangs. I grabbed him by his fur and dragged him home. Pan Łytek, whom I asked to get me a rope for a leash, suggested that he might be a Gestapo dog who had escaped from Auschwitz. The Gestapo used goats to train their dogs.

Nusia and Pan Kubec took the dog with them when they left for Wrocław to study medicine and chemistry. On the way, the dog saw a goat and jumped out of the speeding train.

In the autumn, Karola Sznepf arrived. Waving an envelope with strange stamps on it, she ran up to Mother, who had come out of the kitchen to see who was at the door.

"Milo is in Tel Aviv!" Karola shouted. "My brother writes that they left Russia with Anders's army and ran away from the army in Palestine."

"Do you remember your uncle?" She looked at me.

"What a question!" Mother said, offended.

In the nursery I slipped a cavalry soldier into *David Copperfield.* Looking at the tin sword sticking out from its pages, I thought about the blue number that was tattooed on Karola's arm. She had told us many times about how they transported her from Płaszów to Auschwitz. She was standing on the ramp, filthy and stinking. An officer was selecting seamstresses.

"*Fach?*" He pointed at Karola with his whip.

"*Advokat.*"

"*Ignorant. Was weist du?*"

She remembered her math lessons.

"*Sinus quadrat alpha plus cosinus quadrat alpha ist gleich.*"

He sent her to the seamstresses.

—

Nusia phoned from the post office to say that she and Pan Kubec had gotten married in the town hall. Mother told her about Milo. When will they see him and be able to tell him everything?

—

In the winter, Nusia and Pan Kubec fled via Czechoslovakia to Munich. There, they got married by a rabbi and enrolled in the university.

—

Michał was knotting his tie in front of the mirror above the telephone. Lifting his chin, he adjusted the knot with his thumbs. Mother came out of the bathroom in a black dress and the nylon stockings that Winkler had given her when he took Nella to San Francisco.

"What's happening about Trzebinia?"

She was trying to see her calves.

"They signed the nomination. You're going to have a villa and a garden."

"Who will take care of it all?"

"A gardener."

The telephone rang. He was connected with Kraków.

"Happy New Year!"

Michał sounded happy.

"The same to you."

I had fat cheeks in the mirror. Recently, Mother's dressmaker had sewn in gores so that I could button my trousers.

"Asylum?! When?" Michał suddenly shouted.

"What happened?" asked Mother.

"Winkler fled."

When the Adler drove up, I put on the coat that Pan Churlusz had sewn. Mother said I could drive with them to the ball. She and Michał sat in back. Soon, the headlights shone on the soccer field and we drove out of Ligota. Where is this Trzebinia? Why do we keep moving from place to place? I drummed my fingers.

On the way back from Katowice, Pan Łytek stopped at a tavern. A half-liter of hot beer with raspberry juice. He poured a glass of vodka into it.

He addressed the woman behind the counter.

"Something for him."

"Tea?" she asked.

"But make it strong."

We stirred our drinks with tall teaspoons.

"Happy New Year!"

"Happy New Year. To you, too, sir."

"You're looking good."

He wiped the foam off his lips.

"Mother says I should eat because I have calcification in my lungs."

"The Director's wife knows what she's doing."

"Where is Trzebinia?"

"Near Kraków."

"Were you ever there?"

"No."

Kopcio Holzman

Nusia's Gymnasium ID photo

Mother and Michał right after the war

Left to right: Me, Michał, Nella Winkler, and Mother

Nusia and Karol

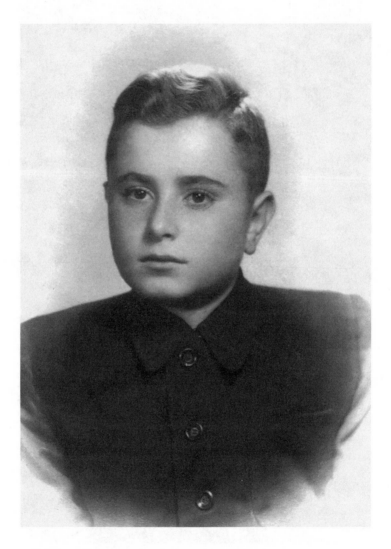

My Queen Jadwiga school portrait

Me in my scout uniform

The cover of Kopcio's book, which features a photograph of Nusia

the oil king's son

In the Morning

Waking up, I saw an empty cage with its door open. The black bird was sitting in a cardboard box on the windowsill. I pushed back my comforter invitingly. He flew down and sat on my chest. Rising and falling with the rhythm of my breathing, he dug in his claws to keep his balance.

I had found him under the chicken coop. Dragging one wing behind him, he was running away from the rooster who even frightened dogs. I carried him carefully into the kitchen.

"That's a jackdaw," Albina identified him.

"Do jackdaws speak?"

"As much as you do." She laughed.

Soon, he started flying around the room. He lived in the box, which held a tiny bowl of water and a plate of grains. Mother was worried that he would fly into other rooms in the apartment and soil the carpets, so she bought him a cage at the Chrzanów market. But he preferred the box.

Ever since we'd moved to Trzebinia, Albina had been our maid. She was eighteen years old. She walked quickly and softly in boots that she wore on her bare feet. Her legs were covered with white fuzz. Her thin, strong hands stuck out from her wide sleeves. Before bedtime, she twined her blonde hair around paper curlers so she could have curls. She wore a kerchief that matched the color of her apron, which she tied in back with a bow. But when she ran out to see Bolek, who had driven Michał back home and was turning around the Fiat in the yard, she pulled the kerchief off her head. She had blue eyes, white lashes, and a sharp nose. When she was happy or upset, her pale, freckled face got flushed.

In the morning, the pillows were beaten by hand to fluff them up and then were aired in the open windows. Goose down whirled among the furniture. Albina picked up dirty shirts and socks from the floor and packed them in among the sheets. She threw the white bundles with their big ears into the closet. She polished the parquet floor by skating over it on felt rags.

Mother crawled under the bed to point out dust, Albina did the same, and the two of them emerged from under the bed, one on each side.

⁓

When I came into the kitchen for breakfast, Mother sat down next to me with a fork and a small washcloth folded in four. Albina took a frying pan off the stove with sunny-side up eggs and hashed potatoes around which shot bubbles of butter.

"Watch out, it will spray you in the eye!" Mother warned me.

I gnawed on bread dipped in fat.

"Don't stain your trousers!" She wiped my chin with the cloth.

I bent over my plate.

"What about this?" She touched a burnt piece with her fork.

"It's the best. I left it for last."

"Michał liked the potatoes yesterday. He wanted more. But I kept them for you."

She stuck the fork into a potato and put it in my mouth.

"Mama!"

"Look at him! How grown-up!" Albina burst out laughing.

Mother unfastened the straps on my book bag. She slipped in my lunch, wrapped in paper.

"Don't give it to anyone. Eat it all yourself."

I went out into the courtyard that was separated from the yard by a carriage house and from the garden by the chicken coop. Once a week Albina ran around in here, chasing the chickens. Throwing herself on the ground, she smothered one and carried it over to the gardener, who was in front of the greenhouse, using an axe to whittle stakes for the tomatoes and beans. She threw the head with its beak into the garbage because Mother couldn't stand the eyes. She poured boiling water over the rest of it so it would be easier to pluck. The hen lived with her chicks in the coop. Not long before this, the rooster pecked to death a chick with a white comb.

⁓

I walked out through the wicket in the iron fence. In front of me and behind me children were tramping across the mud that was as hard as rock. The road led uphill, next to Pan Piotrowski's little shop. That's where I would drink an orange soda. A wire clasp freed the porcelain cork, which popped off together with its rubber seal, and the sweet bubbles burst against my nose. Pan Piotrowski and his customers were silent.

Mother had no doubt about it: "They would slaughter us like hogs! I don't trust them at all!"

⁓

The school was on the top of the hill. Weeping willows leaned over the red-brick building with its large windows and sloping roof. The director was Pan Paryzek. A short man. He taught geography and rehearsed the chorus for the ceremonies at the cinema. In our classroom, a map of Europe hung on the wall. A woman's hat pin was stuck through Lisbon.

"Portugal is a poor country. The Portuguese fish for sardines in the ocean. They stop their boats far from the north."

Pan Paryzek tapped his finger above the map.

"There they furl their sails. During the day, they sail out in kayaks and cast nets, and they return at night, sitting on sardines. Sometimes they drown. It's hard to believe, but many of them don't know how to swim. Have any of you eaten sardines?"

No one answered. So I kept silent, too, even though I had eaten sardines in oil and in tomato sauce.

As class was ending Pan Paryzek reminded us about the tryouts for the chorus. Someone asked if the ceremony at the cinema would be on the first of May like in the Soviet Union or the third of May, like it used to be in Poland. Pan Paryzek pulled the pin out of Lisbon, dragged it over the Pyrenees and across the green plains of France, lifted his hand over Germany and slammed it into Poland.

"When I was in normal school, our parents would come to visit us on the third of May. We paraded before them with banners with crowned eagles, thanking God for our freedom. Why should we change the calendar? I have nothing against the first of May. But what's wrong with the third?"

We painted decorations in the corridor. The sky with diluted ink, and the sun with egg yolks. Pan Paryzek stuck his head out from the classroom where the chorus was practicing and said that I would conduct the first corps' song.

On the first of May we walked to the cinema in groups of four. The chorus went out onto the stage while the curtain was still lowered. I hid behind Gustek and Adam, because I had no intention of opening my mouth during the singing. The curtain rose and I saw Mother looking for me. Songs were sung and she still couldn't find me.

Pan Paryzek announced the song of the first corps and left the stage. I came forward and, my teeth chattering, turned to face the chorus. The director was standing behind the singers. Nodding at me, he raised his arms. I did the same. After all, he had said I should just mimic his movements. He dropped his arms. So did I. The chorus bellowed so loudly that the paper sky shook.

The woods around are resounding.
Is it real, or is it a dream?
What does it remind you of,
what does it remind you of,
this familiar sight?

The golden sand of the Vistula,
a village roof of straw . . .
Flow on, flow on Oka River,
broad as the Vistula,
deep as the Vistula.

As we were leaving, Mother went over to the director triumphantly.
"Didn't I tell you? He took piano lessons!"
He bent down to her with an anxious air.
"We don't have coal, Madam."
"I'll have a talk with my husband."

Before our recess Pan Paryzek would close the glass inkwell on his
desk, set aside his old geography book, and prepare to administer a beat-
ing. His victim was usually the shop owner's son.
"Piotrowski, come here! The priest says you're blaspheming."
The children started giggling.
"Your father told me to make a man out of you."
The boy was already standing near the table.
"What do you have in your trousers?"
The children snorted with laughter.
"The last time, you put your notebook there."
"I was stupid."
"Lie down!"
The boy's nose touched the book in which Borysław was still in Poland.
"Three!" The sentence was pronounced.
The director beat him with a reed. Piotrowski turned red, but he didn't
moan. On his way back to his seat, he grinned at me. Because of Michał,
Pan Paryzek didn't touch me. Or Gustek, whom he feared.

For recess we were sent out into the stone courtyard at the rear of
the school. Here, there was grass growing alongside a fence behind which
the director raised pigs inside a red shed. While the teachers opened the
windows and aired out the rooms, the children chewed on bread with beet
marmalade and drank water from the well under our classroom's windows.

We cranked an iron winch to turn the drum from which a bucket was suspended on a rope. The water rocked and splashed in the silver can. Drinking from the cup that was attached to the bucket with a chain, I would look into the bottom, but I couldn't see myself because it was too deep. I could only detect the smell of moss.

Poverty surrounded me. I was ashamed to unwrap my lunch. I didn't want anyone to see the ham or chopped liver and onion.

"You see what they eat!"

Piotrowski looked at my hands.

"Eat!" said Mother. "You have calcification in your lungs. You know what the danger is."

"They laugh at me for being fat."

"Before a fat man grows thin, the thin man will die."

After lunch the boys played rag ball. Piotrowski swayed back and forth inside the goal that was marked off with two rocks. He held out his splayed fingers toward a big boy who, standing on his left foot, was kicking a bundle of rags. Whenever the boy looked toward the goal, Piotrowski froze in anticipation.

"Gustek, goal!" someone shouted in a high voice.

He took a shot and the rag ball flew between Piotrowski's legs.

Gustek Lawrencic was the strongest boy in the school. No one had such muscles and no one could play *cymbergaj,* a kind of table hockey, as well as he could. The coin he struck with a metal comb always scattered his opponent's coins and landed in the goal that was gouged into the edge of a bench. His light hair fell softly onto his forehead and his gray eyes. He walked slowly, like a worker coming home from his shift. It was only when he played rag ball that you could see how fast he was. He was supposed to go to work after finishing school so he could help his mother. His father was dead and his older brother, Władek, drank up whatever he earned. Gustek and I sat at the same desk. But I was friends with his younger brother, Adam, who was one class below ours.

After classes I ran over to Pan Ptak, who lived behind the school and raised chickens. Once upon a time he had been an engineer in a rubber factory, but he had quit work and built a shed with an incubator. Lights were always burning above the trays with eggs. Every few weeks the shells would appear to be etched and then they'd crack open. Beaks and damp, sticky wings would appear. Pan Ptak would throw out the dead chicks and feed the remaining birds until they were covered with feathers. Then he sold them. He knew everything about chickens. It was from him that I learned that birds cannot stand albinos.

Pan Ptak was very tall. He wore a straw hat. He treated me to water with raspberry juice.

"A little more?"

"No, thank you. I have to go now."

"Kiss your Mother's hand for me and give my regards to the Director."

Noontime

The sun was hot over the water and the wind stirred the reeds that grew out of the sand. Their long stems brushed against each other and rustled. Frogs sat among the reeds, their throats throbbing. Only at night or when it rained did they feel safe. The pond was rectangular, like all the firefighting ponds that the Germans had dug around the refinery. Heads of boys with blue eyes and thin, sunburned shoulders stuck out of the water. When they played ducks and drakes with stones that they picked up from the bottom, concentric circles fanned out along the surface. Adam came with his sister; she wore a bow in her hair. He took off his shirt and ran to join the others. She stayed on the bank, tall and thin.

I took off my clothes, too, and entered the pond at the shallow end, where no one was bathing. At first, I moved slowly and carefully, but then I started hopping. Suddenly, I lost the ground beneath my feet and slid down. I tried retreating to the bank. Hopeless. I kept slipping deeper and deeper. Bubbles flew out of my mouth. I felt moisture in my nose and throat. The end! I'm drowning! Out of stupidity! I survived for nothing!

Then someone's fingers grabbed my hair and yanked me up. I inhaled greedily. Kneeling on the bank with my hands digging into the sand, I coughed and spat out water. Over me stood Adam's sister in a wet dress. Only her bow was dry.

"Shithead! You damn shithead!"

I grabbed my things and fled. The boys were swimming toward us.

I got dressed in some bushes far from the pond and started running down the sandy road. I churned up dust behind me like an automobile. Little bushes bounced up and down, and the trees receded. I turned an imaginary steering wheel and imitated the sound of the horn.

"Beep, beep, beep! I'm alive! I'm alive again!"

On the meadows near the ponds lay burned-out casings of anti-aircraft floodlights that had sunk into the ground. I passed the tar-papered bar-racks of the German artillery units where workers were living now. Each family had a room that was entered from the corridor that ran down the middle of the barracks. This is where Pani Lawrencic lived with Władek, Gustek, Adam, and her daughter who pulled me out of the water. Their room was divided with a cloth screen into a bedroom and kitchen (with an iron stove). Between the barracks there was a latrine. A long board with round holes.

We lived nearby, but we were shaded by chestnut trees, acacias, and fragrant lilacs that grew alongside the iron fence. I slowed down and went inside through the back wicket. The large, red-brick villa was overgrown with yellow, green, and red leaves that climbed above the windows. A chandelier hung behind the curtains. The front door was so heavy that not even a grown man could open it quickly.

Through a wide open gate in the fence a coachman was leading in horses from the factory stable. From the coach house that belonged to the villa, he dragged out by its shaft a black, lacquered carriage. He harnessed the horses and waited on the coachman's seat with whip in hand. Mother, coming outside, smiled at him. The carriage dipped when she got in and moved off over the shadows of trees and bright spots of sunlight. The rubber-tired wheels thumped and the horses' hooves thudded.

I caught up with them outside the gate where at night a guard with a rifle and a cranked telephone stood watch. I hopped into the carriage and sat down opposite Mother on the leather-upholstered bench. She looked at me with dread.

"A wet head! Water in your ears! Dr. Głuski says you have delicate ears."

She dried me off with a handkerchief that she took out of her pocketbook.

"I was drowning!" I said.

"You're crazy!"

She put away the handkerchief.

"How can you talk like that? Do you want me to die?"

"Adam's sister pulled me out by my hair."

"You went into the pond? You're not allowed to."

"Near the bank . . ."

"Adam?"

"He was swimming."

"Why didn't he pull you out?"

"He was in the deep water. She was sitting on the bank."

"Does she know how to swim?"

"I don't know."

Driving along an avenue lined with hazel bushes, we passed the gigantic refinery gate with the factory's guard post. The sentries waved at us. Tanks of crude oil rose from the ground, one beside the other. They stretched out in an endless line. Winding iron galleries led across their gleaming roofs. The gravel crunched under our wheels.

We turned right at the railroad station onto the Kraków highway in the direction of Chrzanów and Katowice. An engineer was leaning out of his locomotive, looking at the raised semaphore. We drove for a long time along the edge of the asphalt roadway that stretched out through the fields. When a car approached, we moved onto the shoulder so the horses wouldn't be spooked. Railroad tracks ran alongside the highway, glittering in the sunlight. The coachman and I were silent. Mother wondered how much chickens would cost at the market. Ours were too thin for broth. Finally the road passed under the viaduct and started climbing. The horses slowed and stopped. We were passed by a wagon loaded with potatoes and cabbages. We were in Chrzanów.

Mother's high heels tapped on the sidewalk. Holding hands, we walked past the shops in the direction of the market. A shoemaker was cutting leather that was stretched on a table. A white line had been drawn around a paper pattern. Boys in leather aprons were hammering nails into soles. The glazier's apprentice was fitting windows with new panes into a rickshaw that rode on thick, red rubber tires. The glazier sat on the rickshaw's steps, smoking a cigarette. A priest came out of the soap maker's shop, followed by a boy carrying a sack on his back. They went off in the direction of the church. In the shop window was a pyramid of soaps and candles. One of the candles was thick and tall. When we reached the meat shop, I asked Mother to buy me a roll and kielbasa.

"Michał can't stand it when you eat in the street," she refused me sternly.

"I'm hungry," I said, whining.

We entered the shop. Loops of kielbasa hung on the white tile wall. The butcher used a long stick with a brass hook to take one of them down. He placed it on the counter and started slicing it. He tossed the rosy circles onto one pan of the scale and the other pan with a brass weight slowly rose up until both pointers were at the same height. Then he took a roll out of the basket and with a razor-sharp knife cut it in half.

"Michał doesn't understand what hunger is," Mother said in the street. "Can someone who wasn't there imagine what we lived through? Here." She gave me the roll, stuffed with kielbasa. "Just don't tell him."

Squeezing the roll to make it fit into my mouth, I bit off a large chunk.

"You're going to choke! No one's chasing you!"

—

The market was at the foot of the church. It was swarming with people. A crush, a hubbub, cries. Unharnessed wagons, their shafts up. Stalls with wooden roofs from which ropes of dried mushrooms and braids of garlic dangled. Clay pots with butter submerged in water, slices of beef and lamb covered with newspapers sticky with blood. Sauerkraut scooped into jars with wooden forks, and pickles fished out of the barrel by plunging your arm up to the elbow in their sour bath. It occurred to me that if a pickle slipped out of your fingers and fell down to the bottom it would be hard to find it again.

"Cottage cheese! Sweet as sugar! Eggs, each one large as two!"

A peasant woman held up a chicken that was flapping its wings.

"Yellow, fat! Fed on grain!"

"Would you allow me to blow on it?" Mother addressed the woman.

"Blow as much as you like!"

The woman handed her the chicken.

Mother blew on the feathers, once and then again.

"It's rather blue . . ."

"What do you mean blue! It's yellow, not blue."

"You blow." Mother turned to me.

"Enough of this blowing!" the woman barked, and took back the chicken.

"If you'll lower the price, I'll buy it," Mother said.

"I can't do that, dear, but I'll pluck it for you."

Mother removed her gloves and took money out of her bag.

"We'll stop by for it on our way back."

"Should I pack up the feet?"

"Yes. They're good for soup."

Metal chains with Christs on them hung on nails. Under them were lighters made from cartridge shells and colored wooden toys. A rattle on a stick started chattering.

"A grager!" Mother was delighted. "Just like the noisemakers we used to swing on Purim."

Afternoon

The black carpet that had stretched from wall to wall in Ligota now lay in the center of the living room. And even though the piano with its legs in crystal coasters pressed it down onto the parquet floor, I was afraid that the flower serpents would wrap themselves around my neck.

It was possible to exit from the living room in several directions. One door opened into the hall, from where one could go to the kitchen and laundry room or outside, passing the coat and hat closet. French doors with brass handles opened into the dining room where the chandelier with the deformed eagle hung. On the oval Chippendale table, surrounded by chairs, there was a vase with fresh flowers that the gardener brought in every day. When guests were coming, Albina would open up the table and add chairs from the other rooms.

A door on the other side of the living room led to the bedrooms. First came Mother's and Michał's bedroom, then mine, then Albina's, and, at the end, the bedroom of Michał's brother Julek, who had survived the gas chamber. The Germans, fleeing Mauthausen, hadn't had time to use their Zyklon-B. American soldiers found Julek unconscious under the shower heads. Gangrene was oozing out of his smashed toe. An amputation. While waiting for a prosthesis he wrote to the Red Cross. From them he got our address and had recently arrived in Trzebinia.

The rear wall of the living room had no openings. A mahogany bookcase with several books in it stood against the wall along with two armchairs and a small round table with a black glass top covered with a white lace napkin. The front wall, in contrast, was made entirely of white window frames, brass handles, and glass. The adjoining doors stretched from floor to ceiling and opened onto a stone terrace with iron tables and white wicker chairs; from there you could walk down several wide stairs into the garden.

It was cold and gloomy in the living room.

Stretched out across an armchair, with my legs hanging over the arm rest, I was reading the first volume of *David Copperfield*. The second volume lay on the carpet. I was thinking that someone who needs to be taken care of is not yet safe, and if he is not safe, then he hasn't survived completely. Only grown-ups can manage on their own. I was afraid of sickness, poverty, and war. But I hoped that before the next war broke out I would be too old for the army.

—

Adam appeared from the direction where the sun was shining and came up the stairs, his sandals slapping. He was my height, but a lot stronger. Gustek must have looked like that at one time. I slipped out of the armchair and we went into the garden grounds among yellow, red, and almost black roses.

"Why is your last name German?" Adam asked.

I didn't really have a right yet to the name I was using. Michał said we would take care of it in court when I turned eighteen. He also wanted me to change my first name.

"Witold sounds good," he thought.

"It's my second father's," I told Adam.

"And your first name?"

"It's mine."

On the way to the greenhouse we came across lilies with blue and gold flowers and long sharp leaves that could cut you.

"What happened to your father?"

"A bomb from a Soviet airplane landed on him."

"They flew here, too."

Mother never mentioned Father. Only once, she took his photograph out of her bag.

"Do you remember?" she asked.

I didn't say anything.

—

The greenhouse stood amid low apple, plum, and cherry trees. Empty tin cans from American canned meat jangled to scare away sparrows. Black, rich garden beds stretched all the way to the tall trees; a wire fence wound among them. Water dripped from rusty pipes and fell in droplets on the vegetables. Later, Mother would cut the big heads of cabbage or peel kohlrabi and give me the slices to gnaw on, like an apple.

The gardener came out of the hothouse.

"Did madam send you for something?"

"No."

Far beyond the bean plants climbing up strings attached to stakes, beyond the leafy tops of red potatoes, the green-fingered scallions, the wall of lilacs that began where the trees ended—beyond all this, the mighty distillation tower of the refinery could be seen.

"Let's go to the movies," I proposed. "They're showing *Professor Wilczur*."

"I saw it before the war," the gardener remembered.

"*Wilczur's* not playing anymore," Adam said. "Now it's a Russian film, *Chapaev*."

Walking alongside the tanks of crude oil, we reached the railroad station and turned left in the direction of Kraków. The highway, which ran through the center of Trzebinia here, had sidewalks on both sides. On the right towered the rusty red buildings of the steel mill with their smoking battery of chimneys. Clouds of white smoke merged and floated across the sky. The steel mill was separated from the street by a fence with a large gate that contained a smaller gate through which people entered and left.

The director of the steel mill was Pan Pierzynka, who played chess with me at the little iron table in our garden. Sluggish and fat, he moved cautiously among the ivory figures. Until recently, he was still a worker. He said that in the course of his life he had thrown enough coal into the furnace to cover this entire garden.

"And where is your wife?" asked Mother, bringing over a tray of sandwiches.

"She doesn't have a dress. Just some old rags."

She set down the tray beside the chessboard and pointed upward with her finger.

"Do you know how much the refinery director earned before the war?"

"No."

"Fifteen thousand! Now my husband makes exactly the same amount."

They laughed.

Behind the steel mill was the rubber plant. The plant director was Pan Karol Akerman—pale, elegant, and a head taller than Michał.

"These are his last weeks in Trzebinia," Michał said. "After the referendum he's going to join the Ministry."

"He's younger than you . . . ," Mother sighed.

"Are you badly off?" He was angry.

"I have no one to talk to."

Once, I saw Pan Akerman come running out of the rubber plant and jump into a Willys in which a soldier armed with a machine gun was seated. The Willys also came to pick up Michał. Later, someone called from the guardhouse to say that the Director would not be coming home that night. Mother walked back and forth from one window to another, screaming that she can't stand this.

Akerman's father was a watchmaker. Customers used to come to him from all over the county. Now he repaired watches only for acquaintances. He had a gray beard and wore a violet yarmulke. We would often wait in his workshop next to the cinema until he finished praying behind a screen and came out to us. Mother, holding Michał's Omega in her hand, bent down to greet him. Old Akerman embraced her and kissed her on the head; me, he stroked with his dry, warm hand. He spoke to her in Yiddish and she spoke to him in German.

Leaving his shop, Mother looked around to see if anyone was nearby.

"He said that his son and Michał are madmen! Our feet mustn't remain in this country."

Along the Kraków highway, on the left side, broken fences and empty lots stretched all the way to the cinema. A truck approached from the steel mill with gravel that stank of sulfur. Coal glowed under the steam boiler. The motor rumbled. Cast iron wheels on thick spokes turned slowly. A DKW preceded the truck. Roaring frighteningly, it left a trail of smoke behind it. From the direction of Kraków two cars suddenly appeared, racing one behind the other. Their black paint sparkled and the sun was reflected in their windows. They flew on silently in the direction of Katowice. We watched them head toward the station, until they vanished from sight.

"American!"

A line of boys in front of the cinema moved up to the ticket booth. We also began running in order to avoid having to sit right in front of the screen. Adam was running in his brother's too large sandals. The afternoon sun shone directly on his hair.

We went inside.

The lights went out and only red bulbs burned above the closed doors. A strong stream of light flowed through the dust-filled hall. A minute later variously shaped spots and streaks jumped across the screen; then drums started roaring and black banners with skulls fluttered. White officers in immaculate uniforms and gloves began the attack. Drummer boys beat their drums. The Bolsheviks were lying in the grass, squeezing the triggers of their Maxim machine guns.

"Rat-a-tat-tat!" said the Maxims.

"No-no-no-no!" begged the drummers.

The officers, letting go of their rifles with fixed bayonets, fell alongside the drummer boys. At first, one at a time; then, in entire rows. The Bolsheviks got up from the grass. Their accordions wheezed and a Russian song resounded.

Hey, Chapaev, Chapaev, Chapaev our hero!
Hey, Chapaev, Chapaev, ha, ha!

The film broke off. The clatter of the wobbly reel grew slower and slower. The lights were turned on and the doors were opened to air out the hall.
It was still day.

Sunday Afternoon

Michał had been at the office since morning. I decided to visit him. I left the villa with a book under my arm and, walking among the ripening nut trees, I approached the factory gate. I got into the refinery through the guard's brick hut. A broad avenue led straight from there to the multistoried administration building. Old chestnut trees that blocked the sky grew along the avenue. Huge buildings with pipes and valves coated with thick grease were visible behind the trees. In front of the administration building the avenue circled around a garden bed planted in carnations and then it forked, with one branch leading to the distillation tower and the other to the garage.

In Michał's office the smell of crude oil seeped in through the open window. White and red carnations covered the shadow of a huge tower on which hung ladders and galleries. Pipes wrapped around it; fat pipes on the bottom, but on the dome they wound around like grass snakes around a greenhouse.

"Does Mother want something?" Michał asked from behind his desk.

"No."

"Tell her I remember about the guests."

The siren for the second shift began to wail. The factory guard opened the wicket in the gate. Workers appeared carrying bags of food and bottles of grain coffee. In their wooden-heeled shoes, they waded into puddles in which colorful peacock eyes shimmered. Above their heads stretched pipelines wrapped in tar paper. Steam was leaking from everywhere. Some of the men arrived on bicycles with oilcloth folders fastened to the frames. They placed their front wheels between the narrow ribs of the bike stands. They disappeared behind doors near which there were red fire extinguishers and winches with firefighting hoses.

"Engineer Michalik is here, Director." The secretary opened the door a crack.

"Oh, you have a guest," Engineer Michalik smiled.

"He's on his way out."

Taking care not to stain my white socks, I walked toward the garage. It was a long building with a flat roof. Three narrow pits could be seen through the wide-open doors. A green Studebaker missing the glass in its small side windows was in front of the first pit; a Bedford with fat tires was in front of the second; while at the third, supported by blocks instead of wheels, sat Michał's black Fiat with its hood raised and its doors open.

Bolek wasn't there. The drivers had the day off.

On my way home I thought about Michał. Why did he tap me with a teaspoon that he took out of his glass of tea when I sat staring at dinner?

"Philosopher! Wake up!"

"Why philosopher?" Mother expressed surprise.

"He's in a daze! He doesn't know if he's alive."

He also called me God's horse, three-toed sloth, and prophet.

"Tzaddik Elimelech!" he chanted gaily. "Look at the pelt the boy's blessed with!"

Mother laughed until she cried. There were no jokes, however, about my getting a haircut. Michał lost his good humor and tugged at my hair.

"Too long," he complained. "Take him to the barber."

"Go, comb your hair with water," said Mother.

When I told lies, he lost his temper.

"How much is seven times nine?" he'd ask.

Seven times seven is forty-nine. Forty-nine plus seven is fifty-six. Fifty-six plus seven is . . .

"You're counting in your head."

"I'm not counting."

"Don't lie."

I got a slap on the head. Mother took me to the bathroom, washed and combed me.

"Michał has the heart of a dove, but you mustn't upset him."

"What am I doing?" I complained.

"You're adding, but you have to know the multiplication table by heart. You could wake me up in the middle of the night and ask me how much is seven times seven."

I crossed the courtyard to visit the Lawrencices. They were drinking tea after mass. From above the iron stove on which stood a golden tea kettle, Christ looked on sadly. Another Christ, no jollier, peeked out through the open bedroom screen. Władek, who was just leaving the house, put a mirror and metal comb into his pocket.

"Don't get drunk!" Pani Lawrencic reminded him.

"Don't worry, Mama."

Gustek, Adam, his sister with the bow, and I sat on stools. The chairs were for their Mother and Władek. Pani Lawrencic brought chamomile, sugar, and enamel mugs to the table.

"It's good that our girl pulled you out by your mop," Władek laughed.

"There's no joking when it comes to water," said Pani Lawrencic. She crumbled chamomile into the mugs and poured boiling water over it.

"Maybe your Mother would stop by someday for tea?"

"She's been very busy lately . . . ," I stuttered.

"They drink real tea," Władek said.

I placed my book on the sill of a window through which you could see the barracks. Pani Lawrencic washed floors in the factory dining hall to which vegetables were brought from our garden. If she were to visit us, Mother would receive her nicely. Maybe Michał could even give Władek a better job? But Pani Lawrencic thought that Mother owed her a visit.

"I'm going; my friends are waiting," said Władek.

"I don't like your friends."

"Do you think that Gustek and Adam have better friends?"

"Don't get drunk!"

The door slammed. The bow turned toward her mother.

"He's going to get sloshed like a pig again."

Pani Lawrencic sighed.

"Some more tea, perhaps?" she turned to me.

"But make it strong."

She poured me more chamomile.

—

There was a gleam on the horizon. A storm was coming from Kraków, but it was still far away. Not having any work to do before dinner, which was going to be late today, I set off toward the school. When I stepped over the wavy lines in the dried-up mud, it occurred to me that I had drowned and that this was my next life. Or maybe I had already almost died many times and I would only die for real some other time?

I walked up the hill. Below me was Piotrowski's shop, the barracks, the villa near the refinery, and the railroad station from which trains were taking people away. There was a strong gust of wind and the willows rubbed against the roof of the school. The empty classrooms could be seen through the large windows. Pan Paryzek came out of the school accompanied by two men. They were walking on either side of him.

"Hello."

"My regards to your parents."

They set off down the hill. They grew smaller and smaller until they became three dots near the tanks.

I met Piotrowski in the school courtyard. He had seen them taking Paryzek out of the classroom. We looked through the window. On the still wet blackboard a map of Poland divided into three parts was sketched in chalk.

"What kind of Poland is that?" Piotrowski asked, confounded.

"Why did they arrest him?"

"Someone denounced him. It wouldn't be you, would it?" He twisted his face into a smile.

"You'll regret that!" I screamed in a rage.

Piotrowski turned red. His eyes flashed, like the eyes of the peasants at the wedding of Albina's cousin near Oświęcim. He grabbed me by my shirt and shoved me. My back slammed into the well, from which the bucket dropped with a clang.

"I'll drown you!"

"Let me go, you boor!"

"No, you mangy Jew!"

"Let go of him!" Gustek suddenly shouted from the street.

Piotrowski let go and started to run away, but Gustek caught him.

"I'm going to rip your legs off your ass!"

"I'll never touch him again, I swear to God."

I got up from the ground where I was looking for a button he'd torn off.

Gustek gave me the book that I'd left on their windowsill and returned to his barracks.

My back and throat hurt. When I passed Pan Ptak's house it was growing dark and pouring rain. I remembered the church near the cinema, when the candles in it were extinguished. I had knelt there once and opened my mouth like the others. The priest had drawn a cross on my forehead and placed the wafer on my tongue. Maybe I should go there again? Lightning stitched the sky like white threads. I thought about our little table in the living room covered with a lace cloth. There was a clash of thunder next to the incubator. I ran home under streams of rain, slipping in the mud. The long branches of the willow tree lashed the school. I didn't even notice when I passed Piotrowski's shop.

I pushed the wicket in the iron fence. The gleaming roofs of cars in the yard reflected the light falling from the windows. Instead of going in through the front door, I ran alongside the chicken coop to the kitchen, clasping volume one of *David Copperfield* under my shirt.

Evening

Noise and confusion dominated the kitchen. Pan Pierzynka's and Pan Akerman's drivers along with a soldier who had his forage cap tucked into his belt were sitting at the table, staring at the tray of sandwiches. Albina dashed out of the laundry room with cloth napkins, grabbed the tray, and rushed off to the dining room. Mother, wearing a black dress and high-heeled shoes, ran in to check on the broth.

"Finally, you're here!" she cried out at the sight of me. "Again, your head is wet. Taste the consommé."

I took the spoon from her hand.

"Blow!" she shrieked. "It's boiling hot, you know."

I blew on it and noisily slurped up the consommé.

"Well?" she asked anxiously. "Salt? Sugar?"

"Nothing."

"Splendid!" She was happy. "Change your clothes and comb your hair so that Michał doesn't see you in this condition. Julek has already asked about you."

In the laundry room, where the linen was pressed with an iron with a removable heater, I dried myself off, put on a fresh shirt, and went out to the hall. In the open hat and coat closet all the hooks were occupied.

From beneath a leather coat that I wasn't familiar with, Pan Pierzynka's greatcoat, dyed brown, stuck out. A belt with an empty holster and a four-cornered cap with two bars and a star were hanging on top of the steel mill director's hat. Two caps were above Pan Akerman's trench coat and Pan Ptak's wet raincoat—the felt hat of the rubber works director and a straw hat from which water was dripping. Under Michał's Borsalino hung his dark blue overcoat and Julek's herringbone jacket, with a thick cane hooked onto one of the pockets.

Smoothing my wet hair, I slipped into the living room. It was filled with light and with voices that reached there from the dining room. I took a deep breath and went inside through the wide open French doors with their brass handles.

The table was extended to its full length. Rain was slashing against the windows. With every gust of wind you could hear the rattling of the iron gate, and the light from the lamp that hung on the gate flashed in the windowpanes. Fine porcelain dinnerware, left behind by the Germans, was on the snow-white tablecloth. Flat plates and soup plates, platters and salad bowls, little pitchers and gravy boats—everything shone with the reflected light of the chandelier. Silver knives, large and small, soup spoons and teaspoons, dinner forks and dessert forks all glittered. Serving plates covered with cloth napkins waited on the credenza. They held salads and desserts for later. Next to a sliced loaf of bread I could see the red seals on translucent bottles of vodka.

The guests had just finished the hors d'oeuvres and Albina carried the sandwiches that hadn't been eaten into the kitchen for the drivers. Michał was walking around the table, pouring vodka into the men's glasses.

"A little glass won't hurt," the major said, half in Russian, and clinked glasses with Pierzynka, who was making a bird out of a printed sheet of paper.

Pan Ptak and Julek wet their lips in the vodka and licked them dry. Pan Akerman covered his glass with his hand to signal that he couldn't drink any more. Michał returned to his seat and raised his glass, which Mother had filled with water beforehand.

"To the referendum!" he cried. "Nothing warms us as much as vodka!"

They drank up and exhaled with pleasure.

I heard the creaking sound of leather straps and turned to look at Julek. He winked at me, inviting me to sit next to him.

"I saved a seat for you," he said. "Bring me a slice of bread, because I have to chew on something when I drink."

Pan Pierzynka leaned over toward the major.

"How should this be managed? The engineer says one thing and the accountant something else. Whom should I believe?"

The major unbuttoned his uniform collar. A button with an eagle on it disappeared behind the green cloth.

"Instinct will tell you who's lying."

"What instinct?"

"Class instinct."

Albina brought in a white oval platter with freshly cooked spaghetti. Mother, using two forks, placed the steaming coils on the guests' plates.

Pan Pierzynka drew his nail along a fold in the paper bird.

"It's easier with a shovel than a pen," he sighed.

"Lenin said that every cook can rule a state," the major said, and sucked in a long strand of spaghetti.

"You don't say!"

"Don't be afraid; the Party will help you."

The major unfastened a second button and indicated Michał with his hand.

"The Director understands very well what I'm saying, because he was there during the war. He knows what the Party can do."

"Yes, yes, yes." Michał nodded affirmatively.

Smiling at the major, Julek leaned over to me.

"Who is that prick? A Jew?" he asked quietly.

"I don't know." I shrugged my shoulders.

Albina came in, bending under the weight of a tureen filled with consommé, which she was holding by its porcelain handles with her white fingers. The aroma of meat boiled with carrots, dill, and flame-toasted onion filled the dining room. Mother lifted the lid and started ladling it into the soup plates.

"Gentlemen!" she cried. "Enough politics; the consommé will get cold."

Pan Pierzynka pushed aside his bird. The major bent over so as not to stain his uniform.

"It's not soup, it's a poem!" Pan Ptak licked his lips. "Is it just chicken, or did you add some beef?"

"Whatever I added, I added. So long as it tastes good."

The major handed her his soup plate.

"Seconds are required," he joked.

Drops of rain hammered the windows like drums.

"My toes are killing me," said Julek, wiping the sweat off his face with a napkin. "It's always worst in such miserable weather. Bring me a slice of bread, because soup without bread isn't worth anything."

Albina brought in, one after the other, a platter of boiled potatoes dressed with butter, a salad bowl with green peas and red carrots, a deep platter with delicately sliced raw cucumber in sour cream, and a bowl of steaming red beets. From the credenza Mother served horseradish in sour cream, marinated mushrooms, and cornichons that swam in their jar amid sprigs of dill and bean leaves as if in a small aquarium. Albina appeared again, first with a platter of boiled chicken, and then with the beef from the broth, adorned with celery leaves.

"This is a feast, not a supper!" Pan Ptak exclaimed.

"Like at my mother's," said the major and, having unfastened the third button with an eagle, served himself a fat chunk of beef and a heaping spoonful of horseradish.

"The scoundrel knows about food," Julek whispered. "The fatter the meat, the better. Bring me another slice, because beef requires bread."

Michał poured more vodka, skipping himself and Pan Akerman.

"May it not be the last!" the major said in Russian.

They drank and sighed with pleasure.

Pan Pierzynka picked at his teeth, picked up the paper bird, and started reading out loud what was printed on it.

"ARE YOU FOR THE ABOLITION OF THE SENATE?"

"No one is going to defend a few old farts," Pan Akerman said.

"No one gives a shit about the Senate," the major laughed.

"ARE YOU IN FAVOR OF RETAINING THE SOCIAL AND ECONOMIC REFORMS?"

"No one will give anything back!" said Pan Akerman.

"Even if he wanted to," the major giggled.

"DO YOU WANT TO RETAIN THE WESTERN BORDER OF POLAND ON THE ODRA-NYSA LINE?"

"On the map, we have shifted left. That's a fact," said Pan Ptak.

"Lwów is gone," Mother sighed.

"Lwów is Ukrainian!" Michał cut her off abruptly.

"Yes, I'm Ukrainian! Did you think I didn't remember?"

"Calm down . . ."

"I hate them." Her black eyes flashed.

"Now they're getting smashed from both directions," the major broke in.

"Not enough!" Mother cried. "They're all damn Kruks!"

"And were you ever in Lwów?" Julek asked me.

"No."

"Well, now you never will be. That's a shame; it's a lovely city."

Albina cleared everything from the table but the teaspoons, dessert forks, and vodka glasses, and Mother set out dessert plates and coffee cups. Sugar bowls with cubes of sugar and little pitchers of milk appeared at both ends of the table. The tablecloth was already thoroughly stained; Mother covered the worst spots with napkins.

Michał poured more vodka.

The major unfastened his last two buttons and stood up ponderously. His gun filled out one of his trouser pockets. His cheeks were red and his eyes glittered.

"Dear friends!" He raised his glass. "Poland has returned! But not to those who lost her in 1939. The referendum is clever. Even those who hate us won't vote NO three times."

"There are people," said Pan Ptak, "who won't be convinced by anything."

"This will shut their traps. To the health of those who thought up three times YES!"

They drank up and sighed with relief.

Julek glanced around the table, but there was no more bread.

"I can't drink like this," he said.

Albina entered with an enameled coffee jug.

"God, how good it smells!" Pan Ptak exclaimed.

Mother sliced the sponge cake on the credenza and poured over it a cream made of egg yolks, butter, sugar, vanilla, and beaten egg whites.

"Just like at my mother's," the major murmured and his clouded gaze settled on me.

"And you, *molodets,* are you with us or against us, young man?"

"He conducted the chorus on May Day," Mother said.

"*Pravilno*! That means he's with us! And what will you be when you grow up?"

"No doubt a conductor," laughed Pan Ptak, licking the cream off his fingers.

"He should study and not think about stupid things," said Michał.

"That's right!" the major supported him. "Socialism is knowledge."

Outside the window there were terrifying flashes and the rattling of the gate blended with the booming of the thunder. I looked at the men around the table. Which one of them should I imitate in order to become a grown-up?

Julek asked me to come to his bedroom. He wanted to take off his leg. He leaned on me as we walked through the living room. Where there was no carpet his wooden foot banged and squeaked.

"The major is garbage!" he hissed. "We have to warn Michał."

He removed his belt in the bedroom and lowered his trousers. Wincing from the pain, he sat down on the bed and unbuckled the straps under his knee. Kneeling in front of his swollen stump, I pulled off his shoe and sock from his other foot. He pointed to the place where he had once had toes and said that that's where it was most painful. He lit a cigarette and puffed at it like a pipe, rather than inhaling.

"I'm an old well driller," he said. "Before the war I bought a piece of land. I sensed that there was oil there. And did it gush! Michał was my partner."

He winked at me. "Psst! Not a word about this to anyone! We would have been rich if it weren't for the war. Now, I want to have a gas station. Money changes hands there. Sha! Michał will arrange for me to get a lease there. You'll be leaving here, too. Your mama wants to go to Warsaw. Michał is going to climb high. He'll give them his soul, because he believes in all of that."

He started yawning and said it was time for me to go to my room.

The guests were leaving. Motors were rumbling in the yard. From my bed I looked at the light along the edge of my partly open door. Michał walked past to the bedroom by himself. Soon, along with his snoring I could hear Albina crying and Mother shouting in the kitchen. Then Mother came back and threw off her shoes. The bed creaked. The rain had stopped completely. In Trzebinia everything was clean that night.

The telephone in the hall was ringing. Albina's bare feet pattered. Mother went out of the bedroom. Whispers, and waking up Michał. The shuffling of his slippers and the slapping of Mother's scuffs. Then a long silence until I heard them again.

"He died," Mother was sobbing. "Now, when it's possible to live!"

"He died in his sleep. He didn't feel anything," Michał consoled her.

"He still managed to repair your watch."

"A career is opening for his son . . ."

"He wasn't concerned about that. He wanted to leave. I do, too."

"We're going to leave for Warsaw."

"I don't want to go to Warsaw. I want to leave Poland."

For a while I didn't hear anything.

"Albina is chasing after Bolek," said Mother.

"My Bolek?"

"We'll have to send her away, because she's going to get pregnant and there'll be a scandal."

"Yes, yes, yes."

I was like a stone that has been thrown. Hard, smooth, and cold, I flew fast and high. I couldn't stop near anyone. I opened the window and leaned on the sill. It smelled wonderful. Drops of water were dripping onto the paving stones from the roof. The bird started moving around in his box and then jumped onto my hand and dug his claws in to keep his balance. Suddenly he pushed off and flew away. He did this so softly and quietly that he left not a trace in the air.

Night

We were playing thousand on Julek's bed with greasy torn cards. The king of hearts was missing from the red deck so we used the one from the blue deck, which had only eleven cards. Julek, in his undershirt and long underwear with one leg rolled up, was airing his stump. Flicking his cigarette ash into an ashtray that lay on his quilt, he turned around my notebook so he could see the picture I had drawn of hussars around a column of figures.

"Why do they have wings?" he asked.

"I don't know."

Late at night he sent me out for cognac. Knocking the cork out of the bottle I brought him, he gave it to me to hold so he could shuffle the deck.

My bedroom door was slightly ajar. Lying under the quilt, I thought about why there is no St. Wilhelm in the calendar.

I dreamed that there was a mirror instead of a pane of glass in the window that looked out onto the courtyard. I saw black hair and eyes. Fat cheeks. I felt like throwing up. I woke up.

A loud conversation was going on in Julek's room. There had been a pogrom on Thursday after the referendum. Forty-two Jews were murdered in Kielce.

"You have to consider who did it," said Michał.

"What do you mean, who?! Michał!" Julek expressed amazement. "Do you have any doubts?"

"Our feet mustn't . . . ," Mother began.

I wanted to get up, but there was such a pain in my side that I screamed.

"What happened?"

Mother came running into my room.

"My belly."

The motor wheezed, the tires crunched over the gravel. Every time the Fiat jounced over a rut I felt as if I had a sliver of glass inside me. Lying on the rear seat, I could see the lights burning on the oil tanks. I groaned. Mother asked Bolek to slow down, but he was afraid that he'd burn out the clutch. Finally, at the railroad station, we drove onto the highway. The car raced along the asphalt roadway. In Chrzanów, we stopped in front of the hospital. Attendants placed me on a stretcher.

Covered with a sheet, I lay naked on a bed. A lightbulb inside a white shade was above me. Dr. Głuski, who had once examined my ears, came in, shuffling his feet. He was short, but like Julek he had a large head with curly black hair. He wasn't wearing a tie. Red rubber tubes stuck out from the pocket of his smock.

He kissed Mother's hand and slid a chair over to the bed. He pulled back the sheet and delicately pressed my belly. No matter where he touched, it always hurt in the same place.

"Appendicitis."

"An operation?" Mother asked.

"His belly is hard. Hm! We shall see. Hm!"

"You heard about old man Akerman."

"Infarctus myocardi."

When I was left alone I recalled how Albina, wearing a blouse she had made from a parachute and dyed red, had packed her trunk. On the bottom, she placed her high-heeled shoes, the ones in which Mother had danced in Katowice. Next to them she placed felt gaiters that fastened with thin straps. On top of these she put the dresses, skirts, and sweaters she had acquired over the year. She stuffed her old peasant things on the sides. Mother brought her an overcoat with a removable lining and the valise from Drohobycz, because not everything could fit into the chest.

"Where are you going?" I asked Albina.

"To the village. I was there for a wedding. Don't you remember?"

I could hear horses' hooves. I opened the heavy entrance door and held it so the coachman could carry out the trunk and valise to the chaise. We said goodbye on the stairs. Albina climbed up on a metal step and sat down on the leather seat. Beyond the gate, in the hazel grove, her hand in its red glove waved and was gone.

Falling asleep, I felt that the bed was turning slowly like the kitchen table at Albina's cousin's wedding. I was sitting there among dirty and clean dishes. A marinated ham lay on a platter with cold pierogi. Forks and knives stuck out of the cabbage. The rolls were soaked with red horseradish-and-beet sauce.

Men came in from the cottage next door, flushed from dancing. To cool down, they opened the door into the courtyard. A German shepherd emerged from the darkness. Its thick fur was covered with snow. Steam was rising from its muzzle. Was it a Gestapo dog? The camp was nearby. If the sleigh that had brought us from the station had gone just a little farther, we would have reached the ramp in Auschwitz.

The men wanted to drink. Push away the headcheese and gelatin! Get rid of the poppy-seed cakes and sweet pancakes! Shove them to the end of the table! Give us slippery mushrooms and herrings! Beer, vodka, and home brew!

"The little Jew will drink, too."

"Pure alcohol?"

"A little beer with juice."

Jumping over the high threshold, they went back to where the accordion and fiddle were playing. A blurry dance line of colorful dresses, aprons, and caps. The shrieks of the whirling girls. The men's black jackets like wings over their white shirts. Albina with freckles on her flushed cheeks.

Dr. Głuski opened the window. A moth flew into the room.

"It's soft. Hm! It doesn't hurt?"

He examined me for a long time.

"With hair like that . . . And eyes . . . Hm! It wasn't easy. But they didn't succeed!" he shouted triumphantly.

His face wrinkled and he burst out laughing. A rumbling "Ha! Ha! Ha!" flew out of his open mouth. His stethoscope bounced playfully. I squealed with glee, although I didn't know what I was laughing at. Nor even if I felt at all jolly.

"Hee! Hee! Hee!"

Suddenly his bass voice fell silent. But I kept on giggling.

"*Fortuna tibi est*," said the doctor.

He wrinkled his face and again roared with laughter.

I stayed under observation for a second night. The lamp shade was already full of insects. How had they gotten in? Yawning, I looked at a Tarzan comic book that Mother had bought at the market in Chrzanów. English words in little clouds emerged from the mouths of people and animals. The drawings were all alike. They differed only in their texts and background details.

Sometimes, however, the perspective changed and then I had the impression that I was in the jungle. With a monkey's eyes I looked down from the top of a palm tree onto Tarzan, who was standing below. I also observed from the interior of the jungle a snake's giant eye looking in. Or I was a frog. The three-toed foot of a stork was immersed in transparent water that was drawn with thin horizontal lines. The stork's long beak hung above me.

When I came home from the hospital Julek was no longer there. He had left for Kraków, where he'd gotten a gas station to run. The rains began after his departure. The wind stripped the trees of their leaves and they clung to the large windows in the living room. Heavy drops struck the little iron tables and wicker chairs on the terrace.

Bolek was admitted to the Kraków Polytechnic. Mother said that Michał had arranged that for him. The new driver, who came from the army, wore a uniform and helmet.

Engineer Michalik left for Kraków. He returned to his old position in the Central Directorate of the Petroleum Industry. Michał didn't try to retain him. He himself was leaving Trzebinia and oil. He forbade me to speak about this, though, until a new director was confirmed.

Mother became upset about how she would manage to pack up our things without Albina. Michał said that Hartwig would do everything. Specialists would wrap each glass in paper and then place everything in the credenza in Warsaw.

Lying in bed, I considered the past day. Would Adam figure out that something was going on? After school, we sat in the living room because it was raining. I wanted to tell him *David Copperfield,* but he preferred checkers. Mother set down a plate of sandwiches next to the chessboard.

"Why did someone draw a cat in chalk on the greenhouse?" she asked.

"The gardener belongs to a cat religion," Adam said.

"Jehovah's Witnesses," I added.

Then the sun came out and we played in the garden. Running around with long sticks, we shot at each other.

"Rat-a-tat-tat-tat-tat!"

I willingly fell over onto the ground. I didn't care about winning.

Again, I dreamed about the window onto the courtyard. Raindrops were splashing on the chicken coop. Water ran down the iron fence posts. Between them, frogs with throbbing throats came into the yard. Pani Lawrencic was walking down the street alongside the fence with her gold tea kettle and enamel mug. Gustek and Adam were pulling a valise behind her. Their sister with her wet bow skipped along at the rear.

Albina was whispering to Mother that the Lawrencic family was moving to Warsaw. Mother was offended that they hadn't even said goodbye.

I ran out of the house. A chick with a white comb fled from under my feet. Slamming the wicket, I tried to catch up with the Lawrencices, who were walking in the direction of the train station. I kept sinking in the mud.

Pan Paryzek was returning alone from the station. Greeting Pani Lawrencic, he said that they were already releasing the people they had arrested before the referendum. Maybe it was a good sign? They had detained him well after May Third. Pani Lawrencic handed him a cup of chamomile tea. He drank it up and set off for the school.

"Good day," I said.

"Give my regards to your parents."

Near the train Pani Lawrencic turned to face me.

"Tea?" she asked.

"But make it strong."

She picked up the tea kettle. Gustek and Adam pulled her into the carriage. The locomotive released steam. The hair bow moved off in the direction of the steel mill and the rubber factory.

in power

Farewell to Trzebinia

It snowed all night.

The new director sent over workers to clear the yard. A white ravine appeared between the villa and the factory guardhouse, and the rising sun filled it with shade. The hazel trees, weighted down with snow, hung over the ravine.

A watchman, carefully making his way between snowbanks, brought over *The People's Voice.* On the first page was a photograph of Bolesław Bierut. The Sejm had elected him president.

Mother burst out laughing.

"What kind of election is that? One candidate!" She threw the newspaper into the stove.

The next day, I went out to meet the watchman. As I took the paper from him, I slipped and fell down. In the kitchen, the snow that had gotten shoved into the paper began to melt. The eighteen men in the photograph of the new government became unrecognizable from the water. Bony Józef Cyrankiewicz turned stocky. Printer's ink flooded his bald head. Władysław Gomułka grimaced painfully. Hilary Minc, whom Michał admired, split in half, and all that remained of General Rola-Żymierski was his cap with zigzag trim.

Soon an amnesty was announced.

I went out into the courtyard. Snowdrifts glittered under the chicken coop. I made my way to the barracks. I told Pani Lawrencic that death penalties would be commuted to fifteen years or life in prison. People who had been sentenced to ten years would serve five, and if they'd been given a five-year sentence they would go free. But not until April.

"They want to butcher a few more," Władek giggled.

"Shut your trap!" Pani Lawrencic hissed.

Adam unfolded his cardboard chessboard. While we played checkers I thought about why Michał had gone ahead without us. Was it true that freezing weather had delayed the reconstruction of the house in Warsaw? If he abandoned us, we would fall into poverty.

The thaw arrived. Hartwig's truck rolled in through the wide-open gate. Torn-off wet hazel branches hung from it. That night our belongings left for Warsaw. Mother and I lay down on Albina's bed, which was to be left behind in Trzebinia. In the morning we set out in the Fiat for Kraków. At the train station, the conductor unlocked a first-class compartment for us.

Over the Butcher Shop

I awoke when the train was pulling in to the station. The carriages on the next track were rolling past more and more slowly. We stopped in front of a sign that read: WARSAW MAIN—FREIGHT. Mother lowered the window and called for a porter. Holding on to the railings, we descended the steps onto grass. Chains hung between the buffers. The rusted wheels had silver rims. We set off in the direction of the locomotive, which had stopped in front of a knoll that was covered with footprints. Water dripped from the boiler. Suddenly there was a burst of steam. Mother grabbed my hand and pulled me onto the knoll.

The sun was rising in front of us. Brick dust turned the light red. There were two lonely walls left standing nearby. Behind them, to the left, stretched a rubble-covered expanse. Stumps of chimneys, all the way to the horizon.

Michał appeared from the other side of the knoll.

"I hadn't pictured to myself that it would look this bad," said Mother.

"It's better farther away from the center."

Some cars were parked near the knoll. We walked over to a brown one. The driver opened its flat trunk; it had a spare tire affixed to it. While he was stowing the suitcases that the porter brought over, I walked around the car. I stroked the gleaming mudguard and the silver points on the hood.

"What kind of car is this?" I asked.

"French," said the driver.

"What's it called?"

"A Citroën."

Michał suggested I sit in front. The car drove quietly. We turned right and then made an immediate left. A wide street. Trucks and trams were driving around us. Walls stuck up from the rubble. Marble and wooden staircases hung between floors. The sun was reflected in yellow, green, and blue rooms. Craters as deep as several courtyards. Paths through the bricks.

We slowed down as we passed a line of cars parked in front of an apartment building that had survived. Porters were carrying out suitcases. There were soldiers and civilians on the sidewalk.

"What's this?" asked Mother.

"The Polonia," Michał said. "A hotel."

At the next intersection we turned right. There were shops and restaurants in the surviving ground floors. Coats hung inside gates. Clothing and shoes lay in rickshaws with raised umbrellas. Beneath windows through which soup was served in bowls sat women wrapped in army blankets. They had trays with small objects for sale suspended on straps around their necks. Above the ground floors, through holes in the walls, you could see other streets. Soot and dust whirled in streams of light.

People were walking in the roadway and on the streetcar tracks as well as on the sidewalks from which the rubble had been shoved aside.

German greatcoats dyed brown. Green English uniforms with insignia on the arms. Sweaters made from American socks. Riding breeches and jack boots. Forage caps and caps with visors. Short dresses and cork wedgies. Nylons with seams. Broad hat brims. Shoulder bags.

A crowd of children in front of a gate. Security personnel with sticks guarding the entrance to a dark courtyard.

"What's there?" asked Mother.

"The Polonia," said Michał. "A movie theater."

A streetcar rang its bell. The pedestrians got off the tracks. Our driver stepped on the gas pedal with his rubber-soled shoe. The Citroën followed the streetcar. Outside the window, on a wall, a bent blue sign glided past: PIUS XI ST. We were driving alongside street lamps that stuck up out of the ruins. Two apartment buildings. Behind a fence, a statue of the Mother of God. We drove into the square. On the steps of the church, under a tower with a crown on it, people were kneeling and lighting candles.

"The Church of the Savior," said the driver.

We passed the streetcar. White slips of paper could be seen on the gates of bullet-riddled apartment buildings. Boards in windows. Flowers beneath a cross. The next square. Stone boots on a pedestal. The fire brigade. Barracks amid trees. Soldiers with blue bands around their caps. The streetcar terminal. A green gate.

A light went on in a marble townhouse. Michał said it was the chocolatier Wedel's house, which had survived because Germans were living in it. Across from it was the bazaar on Dworkowa Street. Wooden stalls and peasant wagons on automobile tires.

A church in ruins appeared on the left.

"St. Michał's," said the driver.

After that, meadows began. On the right, though, there was still a line of townhouses. They seemed to get lower as we drove along. Among them was a newly reconstructed, bright yellow two-story building.

"Here it is," said Michał.

The Citroën pulled over to the curb. Cement steps led up to a white-painted door. On the wall was a bright blue sign: 102 PUŁAWSKA ST. We got out. It smelled of plaster.

"It's far," Mother sighed. "We came too late."

The building was symmetrical. The sun, rising from the meadows behind the church, was reflected in shop windows on either side of the door. In the shop to the left, below red letters reading STAN. STANKIEWICZ: BUTCHER SHOP, a photograph of Bierut was pasted to the glass. The store on the right wasn't open yet. On its windowpane, which was painted over with whitewash, was one word: RENOVATION. There were balconies above the stores. A curtain flapped in the open door to the balcony on the left. The door to the right was closed. A chandelier hung behind the window.

"Who lives there?" Mother indicated the balcony with the curtain.

"Stankiewicz," Michał said.

We went inside. Halfway up, the stairs reversed direction. Michał took out a brass key.

"They're on the right. We're on the left."

—

When Michał had left for work and Mother began unpacking the boxes in the dining room, I went into the living room. It was fairly crowded in here. There was a towering tile stove in the corner. Between it and the door was a couch. The rolled-up edge of a carpet protruded from under it. Opposite the couch, beneath a window that faced the courtyard, was a piano. On it, a porcelain figurine of a naked woman with red hair. I had seen similar women in the magazines that had been left behind in Ligota.

I stretched out across an armchair. My books were lying on the carpet. I picked up the first volume of *David Copperfield*. Our fates were similar. We both had lost our father. Evil people wanted to destroy us. To understand why we had survived, I had read the first volume during the spring, summer, and fall of the past year. A child's suffering and coincidences. Why didn't anyone say that I had been saved by chance? Everyone spoke of a miracle.

"A miracle, a miracle!" Pan Rygliński had shouted.

"A true miracle," Pani Hirniakowa's mother had wheezed.

"A miracle of miracles," agreed the young Jewish woman who came to Andzia Katz's place to see a Jewish child.

In the winter, after Michał left, I had looked into the second volume. David had grown up. He had become older than me. I started skipping lines and paragraphs. Yawning, I changed volumes. Maybe I had missed something? If a miracle is no different than chance, why does it have a different name? I wanted to ask Michał about that, but he wasn't there. He had surely read *David Copperfield* at the Gymnasium and would be able to answer me.

Mother came in. Upset. Am I deaf? She's been calling to me, shouting, and no response! She told me to take out the newspapers that the porcelain had been wrapped in. Pressing the crumpled copies of the *People's Voice* to my chest, I went downstairs. The courtyard was enclosed by a brick wall that had collapsed in places. Through the chinks created by the missing bricks I could see the neighbors' charred trees. An iron trash bin stood against the wall. I lifted the lid and threw in the newspapers.

From the house I walked out onto Puławska Street and turned right. Malczewski Street began at the nearest streetcar stop. Another right turn. Overgrown gardens paralleled the sidewalk. Broken trees leaned on bushes. Inside the gardens were villas shattered by shells. I detoured around standing water in bomb craters. Behind narrow Tyniecka Street an iron fence encircled a small white building.

On the other side of Malczewski Street, on a small square, behind bicycles lying on the sidewalk, boys were kicking around a rag ball.

"Wanna play?" Big Boy called out to me.

"My leg hurts."

Pretending that I was lame, I returned home.

Mother was grating potatoes. Holding a pot with a dishcloth, she bent over the sink and removed the lid. Steam veiled her face. Shaking the pot to get rid of all the water, she put it back on the stove. When the potatoes stopped steaming, she added a piece of butter, poured in half a glass of milk, and crushed some dill. She mashed everything with a wooden potato masher and put it on a plate. She added chicken livers that she had sauteed with onions in a frying pan. I have to eat liver because I'm pale. She had bought them downstairs from Stankiewicz.

I looked up from the plate.

"He's nice," she said. "But do I know what he's thinking?"

In the afternoon, Karola Sznepf came over. She was now an attorney in the Ministry and was living in the Polonia Hotel. Mother brought her in to the living room. They sat down on the couch. I turned the armchair around to face them. The sunlight, streaming in from behind the piano, turned them golden. Karola was wearing a brown polka-dot dress. Mother noticed a flake of soot on one of the polka dots. She blew it off and said that there's soot everywhere. Michał has to change his suit every day. When would they get rid of these ruins?

"Never," said Karola. "Illiterates are in charge. My boss doesn't know what a typewriter is. The 'director' is the same. Besides which, everyone steals. Yesterday, I forgot my glasses. I go back to the hotel. There's a man's coat in the closet! I check the door. It's my number. I start screaming. The manager comes running. 'I didn't know that you'd need your room during the day. You should have warned me.'"

"Russian tricks," Mother sighed.

"I don't care." Karola waved her hand dismissively. "I'm waiting for my brother to take me away. Tel Aviv or New York."

"Milo got married," Mother said.

"I know. To a Sabra."

Mother got started on a new subject.

"Just imagine, what nerve! Gomułka's wife is insisting that Michał change his last name. Why should people say he's either a German or a Jew? 'Subjectively' it's meaningless, but 'objectively' it doesn't serve the cause."

"She's an antisemite!" Karola was indignant.

"She's a Jew." Mother shrugged her shoulders.

"How do you know?"

"Michał saw her."

The kettle began to whistle in the kitchen. Mother brought in the tea.

"I didn't have time to bake anything," she explained. "I don't even know if the oven is any good."

"Michał has a heart of gold," Karola declared.

"He trusts everyone," Mother sighed. "He hired a right-wing nationalist who used to march around Borysław before the war in a fraternity student's hat."

"He's an idealist."

"He works like a dog. And I can't make ends meet."

"Under communism, everything will be free," Karola joked.

"In the meantime, I have to pay Stankiewicz for the parquet floor."

"Why Stankiewicz?" I asked, surprised.

"He owns the building," Karola explained. "I drew up the contract."

"He knows!" Mother waved her hand. "Only he doesn't remember. I have such problems with him! He loafs around all day. He does his homework at night, while Michał eats dinner. Endless quarrels. One shouts, 'You're making a mess!' And the other, 'I'm not!' As long as we were by ourselves in Trzebinia, I had peace. Now it's beginning again."

"Get your work done during the day," Karola advised.

"Michał is nervous," said Mother. "And he," she pointed at me, "he doesn't love anyone."

"He'll become wiser."

"When?!" she expostulated. "He's already eleven!"

I went into the dining room. The door to the balcony was open. The eagle on the chandelier looked out at the treetops swaying alongside the streetcar tracks. I slipped outside. Beyond Malczewski Street several other streets were visible, also going off to the right. On the other side of Puławska Street there were only meadows. The shadow of a cloud that was approaching from the Vistula quickly covered them.

There was a flash. Suddenly, I caught sight of hussars. They were riding in the direction of the Church of St. Michał. A column emerged from meadows even farther away than the streets I could see from the balcony. The horses' enraged eyes. Their manes blowing in the wind. Their rumps and tails. Knights in armor. Golden helmets and swords in their gloves. Cloaks down to the ground. Among them, clinging to the saddles, ran the soldiers with the neck-protecting hat brims that I'd cut off in Ligota. Bayonets as thin as stingers clanged against their helmets decorated with tiny eagles.

There was a flash. Crowned eagles. Black berets. Green uniforms. Horses' legs and heads in German helmets with red-and-white bands flashed by in the tall grass.

There was a flash. The hussar who was riding at the head turned back toward me as if he wanted to tell me something.

I heard the clopping of hooves on the roadway and looked down. A small horse was pulling a cart loaded with something black. Beside it walked a peasant holding the reins. When they disappeared under the balcony, I lifted my head. The hussars were gone. The cart was driving out from under the balcony.

"Soil!" cried the peasant. "Soil for flowers."

I ate refried potatoes and went to sleep. I dreamed that green boys cut out of paper were running around under the bed. Joining them, I noticed that their backs were stamped with the letters UNRRA. They kept coming close to each other and then separating. Pale children flitted among them. I woke up in a sweat. I was sure that Germans were filing in under my bed.

At Queen Jadwiga School

In the morning we went out onto Puławska Street. Mother was wearing a yellowish suit with brown stripes, and I had on plus fours with buckles. I had a backpack on my back. We crossed Malczewski Street. Behind an iron fence, deep inside a courtyard overgrown with trees, was an apartment building with several stairwells. A radio played softly through an open window on which was a flowerpot full of geraniums:

> Our blood has long been spilled by butchers,
> The people's bitter tears still flow,
> But there will come a day of reckoning
> When we will be the judges!

We turned onto Woronicza Street, which I had seen from our balcony. Mother straightened my hair and smoothed my eyebrows in front of Queen Jadwiga School.

The homeroom teacher was a priest. We met him in an empty classroom; the children had gone outside for gymnastics. He transferred his rosary to his left hand and greeted us. I took off my backpack. He asked what I was reading.

"*David Copperfield,*" Mother answered.

"A sad book."

Mother leaned over to the priest.

"Only he and I survived," she said softly. "Of our entire family."

"Dreadful times."

"I don't want anyone to pick on him."

"Who would pick on him?" the priest asked, taken aback.

On the playing field the girls were playing with a tennis ball. The boys were standing in line at a distance from two poles across which lay a thinner pole. The priest introduced me to the gymnastics instructor and went back to the building.

"Go to the back of the line," the gymnastics instructor advised me, and blew his whistle.

The boy at the front of the line, wearing a white-and-red armband, jumped over the crossbar and came to stand behind me. A whistle. The next boy. Soon, I was in the middle of the line. I looked at the pole. It came up to my belly button.

"Now you." The gymnastics instructor indicated me with a nod of his head.

I knocked down the crossbar.

"Again."

Lifting my legs high, I set off down the same path. The buckles on my plus fours jingled ever so softly. I didn't know how to push off from the ground. I knocked it down again.

"I can't."

"You can," said the gymnastics instructor. "If others can do it, so can you."

Starting out, I decided to push off with my right foot. However, I heard the girls laughing, lost my concentration and stopped in front of the crossbar.

"Take a rest," said the gymnastics instructor.

⸺

I sat by myself on a school bench. The boy next to me moved somewhere else. I could hear the scratching of pen nibs against the walls of inkwells. Only Michalski, who sat in front of me, had a fountain pen. The class monitor, who wore a white-and-red armband, shot paper pellets at me. I put them into my pocket.

The last class was about behavior. The priest sat on his desk and, swinging his pointy shoes, which stuck out from under his soutane, asked the girls what had happened in class recently. They complained that the monitor had drunk up the ink from the inkwell on the teacher's desk.

"What do you mean, drank it up?" The priest was astonished.

The children began to giggle.

"It was empty," the monitor grunted.

The priest sent him to get ink. The monitor returned with a large bottle and filled the teacher's inkwell. The priest asked him to check the students' inkwells. Going from bench to bench, the monitor topped up the ink in the inkwells. He started pouring ink into mine, too, even though it was full. The ink started flowing in the direction of my notebook. Afraid for my plus fours, I jumped off the bench. Michalski rescued the notebook with his left hand.

"What's happening?" asked the priest.

The children roared with laughter.
"It was full," grunted the monitor.
"Apologize!"
The priest stopped swinging his legs.
"Why did he come here?"
"And where else should he have gone?"
"To Palestine," whispered the monitor.
"To where?" The priest hadn't heard him.
"I said 'I apologize.'"

On the street, I took my lunch out of my backpack and unwrapped it.
"The Jews killed Jesus," the monitor growled behind me.
My mouth was stuffed with bread and ham.
"Russian flunkeys!"
I swallowed.
"Communists!"
"I'll tell the priest!"
He left me alone. I went back to eating. Near the fence, behind which stood the building with several stairwells, I threw the paper that smelled of ham into the bushes.

From then on, I remained in the classroom after our lessons were over, waiting until the children left the school. One day (it was raining then) I saw through the window that the assistant director was stopping the children as they left and directing them back to the building. Curious, I slipped out into the corridor. Everyone was going to the gym. I joined them and sat down under the ladders from which thick ropes dangled. The boys wrapped them around their necks and pretended to be hanged men. There were bursts of whispers and giggles. The janitors brought in a wooden table from the teachers' room and set it down next to the leather horse that was used for practicing jumps. The windows were closed. It grew hot and stuffy. The wet assistant director and a man in a leather coat appeared. They climbed up on the table.

"Yesterday, near Baligród," the assistant director began loudly and funereally, "General Karol Świerczewski was murdered. The legendary 'Walter,' leader of the International Brigades in Spain and the Second Army of the Polish armed forces, perished from the bullets of reactionary forces. Armed underground bands have bitten the hand extended to them."

The man in the leather coat leaned over toward the speaker.

"Open the windows!" shouted the assistant director.

The janitors started rushing along the walls. Drops of water fell into the hall along with cold air. There were squeals. The man in the coat raised his hand. In the silence that ensued the howling of factory sirens reached us.

"They are weeping like that everywhere," he said.

—

After the meeting I went back to our classroom. I wiped the blackboard with a wet rag and started drawing. A white sky blurred in the damp blackness. On the grass, made with light strokes of chalk, horses were running. Their powerful muscles were covered by dust that looked like fur. A hussar, who was watching me, his head bare, rode along shouting orders. He had pulled out his sword in the direction of the clean blackboard where the ruins of St. Michał's Church were supposed to rise. The eyes didn't come out well. I made him a helmet with a plume, and then I lowered his visor.

"Can I change something?" I heard Michalski's voice behind me.

I turned around and backed away. Michalski rubbed out the visor and picked up the chalk with his left hand. He had marvelous moves! Ping! Ping! Ping! I saw eyes between his fingers. When he brought his hand down in order to draw the nose, white veins appeared around the eyes.

"It's not easy with chalk," he said.

"Paper's too small."

"I have bristol board at home."

—

He lived in an apartment house that had several stairwells. He took out his key on the second floor. We went inside. The entryway was dark. When he turned on the light I saw a painting in a gold frame. Enormous chestnut trees were golden and green in it. In the center was a pink palace. A woman, her head bowed, was visible beneath a colonnade. A courier with a basket of flowers on his head was running into the palace. A gas lamp was burning. Rain was drying on a rust-colored blue and gray roadway. But there was something astonishing in this picture. Suddenly, I realized that it was a mirror. The real picture was hanging on the opposite wall. I turned my head.

Michalski smiled.

"Spring 1905," he said. "My grandfather loves it."

Cossacks in long overcoats and round caps with blue brims were riding alongside the palace. Rifles stuck out from behind their backs. They had whips in their hands. Two in front. On chestnut horses with white spots near their hooves. Two in back. One on a white horse and one on a piebald. They were looking around suspiciously. Boys were walking among the Cossacks. One was wearing a coat, a cap, and shiny boots; the other, a jacket and rumpled shirt.

"They arrested Grandpa."

"When?" I felt frightened.

"Then." He pointed to the picture.

"Siberia?"

"He was blacklisted."

We went into the main room. Here, too, it was gloomy. The window was shaded by the leaves of trees outside. Michalski turned a switch again. I bent over a sheet of bristol board that was lying on the table. Behind a huge tower on a hill the sun was going down, painted yellow. Crystals glittered in stones that were piled one on top of the other. High up on the galleries halberdiers, the size of shirt buttons, were standing. Walls behind which green roofs could be seen were attached to the tower. A road descended from the hill. Winding through trees, it acquired colors. Grass and sand appeared. Knights were riding downhill. The horses' hooves merged with each other. Wind ruffled their manes. Swords dangled from straps. Exhaustion bowed the riders' backs. They had no helmets. Their blond curls fell onto their shoulders. The front rider had a crown on his head. Rubies and gold.

"The return of King Arthur," Michalski said.

"From where?"

"From war."

From then on, we left school together. We drew until dinnertime, and then again until evening. The lamp was always on. Shadows of heads moved across the bristol board. Kneeling on chairs that we pushed together, we kept on sketching. He drew people; I drew horses. I left the eyes for him. We changed places. Our shadows merged.

"Why is it so empty between the horses?" asked Michalski.

"Soldiers and insurgents are going to be running there, holding on to the saddles."

"Flight?"

"The hussars are rounding them up."

While he drew, Michalski told me about his grandfather, with whom he was living. (A photograph of him in a judge's robes hung on the wall: gray-haired, a scar, obscured by binoculars, cut across his eyebrow and cheek.) During the school strike, he had left for the Austrian partition, since he was blacklisted.

"What was the strike about?" I asked.

"About the right to learn in Polish."

He finished Gymnasium in Kraków. He went to Vienna to study law. Law firm. World war. The Brusilov offensive. Siberia. Revolution. Escape to Poland. The Bolshevik war. The Miracle on the Vistula. Wounded at Komarów (a Cossack struck him across the face with his saber). Convalescence. Appointment to a judgeship. The September defeat. Prisoner of war camp. Warsaw's ruins. Searching for his daughter and grandson. His daughter's tuberculosis. Powązki cemetery. A package from London. His son's medals.

We finished the sketch. Now to the painting.

Michalski wasn't in school. The monitor started shooting again. After school, I went to the apartment house with the several stairwells. I knocked. Silence. I went out into the courtyard. Through the window with the geranium the radio was still playing:

> Onward, then onward, lift up our song!
> Our banner flutters above the thrones,
> It carries the thunder of vengeance, the people's anger,
> Sowing the seeds of the future.
> And its color is red,
> For on it is the workers' blood!

Our priest was walking on the sidewalk that ran alongside the iron fence. He was holding a rosary in his right hand. I caught up with him at Malczewski Street. Hearing my footsteps, he turned around.

"Excuse me, Father, but what happened to Michalski?"

"He's not going to be coming back to us."

"Why?"

"He moved away."

"Where to?"

"To Tarnów. To his aunt."

"Why?"

"They arrested his grandfather."

"For what?"

"He was a judge."

The number 4 streetcar from St. Michał's Church was approaching. Its brakes squealed. Sparks showered down from its pantograph. The stop. People getting off. People getting on. Ding-ding-ding! Departure. The priest patted me on my back with his free hand. We crossed Malczewski Street.

Near the butcher shop I slipped my hand into my pocket. Full of pellets. It's good that Michał is an engineer.

"Is there a St. Wilhelm?" I asked.

"Wilhelm the Conqueror," the priest smiled.

"How many saints are there?"

"Oh, very many!" he said, imposingly. "In heaven, everyone is a saint."

In front of St. Michał's Church he raised his hand that held the rosary and, extending two fingers, made the sign of a small cross in the air. I wanted to ask him if he knew Michalski's address in Tarnów, but he disappeared inside the newly rebuilt gate. Playing with the pellets in my pockets, I set off for home.

I thought about death. The first time it appeared, it was in the gondola beneath a zeppelin on the smooth, cold pages of the German lexicon. During the Russian times it had inhabited the police building on the other side of Pańska Street. It entered our courtyard with the Germans. Stinking of carbolic acid, it opened the door to our apartment. In the cellar, it bent over the bucket that was filled with excrement. Since then, I had seen it everywhere. It fired from a pistol while sitting on a horse; it pulled the shoes off Mother's feet. It looked under the bed and into the garret. It stepped on my feet on Pańska Street when we walked behind the wall of people's backs. Coughing and spitting blood, it had come to the attic. It wore a yellow tie. It even crawled into the well. After the war it looked for a flowering fern and peeped out from the pages of the art magazines. Was it death who had dragged me down into the pond in Trzebinia? But I hadn't seen it then.

Before we left for Warsaw I had gone to the pond. Dried reeds stuck up out of the ice. Water dripped from them. The children were sliding about in their boots. Where were the frogs?

In the dining room, Mother was unwrapping a package. The newspaper it was wrapped in carried an enormous heading: AMNESTY. FIFTY-FIVE THOUSAND RELEASED. She pulled out a box with Hebrew lettering. Matzoh! She smiled. She wouldn't eat bread during Passover. She told me about her trip to the synagogue on Twarda Street. Appalling ruins! The sanctuary was destroyed. They were distributing matzoh from Holland in the adjacent apartment building.

In front of the synagogue, Jews who had been expelled from Russia were milling about. Mother recognized someone named Kac, also Ajdman, and Kornhaber, who lost all his teeth in Siberia. Awrum Horszowski showed her his frost-bitten hands and told her how they had baked bread out of sawdust. Elder Hauptman cursed the war in Manchuria. They were all preparing to go to Palestine. Even Frydlander, whose orthopedic shoe was falling apart, was setting out. In Russia, everything was free, but they didn't have shoes. He hoped that he would meet some rich man with a soft heart at the Wailing Wall. Langerman, Szwarc, and Semil . . . These names sounded normal on Mother's lips.

She decided to darn our stockings so that nothing should have holes in it for the holidays. She told me to turn the pockets of my plus fours inside out. Maybe they're torn. She's already mended them once.

The paper pellets fell out onto the carpet.

"What's that?" she asked.

"Pellets."

She went to fetch a broom and dustpan.

Two Michałs

The school year ended. I was advanced to the next grade. Michał gave me a leather ball and a silver pump. The ball was light and hard. I bounced it on the floor. I kicked it. It struck the piano, which emitted a thud. Mother said you don't play in the house. I put the pump next to the red-haired woman and went out to play in the street. The opening into which the bladder fit was laced up with a strap. I wanted to see the knot, but it was underneath the outer skin. I was interested in knots because I still couldn't tie my shoes. (In the morning I would go into the kitchen and put my foot up on a chair.)

The holes left by the bombs on Malczewski Street had dried up. I was standing near Tyniecka Street. The boys interrupted their game and crossed over to my side. Big Boy sniffed at my ball.

"It's genuine!" he said. "There's a nipple under the lacing."

"What for?" someone asked.

"So it can be pumped."

I handed him the ball. He stroked it gently, then threw it in the air. It flew across the roadway. Before it touched the sidewalk, though, he caught up with it and kicked it. It flew up again. This time over the electric wires. It stopped dead in the crowns of the trees and then began to fall. The boys waited. A header. A swing. A kick. It fell into the bushes. I started running, too. But I couldn't catch up with it. Big Boy kicked it toward me. I kicked it back the wrong way.

I retreated to the sidewalk and clasped my hands behind my back.

In the morning I smelled an omelet cooking. I threw off my quilt and went out into the corridor. Between the dining room and the front door, opposite the telephone, stood a bicycle with a small motor. It had fins like the steam machine in Ligota. I touched the right handlebar. It turned. I stroked its shiny leather saddle. Mother appeared in the kitchen door, blocking the light with her body. The silver spokes in the wheels turned gray.

"Did you see it?" she asked.

"It's beautiful!"
"Michał brought it last night. He's always thinking of you."
"Can I ride it?"
"After breakfast."

I placed the bicycle on the roadway next to the curb. I cautiously put my leg across the frame and pressed down on the pedal. When the bicycle started moving, I sat down on the saddle. Pedaling, I passed Malczewski Street. A car honked its horn. I moved closer to the sidewalk. At Woronicza Street, I pushed down on the lever affixed to the front fork. The motor roared. I started pedaling. It flung me forward. I stopped pedaling. A bicyclist stared at me as I passed him.

I noticed a street leading off to the left. The meadows ended there. I switched off the gas, braked with the pedals, and, making an arc, set off in that direction. The harsh morning sun shone right into my eyes. I raced downhill, zigzagging between rocks and dried-up mud.

Just a few houses. Mist was rising from the garden beds. I looked around. The hills I was riding down blocked my view of the city. I rode out into an open space. Huge trees stretched across the road. They hid the sun. The highway ran between them.

I turned right. Stinking DKWs, boxy Hanomags, Opels, and Citroëns were passing slow-moving peasant carts. Even black Demokratkas, which I had seen for the first time near the cinema in Trzebinia, were on the road. I gave the bike some gas and wiped my hand on my shirt.

I thought about why they use a different word for "eraser" in Warsaw. On which side do left-handed people have the gas lever? And can Father have green eyes in a black-and-white photo?

Under a sign that said WILANÓW I noticed a little dog. I stopped and picked him up. He wagged his tail. I put him inside my shirt. We returned home together. Mother fed him. He fell asleep near the armchair, resting his head on the books.

In the afternoon, Karola came to visit. The dog ran over and started pawing her. She drove him away, crying out that "he stinks something awful."

In the evening, he sat down under the table in the dining room. Feeding him a pancake, Michał smiled and started telling us about his mutt in Ratoczyn who was always hungry. He and Julek decided to test the dog's appetite. They gave him a heaping bowlful of cornmeal mush and sauce. He gobbled it up. They gave him more. He licked it clean. They filled it again. He began to squeal, but he didn't walk away from the bowl. He cried and he ate.

"What was his name?" I asked.

"Who?"

"The dog."

"He didn't have a name."

From then on, we traveled together. He rode in my backpack, which hung from the frame.

One day, I again rode downhill to the big trees that lined the highway. Under the sign that said WILANÓW a truck that had been converted into a bus started to pass us. Its diesel motor roared. Its mudguards and the flags fastened onto the headlights shook. People were standing in the back on its iron steps. I felt sick from its black exhaust. I rode across the shoulder and, laying the bike down in the grass, pulled the dog out of the backpack. When I let go of him, he started running full speed ahead toward the next town.

"Dog! Dog!"

I called him for a long time. He didn't even look back.

I set out for Malczewski Street with my ball. When I saw the boys circling the square on their bikes, I turned off the motor and started pedaling. They moved toward me.

"A race!" Big Boy shouted. "Who'll reach the end of the street first?"

They stood up from their saddles and started pedaling with all their might. I pushed the lever forward. They didn't have a chance. We rode back to the square slowly. I left the ball with them and rode off by myself for an outing. I found a grass snake in the ruins. What had it lived on among the stones? Going home for dinner, I dropped by Malczewski Street.

"The cyclist is here!" Big Boy shouted, and handed me my ball.

Vacation was over. Michalski didn't come back. I told Mother about the monitor. Michał found a school in the Żoliborz district. It was called WSFCS. It was far away, but without religion. Unfortunately, they didn't have an opening. However, in October one of the students was supposed to go abroad with his parents to a diplomatic posting. They promised that they would telephone.

"What is WSFCS?" I asked.

"It stands for Workers' Society Friends of Children School."

While we waited to hear from them I "attended" the school on Woronicza Street from time to time.

Mother set the table for dinner, but only for Michał and me. Where she usually sat she set a baking pan in which there was a silver candlestick holding four candles. When the first star appeared she opened her handbag. I was terrified that she would take out Father's photograph. Instead, she pulled out a flowery kerchief, put it on her head, and lit the candles. For her mother, murdered in Bełżec. For her father, who died of dysentery in Flossenburg. (He was sent to the stone quarry from the office because he broke his glasses.) For Bronek, who had been so terribly ill. And for Romuś.

Michał's voice reached us from the street. He was telling the driver that he wouldn't need him any more today. The car door slammed. The doorbell rang. Greetings. His overcoat. A glance into the room. How long was she going to fast? Did she remember that we're going to the Rosenthals? Hand washing. Finally, dinner.

Mother dipped the ladle into the tureen. A carrot, pushed aside, floated between a potato and a piece of celery. The light of the four flames and the seven bulbs in the chandelier (one had burned out and it was impossible to buy a replacement) flickered on the surface of the soup.

We took the number 4 streetcar to the bazaar on Dworkowa Street. We crossed to the other side of Puławska and approached the Wedel townhouse. Michał knocked on the gate. A soldier's face with a leather strap under the chin appeared in a small barred window. Standing on tiptoe, Michał informed him whom we were going to visit. The soldier disappeared. We walked up and down the sidewalk.

"Eternal waiting!" said Mother.

Michał shrugged. "They're being cautious." A key grated. A soldier in a cap with a blue rim opened the gate. We went inside. A civilian was sitting next to the telephone in the wooden booth. Michał doffed his Borsalino. The civilian didn't even move. We started walking up the marble stairs.

Old man Rosenthal clenched his fists on the armrests of his chair. Horse hair was sticking out of the cloth upholstery that rose high above his gray head. He bent toward us with a smile, pulling back his slipper-shod feet that he'd propped on a footrest.

"My rheumatism's killing me," he said.

We sat down on uncomfortable chairs. I swung my legs back and forth under the table. A porcelain socket with a lightbulb in it dangled from the ceiling on a wire. Next to his armchair, on a bookcase filled with books, were portraits of Marx, Engels, and Lenin in his cap. A photograph of Stalin hung on the wall.

We could smell coffee. Pani Rosenthal carried in a coffeepot and a small pitcher of cream that she had purchased that morning on Dworkowa Street.

"*Niemals kann man wissen was wird es heute sein,*" she sighed. "One can never tell what will happen today."

"*Solche Zeiten haben wir.* Such times we're living through."

Mother slid her cup over to me.

Licking my lips, I smiled at Stalin.

The Rosenthals had met in a cable railway car attached to the great wheel of the Riesenrad.

He had wound up in Vienna after the Russian defeat in the war with Poland in 1920. The Comintern had sent him there. That day, he had spent many hours trying to convince the Austrian comrades that nothing could delay the revolution in Europe. In the evening, he went to the jolly little town in order to unwind.

She was born in that city and had come to the Prater that evening by fiacre because she was bored to death in her parents' confectionary shop on Kärnterstrasse.

He invited her to the hotel café. The waiter placed a coffeepot, two cups, and a small pitcher of cream before them on the marble table top. He laid out silver teaspoons on embossed napkins.

Several days later a telegram arrived from Moscow: SUSPEND NEGOTIATIONS STOP RETURN IMMEDIATELY STOP. They went together to the Polish embassy to get her a transit visa. But the consul didn't want to listen to any arguments. Only when she began to cry did he take pity on her and stamp her passport.

They left for Moscow in a sleeping car.

Several months later the postman brought an envelope with stamps depicting hammers and sickles to the confectionary shop on Kärnterstrasse.

I went over to the bookcase and started to examine the titles embossed in Cyrillic letters on their spines.

Nikolai Gavrilovich Chernyshevsky, *Chto delat'?—What Is to Be Done?*

Maksim Gorky, *Mat'—The Mother.*

Nikolai Ostrovsky, *Kak zakalialas' stal'—How the Steel Was Tempered.*

Iosif Vissarionovich Stalin, *Natsional'nye voprosy i Izbrannye sochineniia—Nationality Questions and Selected Works.*

Vladimir Ilich Ulianov-Lenin, *Chto delat'?—What Is to Be Done?* (again!), *Gosudarstvo i revoliutsiia—State and Revolution,* and *Imperializm poslednim etapom kapitalizma—Imperialism as the Final Stage of Capitalism.*

After a bottle of ink and a glass holding pens and colored pencils, gold Gothic letters began.

Karl Heinrich Marx, *Das Kapital—Capital, Kritik der politischen Ökonomie—A Critique of Political Economy*, and *Die Klassenkämpfe in Frankreich—Class Struggles in France*.

Friedrich Engels, *Anti-Dühring*.

The Communist Manifesto in a red binding. Loose papers and notebooks tied up with ribbons were stuffed among the German volumes. I also noticed a few Polish books: *Traps, Fire in the Marshes, From a Hospitable Land to Poland,* and *Feather in the Whirlwind.*

Rosenthal addressed me. "Do you know languages?"

"I'm studying Russian and French."

"French! What for?"

He handed his wife his empty cup and pointed at the books.

"Everything about revolution is in Russian and German."

"German!" Mother's eyes flashed.

Rosenthal shook his finger at her.

"Hitlers come and go, but the German people remain."

"Who said that?" Mother bristled.

"Stalin."

"I'm not a communist," she smiled.

"I'm going to a new school," I said.

"What kind of a school?" Rosenthal again turned to address me.

"The WSFCS in Żoliborz," Mother answered for me.

"Many comrades are sending their children there," Rosenthal acknowledged with a nod of his head.

"Two streetcars. Maybe Michał will drive him there."

"What do you want to study?" Rosenthal screwed up his eyes.

"History."

"Chemistry's better," Michał interjected.

"You'll be teaching someone else's children!" Mother warned me.

"Not necessarily," Rosenthal smiled. "I'm also in history."

He asked me what I was interested in.

"Knights."

He nodded. "The Middle Ages."

"And what was before that?"

"Antiquity," Mother replied.

"In the beginning," old man Rosenthal lifted one finger, "there was primitive communism. Then the world divided into the rich and the poor. Profit. Alienation. Hatred. History is the history of class struggle. Spartacus, peasant rebellions, and the French Revolution, 1789. Capitalism. The proletariat. Marx and Engels write *The Communist Manifesto.* The Spring of Nations, 1848, the Paris Commune, 1871, and Bloody Sunday, 1905. Imperialism. Bolsheviks. Lenin's theory of revolution in one country. Finally, October. He"—he aimed his finger at me—"will see communism! The world revolution is approaching. Yesterday, in Wilcza Góra, the bell was rung at the funeral of imperialism. Four years and four months after the dissolution of the Comintern the Cominform arose. They tried to seduce us with the Marshall Plan. They threatened us with a hundred atom bombs. They created Bizonia. In vain!"

He pulled out a copy of *The People's Voice* from a volume of *Das Kapital.*

"Andrei Zhdanov said that 'danger for the working class derives from an underestimation of their own power and overestimation of the power of the imperialist class.'"

"But that's war!" Mother was frightened.

"Some comrades believe that it is inescapable."

—

We waited by ourselves at the streetcar stop.

"A lunatic!" Mother said.

"A theoretician. He prepares entries for the card index in the History Department."

"I don't want a war!" she screamed.

"There won't be a war!" Michał said impatiently. "The old man's out of his mind with joy because of the founding of the Cominform. Yesterday he wore me out with his reminiscences of 1920."

Since the streetcar didn't come, Michał started telling us about how Rosenthal had driven in a Ford behind five Russian armies approaching Warsaw. Packages containing copies of the "Manifesto of the Interim Revolutionary Committee of Poland," which Julian Marchlewski had given him in the Branicki Palace in Białystok, bounced around on the ruts. Dampness ruined the dye. The signatures of Dzierżyński, Kon, and Próchniak became illegible. A troop of fifty Cossacks trudged along behind the car.

In the evening they stopped in front of a burned-out church near which there was an apple orchard. Exhaust fumes assaulted his nose. The Ford's yellow headlights illuminated the toppled church tower. A bell dangled from a chain, touching the ground.

They made a fire. They ate bread and apples. They drank vodka. The horses chomped on oats in bags tied to their heads. Guards stood one-hour shifts.

The Cossacks' commander found a young priest in the orchard.

"What are you doing here?" Rosenthal asked the priest, yawning.

"I'm waiting until our forces return. The parish priest is in the army. I'm looking after the church."

"Is he a spy?" the commander asked.

"A fool!" Rosenthal laughed.

"All priests are enemies of Soviet power!"

They added kindling to the fire. The flames soared.

"A Jew?" Rosenthal asked quietly.

"A convert," said the priest. "Are you a Jew, too, sir?"

"No!"

"A Pole?"

"A communist," Rosenthal said.

In the morning, the Cossacks shot the priest.

"He was a magnet for trouble. I have to answer for you with my head," the Cossack commander explained.

The number 4 approached. We got into the first car. Before the conductor could punch our tickets, it started moving. Grabbing the leather straps, we made it to the benches. The car was empty. No one was waiting at the stops. The wheels made a horrible noise. The Church of St. Michał loomed up.

"War." Mother shook her head. "One shouldn't say such things. Tomorrow is Yom Kippur. What if God should hear and inscribe it in his book."

"He babbles about whatever his saliva brings onto his tongue."

"I don't believe in any priest who was a Jew, either."

"He makes things up." Michał waved his hand dismissively.

"Let him interfere with someone else's child!"

From the speeding streetcar I could see our yellow window with the chandelier.

Pan Krauz, Michał's boss in the Economics Division of the Communist Party of the Polish People's Republic, came for dinner. Mother served red borscht, beef with beets, and cranberry kissel. It was a farewell dinner, because Michał was leaving for the foreign trade department. The conversation turned to Russia, where both men had spent the war. Michał reminisced about Orsk. The snow-covered huts. The refinery. The columns of *zakliuchennye*—meaning "incarcerated" in Russian. (I had thought the word for them was *plennye*—captives.) Pan Krauz drank his tea and pushed aside his glass.

"An embargo," he said suddenly.

"What's on your mind?" Michał asked.

"The Americans want to proclaim a ban on the sale of strategic goods to the Soviet Union. That will create an opportunity for us to be of service to our comrades. We'll do the purchasing for them. Officially and under the counter."

"More?" Mother leaned over him with the teapot.

"I learned about teas in Kazakhstan," he replied in Russian.

At night, the telephone rang. The shuffling sound of slippers and the clop-clop of scuffs.

"Hello!" Michał picked up the receiver.

"They're connecting me with Prague," he told Mother.

I heard her voice: "We don't know anyone in Praga."

"In Prague, Czechoslovakia!"

"What?"

"Hello!" Michał shouted into the phone.

"It's Milo!"

"Milo!" Mother screamed.

"What's he doing in Prague?"

"He stopped off there en route to Italy."

"To Italy? Why is he going there?"

"To care for the Jews whom they're smuggling into Palestine."

"Smuggling . . ."

"He's going to visit us!" Michał said happily.

"When?"

"Soon. With Dita."

Mother ran down the platform and disappeared in clouds of steam. They emerged together. Milo was wearing a suit jacket (fastened with the middle button), a snow-white shirt, and silken tie. Dita looked beautiful. Her black hair fell onto her back in waves. We climbed the low hill. Mother showed them the ruins of the ghetto. Unfortunately, the day was gray and the expanse of the ghetto to the left was concealed by fog on two sides. Only the nearest chimneys were visible. As we approached the Citroën (from the Ministry), Dita glanced at the driver.

"I wouldn't go alone. He might knife me!" she whispered in Russian.

It turned out that she knew Russian from her home. Her parents had emigrated before the revolution. Now they grew oranges.

She got into the backseat. Milo and Mother followed her. Michał sat me on his lap. The car set off. It started raining. The driver turned on the windshield wipers. It was pouring in Union Square. The barracks vanished in the streams of water. There was a traffic jam at Dworkowa Street.

The dining room table was set for five. Porcelain plates and silver cutlery glistened under the chandelier. Not as brightly as before, because yet another bulb had burned out.

We sat down at the table. We had carp in aspic for an appetizer. (Until yesterday, it had been swimming in the bathtub. It was killed with a blow from a rolling pin. Now it was lying on a platter, decorated with parsley and carrot slices.) We ate carefully, setting aside the bones on the rim of the plate. Michał got the head, which was his favorite part. After the carp Mother brought in mushroom soup. Almost black. Bright yellow dumplings floated among the boleti. She added fresh-from-the-oven potato dumplings to the soup. A pat of butter was melting on top of each dumpling. Then we ate chicken risotto. (Nusia had sent the rice from Munich. The package also contained a note with the news that they had received an American visa.) For dessert there was a torte made from nuts ground in a meat grinder.

"You're living OK!" Milo said. "But can you trust the Poles?"

"Why not?!" Michał bristled.

"Ask Andzia. She was here."

"We're building a new world."

"Ruins, rags, and lines."

Milo looked out through the balcony door.

"It's our country," Michał said.

Mother slid the sugar bowl over to her brother. Stirring his coffee, he said that soon a Jewish state will arise. It will be rich and strong. For now, however, they have to fight. The English don't want to let Jews in; they don't want to offend the Arabs. He himself is in Palestine illegally.

"So what passport did you leave with?" asked Michał.

"A false one."

Toward the end of October I started getting anxious. Why aren't they telephoning from the new school? Sitting in my armchair, I leafed through *The People's Voice.* The Polish Workers' Party and the Polish Socialist Party's youth organizations had signed an agreement to cooperate with each other. I looked at the date. The following Saturday would be my birthday. The telephone rang. I slipped out into the corridor. Mother had just replaced the receiver.

"Kopcio," she muttered. "He's in the hospital."

"What happened?"

"A stomach ulcer."

She said that Kopcio was waiting in the garden of Dr. Płocker's clinic. On the corner of Malczewski and Tyniecka Streets. She asked me to go because she didn't have the strength for this.

"They published his book," she added as I opened the door.

"What's it called?"

"*Earth Without God.*"

"Does he write about us?"

"Not in the best way."

A thin man in a bathrobe and slippers was standing behind the iron fence.

"You've grown." He nodded at me. "Who sent you?"

"Mother."

"She couldn't come herself?"

"She's busy."

"You're in a hurry, too?"

"No."

He handed me fifty złotys through the fence.

"Get me change," he said.

I went to the butcher shop. The smell of blood. I handed Pan Stankiewicz the banknote. He wiped his hands, took out his wallet, and gave me a stack of colored bills.

"Your mother says you're changing schools."

"Yes."

"Why?"

"They bully me."

"They won't over there?"

"No."

"Because?"

"They're better."

Kopcio was waiting near the fence.

"I thought you weren't coming back."

He counted the money.

⁓

The day before my birthday, at breakfast, Michał handed me a present. I ripped open the gray paper. Inside was a book by Stalin: *Problems of Leninism.* I took it to the living room and placed it next to the bicycle pump. When I returned, Michał snorted with laughter.

"Ariel!" he shouted.

"Why Ariel?" Mother asked, surprised.

"A mindless spirit! A grasshopper. He was fooled."

"You'll get presents tomorrow," Mother added.

I went out onto the balcony. Leaning on the cold balustrade I looked straight ahead. There were leaves on the tracks. The passing streetcars blew them to the sides. Electric wires shone among the branches. Behind St. Michał's Church birds were congregating on the yellowed meadows. I slipped my hands into my sweater sleeves and raised my head. Blinded by the sun, I closed my eyes.

On the balcony Pan Churlusz appeared. He was wearing a black suit and a vest with a gold chain. A stethoscope hung around his neck. When I said I was healthy the stethoscope changed into a tape measure. He tapped with a pointy pencil on his notebook in which striped suits were sketched. (I had recently seen just such suits in pre-war fashion magazines in a stall on Marszałkowska Street.)

"Children remember," he muttered.

"Eh, so what!" He waved his hand. "*I* remember."

"And what about the coat cut from the greatcoat?" He smiled bitterly.

"I outgrew it."

The pencil changed into a sword. The master attached six metal buttons. On the left collar he had three stars, on the right, two, because he was standing sideways. Even though he was wearing his Austrian uniform he reminded me of the hero of *A Farewell to Arms,* which was playing at the Polonia. On his breast he had a medal that changed into a king of hearts and, whirling in the air, fell into the street.

And then the master slowly started to rise up. First his head, with its blond hair, passed by, then his vest with its satin back and long arms and legs flung out to the side. He looked like a silhouette cut out of paper. The wind took him. He flew high up and disappeared over St. Michał's Church.

I heard the slamming of car doors and the roaring of the departing Citroën, and opened my eyes. Mother came out of the dining room and slipped fragrant jelly doughnuts under my nose.

"They're still warm," she said. "How many?"

"Two."

"Tea?" she asked.

"But make it strong."

The Atheists' School

To the memory of my father

Who will bear witness to these times?
Who will record them? Certainly none of us:
we've lived here too long, we've soaked the epoch
up too well, we're too loyal to it to tell the truth

. . . .

Hatred, scorn, lies—for so many years,
so as to survive and stay pure. But it can't be done:
survive and stay pure. At best—survive.

BRONISŁAW MAJ, FROM *WSPÓLNE POWIETRZE* (COMMUNAL AIR)

myopia

A Funeral Procession

I didn't know where I was.

In the roadway, rinsed clean by a recent rain, pieces of smashed tombstones sparkled. Fragments of basalt and marble with Hebrew lettering formed a strangely shaped mosaic. I didn't understand the meaning of the preserved words; I knew, however, that broken apart they no longer formed sentences. At best, they were fragments. Minus predicates. Minus tense.

A funeral procession was wending its way ahead of me. At that moment it was approaching the brick wall that spanned the street. The people, heads bowed, were disappearing into a small passageway. It was more like a hole than a gateway, and above it hung a white-and-red plaque: JEWISH CEMETERY.

I followed them inside. Only now did I realize there was a plank coffin at the head of the procession. Four men were carrying it. Their long shadows slid along the earth and the mounds. Was this a funeral? My father's? But where and when? If in Borysław, then Grandma Minia, who died right before the war, ought to be lying in one of the graves we passed. But only Grandma Minia. The other members of my family were taken to Bełżec and Płaszów, where flames consumed their bodies.

But what about him?

I looked at the coffin. If there's a coffin there must be a body. How had he died? I couldn't remember.

I started again, from the beginning, in order, as if reciting a litany.

The first one they took away was Grandma Antonina. That same day they also deported the elder Unters along with their orphanage, and also Marek Bernstein, my friend, with whom during the Russian time I used to pee over the fence in our courtyard.

After the *Aktion* I'd found myself under the bed at crippled Janka's. "You have to memorize 'Our Father' and 'Hail Mary,' " she'd repeated over and over again. I would stick my head out a little. She would kneel down with difficulty and, touching her hand to her forehead, heart, and shoulders, tell me to do as she did and to repeat after her. "If they catch you, pray out loud," she said.

Mother had disappeared into the ghetto in order to be with Father and, fearing another *Aktion,* came back. Lying on the floor just like me, she'd complained to Janka that Father had no one to perform a pneumo-thorax on him.

The coffin was swaying gently. At times, the rays of the sun were reflected from it as from a mirror.

We changed hideouts.

Grandfather came regularly and paid for us. From him we learned that blind Maciek (the Unters' younger son) was no longer alive, nor was their grandson Romuś, who'd been given to a peasant family for safekeeping. During the next *Aktion,* his mother went out to the Germans of her own accord. So, of the entire Unter family, only the oldest son, Julek, remained. He had joined the Red Army together with Milo, my mother's brother. When they took leave of us they were wearing uniforms with insignia that spelled out "doctor" in Russian.

The coffin smelled of pine. A strange smell in a place where only grass grew and moss covered the stumps of felled trees.

One day, Grandfather brought Father, who was coughing softly, but without let-up. Sometimes he would raise his hand, as if he wanted to ask our forgiveness. Usually, however, he stared at the rafter above his head. "It's the end," he whispered to Mother.

Onward! What happened next?

Engineer Tabaczyński crawled in through the opening concealed by an armchair and said that they'd taken away Grandfather. Mother started crying. And Father? He didn't even stir. Our guest, on his knees the whole time, squeezed the hand that was lying helpless on the quilt.

I looked at the coffin again.

On the left side it was supported by Michał and old Pan Rosenthal with a newspaper protruding from his pocket. *Pravda? The People's Voice?* Or perhaps a copy of the "Manifesto of the Temporary Committee of Revolutionary Poland"? One of the manifestos that Julian Marchlewski had given him in the Branicki Palace in Białystok when Tukhachevsky's army was moving on Warsaw.

But what was my stepfather, a vice director in the Department of Foreign Trade, doing here? And especially Pan Rosenthal? After all, they weren't there at that time! . . .

On the right side, the coffin was carried by Milo (had he come from Tel Aviv?) and by Michał's one-legged brother, whom the Americans had found under the showers in Mauthausen. Mother told me that he had hidden under a freight car during a bombardment. The train had moved suddenly and a wheel crushed one of his toes. He went to the gas, but the

Germans hadn't had time to throw in the Zyklon. Unfortunately, gangrene set in.

He rarely visited us, busy as he was with the gas station that he managed in Kraków. When he was in Warsaw he prayed in our dining room every morning. He would take out a satin yarmulke from a tiny case and place it on his head. Then he'd extract two black cubes with leather straps. He tied the first to his arm at the level of his heart and fastened the second to his forehead. Finally, he pulled out a silk shawl, threw it over his head and shoulders, turned to face the Church of St. Michał (according to him, that was the direction of the Temple in Jerusalem) and, his prosthesis creaking, prayed for a long time.

"What's that?" I asked, when he stopped rocking.

"Tefillin." He handed me the cubes.

"Why are there two of them?"

"You shall wear My commandments on your forehead and near your heart," he recited portentously.

I weighed them in my hand. "They're empty . . ."

"No, no," he shook his head. "There are miniature parchment scrolls inside them with words from the Torah."

Mother was walking behind the coffin in a black fringed veil. On her feet were the same shoes with the twisted heels in which she'd fled with me across the river to the Aryan side. How strange. After all, the right shoe had remained there in the mud . . . .

Next to Mother, her friend Karola trudged along. She was constantly straightening her glasses and checking the button at the back of her skirt. There was no mirror in her room at the Polonia Hotel, which the Ministry rented for her. She'd probably come by streetcar. At least, she hadn't had far to travel.

Yes, but is this cemetery in Warsaw?

At the end of the procession came my old classmates: Adam Lawrencic from Trzebinia and fair-haired Michalski. What was his first name? I used to draw pictures of winged hussars with him before he left Warsaw after his grandfather was arrested.

Something cold and wet touched my foot. I looked down. A German shepherd! He was wagging his fluffy tail. The same dog who attached himself to me in Ligota and then slept on our balcony next to my bicycle.

The same one? In that case, everyone, even a dog, knew about Father's funeral. But no one had informed me! Why? How had Father died? Since he hadn't been burned . . .

I raised my head.

There was no procession.

"Where are you?" I called out, but no one responded.

I started running.

"Don't leave me!" I shouted with all my strength, and stumbled over a stone with some Hebrew letter on it. Falling flat on my face, I suddenly woke up.

So it was only a dream! What luck! I felt relieved. Again, I remembered nothing. I was sitting in an armchair with my legs draped across the arm. It was gloomy in the drawing room. Andersen's *Fairy Tales* lay flat on the carpet, its spine facing up. Before sleep overwhelmed me I had been reading about a boy who wanted to know if snowflakes, like white bees, have their own queen. A nice thought.

I went into the dining room.

The Ophthalmologist

A powdery snow was falling.

Mother and Karola were debating whether it would remain on the ground until New Year's. I turned on the light. The bulbs in the chandelier glowed red for a moment and then went out. The glow from a streetlight was reflected in the bronze ball with its curved arms. A streetcar was shedding white dust from the electric wires.

"It's winter," Karola insisted.

"They were longer in Borysław." Mother waved her hand dismissively. "Papa would bring the dog in from the shed. Do you remember Fox?" she asked me.

"No," I replied.

"He remembers what he wants to," she muttered.

I turned the switch again. The lights came on. The table was set with English porcelain with blue pictures. On each plate a team of four horses was pulling a stagecoach. The tiny doors were shut. There were curtains in the windows. On the roof, between the coachman and postillion, several people wearing top hats were seated. Second-class passengers. (The dinnerware wasn't a complete set and only we ate on it.)

Plekhanov's book, *On the Role of the Individual in History,* lay next to a silver fork. Pan Rosenthal had leaned forward in his armchair when he lent it to me.

"Pay attention!" He raised a finger. "Plekhanov changed his views. From 1875 to 1883 he was a Narodnik. From 1883 to 1903, a Marxist. And then he became a traitor! A Liberal . . . a Menshevik . . . An enemy of the dictatorship of the proletariat!" He aimed his finger at me. "Treason grows out of errors." He lowered his hand. "Plekhanov didn't notice the qualitative changes that the creators of Marxism achieved in philosophy, nor the difference between the materialist and the idealist conception of experience." He tapped the book against his chair. "And that left an open window for idealism!"

Pan Rosenthal could not understand why Plekhanov detached dialectics from the theory of cognition; after all, dialectics *are* the Marxist theory of cognition!

"How is it possible! . . ." he shouted, "how is it possible to treat the great Russian thinkers of the nineteenth century like ordinary imitators of West European writers!"

"Then why read this?" I asked quietly.

"*The Individual* is permitted." And he handed me the book.

It was late, and Michał still hadn't come home. Mother started worrying that the roast would dry out. The beautiful veal with no tendons or gristle that Pani Krzakowa had brought her that morning would be wasted. Waiting for our meal, I became hungrier and hungrier. It was many hours since we'd had our dinner.

Finally, the key grated in the lock and Mother ran out into the hall. Usually, I heard the rumbling of a motor and slamming of doors first. Not this time. Probably the wind had drowned them out.

Nowadays, Michał was driven by Dziadzio, the most senior chauffeur in the Ministry. In a black Chevrolet (a "Demokratka") with seats covered in dark-green leather.

When he left work, Michał had seen them putting up a Christmas tree in front of the Ministry building. A *novogodnaya yolka*—a New Year's tree. He recognized it from Russia.

"All the glass balls were red."

He carved a slice of roast.

Mother and Karola hooted with laughter.

"The higher up they are, the fewer there are."

He put some cucumber salad on his plate.

"And a single one on the top."

"Just like in the Party," Karola jeered.

Mother pressed her napkin to her lips.

"Bird brains!" Michał said, offended.

A streetcar was passing. Sparks fluttered down.

"You're buying from peasant women," he said sourly.

"Don't eat," Karola advised him.

The streetcar turned sharply on the loop of electric wires and, with a screech, rolled on toward Śródmieście, the city center.

"Don't read while you're eating!" Michał turned to me.

"You'll stain Plekhanov!" Mother added.

I looked at the chandelier. I'd always liked lamps. But for some time now the little wires in the bulbs had begun to blur in front of my eyes. I'd even mentioned this to Mother.

"Why is he squinting?" Michał asked.

"He can't see the wires," she answered.

"Take him to an ophthalmologist."

On New Year's Eve Dziadzio arrived with a carnation in his lapel. Mother and Michał put on their hats and coats. Wishing me a happy New Year, they left to attend the ball. I went to bed with Plekhanov.

Revolution is the highest right. Why? I'd forgotten. Dialectical thought was difficult.

A year ago, I was drawing hussars with my friend who lived with his grandfather. (A photograph of him wearing a judge's robes and pince-nez hung on the wall.) Kneeling on chairs that we pushed next to each other, we sketched. My friend drew people and I drew horses. Then we colored everything with watercolors, coating the helmets and armor with egg yolk to make them shine.

One day, I brought over a bottle with real gold paint, but no one opened the door. I came back a few days later and knocked until I lost hope. On my way home I saw a priest, our teacher at Queen Jadwiga School. I caught up with him at the nearest intersection.

"Please, Father, what happened to Michalski?"

"He's gone to live with his aunt."

"Why?"

"They arrested his grandfather."

"For what?"

"He was a judge."

I was surprised that the cause of his arrest was just his profession, but I didn't question the priest's words, since I trusted him, nor did I doubt the grandfather's guilt. I immediately recalled the director of our school in Trzebinia who was locked up before all the national holidays.

I kept silent when I got home. Michał didn't like such conversations. I often heard him say through clenched teeth, "We don't know the reasons."

"Reasons can always be found," Karola jeered.

"He believes them." And Mother would lift her eyes to heaven.

Accustomed to the loss of people dear to me, I consoled myself that Michalski was alive (at his aunt's) and I returned to my books. I was reading simultaneously *The Individual, Twenty-Four Scenes from the History of Poland,* and a story by Anatole France set in the future.

The story interested me greatly. Standing on the threshold of a new social system, I craned my neck in order to see what would be. How astonished I was when I figured out that the socialism described by France was boring!

I discussed this with Pan Rosenthal. He waved his hand dismissively. He hadn't read Anatole France, but the French socialists irritated him.

"Why?" he fumed, "Why did Léon Blum not lift a finger when they bombed the Republicans?"

"Blum?" I pondered. "Was the Prime Minister of France a Jew?"

"There's a civil war going on," Pan Rosenthal warned me. "Don't be a foolish aesthete."

True. During the referendum and the elections Mother waited up at night for the lights of the Willys or, muttering curses, ran to the jangling telephone.

It was even worse in Russia. I myself watched the death of Kirov in a film with Polish subtitles. The Leningrad Committee. A muzzle. Smoke! The spinning of a revolver's magazine. The thundering of a train in the night. The elegant interior of the carriage. Beria's pince-nez. Stalin's voice.

Plekhanov dropped to the floor.

I remembered when Mother and Michał drove from Trzebinia to Kraków in the Fiat last winter to go shopping. Wading through snow, I had wandered among the petroleum tanks. They were enormous, but they, too, were threatened by danger. In the spring, one of them was struck by lightning. It burned for several days.

Suddenly, I saw the Fiat coming back. Mother and Michał in the rear window. Perfectly clear, as if without any glass. What happened? I set off running behind the car. I found Mother in the dining room. She was leaning over the table on which her fur coat was lying. It was full of holes.

"A skid," she said. "We landed in a ditch. The windows shattered. Electrolytes. . . ." She touched her cheeks. "It's a good thing that Michał is a chemist. He rubbed my face with snow. Otherwise . . . ," she slipped her finger into one of the holes, "I would look like this fur coat."

I wrapped myself in my quilt. The patterns on the wall didn't look clear to me. Michał is right. I don't read properly. I block the light. I'm ruining my eyesight.

I fell asleep.

I dreamed that I was wearing a Wehrmacht uniform. I had survived, dressed as a German.

From every direction, the Russians were approaching.

Mother was not delighted with the ball. The next morning, frying eggs, she said that there were militia checking documents outside the Ministry. True, they were admitted immediately, but before the war something like that would have been unthinkable.

The sounds of a tango reached them from the conference room. Above the entrance, hanging on a string, fluttered paper letters: HAPPY NEW YEAR. Inside, along three of the walls, were rows of little tables carried in from the cafeteria. An immense conference table stood against the fourth wall. On a white sheet, from beneath which a green cloth protruded, there were towering piles of hors d'oeuvres, smoked meats, pâtés, and yellow cheeses. Layer cakes were placed at both sides, with bottles of vodka and enameled jugs of coffee glittering among them. A plaster eagle and a portrait of President Bierut hung above all of this.

"The Minister. The Soviet higher-ups, the *nachalstvo*." Mother handed me the frying pan. "Sweaty 'specialists.' Coarse wool. Wide lapels. They addressed me as 'Pani,'" she smiled mockingly. "With Michał they spoke in Russian. Not a word in Polish, not even a peep."

They sat down to supper. The more important people were seated farther from the food. Mother and Michał were in the center of the room, next to the Podolskis. He was a doctor by profession. A department head now. Tall, muscular, cultured. A Jew. She wasn't. A nice woman. They have a daughter and a son. They talked about their children.

People danced among the tables. Mother liked the English waltz best. At midnight, waitresses brought in glasses of champagne. The Minister rose from his seat. The toasts began. "To Stalin!" "To Bierut!" Someone started singing the Internationale. Soon everyone was singing.

> Arise, ye prisoners of starvation,
> Arise, ye wretched of the earth.
> For justice thunders condemnation,
> A better world's in birth.

Some drunken bureaucrat whispered into Mother's ear that it would soon be the centenary of *The Communist Manifesto*.

At dawn they played a mazurka.

"People were stamping their feet till I thought my head would burst." She touched her forehead with her fingertips. "Aha!" and she reached for her pocketbook and extracted several cubes of sugar. "Michał put them into his pocket for you."

In February, Michał left for Moscow. Mother ordered a white fur coat.

Negotiations were under way in the Kremlin. Day after long day. There was always something. And receptions at night. Gigantic tables. Batteries of bottles. Vodkas, cognacs, wines. He drank water.

After his return he rested up in the bedroom. He complained that they wanted everything for free. Besides which, why hadn't the letter that he sent from the Metropol arrived? The next day he had pains in his heart. A cardiologist in the government clinic confirmed that it was nerves.

"They followed him without letup," Mother complained to Karola. "They opened his suitcase. They stole his gold Parker pen in the elevator. They created an artificial crush." She gestured with her hands.

"You're surprised?" Karola shrugged.

"He didn't bring the fur coat."

In April, after the death in Kraków of the model miner, Wincenty Pstrowski, Michał visited Budapest. From the high bank of the Danube the parliament building looked spectacular.

From that trip he also brought back greenish-blue Roquefort. Mother, who always unpacked his suitcases, smelled its stench and threw the cheese into the garbage.

In May, he telephoned from Sofia. He'd gotten a fur coat!

We were on our way to the ophthalmologist. Downstairs, Mother noticed a gray envelope in the mailbox and hurriedly pulled it out.

"From the Metropol!" she confirmed. "Two months!"

The letter was inside a substitute wrapping with a stamp that said the original had been destroyed somehow.

"Somehow!"

She opened the envelope inside the Demokratka.

"What does he write?" I asked, watching the speedometer.

"He saw Molotov."

We crossed the bridge over the Vistula and drove to a neighborhood near the Vilnius Station. We stopped on Floriańska Street. Dziadzio cut the engine and got out to open the door for Mother.

The entry was cool and gloomy. We climbed low steps to the ground floor. A rusted plaque hung on the door.

"An optimologist?" I marveled.

"An ophthalmologist," Mother corrected me.

I read it again:

DR. RUTENSTREICH
OPHTHALMOLOGIST

"A Jew?"

"An odd name." She shook her head.

A thin little man in a black suit and a vest with a gold watch chain opened the door. A ruler and a flashlight protruded from his pocket. I glanced at Mother.

"We're here," she said to the ophthalmologist. "We're not too early?"

"Of course not," he smiled.

There was a strange smell in his office. Medicine or mildew? Mother wrinkled her nose. I felt nauseated, the way I used to feel before I learned to drink strong tea.

A chart with a cross section of an eye hung over the desk, along with a board with letters and some kind of a picture. The ophthalmologist drew up a chair for Mother and seated me on a revolving stool across from the chart of the eye. Colored vessels and nerves were clumped in it. However, I couldn't see them clearly.

"The eye is a one-inch ball," he said. "Filled with fluid. The lens is in front. The optic nerves emerge from the back. Their endings change light into electrochemical impulses. However, where the nerves merge into a thick cable leading to the brain, there are no endings. Nothing collects light there. So we don't see everything that we look at."

He placed heavy metal glasses on me in which the lenses could be changed. He covered the left eye with a black disk and turning the stool to face the board, pointed with his ruler to the highest letter.

"E," I read.

He lowered the ruler a little.

"F and P." These letters were smaller.

"Lower." The ruler shook again.

"T, O, and I think . . . Z."

"Lower."

"L or I . . . I don't know . . . I don't know . . . D or O."

"Lower."

I couldn't go any lower.

Then he opened a case with round lenses and slipped one of them into the right eyepiece.

"Now I can see!" I rejoiced.

After examining the left eye in the same way, he turned to Mother.

"Myopia," he said. "He sees, but only what's in front of his nose."

"How many diopters?" she asked.

"Minus four." He turned me toward the picture.

A majestic old man in a red habit was bent over a pulpit on which lay a manuscript. In his right hand he held a small pen. With his left, he was propping up his bald head with its gray beard. Vessels with black and red ink were fastened to the pulpit. Eyeglasses, draped over a nail, and scissors with open blades cast a shadow on the date: MCCCCLXXX. The pulpit rested on a table that was covered with a patterned carpet. Red and gold ornaments were artfully intertwined. From beneath the carpet a cope with gold fringes protruded. Both a thick candle and an oil lamp with a golden shade had sooty, black wicks. The light that fell on the man who was writing came through an unseen window.

"Who is that?" asked Mother.

"St. Hieronymus. The patron of opticians."

"Aha . . . ," she mumbled.

"He translated the New Testament from Greek."

"Aha . . ."

"And the Old Testament. From Hebrew."

"Oh!"

"Who painted it?" I asked.

"Ghirlandaio. A thousand years after Hieronymus's death."

"The patron of opticians . . . ," I repeated softly. "Why?"

"Eyeglasses," he explained. "The first painting in which there are eyeglasses."

He took the flashlight out of his pocket and shone it in my eye.

"Don't close your eye," he requested. "I'm examining the back."

"Well?" Mother asked, interested.

"It's fine."

He took out of his desk a large card that was covered with swarming yellow, red, and bright green dots. The majority were red.

"What do you see?" he asked.

"Dots."

"Nothing else?"

"Nothing."

"He's color blind," he stated. "He mixes up the reds."

Suddenly I realized that some of the dots were pink and formed the numbers one and seven.

"Seventeen!" I said, amazed.

"That's right."

He took out the ruler again and measured the distance between my pupils.

"Doctor." Mother couldn't restrain herself. "What's that smell?"

"Camphor. I forgot to close the box."

"It evaporated . . ." Mother opened her pocketbook.

"It's gone."

Examination

I missed Michalski. I missed not only our drawing together, but also his protection. When he was there, no one dared to touch me. After his disappearance I was picked on more than ever.

"Russki lackey!"

"Communist!"

"Go to Palestine!"

Attending religion class didn't help. "The Jews murdered Jesus." As soon as the priest turned to the blackboard, I would feel paper balls striking the back of my head. Finally, I complained to Mother, and Michał found a nonsectarian school in the Żoliborz district. It was called WSFCS.

"What's that?" I asked,

"Workers' Society Friends of Children School."

Unfortunately, they had no openings. I waited all winter and spring. I went to school irregularly. From morning till night, I read in my armchair.

Only after Michał's return from Bulgaria did a letter arrive from the principal in Żoliborz. They could admit me for the new school year. Was I interested?

"You go with him," Mother said to Michał.

The school was located on Feliński Street. Dziadzio stopped the Demokratka on the opposite side of the street. Michał gave me a gentle nudge and we crossed the street.

Alongside wire netting that surrounded the schoolyard children crowded around a woman wearing an apron. Bent over a pink block that was lying on a card table, she was chopping off shapeless slices with a cleaver.

"Candy!" she was shouting. "Sweet candy!"

The children slipped money into her pocket, took the chipped-off slices from the table, and put them into their mouths.

The rising sun illuminated a gray building. Panes of glass sparkled within white window frames. The gate was wide open. We stepped into the courtyard. There was a vegetable garden on the right. Little cards with Latin letters hung on the plants.

We turned left.

The cloak room was located just past the door. The girls were putting on slippers and the boys were tying felt coverings over their shoes. We went upstairs. Michał located the principal's office, straightened his tie, and knocked discreetly. An elegant woman with long, thin legs opened the door.

She introduced herself. "Lidia Pawelcowa."

Michał kissed her hand.

She gestured toward some chairs. We sat down. She herself leaned against the desk where, next to two ink bottles, one containing black and one red ink, lay a cardboard portfolio. She picked it up, unfolded it, and glanced at the papers.

"Two grades skipped . . . ," she announced without enthusiasm.

"In '44 and '45," Michał explained.

"No gaps?" she asked.

Michał looked at me.

In Borysław they had transferred me from the third to the fourth grade. I still remembered the brick school building. Above the roof rose tall chimneys between which a red flag waved. Portraits of Marx, Engels, Lenin, and Stalin hung above the entrance doors. In class, the teacher read aloud the same lines several times over so that we could memorize them. No one had notebooks or pencils. But in '45 . . . in Ligota . . . I had no memory of that. And afterward? . . . But she wasn't concerned about those kinds of gaps.

"I think not," I said.

"No." Michał waved his hand.

"If we accept him," the principal shook her head, "he won't be even sixteen before he graduates."

"What do you propose?" Michał was getting anxious.

"He should repeat the eighth grade."

"It's a waste of time. Poland needs educated people."

"The Minister's permission will be required for him to take the graduation exam."

"We'll cross that bridge."

The principal walked around the desk, set down the portfolio, and, taking a black fountain pen from a drawer, signed her name energetically.

The Grand Hotel

In July we left for the seashore. The names of stations that our express train was racing past flashed by outside the windows of the carriage: Legionowo, Ciechanów, Mława. We stopped only when we reached Działdowo. And again in Iława and Malbork.

The dining car had veneer paneling. Only the grab bars above the bench backs were made of metal. However, whenever the waiters opened the swinging doors abruptly, the steel box of the car appeared. I lifted the tablecloth. Steel also shone on the edges of our little table.

Pan Cukrowy, a tall, thin man puffing away on a Lucky Strike, was traveling with us. The ash on the end of his cigarette changed alternately from glowing red to gray. Blue smoke fell on Michał, who was seated next to him.

Mother glanced at both men.

"The vice-directors' bench," she smiled, and handed me a menu.

After cube steak with French fries, both she and Pan Cukrowy ordered coffee, Michał ordered tea, and I cake with whipped cream. Waiting for dessert, I opened "Poem about Lenin." Was it possible that Mayakovsky joined the Party at age seventeen? I glanced at the introduction. It was.

—

"Poem" was given to me by Pan Rosenthal when, returning *The Individual,* I asked him why Plekhanov felt such hatred for the opponents of socialism.

"There is no mercy for enemies," Pan Rosenthal said ominously.

"It's possible to be mistaken," I observed.

"You can't make an omelet without breaking eggs."

"Some people advise love for one's neighbor."

"Are you counting on a reward in heaven?" He laughed, and handed me a book covered in gray paper. "Love is revolution!" he shouted.

—

While drinking his tea, Michał told a story about a high school outing to the Baltic coast.

They'd reached Gdynia at night. They slept in the Maritime School. The next morning they toured the port in a motorboat. That's how they passed the first day. On the second, they went by boat to Hel. The Baltic was gray and smooth. They walked to the end of the peninsula along a sandy road. They ate fried flounder and returned to Gdańsk by train. Again they arrived at night. They could hear shouting and singing all around. People were marching down the street carrying torches. Red banners with black swastikas inside white circles hung from apartment houses. Hitler had become Chancellor.

"And were you in the Grand Hotel?" Mother asked.

"No."

"Now he will be." Pan Cukrowy took a deep drag on his cigarette.

We arrived in Sopot in the late evening. Karola, who had rented a room in the city, was waiting for us on the platform. Mother took her arm and we followed our porter to the taxi stand.

Outside the windows of the small Opel white buildings with the lowered blinds of shops slid past. Jammed inside the cab, which stank of gasoline, we rode downhill toward the sea. The yellow headlights of the BMW that carried Pan Cukrowy flickered in the mirror. At the end of the street Karola pointed out a clump of trees.

"The jetty," she said. "But it's dark now."

"What's a jetty?" I asked.

"A long pier."

The driver extended his left turn signal. A lot of lights appeared among the trees. Soon a large building loomed up. Red roofs shone in the glare of the headlights. I adjusted my glasses.

"Well?" Karola asked.

"Ho, ho," Mother voiced her amazement.

The driveway, with huge revolving doors at its highest point, rose and fell in an arc. We drove up alongside parked automobiles. Porters emerged from the side door with a gold cart. Michał pushed the thick pane of glass. A carousel of glass and bronze began to turn.

The interior of the Grand Hotel was immense. People were walking on the wide spiral stairs to which a red carpet was affixed with gold rods. A balustrade wound alongside the stairs, encircling the chandelier that hung from the ceiling. Shadows moved on the marble walls.

The letter *E* shone above the elevator. The doors, covered with gold metal plate, slid open silently. We rose up to the second floor as if in the gondola of a hot air balloon. The end of the trip. We exited directly across from the chandelier. Crystals swayed among the lightbulbs. The polished surfaces sparkled with the colors of the rainbow. Here, Pan Cukrowy took leave of us.

Walking behind the gold cart, we reached a cream-colored door with our room number on it.

I went out onto the balcony. It hung above a terrace that was surrounded with bushes. Beyond them a beach full of wicker baskets stretched out. Light flowed out of the ground floor and I could hear the clinking of dishes. On the right, a long row of lamps cut into the sea.

"The jetty," I thought.

When I reentered the room Karola was already gone. Mother led me to the bathroom. Hot water was steaming in the tub. Thick towels were draped over brass towel rods.

The next day, Michał was summoned to Warsaw. The Central Committee of the Polish Workers' Party had decided to debate the problems of foreign trade prior to the approaching Party Congress.

"They don't let you live," Mother complained. "It's true drudgery."

"It's socialism," Karola jeered.

On the beach I wore an orange cap so Mother could see me easily. If I went too far she would walk down to the shore and call to me, shouting over the noise of the water.

I was searching for jellyfish, which rose and fell with the waves. It seemed to me that something was pulsating inside them, especially when I looked at them in direct sunlight. They slipped through my fingers and fell into the water.

Pan Cukrowy arrived. Wearing bathing trunks, with a towel on his arm, he sat down next to Mother and lit a cigarette. I took off my cap so Mother wouldn't be able to detect me, took my glasses out of my shorts pocket, and put them on. Immersed up to my neck, I observed them intently.

When Mother decided to get married again (already in Borysław), she explained that she was doing it for me. "Everyone says I shouldn't think about myself, because you need a father." Then Michał took me for a walk and said that your Mommy, after what she lived through, also deserves something. Moving my arms in the water, I blew bubbles with my mouth. He loved her. And she? She flirts! Kicking off from the bottom, I moved toward the beach. I was already close when Karola appeared on the beach. I came out of the water and started building a sand castle. Then I stretched out beside its ramparts. It was hot. I laid my head on "Poem."

In the sea, children were tossing around a red ball. For them, I'm a zero, I thought. I don't swim. I don't jump. I don't dig. All I do is read or draw. And not even humans, but dwarfs, small, ugly creatures.

The white jetty stretched far into the sea. The wind carried the smell of the tar that covered its supports, which were driven into the sea floor. People were strolling slowly along the white barrier. In the distance, on the horizon, there were several motionless ships.

Oh, to swim there and return under water! To surface among the children right under their falling ball and strike it high with a "header"! Sure! But how could I do that?

Sinking in the dry sand, I set off in the direction of Orłowo. Suddenly, I smelled the aroma of a smokehouse. In the shed, under a plywood roof, eels hung on rows of ropes. Golden-brown, they swayed gently, their heads pointed downward. I bought one and, leaning on the counter, started carefully separating the skin from the meat. I threw the remaining bits to the seagulls, which fought over them near the wire trash bin. They ate greedily and then cleaned their bills in the sand.

I returned through the woods. It was cooler among the trees. I caught sight of a Subcarpathian sheepdog under a pine tree. Its black eyes followed me from within its thick white coat. "He's lost," I thought, and went closer. When I touched his collar in order to locate his license tag, he caught my hand between his teeth. He held fast and wagged his tail. I froze. What to do? Suddenly there was the sound of a whistle and the dog ran off to its owner.

Rubbing away the tooth marks, I set off. Soon I came to the tennis courts. A match was still in progress, but the disappointed public had already begun walking out. I stopped to watch near the wire-mesh fence. Władysław Skonecki was playing against a giant Russian. The people who had decided to remain in the stands were focused on the white ball flying back and forth above the red court.

A gong! The maître d'hôtel struck a golden disk three times. I took my place at our table in the restaurant. Mother came over. Elegant. One waiter took our order; another served hors d'oeuvres. I removed the lid from a silver bowl. An egg yolk, a slice of onion, and a sardine in oil lay on top of raw meat. Mother turned her head away in disgust.

They brought the soup. My glasses got fogged up from the steaming consommé. While I wiped them with my pink napkin, Mother dipped a spoon into my soup plate.

"Consommé!" she snorted. "It's ordinary broth."

Pan Józio's Gallery

We didn't have many friends.

Cesia and Józio Barski rented a room in an old apartment on Hoża Street. She was an engineer and worked in some kind of chemical laboratory, and he dealt in paintings. The Krasnowolskis had a private house in Saska Kępa; Dziadzio drove us there by way of the bridge across the Vistula. Pan Odwak and Pan Drobot used to drop in just for a visit. Jurek Łobzowski, however, Michał's friend from high school and the Lwów Polytechnic, who, in 1938 when fraternity members wielding razor blades invaded their laboratory, grabbed a bottle of hydrochloric acid and shielded Michał, would get a special invitation to dinner from Mother personally.

She told me that during the Occupation Jurek was in charge of feeding the lice in the lab of some professor who was seeking a cure for typhus. Once, as he was returning from this "job," some *szmalcownicy,* men who extorted money from Jews in hiding, dragged him inside a gate, assuming that he was a Jew. Jeering at them, he unbuttoned his fly.

Michał said of him, "He's very competent, only he's not in a hurry." Jurek hadn't completed his studies before the war and only now was he working toward his degree by taking evening classes.

Aside from Karola, the people we saw most often were Lusia and Zygmunt Wierusz, and the least frequent were old Pan Rosenthal and his wife, who, like Mother, had been born in Vienna. (They conversed in German.)

—

After our return from Sopot, Mother announced that we had to see people more often. True, Karola was enough for her, but it was necessary to think of others. However, when Michał was summoned to the Ministry on the next Sunday, she organized a darning session out of spite. First she phoned Karola at the Hotel Polonia, and then she pulled her underwear off the clothesline in the bathroom and carried it into the living room. She threw her transparent stockings, black socks, and pink underpants onto the sofa and took her sewing box out of the bookcase. A pin cushion with needles in it shone red among the spools of thread and her thimbles gleamed like silver.

Soon, Karola appeared with three pears she had purchased outside the hotel. Mother unwrapped the newspaper they were packed in, washed them, and set them on a plate.

I looked at the fruit.

"Take a napkin," she said; "you're going to drip all over."

Turned to face the window, she was struggling to thread a needle.

"You need glasses!" Karola laughed.

"Never!" Mother speared the thread through the sparkling eye and bit it off.

After I ate the pear I set off for the Barskis'. I ran up the shrapnel-splintered stairs to the second floor and rang the lowest buzzer. Pan Józio opened the door. He was holding a tiny broom made of feathers, which he used to shoo away flies. When I crossed the marble threshold with its colorful veins, he stroked my face. We entered a long, dark corridor. Oil paintings hung on the walls. Portraits of women and of men. Horses. Landscapes with peasants. The paint was peeling from gilded frames. Looking at the empty spaces left by the canvases he had sold, I wondered if likenesses of our acquaintances would be suitable for this collection.

Pan Józio pointed at the newest picture with his little broom. He'd purchased it for very little and already had a buyer. Against a tall wall, in the snow, a boy was standing, dressed in plus fours. A violet jacket. A beret pulled down onto his right ear. A rifle in his red hands.

"*The Young Eagle,*" Pan Józio explained. "A copy of Wojciech Kossak's painting."

Crossing the line of fire, we entered the main room. It was flooded with sunlight. Watercolors, for which the corridor was too damp, were hung everywhere. Light, reflected from the glass of the paintings, fell on the furniture, lamps, and bibelots. Cracks and holes in the parquet floor appeared as black spots. Worn carpets lay under a desk with curved legs and a bronze-colored piano. On the piano, next to photographs of Pani Cesia's parents, who had been deported from the ghetto in the same *Aktion* in which Pan Józio's first wife perished, stood a jar filled with colored balls. The rays of light passing through it cast their colors onto the brass lamps with their satin shades. Between the lamps, on a soft couch, Pani Cesia was reading a book.

"We have a guest," Pan Józio informed her.

She put the book down on a low table and, distracted, went behind the Chinese screen where a tea kettle was boiling on an electric hot plate. Bowing my greeting, I followed her with my eyes. Soon, she carried in a porcelain pitcher and Pan Józio set out gilded tea cups and a sugar bowl.

Waiting for the tea to steep, I cast a glance at the piano. Were it not for the jar, the little balls would scatter over the floor and disappear under the furniture. And what of us? Are we also sitting inside some kind of vessel that guarantees our existence?

Pani Cesia lifted the pitcher and looked at me inquiringly. I nodded. While she poured the tea, I picked up her book. Anatole France, *L'Île des pingouins.* I turned the cover page. In the center of the gleaming white paper was a photograph of a distinguished gentleman with an unusually long face and long nose. Fluffy white hair, moustache, and beard. He was gazing into the space above my right ear.

Brushing flies away from the sugar bowl, Pan Józio asked me what were my plans in life. I had none. So instead, I immediately started dreaming up various stories.

"All right." He waved the broom. "But what do you want to be?"

"A writer," I shot back without a moment's hesitation.

The following Sunday, Dziadzio drove us to Saska Kępa.

The Krasnowolskis were in their garden. We greeted each other under an apple tree. He was a director. He was soon to become the commercial councillor in London. He was tall and stout. A Pole. She was not. She had survived, along with her sister.

The host tore off a red apple, cut it with a penknife, and handed everyone a slice.

A rope for a volleyball net was strung between the trees. The men were not wearing ties. The ladies were barefoot. Pani Krasnowolska's sister, bronzed from the sun, was dressed in a beach outfit. When she jumped, her white breasts popped out from the bodice. She hastily covered them up.

They kept on playing.

Soon, Odwak and Drobot visited us. The former was big, jolly, and had a moustache. The latter was tiny, nervous, and spoke softly. Both were bachelors. They survived in Russia. Michał had met Odwak only after the war and referred to him as "the hermit." Drobot, on the other hand, he remembered from the polytechnic. "An electrical engineer," he said about him. "Very gifted."

Pan Odwak handed Mother yellow roses. She put them in a vase and filled it with water. Little air bubbles appeared on the thorny stems. Then Pan Odwak took out a bar of chocolate in a silver and violet wrapper and gave it to Mother.

"Lindt!" she exclaimed happily. "Bitter."

"*Luche vsekh,*" he replied in Russian, "the very best," and lit a Chesterfield.

Pan Drobot took out a mechanical pencil, slowly advanced the graphite tip, which was thinner than a needle, and drew a line in the notebook in which I sketched my little people.

"H5," he confirmed. "Very hard."

Putting away the pencil, he said that *Pravda* had criticized Israel.

Michał bridled. "Cosmopolitans, not Jews."

"Some writers were arrested," Pan Drobot added.

"Who says?"

"London."

Michał waved his hand dismissively.

"They're making a mountain out of a molehill. Besides which, this is Poland, not Russia."

—

Toward the end of August Mother invited Jurek Łobzowski for dinner. In the morning she grated potatoes, mixed them with egg yolks, onion, and oil, and poured the pink mass into a baking pan. Next, she sliced boletes into a pot, sautéed them in butter, and poured sour cream over them. She put both pans in the oven and soon the entire apartment was filled with the aroma of kugel and smothered mushrooms.

While waiting for Jurek, I read Andersen's *Fairy Tales,* and then started drawing. A large sleigh. Two little people on the bench: the coachman and a little boy huddled up from the cold. I rubbed out the driver and drew him again. This time he was standing, holding a white fur in his hands as if he wanted to cover the boy with it. The reins dangled from the front of the sleigh. Ahead were tails, the horses' back legs, and a snowstorm.

When the bell sounded, I threw everything onto the carpet and ran to the foyer. Michał unhooked the chain and let the guest in. The stuffed briefcase that Jurek placed under the coat tree surprised me.

Mother asked us to come to the dining room.

"I don't enjoy grating." She uncovered the baking pan. "It's easy to cut yourself."

"Nowadays, everywhere is unsafe." Jurek handed her his plate.

She placed a portion of kugel on it.

"They're terribly stiff," she muttered. "Karola says they swallowed sticks."

"Who?" He cut a slice.

"The communists."

"I don't like them." He made a face.

"What about Michał?"

"What kind of communist is he? He wouldn't hurt a fly." He helped himself to mushrooms. "I just don't understand why he dropped chemistry. Those who can't do anything cling to the trough. But he! He's first rate!"

"Central planning is the foundation," Michał responded. "Free competition is a waste. Soon we'll have economic development such as capitalism can only dream of."

"God willing." Jurek gulped down a hot mouthful.

Mother poured cherry compote into glasses.

"Industry will swallow the landless peasants." Michał pushed aside his fork and knife. "The structure of the country will change." He raised his glass. "A new intelligentsia will arise from the sons of the unskilled laborers, the *chernorobochie,* as the Russians refer to them."

"What's wrong with the old intelligentsia?" Jurek took some more kugel.

"Antisemitism will end," Michał went on. "The youth will forget about Jews."

"You believe in miracles?" Jurek eyed the mushrooms.

"At best, the people here will pretend." Mother pushed the pot closer to him.

"What's most important is that it's begun." Michał drank up his compote. "People are changing."

After dinner, Jurek took out boxing gloves from his briefcase. The soft red leather shone like velvet. We went into the living room. There was flypaper hanging from the ceiling. Jurek removed his tie and shirt. He put on the left glove. He gave me the right one. He was Michał's height, but more muscular. He ordered me to attack. The piano strings vibrated and the untied strings of the gloves fluttered. But still I couldn't manage to touch him. He held out his hand and said I should hit it.

"Straight punch!" he yelled. "Straight punch and a hook."

⸺

On the first Sunday in September we drove to Łazienki Park. Dziadzio parked the Demokratka alongside the iron fence. On the other side of the paling people were strolling around a large square. Mother gave Michał her arm. We set off down the wide sidewalk toward the open gate. A moment later we caught sight of Karola. She was waving a small book in a dark jacket. It was a pre-war Warsaw Baedeker with black-and-white photos. She'd found it at the reception desk in the hotel.

Walking along the square, we studied an old photograph of it. A statue of Chopin, seated beneath a carved tree with his left hand on his knee, could be seen. The fingers of his right hand were spread on an invisible keyboard. I raised my head and looked around for the statue.

"The Germans blew it up," Michał said.

We turned right beyond some large willow trees. We started walking downhill on paths strewn with red crushed glass. The leaves of oak trees and maples were swaying against the sky. We reached a pond. In its water the shadows of the trees were trembling.

Karola opened the Baedeker.

"Łazienki was the property of the royal family. In 1815 the Poniatowskis sold it to the tsar."

Scaffolding surrounded the blackened ruins of the Palace on the Island.

"The Germans burned it," Michał said.

The sun cut through the leaves. Its thin rays bore into the glass chips and the dark-green grass where squirrels were leaping about.

Unexpectedly, the Wieruszes and their daughters emerged from a shaded lane: large-eyed Bogusia and Haneczka, who was born after the war. Pan Zygmunt made a slight bow. Pani Lusia held out her hand to me. Spots of light were jumping over her dress. She had thick black eyebrows.

They had survived on an estate. He grew a moustache and managed the property. She never went into the village. The peasants were afraid of the Home Army men whom the manager fed.

"She bleached her hair," Mother said once.

"Her eyebrows, too?" I asked.

She didn't know.

Now, Pan Zygmunt was a director. "A mechanical engineer," Michał explained. "Very talented."

"But not a talker," Mother added. It amused her that Pan Zygmunt didn't eat pork. Once, she'd invited them to dinner. Pani Lusia wrinkled her nose even before she crossed the threshold.

"What smells so good?" she asked in a whisper.

"Pork roast," Mother replied just as softly.

"Tell him it's turkey."

We started back. Walking up the hill, the women kept looking around for Jews. Whenever they noticed someone, they debated where he'd survived. Probably in Russia . . . .

The men talked about Gomułka's expulsion from the Politburo. I pricked up my ears. Yesterday, when I was already in bed, Michał had said that he didn't understand what was going on. Mother rattled the dishes. "Whomever *batiushka* doesn't like, *poshyol von!*" she said in a fury. "If Little Father doesn't like someone, out with him!"

"It's just the beginning," Pan Zygmunt muttered.

"I guess so." Michał clenched his jaws.

there was nothing between us

A Drop of Socialism

It was drizzling. I set out for school in the Demokratka. Streetcars draped with wet people were creeping along Puławski Street. On Marszałkowska Avenue several boys ran into the street. Dziadzio blew the horn. They jumped away, threatening us with their fists. The bell was ringing in the Church of the Savior. At the intersection of Marszałkowska and Jerusalem Avenues a policewoman held up her white-gloved hand. Lodzia. I recognized her from a newsreel.

She turned around gracefully. A change in the direction of traffic. The Demokratka thudded on the tracks. On the right, the sun was rising over the ruins. The rain had stopped. Dziadzio turned off the wipers. On the left, an empty space. I'd seen in *The People's Voice* a sketch of the gigantic building that was going to be built there.

On Bank Square a Chausson bus was leaving from the stop across from the burned-out Mostowski Palace. Dziadzio attempted to pass it. When we were halfway past the bus the driver noticed us in his mirror and stepped on the gas. Clouds of black smoke billowed out of its exhaust pipe. We had to slow down. Only after we passed the viaduct over the Gdańsk Station did the Demokratka jump ahead.

Dziadzio circled Wilson Square and turned into Feliński Street, but he stopped the car far from the school.

"That's the Director's orders," he explained.

In the coatroom I pulled out felt shoe wrappers from under the bench and fastened them to my shoes with long ribbons. I stood up cautiously. In my former schools we didn't put anything over our shoes.

"Where is IXb?" I asked the custodian.

"Over there." He pointed down the corridor with his chin. "At the very end."

But the end couldn't be seen because the corridor turned to the left. Between the coatroom and the turn it was filled with children. Colorful suns and flowers twinkled, embroidered on the girls' slippers. The boys in their felt shoe covers resembled skiers. Touching the walls, I began sliding, too.

In front of the toilets I heard Russian. Two pupils emerged from its dark interior, talking about the eggplants in Samarkand. I stopped to let them pass and observed them attentively. Jews! I hadn't known any Jewish boys until then. I had seen them only in photographs that had survived or in Łazienki Park. My heart began beating faster. Another one was coming from the opposite direction! He was joking with non-Jews. I set off after them. That way, I returned to the coatroom and had to complete the entire route again.

Several Jewish girls were going into IXb, but none of the boys was a Jew. Neither fair-haired Suchocki nor Łopatka with the upturned nose, nor skinny, tall Żuk, whose voice was changing. Welcoming me, they asked who I would like to sit with. Astonished by their kindness, I chose Suchocki. Could it be that they didn't realize? Out of the question. In Borysław, Krosno, and Ligota, everyone kept a distance from me. In Trzebinia I was friends with Adam Lawrencic and in Warsaw with Michalski. As for the rest . . . There's no use talking about it. But here . . .

During breaks between classes I looked around carefully. If I thought someone looked like a Jew, I went over to him and, introducing myself distinctly, waited for him to ask where I survived. No response. A total lack of interest.

After classes I went home by streetcar. The carriage swayed violently. Hanging onto the step, I clutched the metal handrail. At each stop I had to make sure that the passengers didn't knock me down as they got off. It was raining again in Śródmieście. I was afraid that my glasses would fall off my wet face.

Why wasn't there a Jewish question on Feliński Street? What was the reason for that? Only when we reached Puławski Street did the thought occur to me. This school was a drop of socialism. Michał was right. It had begun!

In front of our building I jumped down onto the grass.

"Well, how was it in school?" Mother asked.

"Okay."

"Are there any Jews?"

"It's hard to tell," I mumbled.

"But you've got glasses," she declared ironically.

Through the windows of the biology lab on the fourth floor a sun-scorched Michurin garden could be seen: blackened Siberian grains and yellowed potato-tomatoes. In the late spring, when Michał had taken me for the conversation with the director, everything was still green behind the wire fence. But it had dried up over the summer. Even the cards with

Latin names had faded. On the windowsills, however, there were flower-pots with the new hybrids, and the stems were tied with strings to help them grow together better.

We sat at small tables. Navy blue pinafores, white collars, and hair bows moved above the notebooks, pencils, and chalk. Anielka Klepacka (from the Children's Home) opened the window. The voices of children playing in the schoolyard reached us. Freckled Abramowska lent Zosia Weiss blotting paper to clean her pen nib. Ania Wendek was at the sink, rinsing out gallipots that had contained protoplasm.

Pani Pomorska walked up and down beside the windows. They said she hung a carpet out her window out of respect for the Corpus Christi procession. She raised her legs high, like a soldier on parade, and held a ruler in her hand.

"In the spring," she pointed to the flowerpots with the ruler, "we will transplant all of these into the garden!"

"Last year's dried up," Żuk squeaked.

"What of it?" said Pani Pomorska. "Let's beat our breast. We didn't take good enough care of them."

"They all dried up." Żuk didn't back down.

"If scientists lost interest at their first difficulties, humanity would have gotten nowhere. Now it is believed," the teacher balanced on one leg, "at least that's what they're saying in the office of public instruction, that it's environment, not genes, that decides inheritance." She started walking again. "Mendelism, Weismannism, Morganism are false Western theories. Michurin, on the other hand, and especially his student Lysenko, have grown new plant varieties by manipulating the environment. We, too, shall succeed. Olga Lepieszyńska tore apart jellyfish . . ."

Żuk chortled in a deep voice.

"What are you laughing at?" asked the teacher.

"You said it was hydras . . ."

"It's all the same." She bit her lip.

"Not to the jellyfish."

The class erupted into giggles. That was too much. The teacher slammed the ruler into her open palm.

"Notebook!" she shouted. "Homework."

And she started underlining errors with a red pencil.

Pan Rosenthal believed that genetics is a political science. Once, he took down Engels's *Anti-Dühring* from the shelf and extracted from it a photograph of a monument on which Stalin, with an ear of corn, and the botanist Lysenko were seated in stone armchairs. Tapping his finger on the deserving botanist's head, Pan Rosenthal asserted that communists are changing not only history, but nature as well. New grains will come up even where there is only a short summer and a long winter instead of four seasons.

Next, he read something in German and looked me in the eyes. Whoever wants to understand how a cell arises from a simple protein must investigate all the developmental phases of living matter. "Alas!" he raised up his hands, "alas, naturalists didn't study Engels properly!" Only when Lepieszyńska undertook a solid reading did she understand that in order to achieve "the essence of life" one had first to destroy the cellular structure of the organism. So she ground up a freshwater hydra in a gallipot and spun the protoplasm out of it. Then new life grew out of the transparent fluid. Pan Rosenthal slipped the photograph back into the book. "That's what studying the classics gives you!" he finished triumphantly.

From biology lab we ran down to the ground floor. Past the toilets the corridor led to a hall with columns between which hung a red cloth with the slogan:

ACHIEVE A SCIENTIFIC WORLDVI

A girl was standing on a chair and holding up the remaining letters. Scissors glittered on an open piano among scraps of bristol board.

An assembly was held here every morning. A girl or boy wearing a red tie would read off news bulletins from a card. Picasso in Warsaw, Paul Robeson at a publishing house, Gomułka's errors, the struggle with kulaks, the priests' trials, and death sentences for the criminals from the underground. Next, a communiqué about the removal of rubble, the command "Attention!," several rhythmic chords, and a song set to a tune from the film *The World Is Smiling:*

> With victorious step we stride into the sunlit world,
> Raising our heads and our fists up high.
> We are carrying new life and a new order,
> And above us, like a banner, floats our song.

Past the columns the corridor turned left next to IXc, where meetings of the Union of Polish Youth were held every day. Recruitment was going on. Light penetrated through the window in the door.

At the end of the corridor, facing each other, were rooms IXa and IXb. The best students went to IXa: Owadowicz, Jakubow, and Zabarnicki.

They impressed me, but I couldn't compete with them since I didn't study at all. At home, all I did was read and draw pictures of ancient galleys filled with little people and maps of naval battles.

We entered IXb. A vacant podium. A dirty blackboard. Three rows of desks. I sat down next to Suchocki against the rear wall, which was dedicated to the heroes of labor. Above us hung a "Thermometer of Productivity" of the brigade leaders Ambroziak and Moskalik along with a poster of happy bricklayers. At the top of the wall they were applying mortar with trowels. Their helpers were climbing the scaffolding with wooden yokes across their shoulders. Each man was carrying twenty-three bricks.

The next class was history. The theme: the Punic wars.

I had already read *Twenty-Four Scenes from the History of Poland* at Queen Jadwiga School. I had looked at the illustrations in that book with pleasure. They were reproductions of paintings that mainly depicted battle scenes. I would imagine that I was wandering around among flashes of iron, crushed armor, and white puffs of cannon smoke. The illustrations from *Twenty-Four Scenes from the History of Poland* had imprinted themselves into my memory so powerfully that later on I would associate them with books I read, and even with films, about the Second World War.

I knew the ancient world from reading *The Greek Myths.* It lay at the foot of the mountain from which the gods had descended (in the book there were photographs of their statues) in order to settle their accounts by means of humans. The great heroes perished in torment, and although they lived forever after in Hades, I sympathized with them, recalling how I myself was afraid of suffering and even more so of death.

History was taught by Professor Rybka. Slim and elegant. His closely trimmed moustache and beard held flashes of silver. When he lectured (he spoke softly, with his eyes half-closed) figures from thousands of years ago, unlike either the gods or the knights from *Scenes,* appeared before my eyes.

There were no textbooks, so we had to take notes on everything. In order not to waste time dipping our pens in our ink wells, we wrote with pencils.

Sometimes Professor Rybka interrupted his story and, like a magician who pulls an ace of spades or a colorful scarf from his sleeve, he'd pronounce some Marxist theorem that sounded like one of Kepler's or Newton's laws. Then I'd call to mind the old watchmaker in Trzebinia, Pan Akerman, who, shortly before his death, had looked at Michał's Omega through his loupe. It seemed to me that I could detect the steel springs, the golden cog wheels, and the trembling pendulum of history's inner works. And if I already knew that thought from *The People's Voice* or Pan Rosenthal's books, I would smile in my soul.

Professor Rybka placed one leg over the other. The wooden studs in his leather sole glistened. He straightened his glasses.

"He's going to ask us questions," Żuk whispered, noticing that the professor was taking out his ledger.

"Dichter!" I heard.

I handed him my notebook with the map of Heraclea and a ship equipped with a gangway with a sharp hook.

"Where did the Romans defeat the Carthaginian fleet?" he asked.

"At Heraclea . . . ," I began, but he didn't let me continue.

"How?" He put his hand to his ear.

"They threw gangways across. The soldiers ran up from below the decks onto the enemy's ships and slaughtered everyone."

I wanted to tell him more. "Sicily became a province . . . ," I began, but Rybka gestured impatiently and gave me back my notebook.

Then he opened his ledger, bent over its pages filled with writing in green ink, and began his lecture. Soon, I could see the Spanish mountains, leather tents, and the Africans exuding their hunger for revenge.

"In 221 B.C.E. Hannibal was the leader of the Carthaginians." Rybka looked up at us. "And although individuals do not decide history, one must say a few words about Hannibal," and he bowed his head. "He was a magnificent leader! A runner, rider, and swordsman; he knew Greek and he'd studied the Hellenic wars. When necessary, he combined courage with clear thinking." The professor took out his handkerchief and started polishing his glasses.

Rustling and coughing could be heard. Several pupils, taking advantage of the interruption, sharpened their pencils. Grażyna Kownacka (from the Children's Home), the tip of her tongue protruding, was rubbing something out with an eraser.

"Hannibal set out from Spain and crossed the Rhône." The professor put away his handkerchief. "Because the river was too deep for the elephants, and a pontoon bridge would not have held their weight, he had them wrapped in inflated bladders and towed across to the opposite bank." He squinted, as if he had thought up that stratagem himself. "Soon the twenty-six-thousand strong army with two dozen elephants crossed the Alps. Defeats descended on the Romans. They encountered the most terrible one near Cannae. At that time, the Legions were commanded alternately by the Consuls Paulus and Varro. Paulus was afraid of the African cavalry, but Varro, who was the leader that day, ordered them to advance. On the next day, Paulus was supposed to attack. Seventy thousand Romans struck the center of the Carthaginian crescent . . ." He turned the page. "When the Spaniards and Gauls who were fighting there retreated, drawing the enemy into a trap, the cavalry that had been positioned in the flanks surrounded the Legions. It seemed to the men who observed the battle from the surrounding hills that the earth had swallowed the Roman army."

Carried away by his own description, the professor picked up the pace.

"Slower!" voices called out.

He didn't even lift his head.

"Not wanting to lose any time, the Carthaginians slashed the fleeing soldiers' tendons below their knees." An expression of contempt and disgust appeared on Rybka's face. "Only later did they come back to finish off the wounded. Sixty-eight thousand Romans died. Paulus, too."

Silence ensued. Żuk rubbed his tired fingers.

"*Peredyshka*—a break," he said happily, but the professor began again.

"Terror descended on the City." He chewed his moustache. "Not one of the consuls wanted to command the Legions now. Then a young tribune volunteered who had survived the slaughter at Cannae. The Senate reluctantly confirmed him. It was Scipio, the future conqueror of the Carthaginians."

Noticing that he had closed his ledger, I put down my pencil and started drawing little people with my pen. Romans were fleeing across the page. Behind them, among the letters, the Cathaginian cavalry galloped, trampling discarded sandals and the wounded.

"Although Hannibal was a military genius . . . ," Rybka looked at us with his gray eyes, "historical necessity was on the side of Rome, which was economically more advanced."

Pan Rosenthal had used that same term when I complained to him about Michalski's grandfather. I'd heard then that communists are always right. Because they are guided by reason and not by sentiments, and therefore they know what was and will be necessary. Also, I had no need to be upset about dictatorship and force, because they are transitory phenomena, insignificant in the long run.

"*Nie razmenivaisia po melocham*," he'd added in Russian, noticing that I'd made a face. "Don't waste your talents on trifles. Excessive sympathy and delicacy have already destroyed many people."

I stopped drawing.

The professor turned to the blackboard and wrote:

THE PUNIC WARS: JUST OR UNJUST?

Placing the dot under the question mark, he broke his chalk on the greasy surface and sent me to the bathroom to wet a rag.

I hurried back. Drops of water dripped on the floor and onto my felt shoe covers gliding over it. What would Professor Rybka say? My heart was fickle. On the sea I empathized with the Africans; at Cannae, with the Romans. But knowing the tragic fate of Hannibal, I felt that during the lecture about the destruction of Carthage everything would change again. "He who is guided by emotional reactions," said Pan Rosenthal, "will never understand the mechanism of history."

I pushed on the door handle. The pupils were alone. The professor had been summoned by the principal. I wiped the blackboard and sat down. Suchocki was reading an astronomy monthly. The constellations looked like traces of a spider that had escaped from an inkwell and, drunk with ink, was wandering aimlessly on the paper.

When I arrived at the meeting of the Union of Polish Youth, the red cloth had just been pinned up. However, soon the classroom filled up and the members of the School Administration took their seats on the podium. The meeting was led by a boy whom Suchocki called Vladimir. Exhausted eyes. Unshaven cheeks. A future Party secretary. Of a district . . . the capital . . . the Central Committee!

I knew them from the movies. Taciturn. Possessed of an iron will. They knew everything. Their wisdom did not derive from schools, however. Before the war, instead of attending high school they had spent time in prison.

Like poets and painters, the secretaries had talent: the ability to understand life within the categories of dialectical materialism. Often, after leaving the movie theater I would attempt to reconstruct the flow of their thinking. But I would get lost in the details. Pan Rosenthal believed that one can compensate for the lack of a compass with work. I doubted it. I felt that I didn't have talent. I just wished that the secretaries would like me.

After shedding light on the international situation, Vladimir discussed the upcoming United Congress of the Polish Workers' Party and the Polish Socialist Party.

"The workers are demanding the merger of the parties." He brandished newspaper clippings.

Laughter.

"Don't be children," he said contemptuously.

I thought him more interesting than the top students from IXa. I didn't know how well he did in his studies, but that wasn't important since Vladimir's position didn't depend on grades. I started picturing his room to myself. First, a shelf with Marxist books; he knew and understood all of them. Then a desk covered with papers on which, in a silver frame, was a photograph of a man in uniform. I gave free rein to my fantasies. His father, a colonel, had fallen in battle at the Odra River. I preferred that Vladimir should live alone with his mother.

The question-and-answer session began.

A girl raised her hand. "Why should we care about politics? Isn't it enough to study well?"

"No," Vladimir explained. "From time immemorial some people have exploited others. Now, when the chance to build a just social system has arisen we must be politically engaged! Everyone must do this, or we'll squander it all."

"Can Catholics belong to the Union of Polish Youth?"

"Who do you think the 'patriotic priests' are with?" Vladimir thrust his hands into his jacket pockets. "With us!" he smiled triumphantly. "But we will nip in the bud all antisocialist demonstrations carried out under the cloak of faith," he added threateningly.

A pale boy with a bushy head of hair stood up from the last bench and for a long time didn't speak, giving rise to giggles and curiosity, but then, rolling his *r*'s, he began a peroration.

"My frrriend," he looked at his hands as if he didn't know what to do with them and, mimicking Vladimir, thrust them into his pockets, "let's call him young Count P.," he stared slack-jawed at the ceiling, "lost (or, rrrather, his parrrents lost) theirrr estate. Can he, this frrriend (our fatherrrs knew each otherrr verrry well before mine died in an automobile accident)"—he paused—"can this frrriend, I mean, could he, if he so wished, he hasn't said anything to me afterrr all about wanting to, so perrrhaps he doesn't want to at all and I'm taking up your time, colleague, unnecessarrrily"—(in the meantime, the classroom had become absolutely silent)—"in a worrrd, if he so wished, could he join the Union of Polish Youth?"

"His class background . . . ," Vladimir began.

"Puh-lease, puh-lease . . . ," the boy drawled. "So then, it's not forrr *bialorrruchki,* for those whose hands arrren't calloused."

"The Union of Polish Youth is for everyone. Except our enemies."

"Who decides?"

Vladimir made a broad gesture that indicated the entire class.

"A secrrret ballot?" the boy mocked him.

There was absolute silence.

"Who is in favor of the Count?" Vladimir suddenly shouted and no one, not even the pale boy, raised his hand.

"Nothing's going to destroy this damn system now," Mother had sighed when, strolling on the jetty in Sopot, we looked for ships on the horizon. Water was splashing against the supports sunk into the seabed. It came in waves. The gray sea was everywhere.

While I was listening to the questions and answers I remembered again about "historical necessity." How gracefully Professor Rybka used that concept! But Pan Rosenthal, although lacking in elegance, said exactly the same thing. Dialectical materialism explained history with incredible ease. It was the key to every epoch. Only, the results of force depressed me. The fate of jellyfish was irreversible.

Recently, Mother had baked meringue kisses for dessert. Eating her fill of them, Karola made fun of economic sabotage.

"Illiterates are installing innocents in order to conceal their own incompetence."

Michał picked up his teaspoon.

"He sees nothing." Mother pushed the sugar bowl over to him.

"Because he doesn't want to." Karola wiped white crumbs off her lips.

"Kraków wasn't built in a day." Michał stirred the straw-colored liquid and pointed to me. "They will correct our mistakes," he said.

Through the window in the door I could see the hall ceiling with a single bulb in a porcelain socket. Admission into the Union of Polish Youth had gotten started.

"Class background?"

"Working class."

"Worldview?"

"Scientific."

"Why do you want to join?"

"I love People's Poland and yearn to fight imperialism."

Vladimir looked around the class.

"Who's in favor?" he asked.

Applause.

"By acclamation," he said. "Next."

Under the heading of new business it was proposed that we should vote on everyone at once. Vladimir didn't know if that conformed with the statute. When he hands in the list of those who have been admitted for confirmation "at the District Committee," he'll inquire if that's permitted.

"Anything else?" He leaned against the podium with his hands. "I don't see anyone."

He handed out brochures for the candidates and asked everyone to stand.

Forward, youth of the world,
May our victorious march unite us,
The years of dread shall pass,
Hey, you who are young, stand with us and fight!

The next day, I went up to him. His large hands protruded from the unbuttoned cuffs of his black jacket. He was leaning against a column, conversing with two girls. One of them had a blonde braid and the other black hair cut in a bob.

"One hundred years ago," Vladimir raised his hands high, "Marx and Engels wrote *The Communist Manifesto.* It's frightening to think what would have happened without it."

He reminded me of the drunken bureaucrat from Mother's story about the New Year's Eve ball. I swallowed my saliva. A superficial resemblance of situations. Nothing more.

How to awaken their interest? I was short and ungainly, and to make things worse, I had a squeaky voice. Even my class background left something to be desired. True, Michał was a vice director, but Vladimir undoubtedly knew more important people.

"Did Pstrowski's heart burst?" the blonde-haired one piped up unexpectedly.

"From illness, not from work," Vladimir explained calmly. "The shock workers took an oath over his coffin to follow in his footsteps. The Bugdoł brothers swore to . . ."

"The individual means nothing," the dark-haired one nodded meaningfully.

"Not always," the blonde protested.

That's when I made my decision.

"The individual is zero." I softly spoke the words I had memorized from Mayakovsky's *Poem about Lenin,* and when I noticed that they were looking at me attentively, I began speaking with increasing confidence:

The individual is zero,
                    The individual is nonsense,
    Alone—
            He won't move
                    A five-inch log
    Though he be
            A great
                    Figure,
    Not to speak of raising
                    A five-story building.

"Mayakovsky," Vladimir said respectfully.

I kept going:

> And when we come together
> > In the Party
> > > To join the battle—
>
> Then fall, enemy,
> > Lie there and remember!
>
> The Party—
> > Is a million-fingered hand,
>
> Clenched
> > Into one
> > > Crushing fist.

"Join us," the black-haired girl urged me.

On Sunday, with my lunch wrapped in paper, I went off to work on rubble clearing. In my pocket I had the key that Mother gave me just in case.

Children from various schools were emerging from the ruins and gathering near two flags: a Polish and a red flag. The director of the rubble-clearing operation made a speech. Only bricks that are suitable for reuse should be collected. The rest should stay there. Even so, two hundred hectares can't be cleared out. That would require ten thousand people and seven trains over three years. The Muranów district will stand on a four-meter-deep layer of the ghetto. An economically and historically appropriate decision. He divided us into three groups. The first picked up the bricks. The second passed them from hand to hand. The third stacked them.

Rusty streams started flowing.

We moved mechanically. The sun dragged red dust behind it. At noon, a whistle. A break. We unwrapped our lunches. Those who lived in the Children's House had brought bread with blood pudding and tea in bottles. While eating my lunch, I kept shooing away the flies that were circling around. Staring at the two lone walls near the train station, I pictured to myself the housing development that the director had spoken of. A department store. A theater. Gardens here and there. Apartment houses in the gardens. Quiet and cleanliness. Studio apartments a year from now. Two-room apartments later.

Vladimir approached me.

"Actually, you're not a member yet." He placed his hand on my shoulder. "However, in view of your ideological maturity we want to refer you to the scouts."

"That's for children." I made a face.

"Red scouting is not for children," he bristled. "Have you read the brochure for candidates?"

"Yes."

"Then you know what discipline is."

"Fine," I nodded. "When?"

"After the rubble clearing."

I touched the key in my pocket.

The scouts' headquarters was housed in a villa on a crooked lane that came off Feliński Street. I brushed off the brick dust and knocked on the door. The sounds of a conversation reached me from inside.

Seated around a table on which was a basket covered with a red kerchief were four boys who were significantly older than me. I introduced myself. One of them pushed over a chair for me.

"From Feliński Street?" The most important one removed a cigarette butt from his lips.

"Yes."

"Eighth class?"

"Ninth."

"Fifteen?" He studied me carefully.

"Thirteen."

"Sit." He knocked the ash onto the floor. "We welcome everyone," he shrugged. "The pledge is a little different. Now we're serving 'People's Poland' and not 'God and Country.' We wear red scarves." He uncovered the basket in which lay oxidized crosses. "We don't tolerate competition. Anyone who pins on a cross can kiss it goodbye. If he doesn't hand it over voluntarily, we'll tear it off his shirt. Baden-Powellism is counter-revolution."

He took three crosses out of the basket. "Junior . . . Scout . . . Youth . . ." He threw them, one after the other, onto the table.

The first one had a gold lily, the second silver, and the third just the inscription "Be alert." I picked up the Youth cross. A number was engraved on the back.

"What's that?" I asked, adjusting my glasses.

"They were numbered," the boy seated opposite me said.

"How do you know?" the Most Important One laughed.

"I remember," the one across from me giggled.

"And what did an Eagle Scout have?" the Most Important One continued, clowning around.

"A gold lily in a gold circle," the boy sitting on my right replied.

"What about a Scout of the Republic?"

"The same inside a gold wreath," came the answer from the left.

The boy sitting across from me saluted.

"With two fingers?" he asked. "As before?"

"No," replied the Most Important One. "With the entire hand across the forehead."

—

I returned home by streetcar. The carriage was shaking every which way. The ceiling light fixtures were black with flies. I didn't want to disappoint Vladimir, but I swore to myself that I would not repossess crosses. Take them away from younger boys? Then how would I be any different from Piotrowski, who had tried to shove me into a well in Trzebinia because I was a Jew? Take them from older boys? They would not surrender them easily and could beat me up. Mother would see my bruises and that would be the end of the Union of Polish Youth.

—

I unlocked the door quietly and went inside. Without turning on a light I hung the key on the coat tree. A strip of light was visible under the closed dining room doors. I pushed down on the door handle. Mother was seated on the left side and Karola on the right side of the table. Michał, his back to the balcony, was concealed behind a newspaper. Taking my seat, I removed my glasses and rubbed my eyes.

Mother looked me in the eyes. "They're red."

"From the dust," I explained.

"Maybe his lenses are wrong." Michał rustled the paper.

"Are you seeing all right?" Mother served me barley soup with carrots.

"Fine." I pushed the carrot over to the rim of the plate.

"It's good for your eyesight." She pushed it back.

I took my first spoonful.

"Everyone's joining the Union of Polish Youth . . . ," I began.

"You have time," Mother interrupted.

"It would be better for him not to stand out," Karola interjected.

"Stand out!" Mother shrugged. "People hate them."

"Not in that school."

—

The next day, there was a math quiz. Suchocki was the first to finish. He checked his answers, handed in his notebook, and immersed himself in astronomy. (He was better in mathematics even than Owadowicz, who aced everything.) Zosia Weiss and Abramowska finished after Suchocki. I was fourth. I immediately started drawing elephants crossing the St. Bernard Pass. Suchocki brushed his fair hair off his forehead.

"Their tails are like integral symbols," he laughed.

We left school together. The leaves were falling onto Feliński Street and piling up against the gardens' fences. Scattering them with my shoes, I asked Suchocki if he liked the candy sold by the woman vendor.

"I'm going to naval school," he answered on a different topic.

"But what about graduation?" I asked, astounded.

He started walking faster.

"Astronomy?" I wouldn't give up.

"I prefer to sail around the world."

I thought that I would lose him, too, and fell silent. Only at Wilson Square did I speak again.

"I'm joining the Union of Polish Youth," I informed him.

"Why?" He shrugged.

"One has to choose."

"That's a strange rule."

"Plekhanov said that revolution . . ."

"Who's Plekhanov?" he interrupted me.

"Someone," I stammered.

The windows of the Universal Department Store were covered with doves that Picasso had painted in Warsaw.

"They're arresting people all the time . . ." He didn't look me in the eyes.

" 'The class struggle intensifies the closer we get to socialism.' "

"Plekhanov?" he laughed derisively.

"Stalin."

A Ship in the City

The streetcar came to a halt between stops in order to allow the people who were returning from the Primate's funeral to cross the tracks. Outside the dirty windows colorful kerchiefs on the women's heads and men's black hats decorated with shells and feathers moved by slowly. Cardboard rectangles with the names of parishes swayed above them.

Some of the mountain folk had knives like the Finnish knife I'd received the day before as a birthday gift.

The shop on the ground floor was closed. Beneath the red letters, STAN. STANKIEWICZ BUTCHER SHOP, hung a placard: CLOSED. Bierut's photograph had been replaced with the obituary notice for Cardinal Hlond. A dust-covered announcement lay in the neighboring shop window: FOR RENT.

I ran upstairs and started ringing the doorbell over and over again. I expected that Mother would take her time coming to the door from the kitchen, let me in, and say that her ears were ringing. That was our ritual. This time, however, I heard her running and so, disturbed, I released the buzzer. She opened the door a crack and placed her finger on her lips.

Michał was at home. He was sitting in the dining room with a scarf knotted around his face. Its shaggy ends dangled over his ears. His jacket hung over the armrest of his chair, its sleeve brushing his leather briefcase. His silver Omega and green Pelikan lay on a pile of typed papers. He had a blue-and-red pencil in his hand. He put it down, covered his mouth, and said something to Mother indistinctly.

With my eyes fixed on his snow-white shirt and his tie with its yellow polka dots, I retreated to the kitchen behind her.

"What happened?" I whispered.

Handing me a plate with a steaming sausage, she said that Michał had experienced a spasm while shaving. His mouth was twisted.

She clutched a loaf of bread to her breast and cut off a thick slice. Then she took out two jars of horseradish from the credenza.

"White or red?" she asked, holding them up.

"Red."

She unscrewed the lid.

When the spasm wouldn't stop, they went to see a doctor. He was actually a cardiologist (the one who had treated Michał after his return from Moscow), but they had faith in him. He saw them immediately. He asked her to take a seat on his leather couch and told him to undress. He tapped on his joints. He drew crosses on his arms and thighs. Finally, he gave them his diagnosis. Damage to the facial nerve. Injections of vitamins B1, B6, and B12, along with warm compresses.

It's all because of that job! Had I noticed the briefcase filled with papers that Dziadzio had brought over from the Ministry?

"Dr. Lis will be coming here any minute now." She put another sausage on my plate. "He's a lucky one! The war found him in Switzerland. He was studying there, like Milo in Italy. Now he's employed at the headquarters for pharmaceutical imports; he's in charge of importing PASS.

"PASS?" I looked up from my plate.

"It's a drug for tuberculosis," she explained in a low voice.

"Injections?"

"I don't know. Ask him."

The doctor was a young man. Dressed in a dark suit. He removed the scarf from Michał's head and touched the sick cheek. He took out a metal box from his zippered bag and extracted from the box a small glass cylinder into which he inserted a plunger with a silver handle. He fitted a needle into the other end of the cylinder. Flicking his fingernail against ampules containing clear, yellow, and pink fluids, he snapped off their necks and they broke with a cracking sound. A nasty odor emanated from them. He drew the fluids into the syringe and pressed on the plunger until a drop flowed out of the tip. Michał rolled up his sleeve. The doctor inserted the needle.

"Do you have children?" Mother started in.

"A son and a daughter." He pulled out the needle.

"Any photographs?"

He took out his wallet and handed Mother two prints.

She looked at them and raised her worried eyes to the doctor.

I craned my neck. The boy looked normal, but the girl had a strange smile and slanted eyes.

"Alas," he stammered, delicately tying up the scarf.

Mother spoke after a rather long silence. "Where do you see patients?"

"Nowhere." He held out his hand for the photographs. "I import PASS."

"Injections?" I asked.

"Pills." He zipped his bag.

Mother offered him tea, but the doctor thanked her and said no. Last Sunday, when they were moving the Primate's remains from the Elizabethan Sisters' Hospital, he'd gotten stuck in Union Square. Today, the crowds were even larger.

—

The next day, when I came back from school, Mother said that Michał had swallowed only a couple of spoonfuls of oatmeal. Nevertheless, he'd been working since morning. The doctor had been there already.

I went into the dining room. It was gray in there. Not even the jar of little colored balls next to which Pani Cesia read her French book could have lent it any color. Rain was falling outside the window. Water was running down the panes and splattering on the balcony railing. It dripped from the branches and the electric wires. Fog concealed the opposite side of Puławski Street and the Church of St. Michał.

With my notebook and two ink bottles I sat down across from Michał. Between us, the veneer glistened. I peeked at him. Short fingers with neatly trimmed nails. A gold ring. He was writing with his Pelikan in the margin of a typed document. The letters dried quickly, losing their sheen. He put down the pen and picked up the two-colored pencil. He drew a blue line around a fragment of text and added an arrow up to the top of the page. Then he turned the pencil upside down and underlined a few words in red.

I had an assignment to write a composition on "The maturation of peasant consciousness in Wanda Wasilewska's novel, *Fatherland*." I didn't know the book, but that didn't matter. Our Polish language teacher had been replaced with a teacher in training, who was acquiring pedagogical experience in our school. As a rule, he didn't read our compositions. Especially those written illegibly. I opened my notebook. No. Polish, no. Something else. But what?

Rocking back and forth, I drew little people mechanically. They looked like flies between the violet lines. I gave them caps and hats.

Unexpectedly, a certain sentence popped into my head. It had nothing to do with *Fatherland,* but it sounded good. I dipped my pen. On paper, however, it no longer pleased me. I started reworking it. I crossed it out. I started over. So as not to get lost in what I was doing, I alternated black and red ink. Soon the little people were inside a thicket of letters, crossings out, and scribbles.

In the very center of the city people are hammering copper nails. They are standing on scaffolding, sitting astride beams and working in silence. The hull of the ship already reaches the highest stories. Its gigantic cedar keel penetrates the pavement. Boulders from stone quarries, dragged here during the night, support its sides. There's still a long way to go before construction is completed. Only the prow is ready. It is crowned with the figure of a woman with a beautiful, though menacing, face, one arm raised high. The pleats of her wooden dress tower. Who builds like this today? Far from the sea. Why?

It was time for dinner. We gathered up our belongings from the table and transferred them to the credenza. In the meantime, Mother covered the table with a tablecloth and served out borscht with dumplings. Michał could barely open his mouth. She fed him with a spoon. Yet not long ago he'd been laughing out loud in Łazienki Park, revealing his gold tooth. What had made him laugh then was a story about the two Drobots that Pani Lusia told him.

Pan Drobot, on a visit to Warsaw, had stayed at the Wieruszes' home. During the night, Lusia wanted to get a drink. She went into the kitchen. On the way, she noticed their guest entering the bathroom. Suddenly the living room door opened and a second, identical Drobot appeared in it! Terrified, she fled to the bedroom.

"There are two of them!" she awakened her husband. "Or else I'm having hallucinations!"

"His twin," Pan Zygmunt muttered in his sleep. "He arrived when you were already asleep."

I took a spoonful of borscht, but before I put it in my mouth I caught sight of another Michał at the table. Instead of the tablecloth, a manuscript lay before him. His back to the credenza, he was writing something rapidly with a goose-feather quill. Or maybe it was just a pelican's feather? He paid no attention to us. He started a new line immediately after placing a period.

That's how I had once imagined Mickiewicz bent over his epic poem *Pan Tadeusz*. I had thought at the time that the poet created without stopping for breath and that as soon as he finished one book he would go outside to breathe in the fresh air.

Suddenly, the second Michał laid down his pen and stretched out his hand toward me. For a moment, it seemed to me that he wanted to slide the inkwells closer to him. He was reaching for the notebook, however. I moved abruptly, as if to stop him. Drops of borscht splattered. It was the dumpling falling off my spoon into the soup plate.

The tips of the shawl turned in my direction.

"The tablecloth!" Mother held her head. "I had a feeling he'd stain it."

When the whole affair exploded, journalists arrived from everywhere. From every country. They couldn't believe it. They thought it was a fairy tale. It can't be! In the very center of the city? Impossible! Thousands of questions formed on their lips. They, however, did not want to give interviews. They came every day, gloomy, ragged, and set to work. Silent. Implacable. Until the journalists gave up and went away. With a collection of photographs, to be sure, but without any explanation.

After dinner came tea. His, straw-colored; mine, reddish-black. I slipped a rough lump of sugar into my mouth and reached for another. Once, in Ligota, one of our sheets that was drying on the balcony had fallen onto the wolfhound who slept near the bicycle. Frightened, he'd run into the hall, dragging a white train behind him.

That image could serve as a model of memory. We remember the floorboards that the cloth covers at a given moment. We forget the boards that were behind it. The dog, however, is running in the direction of new boards of memory.

But that's only a simplification. The movement of the cloth doesn't explain everything. One board is not the same as another. True, silhouettes and eye colors from Borysław had disappeared, but I still felt the fear and the smell of war.

Mother started clearing the table.

What happened before they went out into the square? There are different versions. Some people insist that they had already been meeting in secret for a long time. They had been collecting etchings and plans on parchment. They traveled to England and to Venice—countries famous for sailing and for wars at sea. They stockpiled wood, nails, and wax for sealing cracks. They even stole a loom so they could weave the canvas for the sails from plant fibers. They drew on sand, rubbing out unsuccessful marks with their shoes. And thus, centimeter by centimeter, a precise plan arose on graph paper. Others, however, say that nothing of the sort happened. They insist that they started without any preparations. Just like that, quite simply, from day to day.

Grammatical corrections, unsuccessful formulations, and the usual scrawls occupied almost an entire page. I tore out the page and, using scissors, cut out several sentences that I wanted to preserve. Then I pasted them onto the next page. Now the first had more room. Waiting for the paper to dry, I tried to read the entire newspaper that was lying next to Michał.

Usually, I looked at *The People's Voice* with Mother. She read mainly the obituary notices and I read the headlines and the beginnings of speeches. That's how I learned that truth and absolute morality do not exist. Every social class has its own.

"What class do I belong to?" I asked Pan Rosenthal then.

"None." He turned his head. "You come from the working intelligentsia, and that's a group. However, through Michał you're connected to the avant-garde of the proletariat."

It was dry. I grabbed a pen.

> *How many of them were there in the beginning? A dozen? Perhaps two? Now there are hundreds already, if not thousands. They don't all come to the square. Many of them work at home or in distant bays they pull from the water pieces of old shipwrecks run aground on sandbars. Even children collect copper nails. Entire families have followed their men. Only sometimes a wife flees to her mother, crying that her husband has lost his mind. But little is known about this because such women pack up their stuff and leave the city.*

Michał had tears in his eyes when he spoke about Mickiewicz or Orzeszkowa or Prus. But I never saw him reading those nineteenth-century authors. In general, he had no time for books. He wasn't even interested in the poems of Władysław Broniewski, whom he saw at embassy receptions. Yet once when Mother and Jurek Łobzowski, reciting verses they had memorized in high school, got stuck after the first line of Asnyk's "Vain Regrets," Michał, without laying aside his newspaper or hesitating for a moment, took up the broken thread:

> The world, moving backward, won't return to you
> The ranks of vanished apparitions . . .

My pen started wandering. I asked myself, for whom was I writing. And why? Who are really the builders of the ship in the city? Why did I panic when I imagined that Michał wanted to look into my notebook? I could have said that it was an exercise. A free topic. He doesn't know what they assign us.

Again, little people in caps gathered. I bombarded them with drops of red ink.

> *They finish work at dusk. They put down their hammers, saws and axes, descend the rope ladders and return to their homes. But even then they*

are silent. Does something unite them other than work? They are becom-
ing more and more alike, almost identical, but what does that mean?
Are they capable of laughing or crying? Do they know joy and fear? Are
they afraid of death—like me?

The teachers had a productivity workshop and we were dismissed from school early. I decided to go to the movies. An Italian film, *Shoeshine,* was playing at the Palladium. I took a bus there. A crowd in front of the theater. It would be necessary to stand in line for at least an hour. I hopped on a streetcar. It was several stops to the Polonia. A poster advertising Russian language courses on the radio hung next to the ticket booth. I bought a ticket without even knowing what was playing.

On the screen trains were transporting Komsomol youth to Magnitogorsk. Inside the cars, boys were shoving each other to reach the windows. Foundries rose out of a fiery glow above the steppe. Huge as churches. Soon, the new arrivals were sifting coal into large ovens or tipping over vessels with long spouts from which streams of metal poured into molds dug into the earth. Cranes lifted the cooled castings and brought them to where the steel was tempered.

At night, the boys wrote letters. Postmen on motorcycles delivered them to girl tractor drivers. In the evenings, the girls picked cherries in the orchards and sang dumkas. Toward the end of the film men pinned on medals and women braided their hair. The pioneers knotted their scarves. Party secretaries came onto the stage. Processions began to move. Hammers and sickles waved.

After leaving the theater I thought about why things are as they are. Just as they are and not otherwise. Did what had happened have to happen?

"In history there are no accidents," Pan Rosenthal insisted once.

"You could fall under a streetcar," I said.

"That's not important." He waved away my doubt. "Laws have a statistical character. The individual's fate doesn't count. Neither one stroke of luck or another. Only the average is significant. Study the classics, read Soviet literature, go to Mosfilm movies, look at the art in *Ogonyok,* and eventually you'll understand the mechanism of history."

Mulling this over, I came to the Square of the Savior, and from there, past a line of poles decorated with red banners, I reached the Polytechnic. In front of Main Hall workers were raising and lowering flags on flagpoles. The building was covered in scaffolding. They were plastering its facade. Under the dripping lime boys in green shirts and red ties were running back and forth, carrying chairs into the auditorium from trucks.

I observe them. The sun has already set beyond the city. A rusty red
hangs over the square as if the buildings surrounding it were on fire.
Heavy buses turn in all directions, emitting black sooty smoke. Their
passengers look straight ahead, showing no signs of life, or are asleep on
their feet. Some of them are reading newspapers. No one glances at the
square. Those times have long since passed. At most, occasionally, a child
does, who was born not long ago and is seeing this for the first time.
Its mother nervously pulls it away from the window. Does she fear the
magic of the view? Is she anxious about her offspring's future? Does she
want to avoid questions, not knowing the answers? Cars are moving
slowly. Some have already switched on their headlights.

After the joint session of the Central Committee of the Polish Workers'
Party and the Central Executive Committee of the Polish Socialist Party,
Michał's mouth began to return to its proper position. Soon he removed
the scarf from his head.

"What are you writing?" he asked me all of a sudden.

"Polish." I placed my hand on the text.

"A composition?"

"Yes," I mumbled uncertainly.

"On what topic?"

"How ships were built."

"When?"

"In ancient times."

"What are they really teaching you there?" he laughed. "Is it a maritime school? Read me a section."

"When I'm finished." I shut the notebook. "It's not ready yet."

"It's been going on for quite a while." He shook his head. "What about
your math?"

"I did it in school."

"Show me."

"It's in my school desk."

He gave me a penetrating look.

What will happen when they finish their work? Will they part forever?
Will they begin a new construction project? Where? In which place in
the city? Or maybe they'll wait? For a flood. A deluge. The ship will be
lifted up and float away. A terrifying thought. Although at the same
time, a beautiful one. The entire city under water, nothing protrudes
from it now, not even the tallest chimney, but the ship rides proudly on

the stormy waves. The wind fills its sails. The wooden woman points the way.

Karola arrived with the news that three hundred thousand members were expelled from the Polish Socialist Party.

"A *mikvah*!" she observed, laughing.

"I don't understand." I raised my head from my notebook.

"They're cleansing themselves before marrying the Polish Workers' Party."

Mother sighed.

"Before I married Bronek," she said, "Papa bribed the bathhouse attendant. For five złotys I got a certificate saying that I'd been in the *mikvah*, because the rabbi wouldn't marry us without one."

> *For the time being, however, there's a drought. Heat pours down from the sky. Not even the tiniest cloud covers the azure. Faces, arms, and backs are drenched in sweat. Sometimes, voices fall into the rhythmic hammering of the tools. They are not words, however, and definitely not a song. Rather, a groan or a sigh. Sounding, sometimes, like a sob. If only it were dusk, if only it were dusk!*

There was a cloudburst after school. I arrived home wet. Wiping my hair with my sleeves, I ran upstairs. The door was locked. Where was Michał? I was overcome with terror that something bad had happened. All because of that "Ship in the City"! A free topic! Why was I writing such nonsense? I went down to the courtyard and threw my notebook into the iron trash bin.

Soon the gate creaked and I could hear the clacking of Mother's high heels.

"Where's Michał?" I asked in a whisper.

"At the office." She closed her umbrella. "What of it?" She gave me a look.

I shrugged. "Nothing, nothing."

Opening the door, she said she'd been with Lusia at Gajewski's for sweets. They had a large selection but most of it she wouldn't even put in her mouth. They make their éclairs from yesterday's leftovers. The cakelike ones are just butter, and the jelly doughnuts are rancid. But people will eat anything. Even roses made of cream. Not she! She'd hesitated for a long time over what to choose: a cream puff with whipped cream or a napoleon with pudding? Neither looked safe.

"So, which did you choose?" I asked when we went into the kitchen and Mother started making me an omelet.

"Both."

While I ate, she told me that it had been pouring cats and dogs in Śródmieście. Above the toy store, workers had hung a banner:

POLAND'S INDEPENDENCE IS THE PEOPLE IN POWER

What a slogan! A long line of people were standing on the sidewalk. Every so often one of them would run out of the store and, covering his head with a rocking horse, race to catch an approaching streetcar.

"Only horses! Who's planning this?!"

And Michał? He doesn't let her say a word against them. And he yells at her to calm down because they'll arrest her. She lowered her voice. Before they threw Masaryk out the window it would have been possible to make their getaway via Czechoslovakia. She wanted to. But he! "You've starved enough. You've suffered enough," he repeated over and over. "Here, we're set up. Over there? Who'll give me a job?"

"Lusia says Zygmunt is afraid, too." She took my empty plate.

In the evening I stole out to the courtyard. I retrieved my notebook from the trash bin and came back to the living room. I sat down in the armchair across from the mahogany bookcase. I caught sight of Stalin's *The Problems of Leninism* behind the thick glass panes. I was given it for my last birthday and I'd competely forgotten about it. I placed the notebook on the little table with the black top and took a pencil stub out of my pocket.

> *In the very center of the city they're banging with hammers on copper*
> *nails. In the square stands a ship. Not a ship; the skeleton of a ship.*
> *The naked ribs and beams form an immense grill. Seen through it, the*
> *buildings on the other side of the square appear somewhat smaller. I*
> *slowly lift my eyes to the deck and the masts. The sails are not billowing.*
> *They are still missing.*

I put down my pencil. Nothing else came into my head. Perhaps I'll return to it someday and write a continuation? For now, I slip the notebook into Stalin's book and replace the book on the shelf.

Michał came home late. Minc, the Minister of Industry, had summoned him.

"Did you eat?" Mother asked.

"Yes," he answered her.

"What?"

"*Boeuf à la Strogonoff.*"

"What's that?" She made a face.

"Beef cutlets."

"Fried?"

"Smothered."

"In sauce?"

"Mushroom."

"Let's move to Śródmieście," she said suddenly.

"What for?" he asked, astonished. "You have Dziadzio."

Christiania

After the Congress of Unification, Michał asked Mother if she'd like to take a trip with me to Karpacz for the holidays. His department head, who'd been assigned a room there, had fallen ill, and now two places were available at the *pension*.

"Near Legnica!" Mother made a face. "With Russians."

"There aren't any Russians!" Michał said irritably. "It's a spa."

The next day she bought me metal-banded ski boots. A thick tongue stuck out from beneath leather laces.

"They pinch," I groaned.

"They'll loosen up," the shoemaker assured me.

Next, we stopped in at a clothing store. Six sales ladies and a bakelite mannequin.

"Wool socks." Mother pointed at me.

"There aren't any," the sales lady said.

"What do you have?"

"Foot-wrapping cloths," she giggled. "They made a mistake. They were supposed to go to the countryside."

I noticed green shirts.

"Too large." Mother shook her head.

There were ties on the counter.

"Too long. Anyway, they're already unraveling." She pulled a red thread out of one of them.

The compartment was full until Wrocław. After that, we had it to ourselves. Mother stretched out on one seat. I sat down next to the window. We were reflected in the glass, disappearing only at illuminated crossings. Gate keepers jingled bells beside the lowered crossing gates.

I played with my Finnish knife. Its bone handle with colored veins was like the marble threshold in the Barskis' apartment. I stroked it for a long time. Then I pulled out the blade from the leather sheath. It gleamed like a mirror. To test if it was sharp I picked up a copy of *The People's Voice* that was lying on the seat. It smelled of kielbasa and pickled cucumbers. On the front page was a photograph of the Warsaw Polytechnic auditorium. The delegates were seated on chairs. I cut them away from the white podium on which President Bierut, in dark glasses, was standing. He was surrounded by empty armchairs and clusters of banners with illegible inscriptions. Above him, seven more flags hung down from the crowded gallery on the second floor. On the left hung his portrait. On the right, Premier Cyrankiewicz's. One floor higher, one above the other, were four short names:

MARX

ENGELS

LENIN

STALIN

In the Wałbrzych train station Mother said that many Jews lived there. On the platform in Jelenia Góra Russian soldiers were milling about. At midnight, just as Stalin's birthday was beginning, we entered the mountains and the train slowed down.

I was thinking about assimilation, the class struggle, atheism, and memory—about everything at once. I kept separating these ideas like copper wires from an old cable, but the coil just kept curling up.

Once, Karola had said that there are three ways of getting rid of Jews: assimilation, Madagascar, and Auschwitz.

"*Judenrein*," Mother added.

"What about *Meir Ezofowicz*?" Michał expressed surprise. "He left the ghetto himself in order to break with ignorance and fanaticism. No one forced him to."

"That's ancient stuff. When was that novel written?! . . ."

"In 1878," he replied with dignity.

"Don't you think Orzeszkowa was writing about him?" Mother laughed, and recalled how right after the war she'd gone with Michał to see the hut in which he was born. "If only you had seen that poverty!" She clutched Karola's hand. "Exactly like Meir."

Michał and I considered ourselves Poles. He, blond and blue-eyed, did not deny his roots. I, black as tar, when I heard the question "Jew boy?" wanted to lie. I could have, but what for? Every morning I looked at myself in the mirror and for the rest of the day I remembered what I looked like. So I'd reluctantly nod yes, as if to say, 'What can I do?'"

I missed Suchocki. I was depressed by our parting on Wilson Square. Why had I initiated that entire conversation? What had I needed it for?

"The class struggle intensifies the closer we get to socialism." And what did that mean? The better it is, the worse it is?

Mother didn't mince words. "This intensification will lead to war!" she shouted all the time. But did she understand dialectics?

Pan Rosenthal and then Vladimir wanted to know if I'm an atheist. I just smiled. I couldn't even give myself an answer to that question. To give up all hope of seeing those who had died? It was bad enough that I'd forgotten their faces.

Lately, I had started thinking that without memory there is neither a "before" nor an "after." But I was unable to understand what follows from that. Thinking about this, I fell asleep with the knife in my hand.

I dreamed that I heard voices in the attic. I ran upstairs and opened the door with a key on a yellow ribbon. It slammed shut behind me. Darkness. Silence. The smell of medicine. Was it PASS? I brushed against ropes hanging from the ceiling. My cheeks were burning. Mother insisted that every subfebrile state is dangerous. I choked on dust. I started coughing. The stench of phlegm. Pinching my nose, I dropped the key.

The squeal of brakes. It was light already. A snow-covered tablet with the word KARPACZ slowed down and came to a stop. Sleighs were waiting in front of the station. Tucked under a sheepskin, we set off for the *pension.* Invisible birds were chirping. What do they do at night? Do they sleep in the trees?

"Is it far?" Mother asked.

"*Nahe bei der Wang,*" the driver said.

"*Was ist das?*" Mother switched into German.

"*Eine norwegische Kirche.*"

"A church?" She was astonished. "They transported it here from Norway?"

"*Während der Kaiser Wilhelm Zeit.* During the time of Kaiser Wilhelm."

I was sleepy. My eyelids were stuck together. The bells on the horses' necks jingled ever more softly. Suddenly, Mother jabbed me with her elbow. We were driving under an iron gate with a cardboard sign: VACATION RESORT AND CAMP. I rubbed my eyes. The driver led us up a side staircase. His key grated in the lock. Two beds covered with brocade coverlets, night tables, and a wardrobe with a mirror.

"*Gemütlich.*" He smacked his lips.

Finally, to sleep my fill.

—

The smell of breakfast woke me. Mother's bed was made. Had she not lain down at all? With the metal on my boots clacking, I went down to the dining room.

Across from a portrait of Stalin under the slogan

CONGRATULATIONS TO THE PEOPLES OF THE USSR
AND THEIR BRILLIANT LEADER
JOSEPH STALIN
FRIEND OF POLAND

Mother was eating a soft-boiled egg. When I sat down she tied my shoelaces.

The sleigh driver carried in a Christmas tree and leaned it against the wall. Catching sight of the portrait behind the boughs, however, he moved the tree.

"*Das ist ein Jubilar.*" He raised his hands.

Not far from the *pension,* next to the café, above a boarded-up workshop, hung a foot in a sheet-metal shoe. The leg was surrounded by the word HERRENSCHUHMACHER. On the other side of the road was a low hill. Fastening my skis, I walked sideways up to its top. Below were winding streets. Streetlights with smashed lamps. Bowers covered with snow. Everything white. Only the red of tiles on steep roofs. A small church. *Wang?* In the distance, the ski jump sparkled.

I had barely moved when my legs went out from under me. I fell down and lost my skis. Shielding my glasses with my hands, I rolled down the slope. Cold snow behind my collar. I stood up halfway down the hill. I found my skis, tightened the straps, and started climbing up again.

At the top, a young instructor was showing several ladies the basic skiing positions. He was explaining to them that one must always keep one's knees together. I stopped nearby and pricked up my ears.

"We brake with the plow." He brought the tips of his skis close to each other and rode slowly in front of them. "We use a christiania to stop." He pushed off with his poles and, having picked up speed, suddenly made a ninety-degree turn. The snow sprayed. He stopped.

The plow was easy. I tried it and mastered it right away. But the christiania? First, I turned too abruptly and fell over. Then too delicately, and nothing happened. The plow saved me then.

Finally, it worked! I could slow down and stop when I wanted to. Alas, my boots were still pinching me. The Warsaw shoemaker had predicted too rosy a future for them. I pulled out the laces and when that didn't help I looked around for Mother. Black hair and a white fur coat. She was sitting on the terrace. Above her, through a transparent placard:

EXTRICATE YOUTH FROM UNDER THE INFLUENCE
OF CLERGY, IGNORANCE, AND BACKWARDNESS

shone a sign: KAFFEEHAUS. I pushed off. Several plows, a schuss, and a christiania at the café. I stopped beside her table.

"*The People's Tribune.*" Mother handed me the paper with a picture of Stalin. "*The Voice* is already gone." She drew a handkerchief from her bag.

"My boots." I shook them by their laces.

"In the instep?" She wiped her nose.

"Yes."

"In Warsaw, we'll go to the shoemaker." She cast a sad glance at the sheet-metal shoe.

"I'll ski in my overshoes," I declared.

"In overshoes?!!" she shrieked. "You'll freeze."

"They're felt."

"And the skis?"

"I'll shorten the fasteners."

I glided off, following the tracks of skis. The road was covered by shade from the woods that rose up on both sides. The sun shone bright between the mountains. I heard the birds again. They were sitting on snow-covered spruce trees. Gray breasts. Traces of brown and white around their bills. I shouted at them, and when they didn't react, I stopped and, making a snowball, threw it at the tree. Snow sifted off it. They took off, their wings whirring, circled once, and returned to their places.

The ski jump appeared around a bend. Wooden stairs led up to a hut on which a sign was flapping:

FOR AN INTERNATIONALIST ATTITUDE TOWARD THE USSR
AND THE UNITY OF THE ANTI-IMPERIALIST CAMP

Openings could be seen between the letters, cut out so that the wind wouldn't rip the canvas.

Silhouettes of boys showed up black under the ski jump. Squeezing their poles under their armpits, they were gliding down the steep run. However, before I reached them, my feet froze. I started back. Soon I caught sight of the low hill, then the *pension,* the café, and the workshop. The sun was reflected in the metal shoe.

"How are the overshoes?" Mother asked.

"Dry."

"That's good felt."

We went down for supper. The radio was broadcasting Chopin. The Christmas tree was ringed with a paper garland. Candies and star-shaped cookies hung on threads. Among them, firmly seated on zinc holders, candles were burning. Streams of smoke wafted up to the ceiling, bypassing Stalin's portrait.

Everyone was in holiday dress. I hid my overshoes-clad feet under the chair. Green boughs lay on the white tablecloths. Waitresses brought in miniature mushroom pâtés and borscht served in cups. Then dumplings with poppy seeds and wheat with honey and nuts.

"What's this?" I asked Mother.

"It's *kutia*," she smiled. "I had it at my friends' houses before the war."

After the preludes, a chorus started singing a carol. Someone turned up the rheostat.

> Christ is born, he'll bring us freedom,
> Angels are playing, kings are greeting,
> Shepherds singing, cattle kneeling,
> Proclaiming miracles, miracles.

I was reminded of the *novogodnaya yolka,* the Russian New Year's tree, that Michał told me about last winter. I'd have to check if they'd put it up outside the Ministry this year, too.

On the last day of our stay Mother noticed that the shoemaker's was open. She was pleased. At last, someone had taken charge of the shop. Maybe someone repatriated from the east?

"Take him your boots."

There was a card hanging on the door: BOOKBINDER. Could it be a name? Strange. Although I'd heard once about a family of Bookbinders, none of whom had survived. I pushed the door handle. A bell buzzed over my head. A thin man, kneeling among brushes and iron lasts, was opening a metal can. A book protruded from his pocket.

"They pinch." I held up my boots.

"The shoemaker's not here anymore." He tore the lid off. "He fled to Germany."

There was a strong odor. Perhaps the glue that the builders of "The Ship in the City" were preparing stank like that? I sniffed.

"It's cobbler's glue, but it'll do for book bindings." He looked at my feet in amazement. "You're going to freeze your toes off."

"I don't freeze," I said.

"Even in overshoes?" He stood up.

"They're felt."

"Where are you from?" he smiled.

"Warsaw."

"First time in the mountains?"

"Yes."

"Were you on Mount Śnieżka?" He came closer.

"Of course not!" I said. "In overshoes?"

"The peaks are dangerous," he said pensively. "You can fall into a crevass or get lost in the icy interior. Have you heard of the Snow Queen's palace?"

"The one in Lapland?"

"They say it could be anywhere."

"There are no ice mountains in the Karkonosze range."

"Be careful."

"I don't have to be anymore." I started retreating toward the door. "I'm leaving this evening."

"In that case," he took the book out of his pocket, "here's something for the journey."

I looked at the cover. James Jeans, *The Universe.* I hesitated.

"I was going to bind it as an experiment. I don't need it."

"Thank you." I pressed the door handle.

"Goodbye."

—

We boarded the train. The sleigh driver placed our suitcases on the shelf. "*Danke schön,*" he thanked us for his tip. Clumps of steam concealed the platform. The train started moving. JELENIA GÓRA. WAŁBRZYCH. Telegraph poles flashed by rhythmically against the starry sky. Ever since I'd gotten glasses I'd been able to see the stars better, but I wasn't interested in them. Constellations? What did Suchocki see in them? I drummed my fingers on the book. What could I entertain myself with? Mother had packed my Finnish knife in the suitcase.

In Wrocław a fine snow was falling. White dust settled on the windowpane. I opened *The Universe.* Just as in Pani Cesia's French book, there was a photograph of the author in the front of the book. An astronomer was holding his glasses in his hand, and they were casting a shadow on his jacket. He was squinting. Narrow slits between his lids.

Mother believed that near-sighted people shouldn't take off their glasses when they're photographed. She said so in the photography studio on Poznańska Street when the lamps on tripods were turned on. (Then she sent my likenesses to Milo in Tel Aviv and to her sister, Nusia, who had left for New York after the war.)

Looking at the trembling page with the photograph of Jeans, I suddenly saw Anatole France's long face. The writer's eyes were wide open and a little frightening. I turned the page.

> On the unforgettable night of 7 January 1610, Galileo, a professor of mathematics at the University in Padua, looked through a telescope that he had built with his own hands.

I made slow progress. The English names of the astrophysicists and the characteristics of particles were difficult for me. I read some passages several times and marked particularly complicated places with pieces of the parchment in which our sandwiches for the trip were wrapped. I ate rolls with ham and hard-boiled eggs. The snow was plastered to the window. It was warm. The wheels thumped rhythmically.

When I'd finally made it to the chapter about the origin of the solar system, the train began to slow down. The wheels thumped less and less frequently. Finally, the brakes screeched and we stopped.

"Piotrków Trybunalski," the conductor's voice rang out.

Mother's lips moved in her sleep. Soundlessly. Like on Fridays in front of the silver candlestick with four candles. I bent my head down again. From the dense print my eyes caught sight of the name of Kant, whom Pan Rosenthal had called a metaphysician and a transcendentalist.

"All aboard, please! The doors are closing!" the conductor shouted.

The carriage jerked. As we gathered speed, the compartment swayed more and more. The thumping began again.

Immanuel Kant maintained that primeval chaos condensed into nebulae from which the stars and planets erupted. Half a century later, Laplace, using mathematics that were unavailable to Kant, put forth the hypothesis that nebulae, collapsing under their own weight, whirled faster and faster until, under the influence of centrifugal forces, they expelled streams of matter—the future planets.

We were now traveling full steam ahead. The things about which I was reading had taken place somewhere unimaginably far away—or long ago. Meanwhile, it had become hot in the compartment. Rivulets of steam transformed into drops were flowing down the windowpane. I lowered the window. A frosty wind blew in. The lights flickered. A freight train was rumbling down the track paralleling ours. The roofs of the wagons brushed against a cloud, dragging streams of snow behind them.

Mother woke up.

"You've lost your mind! Do you want to get pneumonia?"

I shut the window and went back to my reading.

Nebulae reminded me of whirlpools in the kitchen sink or fireworks on the anniversary of the revolution.

And yet, even Laplace had been wrong, like Kant before him. Jeans demonstrated that nebulae, revolving like gigantic flywheels, would have disintegrated into even parts rather than fling out matter. Assuming that the original rotation was preserved in the revolutions of the sun and planets, he calculated the speed at which our ur-nebula would have had to whirl. Too slowly for an explosion. A lone star could not have given birth to the planets.

I looked out the window again. The snow on the windowpane was melting and slipping slowly down. Steam locomotives were shunting the cars. A large station was approaching.

The planets arose as the result of catastrophes. Collisions weren't necessary. In passing each other, stars produced tidal waves that rose up like mountains and floated away into space. There, they broke apart. Gigantic drops at first raced around both heavenly bodies. Then, they remained in the vicinity of one of them.

A photograph of a boy wearing a scouting uniform fell out of the book. His face was completely faded. Only his glasses and his mouth remained. On his barely visible shirt, the buttons and pointed tip of his scarf showed black. I turned over the photograph. On the back, in round letters, was written: A SCOUT BEHAVES LIKE A KNIGHT.

I slipped the photograph of the previous owner of *The Universe* back into the book.

And what would happen if the catastrophe were repeated? Perhaps somewhere not far away a gigantic body of matter is already plunging. We'll enter its corona. It will swallow us. The jar will explode.

Latin Lessons

In January, Mother made a birthday party for Michał. It was especially grand because he had just been named Director and along with that designation came the right for Mother and me to make use of the government clinic.

Almost every one of our acquaintances came: Cesia and Józio Barski, the Odwaks and the Drobots, Jurek Łobzowski, Lusia and Zygmunt Wierusz, as well as Pan Rosenthal and his wife. Only Karola, who'd been seconded to Kraków, and the Krasnowolskis, who had applied for asylum in London, were missing.

The table in the dining room was extended. Twelve chairs surrounded it. Mother seated the ladies, Pan Rosenthal, and Michał on the six chairs that were part of the dining room set; the other guests seated themselves in the remaining chairs. In the center of the table, glittering in the light falling from the chandelier, were two platters with carp in aspic, decorated with parsley and carrot. Poppyseed-covered rolls, freshly baked that morning, blushed rosy in their baskets.

Michał walked around the table and poured vodka into shot glasses.

Pan Odwak had to sit on a kitchen chair. When he pulled it out, it turned out that I'd left the book by Jeans on it. He picked it up and glanced at me.

"Yours?" he asked.

"His," Mother answered.

"What is it?" Jurek Łobzowski inquired, interested.

Pan Odwak handed him the volume, then served himself some carp.

"*The Universe!*" Jurek exclaimed happily. "I've read it."

"There was also another English book about astronomy." Pan Drobot stabbed two forks into the fish. "About gravitation."

"About the theory of relativity," Pan Wierusz corrected him.

"The Party still hasn't issued its final judgment on Einstein." Pan Rosenthal drew out a long bone from the fish and laid it on the rim of his plate.

"What was the name of that Englishman?" Pan Dobrot took some aspic now.

"Eddington," Michał answered, putting the cork back into the bottle.

—

Pan Rosenthal stood up laboriously, handed his wife his cane, and raised his glass.

"To the health of the birthday man!" He wetted his lips. "To a classless world!"

Pan Odwak and Jurek emptied their glasses.

Everyone started singing "*Sto lat, sto lat* . . . , may we all live one hundred years!"

That was followed by noise and excitement. The guests came up to Michał one by one.

"To two hundred!" Mother kissed him.

"Give me your mug, you horse of God!" Jurek threw himself on his neck.

"*Herzlichen Geburtstag!*" Pani Rosenthal whispered.

After offering their wishes everyone took their seats again.

Pani Cesia found the faded photograph of the scout in the book.

"Is that you?" she asked, turning to me.

"No." I shook my head.

Mother took the photograph from her.

"Then who is it?" she asked.

"I don't know," I shrugged. "It was inside the book."

She gave the photo to Jurek, who examined both sides.

"A pledge," he declared. "Before taking the oath."

"How do you know?" asked Pan Rosenthal, interested.

"There's no cross."

"What's that on the back?" I asked, pointing to the inscription.

"The fifth rule of scouting." Jurek tapped his finger on the yellowed letters.

—

Toward the end of the birthday celebration, when the guests were drinking the last of their coffee and licking the nut torte off their forks, Pan Odwak offered Jurek a Chesterfield. Clouds of smoke filled the dining room. Jurek walked over to the balcony door with uneven steps and opened it a crack.

Mother looked at the exhausted revelers.

"This isn't how I imagined it . . . ," she began.

"What?" Pani Lusia roused herself.

"What it would be like after the war."

"I didn't imagine anything," Pan Józio said.

"Nor I," Pani Cesia admitted.

"They don't want us." Mother lowered her head.

I felt a cold draft and closed the door.

"The achievements of the system will soon convince everyone," Pan Rosenthal assured her.

"That's not the point," Mother muttered.

"And what is?"

"They don't want us," she repeated.

"What does that matter!" He waved his hand dismissively.

"She's speaking about Jews," Pani Lusia said impatiently.

"They dehumanized us," Pani Cesia sighed. "And it's still going on now."

"What?" Pan Rosenthal couldn't get what she was saying.

"We should emigrate," Mother declared.

Pan Rosenthal turned red in the face.

"The duty of communists . . . ," he began, but Mother didn't let him finish.

"In my family there were no communists!" she said coldly.

I froze with a piece of torte in my mouth.

"Andziu!" Jurek Łobzowski wailed. "You're not going to leave me all by myself?"

Everyone burst out laughing.

Karola's absence reminded me of Latin.

Ever since she'd left I hadn't once opened my textbook or reader. Karola knew Latin very well and regularly helped me do my lessons. I had gotten so accustomed to this that when she wasn't there I stopped working entirely. "She abandoned me," I thought, although I knew very well that she had fought against being "exiled to the provinces."

In the meantime, the teacher questioned us at almost every lesson. A couple of times I got out of it with colds and headaches, but then I no longer had any good excuses and I lived in terror. During question time, waiting for my name to be called, I counted nervously just as we had done before a bomb fell: "One, two, three, four, five . . . Leszek Owadowicz!—Good, it worked.—One, two, three, four, five . . . Marek Jakubow!—Ooof!"

The backlog was growing. What to do? Start studying by myself? I didn't particularly like that idea.

"When is Karola coming back?" I asked Mother.

"In May," she replied. "Why do you ask?"

"No, it's nothing," I mumbled. "I'm just asking."
I decided to wait.

But it didn't give me any peace. Why, in any case, had I signed up for Latin? "*Mertvyi iazyk,* a dead language," Żuk had laughed when I told him about my decision in Russian class. In a sense, he was right. In addition to Latin, we could choose as our second language French, German, or English. Wouldn't it have been better to study the language of Jeans and Eddington? Frankly speaking, I went to Latin in order to observe Owado-wicz, Jakubow, and Zabarnicki. I was also fascinated by the teacher.

Even before I decided on Latin I had seen her at morning assembly, which was devoted to the top students. Short, with smoothly combed hair. Wearing a navy blue suit and white blouse. Under her neck she had a metal daisy with sixteen (I counted them later) petals. Bent in the shape of the letter *S,* they clung to each other. Droplets were engraved on the petals and surrounded the polished center of the flower.

She had a calm, powerful voice. Her language was precise. Transferring her glasses from hand to hand, she spoke about the children of poor families. Now they are studying free of charge, but before the war it was different. Many just languished because they didn't have the money for tuition. (Mother also recalled that she wasn't admitted to school when Grandfather was late in paying.)

"Everyone ought to have the right to a decent life." The teacher put her glasses on. "Isn't that so?" She smiled. But her eyes, like my Mother's, were sad.

It was a strange speech. Without big words and concluded with a question. Pan Rosenthal wouldn't have been enthralled with it. After all, he used to repeat, striking his thumb against the arm of his chair, that one must not lift one's eyes from the compass on which the word "revolution" is chiseled. Agitate! Agitate! Agitate! But she?

"Who's that?" I'd asked Żuk then.

"The Latin teacher." He shrugged. "You don't know?"

Did Vladimir remember that he'd sent me to the scouting association? Or did he, perhaps, give up on me, seeing that I was doing nothing? At any rate, he never mentioned anything about it, and recently had proposed that I should edit a wall newspaper. Pleased, I went home and got down to work. I began by forming the letters for the title. I took the shape of the type face from the masthead of *The People's Tribune.* I measured the letters in the newspaper precisely, after which, with the help of a compass and a French curve, I plotted their enlarged shapes on red paper. My yellow Hardtmuth mechanical pencil with an H5 lead, a present from Pan Odwak from his trip to Czechoslovakia, left a barely visible trace. Some of the letters fitted perfectly immediately. Others I constructed from fragments of the remaining letters. Late at night, I cut them all out with a razor blade and placed them in a book to keep them from being crushed.

The next day, I left home early. The streetcar, arriving from the terminus in Wierzbno, was almost empty. I took a seat next to the window and placed the tube of bristol board, wrapped in newspaper, on my knees. After several stops it became crowded. Unwilling to give up my seat to anyone, I stared out the window. It was snowing. There was no wind and it was cold. The snowflakes were settling on the trunks of cars and the caps of pedestrians. They were piling up on the sidewalks. In Śródmieście, it was already snowing so heavily that the shop windows were beginning to disappear.

The trolley moved quickly and quietly. That's how the white-laquered sleighs from Andersen's *Fairy Tales* might have driven, the sleigh on which the Snow Queen abducted Kay. I winced at the thought that a sliver from her mirror had fallen into his eye.

I stood up near Gdańsk Station and, holding my tube upright, began squeezing my way through to the front. I got off on Veterans' Square. The snow crunched under my shoes.

Our classroom was dark. Ice flowers glistened on the windowpanes. I turned on the lights and, unrolling the sheet of paper, fastened it to the wall with thumbtacks. I pasted the red letters onto it with flour-based glue and, taking a step backward, looked closely at my work. Something was missing. But what? I took a soft pencil and began drawing little people. They were walking in single file. Each one supported one letter of the title.

Voices could be heard in the corridor. The girls showed up. Then Żuk and Łopatka were standing behind me.

I took chalk out of my pocket and made the little people more distinct, giving them various details.

On the left side of the newspaper I placed a list of the top students and surrounded it with flowers. Near the names of the girls Abramowska and Weissówna I colored the centers of the daisies yellow. On the right side, I attached a caricature that I'd cut out of *The People's Tribune* depicting Cardinal Mindszenty and Marshall Tito with a bloody axe. In the center, inside a border of loops, was a photograph of a Chinese who was painting a portrait of Stalin on a grain of rice.

"What's he doing?" asked Żuk.

"Making a birthday present."

"It already was his birthday."

"For his seventieth," I explained.

"He's already started?" Żuk laughed.

The bell rang. The first lesson that day was Polish. A teaching intern, whom Żuk called "the wood grouse," was going to teach us. The topic: Socialist realism. The wood grouse had promised that he would bring new poems.

I sat down in the last row. I crumpled the damp newspapers and put them in Suchocki's empty seat. Then I slipped my hand under the desktop and touched the book that was lying there.

The Universe . . . The collision of heavenly bodies was inescapable. Everything was only a matter of time. Cosmic catastrophes, however, did not remind us of the explosion of bombs. They were, rather, epochs of mutual penetrations. Anyway, considering the enormous distances before something like that will begin, millions of years will pass and we'll have time to escape to the stars.

I remembered Latin. Today, after our long break. In the same classroom where the Union of Polish Youth meetings took place. On the other side of the corridor. What should I say if she calls on me? The newspaper!

The door opened wide and the intern appeared in it. He had a battered briefcase and acne on his face. His long, red neck protruded from a coarse wool sweater. As he entered, a large fly flew in behind him and, buzzing loudly, started circling the classroom. It struck the windows several time and then froze, motionless, on the window frame.

A winter fly! When I'd fought with Jurek Łobzowski in the living room recently, I'd caught my boxing glove on a strip of flypaper. Tearing off the honey-coated tape, Jurek had said that often an insect will hatch in winter from an egg that was lying behind the stove. After returning to the dining room I'd asked Michał what he thought about that.

"There are no flies in winter," he proclaimed.

"And thank God for that!" added Mother.

The intern threw his briefcase on the desk.

"One month ago a Convention of Writers took place in Szczecin," he began. "The participants embraced socialist realism. Without going into details, which are too difficult for you, I can say briefly that 'writers are the engineers of human souls.'"

Żuk giggled. The girls, who were busy reading or doing their homework for other subjects, looked at him disapprovingly. Boy, is he going to get into trouble! But the intern didn't notice anything. Abramowska and Weissówna went back to working on math. Ania Wendek started coloring worms on a cross section of an apple that she'd copied from her textbook. Anielka Klepacka opened a novel.

Without letting go of the book, I shut my eyes. Stars, planets, and even asteroids shared immense distances. I was flying among them, alone, like a fly in winter. Where to? Why? For what purpose? I recalled the night in Trzebinia when Pan Akerman died (*infarctus myocardi*). I had imagined then that I was like a tossed stone and I yearned for some hand to catch me in my flight.

The intern pushed his chair back.

"Socialist realism is not a simple continuation of previous literary directions," he said. "It's a qualitative leap. The proletariat, who have changed the course of history and now are designing new channels for our rivers, yearn to read works that glorify the grandeur of our times." He raised his voice. "Books ought to encourage us to march! This can't happen, however, at the cost of vulgar simplification of reality. Varnishing and schematism are unacceptable."

The fly took off, fluttered across the classroom, and landed on the open notebook of Łopatka, who sat in front of me. Its black-and-green wings shimmering, it moved sluggishly in the direction of the lesson topic that he'd written out at the top of the page. A freckled hand slid stealthily behind it. Along its calluses (from the gymnastics parallel bars) ran a clear life line. When the fly crossed the word "realism," Łopatka caught it. A loud buzzing issued from his clenched fist.

The intern didn't notice a thing.

"It's in the nature of things that a communist is a positive character," he continued cheerfully. "Our hero does not yield to temporary difficulties. The road to the New is paved with class optimism. What about suffering? Loneliness? Poverty?" he asked rhetorically. "Those are bourgeois anachronisms! In our system there is no place for 'the tragedy of human fate.'"

And he started telling us about Nikolai Ostrovsky, a youth from Shepetovka in the Ukraine, who, guided by his infallible class instinct, had fought in Budyonny's cavalry. Wounded many times, plagued by constant operations, paralyzed, losing his sight, finally completely blind, he dictated his memoirs. His personal misfortunes did not cloud the optimism of his novel. Generations of Komsomols grew up on his *How the Steel Was Tempered*.

I suddenly saw the bookcase at Pan Rosenthal's. *Kak zakalialas' stal'—How the Steel Was Tempered*. Between Stalin and Gorky.

Flying, I thought about whether it's possible to string up a net in space. On what? I started searching for points to pin it to. Pan Rosenthal didn't like it when I "got bogged down in details." He insisted that I couldn't see the forest for the trees. "Oh, what's the use!" I sighed to myself. "There won't be a hand there!" I gave my fantasies full rein and immediately espied iron links. They were sparkling with the reflected light of the stars. I caught one of them and stopped. Now what? Should I hang in infinity? I spread my fingers wide and glided on.

The intern pulled from his briefcase sheets of paper with poems on them.

"Literature should popularize the Party's program. It should be a clarification of Marxism-Leninism." He pulled his chair closer. "The Party ennobles our thoughts. It gives us joy in life. It teaches us to love Mickiewicz and Chopin."

He picked up the first sheet:

> We have returned transparency
> To the rivers—and greenness to the trees.

The fly struck the windowpane and fell onto the sill. Anielka Klepacka moved away from the window with disgust. Łopatka, noticing that the intern was looking for something in his papers, reached for the fly and placed it on my notebook.

I drew a fence around it in ink. Little people behind the pickets. One, two, three . . . I didn't get to do more than that. It came to and flew off.

The intern straightened up.

"We model ourselves on the leading literature of the world," he declared. "The creative stream of Gorky, Sholokhov, and Mayakovsky flows broadly."

He picked up the next sheet:

> To the cooperatives
> of Polish Wysocice
> the path from the Kremlin
> is straight as a ray.

"Literature should be proletarian in content and national in form." He pulled his sweater away from his neck. "That is why we draw from our native well springs: Wasilewska, Broniewski, and others. We also reach for the bookshelf of progressive creators from the west: Aragon, Eluard, Neruda, Hikmet, and Belojanis." He took a deep breath and warned us: "Let us not forget, however, about their bourgeois, biblical, and nihilistic tendencies."

Grażyna Kownacka (from the Children's Home) wrote in beautiful calligraphy: THE DISEASES OF OUR ORCHARDS. Then she put her head down on her arm. The navy blue pinafore rose and fell evenly on her back.

Żuk dipped his pen in his inkwell and flicked it with his finger. The penholder started rotating, drawing a rapidly diminishing cone.

"It's not a question of describing the world, but of changing it." The intern raised his voice. "Writers cannot live in ivory towers. Industry needs them. The Six-Year Plan will soon come into effect. Can it be fulfilled without writers? No," he answered instantly. "The enemy does not sleep. Someone must sound the alarm."

He picked up the third sheet:

> If the tractor cannot plow,
> If the sowing doesn't take place,
> If the norm breaks down in a hand,
> And the foreman stinks of vodka,
> If movement in the workshop has stopped,
> And the motor has burned out its heart—
> It's a fact,
> The class enemy is at work.
> The struggle continues.

Michał also talked about a grand plan that would encompass the entire economy. Every detail. They were working on it day and night. Everything had to be foreseen. He came home later and later. He explained to Mother that the priorities were changing. There was a need for more iron and steel.

"For what?" she asked.

"The international situation is becoming more dangerous."

"They'll lead us to war!" She raised her eyes to heaven.

"There won't be a war," he said impatiently.

She also feared collectivization. She remembered how the Russians closed the market in Borysław. Now again the government was sticking its nose into everything! What kind of a state is it, anyway, that deals in parsley?!

I looked at the intern. He was pimply. Unattractive. A screwup. What would Pan Rosenthal and Vladimir say? "Objectively, he does good work," I seemed to hear their voices. "Personal characteristics are insignificant. The only thing that counts is the Cause." I protested in my heart that it's not enough to want to do something, one must also be competent. After all, it says "from each according to his ability."

The intern put the papers away in his briefcase.

"Writers . . . literati, have to purify themselves." He fastened his watch. "Confess before the Party. This applies particularly to the older ones."

And he recited from memory:

> The Party is a whip,
> It is the beating of our hearts,
> > It is our mother.

Żuk pulled a clownish face and struck his breast.

"Mea culpa," he squeaked. "Mea great, great culpa!"

The intern turned to him furiously.

"What are you doing?" he snarled.

"I'm sorry." Żuk bowed his head.

The bell. Standing up from my desk I told myself that poets are necessary to propagandize for the revolution. I decided I would read *How the Steel Was Tempered* in its entirety, in Polish, since my Russian had been getting worse and worse since our repatriation from Galicia.

During the long recess Vladimir came over and looked at the Chinese man for a long time.

"The seventieth." He nodded approvingly. "It's important!"

We went out into the corridor.

"And why is there nothing about the Six-Year Plan?" he asked. "Nothing! It's fundamental. Steel is our daily bread. Always ask me ahead of time. Two heads are better than one. In the next newspaper include something about meatless days. We have to struggle against enemy propaganda."

We turned around near the columns.

"Aha!" he reminded himself of something. "Who is carrying those letters?"

"Little people."

"Elves," he laughed mockingly.

"For decoration . . ."

"Unnecessary. Totally unnecessary."

The bell. I shuffled over to the other side of the corridor. Everyone was there already. I sat down in back, near the window. The ice on the windowpanes was melting. The sky was turning gold and red. Although the teacher hadn't arrived yet, it was quiet and peaceful in the classroom. Leszek Owadowicz sat bent over his reader; Marek Jakubow was writing out words from the dictionary; others were looking through their notebooks, and those who were conversing did so in hushed voices. I looked at the assigned text. I couldn't understand a single word.

"The newspaper! Only the newspaper!" I thought.

The brass door handle shuddered and the Latin teacher appeared in the doorway. She was wearing the navy blue suit in which I'd seen her at that roll call. Her brooch sparkled. She was holding the class grade book and the reader under her arm. Her pocketbook dangled from her shoulder. We stood up.

"*Salvete, discipuli.*" She let got of the door handle.

"*Salve, magistra.*"

She signaled us to sit down and stepped onto the podium. After she had laid everything down she took her eyeglasses out of her bag and, without putting them on, looked around the classroom.

"The text that I assigned last time," she came to the point immediately, "is from Livy." She turned around and wrote carefully on the blackboard: *Ab urbe condita*—From the founding of the city. "This event took place two thousand four hundred fifty-seven years ago." She put down the chalk. "And yet, the question, 'the public good or the personal good,' is still relevant. After what your older brothers and sisters experienced fighting in the Warsaw Uprising, Livy's hero, more or less their age, should be particularly close to you."

The Warsaw Uprising? Pan Rosenthal didn't express himself particularly favorably about it. "London criminals," he said. "They wanted to overturn history." And Vladimir had declared at a meeting of the Union of Polish Youth that the goal of the Home Army's leadership was to create an accomplished fact and wrench power from the hands of the people.

"They rrrequested on Rrrussian rrradio that the uprrrising should begin," came a voice from the classroom, *r*'s rumbling.

"That's not true!" Vladimir shouted. "The uprising took the Soviet leadership by surprise. Comrade Stalin ordered the Red Army and the Polish detachments that were fighting alongside it to regroup and drive out the Germans."

From the propaganda brochures for editors of the wall newspapers posted where the public could easily read them, I knew that after liberation the Red Army soldiers, the *krasnoarmeitsy,* had removed two million unexploded shells and constructed a pontoon bridge across the Vistula. From Russia had come flour, prefabricated houses, thirty streetcars, and a radio broadcasting station for Raszyn. Comrade Stalin even sent urban planners under the leadership of Nikita Khrushchev to plan the reconstruction of the capital.

And in the streetcars, snatches of conversations reached me through the clattering of the wheels, the squeal of the brakes, and the whining of the electric motors:

> They fired at us as if they were shooting ducks . . . Through the sewers . . . I can still smell that stench today . . . The shell smashed into the corner supporting beam, the furniture flew out onto the sidewalk, but there was no fire . . . I jumped out through the window . . . It killed both nurses, but he's delirious. He's seeing visions of the Russkis on Książęca Street . . . She kept crying that the child was hungry, so I said, "I'll bring you a bit of pumpkin from the garden plot, or some beets or potatoes." "No, because they're winding up the 'cow' and shelling us!" So guess who got hit! . . . By morning it had grown quiet. People emerged from all the courtyards and ruins . . . In single file, in a dense crowd . . . We saw the Germans only on the second day . . ."

On the way home from the clinic (my sinuses were obstructed), I asked Dziadzio where he was during the Uprising.

"Here." Without taking his hands off the steering wheel, he indicated the direction of Hoża Street with his chin.

What was the people's attitude toward the authorities?

"They're dissembling," Mother said impatiently during the endless conversations about antisemitism.

"They'll change," Michał exploded.

Where did that anger come from? After all, opinions about the present and the future were not contradictory. Obviously, Mother and Michał recognized each others' intent more from their expressions and tone of voice than from words. I, too, always applied "they'll succeed" and "they'll change" to the government and communism; after all, I felt that it applied to everything.

Having survived in Borysław and been brought up in Ligota, Trzebinia, and Warsaw, I didn't doubt that Count P. would have won secret elections. On Feliński Street, however, although I always remembered my former schools, I had begun to believe that it is possible to change the world. What did it matter who the passengers in the streetcar would vote for since they didn't know where historical necessity lay? Heart and even common sense are not enough. Only by assiduously studying dialectical materialism could one recognize the truth.

But! But! How, in that case, did simple people who weren't familiar with Engels's *Anti-Dühring* distinguish good from evil? "By class instinct!"

I head the voices of my mentors again. "Absolute truth and morality do not exist. Every class has its own."

—

"During the siege of Rome by the Etruscans," the Latin teacher continued, "Caius Mucius Cordu, with the agreement of the Senate, set off for the enemy's camp in order to kill King Porsenna. Let us begin with the words spoken by Mucius in the Senate. She opened her book. "*Transire Tiberim, patres . . . ,*" she read and looked around the class.

I bent my head down and started counting. What a horrible feeling!

"How did you translate this sentence, Joasia?" The Latin teacher turned to a girl who was sitting on the first bench.

The blonde girl stood up and read aloud: "Senators, I wish to cross to the other side of the Tiber and, if I succeed, to enter the camp of the enemies not like a looter or an avenger of the plundering carried out from that side. I intend to carry out a greater deed with the help of the gods." She straightened her braid.

"Very good." The teacher turned the page. "As we know from our own experience, however, even the best, most thoroughly thought-out plans are not always crowned with success. A thousand causes can contribute to this. Mucius killed a scribe by mistake. He was captured and brought before the king. Let us turn now to Mucius's words that he addressed to Porsenna: '*Romanus sum civis, C. Mucium me vocant . . . .*'"

One, two, three . . . She looked at a girl seated next to the wall.

"I am a Roman citizen, my name is Caius Mucius," she mumbled, not lifting her eyes from her notebook.

The Latin teacher nodded.

"*Hostis hostem occidere volui . . .*"

This time I counted to four.

A tall boy bobbed his Adam's apple and adjusted the thick glasses on his nose. "As an enemy, I wished to kill an enemy and I have no less courage to endure death than I had to carry out murder."

I had the impression (and it was not the first time this happened) that everyone was speaking in verse. Both in Latin, which I didn't understand, and in Polish. There was something thrilling about this, and I envied those who were capable of reading and translating fluently. Besides which, I was captivated by the teacher's voice.

I had to finally buckle down to studying! And not wait for Karola's return!

"*Et facere et pati fortia Romanum est . . .*" The Latin teacher looked up from the book.

One, two, three, four, five . . . She was looking at me.

I stood up and, staring at my notebook, which was covered with little people, didn't say a word.

"Well, we're listening," she encouraged me.

"I was working on the newspaper," I mumbled.

There was rustling and giggling.

"So, what of it?" She quieted the class with a gesture.

"I didn't have time to prepare."

"It's the same in every class," she said coldly. "If you want to come here, you have to be prepared."

"But I . . . ," I started stammering.

"You could have chosen a different language," she interrupted me. "No one forced you to take Latin. Besides which, politics cannot interfere with studies. Sit down."

She turned her head away. "The duty of a Roman is to act and to suffer," she translated herself. "*Nec unus in te ego hos animos gessi . . .* ," she read after a moment.

I didn't even see whom she called on for the answer.

"And not I alone had such intentions toward you," came the nasal voice of Marek Jakubow. "There is a long line of those who desire the very same distinction."

"The next sentence," the Latin teacher requested.

"*Hoc tibi iuventus Romana indicimus bellum,*" Marek read. "It is we, the youth of Rome, who declare war against you."

I raised my head slowly. The eyes of everyone were fixed on the teacher. She was still standing.

"*Cum rex simul ira incensus . . .* ," she read the beginning of the next sentence and glanced at Owadowicz with a smile.

He stood up and, tossing back his hair from his high forehead, began softly.

"The king, infuriated and horrified, threated Mucius with torture if he didn't reveal everything."

Modulating his voice, Owadowicz addressed Porsenna.

"I am doing this for you so that you might understand how low a price the body commands for those who seek glory," and imitating Mucius, who after these words placed his right arm into the fire that he was to be burned in, stretched out his arm in front of him, his fist clenched.

This reminded me of the old woman who often came to the butcher shop on the ground floor to get bones for her dog. Her husband used to be the custodian of an apartment house next to St. Michał's. (He died of typhus in Miechów where they were sent after the Uprising. She came back and took up residence in the cellar underneath the ruins of her building.)

She would sometimes look at me and fix her gaze on my eyes.

"Our people don't have eyes like that," she said to the butcher.

Before the war she knew many "little Jews." Hitler finished them off. She nodded her head. Of course, they let themselves be slaughtered like sheep. One way or another, death awaited them. They could at least have dragged a few Germans into the grave with them.

"What are you babbling about!" Pan Stankiewicz took down a kielbasa from its hook and, cutting off a few thin slices on the marble counter, threw them onto the scale. Then he took a roll out of a basket, cut it in half, and placed the fragrant slices on the more porous half.

The custodian's wife put the bones into her frayed and darned bag and, hunched over, left the shop.

"She doesn't have a dog," the butcher jeered. "She eats them herself."

He handed me the roll.

I went up to the landing and sat down on the windowsill. Staring at the door to our apartment, I started eating.

Why hadn't I reminded the custodian's wife about the uprising in the ghetto? What would Mucius have done in my place?

The king freed the Roman. Owadowicz opened his fist. His long, spread-out fingers reminded me of Chopin's hand in the black-and-white photograph in the old Baedeker.

"*Trecenti coniuravimus principes iuventutis Romana . . . ,*" he read Mucius's words, and then continued in Polish, "Three hundred of the best of us young Romans took an oath to oppose you in this way. My lot was drawn."

"*Mea prima sors fuit . . . ,*" the teacher interrupted him.

He glanced at the text.

"Right." He nodded. "My lot was drawn first," he corrected himself. "The others will come in their own time."

"Thank you." Finally, she sat down.

Telling us the story of how Porsenna concluded a peace treaty with Rome and Mucius received the nickname Scaevola (Left-handed), the Latin teacher opened her grade book, took a fountain pen out of her bag, and put on her glasses.

"Why do we still understand Livy?" she asked softly. "Have we really changed so little?"

And only then did she start checking the attendance list.

My ears were burning.

In March, Michał left for Switzerland to conclude a trade agreement and to deal with a matter concerning a commuter rail line in Zakopane which Poland had not paid for because the war had broken out.

Soon after, Dziadzio delivered a package of bananas to us that "the Director" had sent via diplomatic courier. A white envelope was attached to the package. The envelope contained a letter and a photograph of the Jungfrau. Michał, stripped to the waist, was standing on its peak.

"He bought a gold Schaffhausen watch," Mother read. "But he had to pay separately for the band. The Swiss are misers." She folded the letter. "You're getting an Omega," she added a minute later.

I tore open the wrapping paper on the package. A sweet smell filled the dining room.

She sniffed. "They're rotten."

They ran through our fingers.

In April, he flew to London.

The next day, his secretary phoned. The Director is in West Germany. Visibility in England was poor. No airport would let them land. They returned to the continent. Fog there, too. They landed in an open field, breaking a wing.

From then on, the telephone rang every day.

"They're waiting for the wing," the secretary repeated.

"It's probably Russian," Mother prophesied ominously. "They have to send it from Moscow."

A week passed before they reached England.

After he returned, Michał said that the Germans had fixed the plane immediately but spent a long time investigating whether the Poles were spies.

He was enchanted with London. His lodgings weren't far from Parliament and he'd had *porridge* for breakfast.

"What's that?" Mother asked with interest.

"Oatmeal. Only better."

In London he'd met Julek Unter, who had been drafted by the Russians in Borysław together with Milo. The sole survivor of the Unter family had left Russia with Anders's army. In Persia he'd fallen ill with malaria and sailed to England on a ship filled with German prisoners of war. He regained his health there. He fought at Caen and Falaise. After the war, he settled in Hastings. He had recently become engaged to an Irish nurse. They were going to be married in a church.

"In a church?!" Mother asked, taken aback.

"He's Catholic."

"Since when?"

"I didn't ask."

From Julek Michał brought Mother a length of light brown woolen cloth; from himself, navy blue silk for a long dress. I received a sweater. Trying it on, I rolled up the sleeve so it wouldn't cover my Omega.

In the morning, Mother made oatmeal for Michał.

"Well?" she asked irascibly. "Isn't it better than that . . . ?"

"*Porridge,*" Michał prompted.

"Yes, that."

"It's different," he weaseled out of it.

She grabbed a clean spoon and, scooping up some oatmeal from Michał's bowl, slipped it into my mouth.

"Taste it!" she commanded.

I swallowed.

"Well?" she asked.

"I don't know what *porridge* is supposed to taste like," I answered, following in Michał's diplomatic footsteps.

"Oatmeal is healthy," Michał suddenly changed his defense.

"That's the point!" Mother agreed.

I glanced at the enameled pot from which she was pouring our coffee and said that I couldn't find *How the Steel Was Tempered* anywhere. Even in the library no one had heard of it.

"What is it?" Michał laughed. "A metallurgy text?"

"A revolutionary novel," I explained.

"Russki. . . ." Mother stirred in the sugar with her teaspoon.

"Yes."

She rolled her eyes.

In May, Michał started bringing home books from the office. Aleksandr Bek, *The Volokolamsk Highway;* Aleksandr Fadeyev, *The Young Guard;* Valentin Kataev, *A White Sail Gleams.* Each of them bore a green stamp: REVIEW COPY. First, I placed them on the carpet in the living room; then, stretched out in the armchair, I read them and, cutting the pages with my Finnish knife, blew the paper dust off my shirt. Done with that, I placed them in the bookcase where they looked more modest than the leather-bound German volumes that Mother had thrown out in Ligota when she noticed the swastikas stamped on their spines.

One day, Mother sent me down to get the mail. I ran down the stairs and opened the mailbox. Inside was an envelope addressed in careful handwriting. I looked at the reverse side. The Latin teacher! I dragged myself slowly upstairs. Mother interrupted her work folding pierogi and tore open the envelope.

"You've been looking for trouble and you've found it," she announced. "She writes that you're not doing any work and that you're in danger of failing at the end of the year. There's only one test left."

She looked at me over the letter.

"Not a word to Michał!" She started throwing the pierogi into a pot of boiling water. "He mustn't be upset."

The next day she went to Feliński Street.

I locked the door with the chain and looked around the entrance hall. Under the coatrack, where my motorized bike had once stood, two umbrellas protruded from the tin bucket. Across from the dining room were the entrances to the living room and the kitchen. The living room door was closed, but a wooden bowl filled with strawberries could be seen on the window sill through the open kitchen door.

Hugging myself, with my arms crossed and hands on my shoulders, I moved along the entry hall. That Latin was going to cost me dearly. I had apparently lost my sense of reality. Just like the Decembrists. I stopped at the end of the hall. On the right was Mother's and Michał's bedroom; on the left, mine. About face. A few steps. I entered the living room.

It was dark and stuffy in there. On the carpet, my Finnish knife glittered among the books. Let it lie there. I stretched out in the armchair and took off my glasses. I put them on again, however, afraid that a piece of plaster from the peeling ceiling might fall in my eye. I slipped my hands under my head and closed my eyes.

Snow started falling from the ceiling. So thick that I couldn't even see the edge of the sleigh that was silently gliding along. The flakes were large, like the chickens of Pan Ptak from Trzebinia, who had given up his profession as an engineer and built himself a shed with an incubator.

"Where's he taking me?" I glanced anxiously at the driver and remembered Janka's words: "If they grab you, pray out loud." But I couldn't remember a single prayer. Only the multiplication table, and that only up to seven. My teeth started chattering. The driver turned around with difficulty, then handed me his whip. "We're driving into a classless world!" he shouted and threw his white fur coat over me. I had the impression that an avalanche had slid down. The cold reached my heart. "It's the end," I thought, but soon I felt fine. When I dug myself out of the snow he was no longer there. The discarded reins were slipping down from the sleigh. I was struggling to pull them in with the whip when the doorbell rang.

—

I dragged myself out of the armchair and walked over to the door.

"Who's there?" I asked softly.

"It's me," came a familiar voice.

"Karola!" I nearly ripped the chain off the door. "Just in time! I've got a D in Latin! Mother's at the school right now!"

I led her into the dining room where the wind was lifting the curtain. I brought over the strawberries, which she was crazy about and, watching as she dipped them in powdered sugar, asked if she had returned for good. She nodded.

I was saved.

Soon a car stopped beneath the balcony. Hearing Dziadzio wish Mother good night, we went out to the entryway.

"Karola!" Mother dropped her keys into her pocketbook. "When did you arrive?" And without waiting for an answer she switched into her complaining voice. "He's facing a grade of unsatisfactory! Can you imagine?!"

"In Latin . . . ." Karola smiled roguishly.

"How do you know?" Mother asked, surprised.

"I found out. Through my ears."

"Michał will kill me!" Mother wrung her hands.

"Don't be afraid," Karola calmed her down. "I'll take charge of this."

We went into the kitchen. The frying of the pierogis began. With my eyes fixed on the frying pan, I listened to Mother's story.

The Latin teacher was waiting for her in the teachers' room. A small woman. In a gray skirt and white blouse. With a metal brooch near her neck.

"Single?" Karola asked.

Mother shrugged and looked at me.

"No," I said. "Married."

She didn't even smile when she greeted her! Got down to business immediately. Your son is not applying himself. In general, he's not studying. And he explains everything with politics. He's doing this, he's doing that. He's editing a newspaper. Only not his Latin texts. In the final analysis, it's his business. He could have chosen a different language. But since he chose this one, his first obligation is to study and not engage in politics.

Mother placed a plate in front of me. She knows this herself. Hadn't she forbidden me to requisition crosses? Hadn't she asked why I needed to get involved with those newspapers? Hadn't she kept repeating that Michał and I had gone mad, because only madmen believe that it's possible to build socialism? She slammed the frying pan. But how could she say this to a stranger? So she had only inclined her head and whispered confidentially that she isn't too strict with me because I had gone through a great deal during the war. And that woman had immediately responded, "He's spoiled!"

"Do I spoil him?" Mother grasped Karola's hand. "You tell me."

"You're going to burn the pierogi!" Karola warned her.

Mother took the frying pan off the stove.

"I got the impression that she doesn't like me. Or you," and she dished out pierogi for me.

Michał came home late.

"Have you eaten?" I heard Mother's voice.

"No."

I smelled roux.

"How are the pierogi?" she asked.

"Excellent."

I pulled the quilt over my head.

"More?"

"What about him?" Michał asked.

"He's already eaten."

He knocked his fork against the porcelain platter.

"*How the Steel Was Tempered* hasn't come out yet. It won't be published for another year," Michał said abruptly.

"What will be published?" Mother asked in an impatient voice.

"*How the Steel Was Tempered.*"

"And why does that concern me?!"

"He asked, so I found out."

"Then tell him, not me."

I crammed Latin every day. Karola explained the grammar to me, tested me on vocabulary, and made me translate at random texts that we'd worked on. Many of them were from Livy. Oh, if only the Latin teacher would call on me now for an answer! I would translate as if reading from a score. At the very least like Owadowicz, and maybe even more fluently! Confidently, rhythmically, almost like poetry! Why hadn't I applied myself to studying earlier?!

Every so often Mother would open the door and bring fruit for Karola and strong tea for me. Then, leaning against the stove, she would repeat soundlessly phrases that she had worked on once upon a time in Gymnasium. I didn't even notice when she left the room. Only afterward, I'd realize that she wasn't there anymore.

We finished studying late at night when we heard the slamming of the Demokratka's door. Before Michał came upstairs, the reader, the dictionary, and our papers were already in my briefcase.

Then, in bed, I repeated to myself sentences from the translations or, turning on the light, I'd run my eyes over the columns of Latin words, reordering them and translating them randomly. If I didn't recognize one of them I looked in the dictionary and began all over again. How many verbs do I know? What is "to remember"? Remember!

The day before the test we worked till midnight. When the clock struck twelve Karola said she was going home to the hotel.

"I think I'll grab a taxi," and she got up from her chair.

"Michał isn't here yet," I protested. "Let's study until he comes home. Dziadzio will give you a ride."

"We've done all we can."

"There's nothing more to do?"

"Not anymore."

After the exam, several of us, the worst students, milled around outside the teachers' room waiting to learn our fate. When Joasia finally brought out a bunch of tests, I snatched the paper from her hand. A C! I slipped the paper into my pocket and walked out of the school. Across Veterans' Square I set off in the direction of the Gdańsk Station. The air was heavy. It looked as if it was going to rain soon.

Striding onto the viaduct I imagined that my limbs were getting longer and my muscles were growing. I could easily leap across a wooden horse now, like Łopatka in gymnastics class. Slapping my hands on the leather mane, soaring across with outspread legs, and a bouncy landing with arms thrust out.

I also had the impression that my eyebrows and hair were growing lighter. What Mother hadn't been able to accomplish during the war was happening now without benefit of peroxide. Blinded by the sun, I closed my eyes. With every step, Śródmieście loomed larger. The palace on Bank Square. The two ghettos. The large one and the small. Along the footbridge connecting the walls Jews were walking, as in the photograph in *The People's Voice*. A patrol appeared on the viaduct. The occupation! But I wasn't afraid of anything. More similar in appearance to Suchocki than to myself, I passed by the Germans calmly. I smiled at the thought of *szmalcownicy* waiting in vain inside courtyard gates.

"I am not who I am." I opened my green eyes.

I was the same. Under the viaduct, alongside a wooden building on which the white-and-red flag was fluttering, freight trains were rolling, their doors wide open.

The streetcar pulled up. I jumped onto the step and, grasping the handrail, pressed myself against other passengers in order to straighten my glasses on my nose. Only when we reached Śródmieście did I manage to get inside. It was turning dark rapidly. The wind was blowing beyond Union Square. The long branches of trees waved above the trolley wires. Rain was pouring down. We rode past the Wedel apartment house where Pan Rosenthal lived. I hadn't seen him in a long time. Grabbing the leather hand-holds, I walked out onto the front platform. The motorman rang his bell at the intersections with Belgijska and Dolna Streets. St. Michał's Church slid past. It was here that the priest from Queen Jadwiga School had lifted his hand and made the sign of the cross over me in parting. How is he? Somewhere in the distance there was a bolt of lightning. The window with the chandelier flashed by. My stop. The grass was sparkling wet. The butcher shop was empty. I ran upstairs.

Mother (*left*) with Cesia Barska in Łazienki Park

Mother (*right*) with Karola Sznepf, her closest friend

Michał

Wikta with her little daughter, Helusia, and Julek

Me at age 14

Helena Liberowa (the Latin teacher)

Portrait taken when I passed the graduation exam

E.

let us love one another

Birthday Conversations

The wind blew up every so often, driving flakes of snow. They flew past the window in all directions. Some of them struck the windowpanes and slid down, accelerating over the wet spots.

Mother and Michał were preparing to leave for a reception at the Soviet Embassy and Karola and I, along with Michał's one-legged brother, Julek, who'd come to ask Michał for help because his gas station lease had been canceled, were playing thousand. The cards were greasy and had red backs, with the exception of the king of hearts, which came from a blue deck.

"Eighty," I declared, laying down a queen of diamonds.

"You have to add something," Julek explained to Karola. We were teaching her how to play.

"What?" she asked.

"A low diamond," I advised.

"What if I don't have one?"

"Then a higher one."

She put down a jack.

"All right then, we're done with the red suits!" Julek slammed down an ace and took the trick.

Mother pirouetted to show off her new dress. A navy blue circle of silk swirled over the parquet floor and then fell gently onto her glossy pumps. She raised her hands and glanced at Karola.

"It's not too long?" she asked Karola.

"That's what they're wearing now."

They put on their fur coats. While fastening his buttons, Michał promised that if he should meet someone from Petroleum, he'd have a chat with him about the lease. But it wouldn't do to get one's hopes up because the retail sale of fuels and oils was being transferred to state control.

We heard the rumbling of a motor and the slamming of a car door. Before Dziadzio reached our floor Mother and Michał had put on their hats and, wishing us a pleasant game, left the apartment.

I walked over to the window.

The balcony railing was covered with frozen snow. Black tire tracks showed up against the white roadway. On the opposite side of Puławska Street, beyond the streetcar tracks, a Christmas tree stood in front of St. Michał's. It had been installed in the morning when I was on my way to school.

The Demokratka rolled out from under the balcony and, spattering snow, pulled away from the curb. Its brake lights glowed red as it approached the intersection and then its left-turn signal came on. Dziadzio crossed the tracks, passed the church, and took off in the direction of Śródmieście.

I returned to our game.

"Where is that embassy?" Michał's brother handed me the deck.

"On Szucha Avenue." I dealt out the cards slowly. "Opposite the Ministry of Education, where the Gestapo had their headquarters."

Like Michał, Julek had lost his wife and several-months-old son during the occupation. The son died first. Mother said they had had to take him from the place where he was hidden because the people there had stopped feeding him. He was no longer in any condition to live and a cousin who was a doctor had put him to sleep with an injection. And how did the wife die? Mother didn't know.

Recently, Julek had married Wikta Astman who, even though she'd been pregnant, had survived and given birth to a daughter right after liberation. The child's father perished and mother and child were all alone. Now they'll return to life. Julek has money.

Mother asked me if I remembered that Wikta had given us fifty rubles on the third day after the Russians arrived. Yes, I remembered that. Lately, I was remembering various things. I had forgotten the faces of the dead for a couple of years but now, when I'd lost hope that I would ever "see" anyone again, the whole process had begun to reverse itself.

The first time I noticed this was while I was looking through *Twenty-Four Scenes from the History of Poland.* One of the illustrations depicted the morning before the battle of Grunwald. At the foot of a hill on which the Polish king stood surrounded by great noblemen, two knights had stopped. White metal shields with red crosses hung from their arms. In their outstretched hands they held gifts from the Grand Master: naked swords in case the king didn't have his own. Contempt and anger were painted on the noblemen's faces. The Lithuanian glowered, thinking about the battle awaiting him.

That's what Moszek looked like when he carried me to our last hiding place—in the well. I sat on him as if on a horse, holding on to his forehead with my hands. Mother ran alongside. We slowed down outside the town and while we were moving alongside the edge of the forest we heard the distant rumbling of an airplane. Moszek craned his neck and headed in among the trees. "It's a Kukuruznik." I didn't take my eyes off him until he sat down. Only then did I calm down and believe that he wouldn't leave me there. Suddenly, the earth shuddered as if something heavy had landed on it. "A bomb!" Moszek screamed, but he didn't even get up; he was resting before the journey.

Since that moment, my memory had been returning rapidly. One day I "saw" Grandma Antonina, who was born in Vienna and who spoke to everyone, except me, in German. Once again, she was wearing her black dress with its button fasteners. Later, I "smelled" the odor of ether, and Romuś came back to my memory. A strange woman was carrying him, asleep, out of the apartment. Grandfather slammed the door behind them, placed the broken ampule in his pocket, took us in with a glance, and slowly removed his wire-rimmed glasses.

We were getting close to a thousand.

Karola gave Julek her cards and looked intently at his bushy eyebrows. "They've gone gray," she sighed. "You look like St. Nicholas."

"It's because of that station." He started shuffling the deck. "Damn the place!"

But at home he had a piece of paradise. Under Witka's care, everything shone. A housewife to the core! And the little one! A marvelous child! She plays Beethoven for days on end. The music teacher can't praise her enough.

"La-la, La-la, La-la-la-la, La," he hummed.

"What's that?" I asked, interested.

"*Für Elise,*" Karola explained.

I looked at her with respect and started adding up our scores. They were jotted down on a sheet of paper with Broniewski's poem, "A Word about Stalin," on it that I had ripped out of some brochure or other in order to copy the piece for my last wall newspaper. Recently, I had become an agitator, and once a week before school began I gave talks in the department store on Paris Commune Square, which people still called by its old name, Wilson Square. I taught the sales ladies about dialectical materialism and how existence shapes consciousness, and after lecturing to them I ran to Feliński Street in order to make it to my first class.

Julek announced that he had won, and pushed the paper away. Karola raised the poem up to her eyes (she wore thick lenses) and started reading it out loud, exaggeratedly accenting the phrases:

"Revolution is the locomotive of history . . ."
Glory to its machinists!
So what if enemy winds should blow?
Glory to the burning sparks!

Pan Rosenthal praised me for placing an excerpt from "A Word about Stalin" in our newspaper. That was the red thread that weaves through the history of the workers' movement! Marx called revolution the locomotive of history, Lenin set the machine in motion, and Kaganovich—not Broniewski, but Kaganovich!—said that Stalin is the great machinist of the locomotive of history.

"When?" I asked, curious.

"For his sixtieth birthday."

"In 1939," I calculated rapidly.

Glory to those who amid fire and frost
Endured like a granite block,
Like will and reason incarnate,
    Like Stalin.

"Beautiful!" Karola put down the paper. "Except that he didn't stand 'amid fire and frost.'"

"What do you mean, he didn't?" I asked, surprised.

"Others stood for him." Julek reached for his cane.

"Drop it!" I shook my head disapprovingly. "They saved our lives."

"Which 'they'?" Julek asked.

"The Russians."

He laughed.

"Not my life." He cut the deck. "Mauthausen was liberated by the American army."

I started dealing the cards again and already, in the first round, the "blue" king fell to me.

"Lucky dog," Julek muttered.

"Are you surprised?" Karola giggled. "Today is Stalin's birthday."

That morning our school assembly was especially grand. Red banners hung from the windows. In their rosy glow, rows of green shirts and red ties could be seen. Between the columns a banner had been strung up on which the following was written in paper letters:

OUR TOP GRADES MAKE STALIN HAPPY

There, where the Latin teacher had once stood, Vladimir was speaking. He kept raising his arms and his large hands protruded from his cuffs. He looked like a rooster attempting to fly. Pan Rosenthal would have had no reservations, however. The orator never took his eyes off his compass on which the word "revolution" was inscribed.

He raised his voice.

"Working people of all the world search for the Kremlin stars and with respect pronounce the most beloved name."

"Stalin! Stalin! Stalin!" we chanted for a long time.

Then the top students declaimed Broniewski's poem:

> The train of history is rushing onward,
> Behold the century's semaphore.
> The revolution has no need of glory,
> No need of grandiose metaphors.
> What it needs is a strong machinist,
> He is the One:
> Comrade, leader, communist—
> Stalin—a word like a gong!

The streets along which I returned home were decorated with red flags. Ruby stars with portraits of Stalin glowed beneath the rooftops. Even on the loudspeakers attached to the streetcar pylons red bows were tied. From everywhere came the sounds of a cantata composed by Khachaturian for the seventieth birthday.

The streetcar rocked gently. Around me, snowflakes were melting on coats and hats. Drops of water dripped onto the newspapers protruding from people's pockets, on which various parts of Stalin's face could be seen.

On Puławska Street, where there were no loudspeakers, the voices of passengers reached me. Closing my eyes, I made an effort to imagine their faces. I rode that way for two stops. Only at the bazaar on Dworkowa Street did I look around again and saw with amazement that no one looked anything like what I had imagined.

Outside, women were milling around near snow-covered stalls. They carried net bags full of potatoes or clutched loaves of bread to their bosom. Mother believed that Dworkowa Street had gone to the dogs. Fortunately, she no longer had to come here because Pani Krzakowa brought us everything.

The streetcar started up.

I thought that seventy is a serious age. What will happen when Stalin dies? Will everything continue as before? Or maybe everything will come to an end? What then? Why do I push myself forward? Jurek Łobzowski had put the identical question to me when I joined the Union of Polish Youth. "Everyone's doing it," I'd snarled at him then.

What would I say now?

Ideas? Yes. Simple and beautiful. First, the original commune. Then the world was divided into the poor and the rich. Profit. Alienation. Hatred. History is the story of class warfare. Spartacus, peasant rebellions, and the French Revolution, 1789. Capitalism. The proletariat in factories. Marx and Engels write *The Communist Manifesto*. The Spring of Nations, 1848; the Paris Commune, 1871; and Bloody Sunday, 1905. The twilight of imperialism and the Bolsheviks. The Leninist theory of revolution. Finally, October and the building of socialism. Stalin.

From the mechanism of history arose the succession of social-economic systems. Inscribing an immense circle, humanity was returning to the commune. Nonetheless, this was progress, because the end differed qualitatively from the beginning. Not everyone understood this concept and before our history exams someone would always ask me what this really means. How were they to know that I, too, confuse the laws of history and commit errors in their dialectical interpretation?

Once, talking with Pan Rosenthal about the fundamental principle of the society of the future, "From each according to his ability, to each according to his needs," I asked him if we would live to see socialism.

"Socialism exists already," he shrugged.

"Where?" I asked, taken aback.

"In the Soviet Union."

"Since when?"

"Since 1936," he replied. "When the peasants joined the kolkhozes everything became communal property."

"How can that be!" I screamed. "After all, they don't have 'according to their needs.'"

"That won't happen until communism."

The crowds beneath the red banners? The Party secretaries on the daises? Most definitely. Power impressed me. I was disgusted, however, by boorishness and didn't believe that the end justifies the means, although Pan Rosenthal insisted that I was confusing Machiavellianism with far-sightedness.

A career? Of course. I'd be graduating in a year. True, I didn't know yet what I would study, but all professions were "political."

Riding past St. Michał's Church, I thought that doctors will do everything to extend Stalin's life, and started pushing my way to the exit.

We continued playing.

Waiting for Karola to bid, I walked over to the window again. It was already dark outside. The streetcar from Śródmieście was approaching. I couldn't see it yet, but it was sending off so many sparks that the sky was lit up every so often as in a thunderstorm.

I closed the curtains, but before I went back to the game I turned on the light in the hallway. I'd been doing that a lot lately, and Mother followed me and turned it off. "This is not a palace," she complained. "Electricity costs money." I was afraid that I would "meet" Father. I had the impression that he was lying in wait in dark places and wanted to strike me. In town, I avoided alleys where wooden annexes and ruins limited the field of vision. I arrived early for the lessons I gave at the department store in order to meet one of the saleswomen and walk with her down the long, gloomy corridor that led to the store from the rear entrance. Wasn't it worth it to turn on the light in the kitchen as well?

"Come on, make a bid," I addressed Karola.

"One hundred?" She laid down the queen and king of clubs hesitantly.

"Sixty," I corrected her; "they're not hearts."

"Since the German state arose . . . ," Michał's brother began out of the blue.

"Two states," I interrupted him, "the GDR and the FRG."

"I'm not talking about Wilhelm Pieck's people."

"Why?" Karola expressed surprise.

"They don't have what they need to cover their asses!" he bristled. "But an 'economic miracle' is taking place in Bonn. Maybe Adenauer will pay something?"

"To whom?"

"The Jews."

"For what?" I asked automatically, still thinking about the light in the kitchen. Only when I realized that they were looking at me as if I were a madman did I quickly add that I wouldn't take even a groschen from the Germans.

"A second Michał!" Julek laughed, and moved on to the question of emigration. "Now that the Arabs have gotten kicked around it should be possible to emigrate to Palestine."

"To Israel," I corrected him.

"La-la, La-la, La-la-la-la, La," he whistled. "But how?"

Mother and Michał came home before midnight. Although they'd only walked from the car to the gate, their coats were powdered with snow.

"Well?" Julek asked.

"There are no more leases; it's over." Michał gestured that it was hopeless.

Mother started telling us about the reception in the embassy. It took place on both the second and third floors simultaneously. Some kind of picture representing Stalin hung in every room. Pan Cukrowy, whom they met as soon as they entered, led them to a hall in which many guests were clustered about a copy of a work recently painted in Moscow. In a gold frame, at the top of a marble staircase covered with a red carpet, stood the generalissimo. One step lower, their eyes fixed on him, members of the Politburo stood applauding. Mother could identify only Molotov, but Michał and Pan Cukrowy knew all of them. Other gentlemen were also pointing out to the ladies the individuals on the canvas, whispering their names.

Mother observed that only Asians were leaning over the balconies in the painting. "Kazakhs!" she whispered to Michał, who pulled her away from the painting.

Russian melodies could be heard everywhere. But they weren't able to make their way to where the band was playing. A lot of Polish and Russian generals. Women in long dresses. "Every one of them!" and she gave Karola a meaningful glance.

"Tables set with food. A kind of buffet," Michał observed. "But in the Kremlin waiters walk around offering food."

The biggest attraction was Marshal Rokossowski, the new Minister of National Defense. I knew from the brochures prepared for editors of news sheets that he had served in the tsarist army during the First World War and had become acquainted with the Bolsheviks at that time. Then he fought with Kolchak and Baron Ungern von Sternberg, was wounded twice, and captured the rail line to Vladivostok from the Chinese.

"Exceptionally handsome." Mother grew animated. "But he blushes like a girl."

Pan Cukrowy said that the marshal (he referred to him as Kostia) is an eccentric with elegant manners. On his staff in Legnica the officers wore white gloves and reported in French.

"Does he look like a Pole?" Karola asked.

"At least he doesn't look like a boor," Mother replied.

"Do you know what he did before?" Karola fixed her eyes on me.

"When?" I didn't understand.

"Before he defended Moscow and Stalingrad."

I shrugged.

"He was in prison!" She spat out the words. "The only thing that saved him from execution was that the Germans went too far. Isn't that so?" She looked at Michał.

"Yes," he mumbled.

"What kind of boots was he wearing?" I interjected.

"Jackboots," Michał said.

"That can't be right!" Mother exclaimed. "I saw shoelaces."

"Stalin slips his trouser legs straight into his boot tops," Karola informed us.

"Not always," I shrugged.

"Look at him, the know-it-all!" she giggled.

"Alas!" Mother waved her hands. "He should only know his Latin that well."

That night I dreamed that a woman wearing gloves pushed the armchair aside and lifted up a trapdoor that was concealed behind it. Through the small opening Mother and I crawled into an attic. There was an empty bucket with a wooden lid beside a straw mattress. A beam stretched above the mattress. I bent over so as not to hit my head on it.

The woman looked in at us.

"Where is your sister Nusia?"

"In a well," Mother replied.

"And Kopcio?"

"Also in the well. He's writing."

"About what?"

"About Jews."

The smell of coffee woke me. Mother and Julek were eating breakfast. The woman in the gloves was probably Pani Hirniakowa in whose attic we had hidden. Right after the war she brought us a bag filled with boxes of matches as a present. "What happiness that you're alive!" and she embraced Mother with her cotton-gloved hands. "He, too! It's a real miracle."

I hadn't thought about her until now. Mother, too, never mentioned the women who hid us. She only said that she had no hard feelings toward anyone who made us pay, she understood those who didn't help (she herself would have been afraid), but she couldn't forgive those who betrayed us.

In the bathroom, I looked at myself in the mirror. I wondered if Nusia liked the photograph that was taken in the studio on Poznańska Street. I still hadn't thanked her for the rice she sent me from America. "All you know how to do is take!" Mother complained.

And Kopcio? Is he alive? They were going to operate on his stomach ulcer in Tel Aviv. His book, *Earth Without God*, was in the bookcase in the living room. Mother said that his description of us wasn't exactly nice.

I went in to the dining room.

"So tell me." Julek removed his suitcase from the chair and invited me to sit down next to him. "Are we going to build socialism?"

"We're on break now," I replied.

Mother poured me coffee.

"Do you remember," she asked, "how Papa brought me coffee with milk and sugar to our hiding place because I wanted to drink it one more time?"

I shook my head no.

"In a vodka bottle," she attempted to help me.

"In the garret," I suddenly remembered, and Grandfather's exhausted face flashed before my eyes.

"You see!" she cried triumphantly. "I always said that he remembers everything."

"He brought morphine then," I said. "In two little cloth sacks."

Julek opened a jar of jam.

"Morphine!" He smeared his bread with the red jelly. "That was a luxury."

—

We were still sitting around the table although no one was eating or drinking anymore. Mother was complaining that it was impossible to talk about anything with Michał because right away he'd start yelling. And what is it that she says? Only the truth.

"It's that job." Julek made a face.

"He works like a dog, but it's not enough for a better life."

"Who earns more today?" He shrugged his shoulders.

"Vice Ministers," she answered. "And private businessmen," she added provocatively.

(I had a feeling that she was going to say something about "private businessmen" because she bore a grudge against Michał's brother for not helping us financially.)

"He'll become a Vice Minister," Julek winked.

"When?"

"The later, the better." He toyed with his cane.

"Have you heard something?" She looked at him suspiciously.

"They're starting to devour each other. They threw out Gomułka because he didn't want collectivization. Now they're starting up with General Spychalski. They've already forgotten that it was his boys who threw the bomb into the Café Club."

I myself had read in *The People's Tribune* that Marian Spychalski "was expelled from the Politburo for political blindness, nationalism, and the expression of erroneous theories about the extinguishing of the class struggle." Similar things were written about the Hungarian Laszlo Rajk and the Bulgarian Traicho Kostov before they were hanged in October and December. How was it possible that in all the countries in our bloc enemies had infiltrated into positions of power?

Mother lowered her voice.

"Imagine," she whispered, "they arrested Dr. Lis, who's as innocent as a lamb. For spying on behalf of Switzerland!" She slapped her forehead. "They even put his wife in prison. And what does she have to do with it? Who'll take care of the children?"

"The Jews are to blame for everything." Julek pulled a clownish face.

"Why?" Mother didn't understand. "Lis is a Jew, after all."

"The antisemites don't care," he sighed. "The Jews are in power. And that's that."

"What about the Jews from Wałbrzych? They live like beggars."

"People see the ones at the top. The poor don't count."

—

Once, in Kraków, I met a Jew from Wałbrzych. Mother and I had traveled to Kraków from Trzebinia to see Karola and to walk around in the Rynek and the Planty gardens. He approached us as we were standing beside the Mickiewicz monument in the Rynek. I was waiting for the trumpeter to appear in the steeple of St. Mary's.

"*Shalom.*" He stroked his golden peyes.

Mother and Karola perked up at the sight of him.

"*Mein kind.*" He stretched out his hand to me. "*Vi hayst du?* What is your name?" he asked me in Yiddish.

Mother told him my name.

"And I'm Elijah." He didn't let go of my hand.

The golden sun slid onto Mickiewicz's head. The shade beside the monument diminished and vanished. Red with embarrassment, I looked around.

"*Ir voynt in Kruke?*" Karola asked, and explained to me that she was asking if the gentleman lives in Kraków.

"*Ikh bin haynt gekimen fun Wałbrzych,*" he answered.

"He arrived this morning . . ." and she broke off, seeing that I understood.

The trumpeter in the steeple played the *hejnał*. A few pedestrians were making their way among the pigeons that were sitting motionless on the paving stones.

"What are you doing here?" Mother asked, curious.

He smiled and again said something in Yiddish.

"He's looking for Jews," Karola translated.

—

"Yes, yes," sighed Julek. "A lot of Jews are connected with this government. From before the war. Who formed the Polish Communist Party?"

"Not just Jews!" Mother bristled.

"Not just Jews, but a lot of them."

"Józio says that they were twenty-five per cent."

"Józio who?" asked Julek.

"Barski. Cesia's husband. Anyway, what kind of party was it? A couple of thousand! And only a quarter of them were. Among the Jews that was just a handful!"

"Not for antisemites."

"Their families were ashamed of them," Mother recalled. "They considered them madmen."

"That's of no interest to Poles."

"But aren't we Poles?" I asked in a hushed voice.

Mother and Julek exchanged glances and laughed indulgently.

"They summoned the most important ones to Moscow and butchered them there," Mother returned to her theme. "I read about it in the paper."

"In which one?" I asked, anxious.

"In *The Moment*." She thought about it. "Or maybe it was in *New Age*, which they used to bring in by the deluxe express from Lwów."

I calmed down. Who cared about pre-war newspapers!

"It's interesting that the people who fled Galicia before the Germans still haven't had enough." Julek spread his hands. "After all that they saw in Russia."

"And what was it that they saw?" I inquired, my interest roused.

"Ask Michał. He was there."

"And thank God for that," Mother interjected. "Otherwise, he would have perished."

"That's not the point!" Julek said impatiently. "They're under the impression that they're going to change the world, that they'll create paradise on earth, but they're only a tool . . . a horse to do the dirty work."

"Michał works like a dog," Mother picked up on the thread.

"It all serves Russia," Julek said.

"It serves the working people." I took up the polemic.

"This system wasn't born here. The Poles don't want it . . . The Russians are using the Jews."

"Oh, sure!" I exploded.

"You'll see! You'll be convinced. When they finally do their thing, they'll get kicked so hard that they won't be able to pick up the pieces."

"So you have heard something after all!" Mother became anxious again.

Julek inclined his head toward hers.

"And what if they make this the seventeenth Soviet republic?"

"This is Poland, not Russia!" I protested.

"Is something brewing?" Mother clutched at his sleeves.

"Brewing or not brewing," Julek twirled his cane. "Do you remember what happened in Borysław? There's one thing I'm certain about: this is no business for Jews. They shouldn't get involved in it, they shouldn't push themselves forward. It will end badly for them."

"Do you want poverty to return?" I asked. "Discrimination? The ghetto?"

"Poverty doesn't have to return. It's already here. All you have to do is look. As for the ghetto, it's you and Michał who are sitting in it. Except that it's of your own free will. You have no idea what people say about you."

"Michał . . ." Mother began.

"Michał should watch out."

"You tell him."

       —

That evening I was sitting in the living room. Mother's, Karola's, and Julek's voices reached me from the dining room. Politics and Jews. Always the same thing. Ever since *Pravda* criticized Israel, Mother had been insisting that *kosmopolity* really means *evrei,* "cosmopolitans" being a code word for "Jews." And although she believed that Germans should all be shot, it was the Russians she was afraid of. London was broadcasting that they were arresting writers in Moscow. Only Jews! An accident? No one knows what will happen. Who will defend us? Didn't Jurek Łobzowski say that it would take a hundred Poles to rescue one Jew, but one would suffice to betray a hundred?

"What's that got to do with it?" Karola asked, surprised.

"Nothing."

       —

What to do? Could one remain a communist without trusting the Russians? Careers aren't made at home. Mother herself said when we were coming back from the Rynek, after we met Elijah, that it was impossible to wangle anything in Wałbrzych.

Outside of our home, however, Jewish themes didn't exist. Not in the school on Feliński Street where I gave talks in the younger classes, supplementing the texts in the brochures with anecdotes from novels and astronomy books. Nor in the department store on Wilson Square, where I spoke to the saleswomen about the creation of added value, using examples from Marx's *Capital* that touched on the production of shoes. Nor in the streetcars that I rode throughout the city.

       —

After Michał's return, when everyone was bent over the barley soup made with broth from veal bones that Pani Krzakowa had brought, Mother said that the Russians do nothing out of the kindness of their hearts. They saved us, that's true, and thank God for that, but she doesn't have even an ounce of trust in them.

"They're plunderers!" Karola shouted. "They grew up under the Mongols' whip and then they subjugated their neighbors. And yet they say that others have designs against them."

"Hitler validated those fears," observed Michał.

"But didn't they love him for two years?"

"To gain time. One way or another," Michał continued, "they have no one to fear anymore. The border of socialism runs through the center of Europe. Russia is so large that no intervention threatens her. True, they lost millions of soldiers, but they gained security for centuries. And that's why they won't retreat even one step."

"Then why do they frighten us with imperialists?" asked Mother.

"In order to mobilize society."

"For what?"

"For work."

Michał wiped his lips with his napkin and turned to the birth of present-day Poland. In his opinion, it was the approach of the Red Army to Berlin, and not the blood shed by Poles, nor their heroism, that had determined our fate. For some people the Russians were liberators and for others enemies, but that was of no importance. One has to look truth in the eyes. Things could not have turned out differently without another war.

"The Allies . . ." he began, but Mother didn't let him finish.

"They sold us out at Yalta," she snapped and walked out to fry the schnitzel.

"They had us by the short hairs," Michał's brother sighed.

I remembered Pan Rosenthal's favorite saying. "No one pulls someone else's chestnuts out of the fire."

"Only Russia," Michał started toying with a toothpick, "guarantees our borders. The West would have given the Recovered Territories to the Germans, but without Gdańsk and Wrocław there'd be no Poland."

"And Lwów?" asked Karola.

"I said that the Russians won't retreat even a single step."

"They're going to turn us into one of their republics," Julek warned.

"Nonsense!" Michał said, offended. "Nothing is threatening us. Unless we bring ourselves to that point by our own brawling. We have to make our peace with the fact that, like the liver or other organs, we are part of a larger organism."

"We're going to kiss their ass," his brother muttered.

"A typical error of Luxemburgism!" I pointed my finger at him.

Rosa Luxemburg's errors were Pan Rosenthal's crown of thorns. What pained him the most was that before her death she had opposed the formation of the Comintern. Why? Out of fear that the *raisons d'état* of the country in which the revolution triumphed would dominate the workers' movement. "How could she!" he lamented, "how could she not see that Russia is the bulwark of socialism! Did she lose her class instinct? Did she forget that the general line is sacred? Only a martyr's death saved her from being expelled from the Party."

I smelled the schnitzel and everything flew out of my head. The others also turned toward the kitchen.

"It's not ready yet," Mother called out, guessing the reason for the silence.

Michał snapped his toothpick and proposed that we start thinking in European categories. It's time to get out from behind Borysław village fences.

"There were no village fences in Borysław," Mother's voice could be heard again. "Maybe in Ratoczyn, but not in Borysław."

Michał let the jibe against his birthplace pass and continued stoically.

"Armed opposition in Poland has been liquidated. Had we not done it ourselves, the Russians would have invaded."

"Why would they have to invade?" Karola raised her eyes. "They're already camped in Silesia."

Mother carried in the schnitzels and for a long time the only sound was the clinking of cutlery. Only after the second course did Michał assert that the initial stage of reconstruction of the country is already behind us. Poland has emerged from the ruins. The Six-Year Plan now embraces the entire economy and will transform it. Soon we will become a modern, industrial country. The foundation for extraordinary economic progress is planning—national and bloc-wide. The Council of Mutual Economic Cooperation in Moscow takes care that industries in the socialist countries don't duplicate each other, which is particularly important for our steel mills. He added that if it weren't for imperialist encirclement, everything would happen much more rapidly.

"And you said that there won't be a war!" Mother interrupted him.

"*Si vis pacem, para bellum.*"

"*Vos hot er gezogt?*" asked Julek, and Karola started translating again. "If you wish for peace, prepare for war."

For dessert we had the Jewish question. Mother observed that no one had ever concerned themselves with the Jews. Michał said she was right.

That's how it was. Now, however, there was a system of social justice and the state was defending all nationalities. It's high time to rid oneself of fear and stop that endless chattering about the Jew this, the Jew that. The river of history will spit out antisemitism.

"La-la, La-la, La-la-la-la, La," his brother hummed.

But socialism cannot build itself. Historical processes have to be helped along. The end of alienation is the beginning of assimilation.

"If I'm not Polish enough for someone, he can kiss my . . ." Karola bristled.

"Mine, too," Mother seconded her.

"I am a Jew," said Michał. "But that doesn't mean that I have something to brag about."

"But I do," Karola insisted.

"And so do I," I heard Mother say.

"What do you two really want?" He was losing his temper. "With such an approach to things it would be best to emigrate."

"How?" they asked in chorus.

Michał restrained himself. It wasn't a matter of national assimilation alone, but also of political assimilation. Struggle itself isn't enough. It's necessary to drag people who are indifferent over to the correct side.

Karola picked up a bar of Lindt chocolate and broke off a piece.

"The Party rules everything," she sighed.

"Not at all," Michał smiled mischievously.

She looked at him uneasily.

"Then who?" Karola wondered.

"The Politburo. The smartest ones."

Why that smile? After all, that's the way it really is. The Party represents the working people, the Central Committee represents the Party, and the Politburo represents the Central Committee.

"If they're so smart," asked Mother, picking up crumbs of chocolate from the table, "then why do they throw mud at each other?"

—

Looking at her, I remembered how she told me that Michał had proposed to her. I was gnawing on a *bolshoi shokolad* that I'd gotten from him that day, and she was picking up the crumbs from the chocolate bar.

Suddenly, Pani Hirniakowa's attic appeared before my eyes with the beam beneath the ceiling! Father was lying on the mattress, coughing constantly. Mother, curled into a ball, snuggled against him, touching her lips to his forehead.

It was from there that Moszek took us away. But what happened to Father?

He'd remained at Pani Hirniakowa's. How could we have known that a bomb from a Kukuruznik would fall on her house?

We reached the well at night.

Moszek started lowering me into the hole. It smelled of moss.

Someone grabbed me by the legs.

"Let go!" Kopcio's voice echoed among the stones.

Through a hole in the stonework surrounding the well I was pulled into the interior. I fell onto Nusia, whose face was wet. Then Mother came down. Nusia flung herself at her. They were hugging and crying.

I saw Kopcio in the morning. He was sitting near the stones that blocked the entrance and writing in a notebook on which a thin stream of light was falling.

"Who's going to read that?" Mother asked from the darkness.

"Jews," Kopcio answered.

"There aren't any Jews anymore."

Karola wrapped the rest of the chocolate in its silver and violet foil and collected the empty glasses on a tray. I sighed with pleasure as, on her way to the kitchen, she turned on the light in the hall with her elbow.

Mother started clearing the plates. She was short and graceful, like a girl from my class. Her short black hair revealed her neck above the collar of her sweater.

"It's late," she turned to Karola. "Spend the night with us."

No Help from Anywhere

The black carpet with two concentric wreaths of rosy red flowers covered the living room floor. In our post-German apartment in Ligota it had fit perfectly. In Trzebinia, it barely filled the center of the colossal drawing room. Here, in contrast, it had been necessary to roll it up a bit to fit it in. This destroyed its symmetry: the side table with the glass top and two armchairs were outside the border formed by the wreaths. From where I sat I could see the mahogany bookcase, the green sofa on the right, and on the left the piano. A porcelain figurine of a naked red-haired woman was on the piano along with a crystal vase in which, instead of flowers, there was a silver-colored pump for a soccer ball. On the wall behind me hung two paintings (also, like the majority of our furnishings, brought here from Ligota). One of them represented bluish mountains surrounding a glittering frozen lake. In the light from the lamp the lumps of congealed paint cast small shadows. There was a time when I thought that my childhood memories were hidden in the depths of that lake and ever since then I thought of this painting as *The Past*. In the other painting, women, no doubt fishermen's wives, were standing on the seashore and looking into the distance at boats with billowing sails. It was impossible to say whether the boats were sailing away or coming in to shore. Whichever direction they were headed in, however, I liked this painting a lot more, and I named it *The Future*.

All winter, no matter how often I looked at the sheet of ice covering the lake, the face of crippled Janka emerged from beneath it, and without even closing my eyes I would immediately start seeing her from below, from under the bed in that room in which I had hidden with my mother.

"Your papa is sick, so Mommy has to go to him in the ghetto," I again heard Janka's voice. "You're safe here with me. We have potatoes. My papa knows your grandpa and can't praise him enough. You will be a man like that, too, someday."

"What kind of man?" I sighed bitterly. I hadn't lived long enough even to know them! And turning my gaze to *The Future*, I thought about the adults among whom I was growing up.

Various ties connected them and for the most part they lived harmoniously, yet an invisible boundary divided them. On one side were Michał's brother and Jurek Łobzowski and also, although in a somewhat different way, Pan Józio and all the women. On the other, Michał and his colleagues from work—Pan Cukrowy, Pan Wierusz, and also Pan Odwak and Pan Drobot. And, of course, Pan Rosenthal.

I felt fundamentally better with the people from the first group who, aside from Mother, demanded nothing of me and were never angry with me about anything. With Julek I played cards or listened to his stories. Jurek Łobzowski always had something that attracted me: sometimes boxing gloves, sometimes chess (which he let me win), or old books that he'd found in secondhand bookstores. Pan Józio treated me with refined politeness, and when I went to see him on Hoża Street he would conduct me through the gallery in his long, dark corridor as if I were a little prince. Karola? She was always friendly; even studying Latin with her didn't bore me too much. Yes, that is all true. But at the same time, their endless bitterness and open dislike for the regime irritated me. They were always complaining and even cursing (Mother and Pani Lusia most of all, and yet, as Michał said, "they took advantage of the benefits of socialism by the fistful"). As for Julek, after the fruitless intervention in the matter of his gas station, he simply foamed at the mouth. Infuriated because they were forcing him into the "building of socialism," he started cursing his persecutors. "They got an urge for pyramids! The shitty pharaohs! Haven't they embalmed Lenin?" I attempted to explain to him what a "planned economy" is, but he only smiled politely and said that the Russians had already made that clear to him by nationalizing in 1939 the piece of land on which he had drilled for and found oil.

"We would have been rich!" he sighed. He decided to return to Kraków.

Mother telephoned Dziadzio so he could drive Julek to the train station.

A moment later Pani Lusia phoned with the news that there were camel-hair blankets in the special store. But only a few. Mother said goodbye to Julek and ran for the streetcar, not even waiting for the car.

She hadn't been gone a minute when Jurek Łobzowski dropped in; he had just received his diploma in chemistry. We made tea to toast his success.

"I still remember how you used to visit us in Ratoczyn," Julek smiled. "You and Michał would study in the pasture while tending the goat."

"That's the way it was," Jurek agreed.

"It was, but it's vanished," Julek sighed, and started massaging his knee.

"Does it hurt?"

"This prosthesis is useless."

"Order a new one."

"I'll do that after I leave."

"Do you want to emigrate?"

"What else? Do you think I'm going to sit here?"

—

All of them, although they were kind to me and entertaining, struck me at the same time—as adults—as not serious. They treated their social and professional positions, their workplaces and, in general, our reality almost as if it were a disaster. Real life began for them only in the evening when they got together to gossip, to mock, and to bitch. I often wondered how much of this they could stand and what they really got out of it. Don't they see that they've gotten stuck in one place and are buzzing like flies trapped on flypaper? Finally, I came to the conclusion that if I were to start thinking like them and to catch their discontent and negativism, I would not go far. And so, slowly, because it was not easy, I started moving over to the side of Michał and Pan Rosenthal.

—

Michał had little time for me and we barely spoke. While I was getting ready for school he, smelling of cologne and with his still-wet hair combed, ate his *porridge,* put on his suit jacket (the golden arrow of the Pelikan always protruded from its pocket), and went down to the car. In the evening, by the time he'd rested after supper and read his *Neue Zürcher Zeitung,* I was already in bed. And if I happened to start talking with him about something, he immediately grilled me about school. He'd ask if I'd already done my reading and, flicking his finger against the arrow on his pen, make faces at Mother to show that he didn't believe me.

Recently, I'd been avoiding him like fire, because, made anxious by the news from Moscow, he could explode very easily. Mother told Karola that the Russians were looking askance at Jews. Officially, everything was supposedly the same as always, but everyone knows what it's like there. Michał showed her intercepts from the Central Committee: London kept broadcasting about those writers. The best thing would be to go abroad to one of their diplomatic posts. She kept begging him to go to the Minister and request a position as trade representative in London, Paris, or Rome, but he "has his honor."

"An idealist," Karola sighed.

"And what do I get out of this?" asked Mother.

One way or another, Michał had a kind of magnetism that attracted me. It was connected mainly with his position and his mind. I had often seen how, in Ligota and Trzebinia, the engineers and refinery workers had greeted him. He was planning Poland's foreign trade. He traveled to foreign countries. Mother had framed his photograph from the Jungfrau and a snapshot from London where he was standing next to Westminster Abbey with Julek Unter. There were days when our telephone rang nonstop. He was always needed. He was supposed to become a Vice Minister.

He excelled in everything. He spoke Russian beautifully, he knew French from high school, and he'd taught himself German in order to read the Swiss newspaper. What a memory! In addition, he knew the complicated chemical formulas of minerals, fuels, and medicines, and skillfully used his slide rule made of fragrant exotic wood with a low coefficient of friction. A smooth white facing, like piano keys, covered the surface of this device on which was carved a scale with numbers more precise than the hours on the watch face of his Schaffhausen. And the poetry! How many times had he helped out when someone, trying to recall some quotation, forgot words or lines! He'd offer the words immediately and without a single mistake.

—

In contrast to Michał, Pan Rosenthal almost always had time for me. Indeed, he seemed to need my company more than I did his. He would phone, invite me, find various pretexts for meetings. Besides which, he treated me like a grown-up. He wasn't interested in my school work. We talked about important matters: historical turning points, wars and revolutions, the future of humanity and of the world. When I visited him he would immediately get up from his armchair, out of which horse hair was always poking, walk over to the shelf, and pull out a book. He recited. He persuaded. He babbled on without interruption.

After a while, however, these perorations became tiresome. Every conversation turned into a monologue full of abstractions and slogans. Besides which, Pan Rosenthal seemed not to think (I didn't realize this immediately), but only to have a ready answer for everything. Once, when I asked him how democratic centralism differs from dictatorship, he responded that the fate of the world depends on several Marxists with great heads. "And the masses?" he went on, although that had nothing to do with my question. "The masses are impotent." The wheels of history grind everything that stands in their way. Only those who run after the carriage, without even seeing the road, will survive. So it's a good thing that someone is sitting on the coachman's bench and holding the reins. Democracy demands dictatorship! That struck me as absurd and I must have made an astonished face, because he added impatiently that that is a typical "dialectical contradiction"—a category that I still didn't understand.

That he treated me as a grown-up also had its bad sides. He was always reminding me that I was "maturing ideologically too slowly," and recently he had actually advanced to denunciation when, at supper with us, he accused me of "a lack of knowledge of the fundamental texts." At my age, he already knew the classics by heart! And I? Nothing. I must make up for it immediately! I must pore over the Marxist books because socialism is science. It is necessary to learn its laws. Laws and commentaries. Commentaries and the general line.

What did it matter that this criticism was of little concern to Mother and Michał and even aroused their anger? (She snorted and went out to the kitchen, and he observed coldly that at my age the most important thing is school, because with poor grades I'll be sweeping the streets instead of being concerned with politics.) I felt bad. I experienced Pan Rosenthal's outburst as a betrayal. Wasn't it enough for him that he scolded me in person? He had to also let his big tongue wag in front of them?

And yet, despite these hurtful aspects of his character, I had a fondness for him. Contact with him gave me a taste of being in touch with something great. Whether he was dogmatic or not dogmatic (an "emeritus apparatchik," Karola sneered), he had still rubbed against something that had changed the shape of the world. Revolution, civil war, the triumphant march into Europe—I knew this only from the movies. He shared with me his faith in the triumph of communism throughout the whole world! Even though I was irritated by him, when I left his home I would think, "There is only one road."

I turned away from paintings and bent over the review copies of novels by Balzac, Stendhal, and Flaubert that Michał had recently brought home from the office and that lay scattered over the carpet. Cheap editions, they fell apart, the text was often smeared, and old reprinted pages appeared instead of new ones. I read those books throughout the spring, patiently cutting the pages with my Finnish knife. Thus, I got to know the streets of Paris, described in detail, and the fields of the last Napoleonic battles in which the wounded were still lying. All those volumes fell apart by degrees and Mother, when she cleaned, piled them up in stacks, mixing up their order and authors.

An unusually interesting world emerged from these readings. In contrast to Soviet novels, whose heroes were always right and who acted for the good of all, here everyone was concerned with his own affairs. No one was completely bad or completely good. Various degrees of everything existed. Out of this a combination of hatred and love, cruelty and mercy, humiliation and triumph was created. I nodded, smiling bitterly, when my fears that love and friendship are risky were confirmed. Strangers cannot be trusted.

These matters so engaged my mind that I wanted to talk about them. So I decided to refer to these readings in my lectures. At any rate, the sources of our so-called examples, or literary anecdotes, were not narrowly defined by the regional center. And so, without asking anyone's permission, I wove into my discussion of the new socialist steel-mill town of Nowa Huta the story of Père Goriot. It was just my luck that Vladimir dropped in on this meeting, and when he heard this at first he just lifted his eyebrows and then he glowered. It didn't help that immediately after he entered I called Paris a metropolis of scoundrels and rich men and emphasized the filth and lack of sewers prevailing there.

"*V chem delo?*" I asked him jokingly in Russian when we went out into the hall. "What's the problem? Is it forbidden to compare a socialist city with a capitalist one?"

"It's permitted, but it's not necessary." He placed his hand on my shoulder. "We propagandists must know such things."

Flaubert's story about the two elderly office clerks, Bouvard and Pécuchet, made the greatest impression on me. Having inherited a small fortune, they waste it on idiotic agricultural experiments, archaeology, chemistry, even historiography. Like an entomologist who removes the chitin shells of beetles in order to expose their insides, Flaubert peered beneath the thick shell of human posturing, all those habits, faces, poses, conventions, and seemingly reached the very essence of what is human. Everything there was inextricably overgrown with stupidity, like fatty tissue. It was possible to struggle against it, but it was an unwinnable war since the destruction of stupidity threatened the organism itself with death. This had never entered my mind. I had thought that stupidity derives from ignorance or is a bad habit from which people can be weaned. I recalled the Latin teacher's rhetorical question about why we still understand Livy: "Have we changed so little?" We haven't changed at all! We are still exactly the same.

And so, since that's how it is, will we succeed in building socialism, which demands the remaking of man, and in a short time, to boot?

But maybe Flaubert exaggerated? I started following every step of that pair of his pompous heroes. I deliberated over all their platitudes. I was so close to them that I felt the breeze when they fanned themselves with their hats, and I grew hungry in the cafés they frequented and fetched a slice of bread and dry kielbasa from the kitchen. I found nothing, however, that would overturn my conclusion regarding stupidity.

Who could help me? Karola and Jurek Łobzowski would only mock me. Vladimir? He would have thought it was all nonsense. Pan Rosenthal? He would shower me with an avalanche of words. Then Michał . . . yes,

Michał! But Michał would probably say that I had my head in the clouds instead of concentrating on something concrete.

"There's no help from anywhere," I thought mockingly.

I curled up in the armchair and as soon as I closed my eyes, I dreamed that I was in Warsaw on the corner of Marszałkowska Street and Jerusalem Avenue. I was hurrying somewhere. Weaving in and out among the pedestrians, I kept changing directions. At one moment I split in two. One went this way and the other that way. I still was observing from my old point of view. So, the one who had gone off and disappeared in the crowd was also me. I was overcome with fear, as if I'd lost or squandered something. Which one of us was genuine? I touched my face and woke up in the middle of the night.

The Death of a Communard

The day Michał left for Beijing to conclude agreements about trade and telephone connections, Pani Rosenthal phoned. (I figured out that it was she because Mother didn't speak German with anyone else.) Pan Rosenthal had lost consciousness while reading in his armchair. He'd come to only in the ambulance. He was in the government hospital and wanted me to visit him.

"A stroke." Mother replaced the receiver. "But he can speak."

The next day, on my way back from school, I got off the streetcar in Śródmieście and walked along Hoża Street to the corner of Emilia Plater. Two policemen were standing in front of the clinic, which was located in the former St. Joseph's outpatient facility. I pushed open the left wing of the double door. I pulled out my school identity card in the vestibule and entered the main hall.

"Who are you visiting?" A man behind a little window lifted his head from a large volume and took my identity card.

"Pan Rosenthal."

He wrote something with a pencil in two places.

"Room seventeen."

He handed me a document.

I passed the entrance to the elevator and a corridor that led off to the right where the pharmacy was located and made my way to the coatroom. Among the fur coats, overcoats, and hats, officers' great coats and caps were also hanging. Beyond the coatroom was a staircase with a slickly polished handrail.

On the second floor I entered a long corridor, found room seventeen, and knocked on the white door. When no one answered I began gently pushing it open.

I noticed a sink and mirror directly across from the door, then an empty bed against the right wall, a table with two chairs, and a window covered by a drawn curtain. Beneath the windowsill was a bucket into which water from a damaged radiator was dripping.

Pan Rosenthal lay on the left side of the room, his eyes closed.

Should I enter or not?

I was still unsure if he really wanted me to visit him. Perhaps it was only Mother or Pani Rosenthal who said he did? Because, really, who was I for him? I tiptoed inside only after a moment's hesitation.

Although I stepped as softly as I could, he opened his eyes almost immediately. I stopped. Then he beckoned me over impatiently with one finger. So he did want me!

I approached the bed. His damp, flabby skin was covered with a thin gray growth of whiskers. Above his head hung an electric wire ending in a bakelite globe with a push button.

"I'm here," I said. "How are you feeling?"

"Moof shair," he bellowed.

"Sure, he can speak!" I thought bitterly.

"Don't worry." I sat down. "Michał had the same thing and it passed."

He turned his head indicating "no" and, twisting his mouth in a pitiful grimace, started speaking passionately.

I understood him, but only with the greatest difficulty. After a while, however, I grew accustomed to his crippled speech and comprehended almost everything.

—

He told me about his childhood. But it was strange. I couldn't figure out who his parents were. What did they live on? And where did it all take place? In Poland? There was no Poland then. So, in Russia. Or in Austria, because apparently not in Germany.

My mother was radiant when she reminisced about pre-war times. Pan Rosenthal seethed with fury. She related anecdotes; he criticized social groups and institutions.

The rabbis deceived the faithful and sucked up to the rich. Even the cheder was a tool of class oppression. Merchants cheated their customers, leaseholders cheated beggars.

It was even worse when it came to the goyim. The church! O, that was truly opium for the masses! Not to mention antisemitism. In the Gymnasium the teachers were fools and hypocrites for whom history was colored pictures.

In the meantime, Mammon ruled everything! The big landowners squeezed the sweat out of the peasants and the bourgeoisie drank the blood of the workers.

Finally, someone informed him that without a cadre of professional revolutionaries things would always be that way. The masses must be enlightened. Teach! Teach! And again—teach!

A nurse entered the room. Pan Rosenthal stopped talking immediately.

"You're not tired?" she asked, checking his pulse. "Perhaps it's time for your guest to go home?"

"No, no," he attempted to smile; "he juf came."

"Don't talk too much." She threatened him playfully with her finger and went out.

He followed her with his eyes, and the moment the door closed he started in again. This time, for no apparent reason, he violently attacked the liberalism of the Polish Workers' Party.

So many comrades have been shot from around a corner, and we make nice to the enemy. We must not forget that those who are in prison today will get out tomorrow and will start murdering again. You'll see what will happen when true collectivization begins. The peasants are dangerous and ignorant. Stubborn and ungrateful. Before the war, because of their poverty, they used to divide a match into four pieces; now, they're not interested in an alliance with the workers.

"They would glab the palty by the thloat!"

It was getting late. A gray border appeared around Pan Rosenthal's lips. He was speaking more and more unclearly.

"Please take a little rest," I interrupted him finally. "Perhaps I should go now?"

The echo of the drops dripping from the radiator seemed somewhat higher to me. The bucket was almost full.

"Come tomollow," Pan Rosenthal whispered.

Mother was waiting for me at home with dinner.

"How is he feeling?" she asked, handing me my soup.

"Bad," I said.

"What does he think about the Chinese?"

"What Chinese?" I asked, surprised.

"They've invaded Korea." She pushed the basket of bread over to me. "Four hundred thousand! All of them volunteers!" She giggled.

The Korean War erupted in June of the year I completed tenth grade. Michał was detained in Warsaw and we didn't go on vacation. All summer I went to the movies and watched news chronicles showing the recoiling barrels of field guns, cowardly South Korean prisoners of war, and the burned-out wrecks of "Flying Fortresses."

Mother was offended. *The People's Tribune* wrote that the Southerners started it but the Northerners are advancing like a knife through butter. They've already captured almost the entire peninsula.

"You said there wouldn't be a war!" she screamed at Michał.

"Is it his fault?" Karola soothed her.

"Then let him say whose it is," Mother demanded.

In September, when the American landing changed the outcome of the war, Mother and Karola predicted an immediate armistice. Michał, however, was afraid that General MacArthur's victories would enrage the Russians.

He was right. The Chinese would not have lifted a finger by themselves. And if this was the beginning of World War III? In three years, I would be of draft age.

The next day, Pan Rosenthal was very animated. The incursion of the "volunteers" had put him into a marvelous mood and reminded him of 1920.

During the Comintern Congress that took place in Moscow's Bolshoi Theater, little red flags were repositioned daily, further and further toward the west, on a huge map that stretched across the stage. The delegates clapped and shouted for the next Congresses to be held in Berlin, Paris, and London. What joy that the Central Committee had finally decided to probe with bayonets as to whether the Vistula River lands, the *privislinsky krai*, as they called them, had matured already to revolution.

"Ovel the colpse of white Poland to the Atlantic!" The old slogans were returning to him. "Forward! To Wilno! To Minsk! To Walsaw! *Fpeliot!*"

He was gasping for breath but he soon picked up the thread.

From the palace of the "sugar king" where the Comintern bureau was located he was sent to Białystok. It was there, in the POLREVCOM headquarters, that Julian Marchlewski had handed him parcels containing copies of the Polish Revolutionary Committee's manifesto. Driving to Warsaw in a rattletrap Ford under the protection of a troop of fifty Cossacks, he read about the nationalization of factories, land, and forests. He was convinced that the proletariat and the landless peasants would greet the Red Army men with open arms.

Piłsudski ruined everything.

———

"A miracle on the Vistula!" Jurek Łobzowski had joked once when, attacking his king, which was hidden behind a row of pawns, I unexpectedly forfeited my queen, with which I'd wanted to declare checkmate, and lost the match.

"You play like Tukhachevsky." He'd patted me on the back and started telling me how the Red Army had descended on Warsaw. They were just approaching the Vistula when an attack force that had formed to the south moved to cut them off on the east. It marched and marched, and still there was no enemy. The soldiers saw that the leader was riding hither and yon in his car and was himself searching for enemy patrols. Not a sign. For thirty-six hours they didn't meet any resistance. The Russians allowed themselves to be attacked from the rear.

"My uncle fought there," he said proudly, and swept the wooden figures onto the table.

For a long time I thought about Pan Rosenthal's stories. Despite appearances, they were not chaotic. Rather, he recalled fragments from one and the same party. But why had he selected me? It didn't give me any peace. Maybe he simply had no one else? Or maybe . . . But I was unable to formulate the question, although I attempted to several times. Finally, I gave up and started thinking about what chess piece I resembled. A king? No. Not a queen. I also didn't resemble a rook, as menacing as a tank. A bishop? Attacking on the diagonal? How could I be! Aside from the pawns, only the knight remained, capable of ducking out of every situation.

"Yes, yes," I mumbled. "Probably that's it."

When I came to the clinic the next time, the other bed was surrounded by a cloth screen. A nurse's white cap was moving about above it. Pan Rosenthal explained in a whisper that the person behind the screen had suffered a heart attack. He'd had it right outside the clinic door. Of course, he didn't have a right to be here, but they were afraid to transport him to Infant Jesus Hospital.

A metallic clank came from behind the screen, after which the nurse left the room with a basin in her hands.

The Bolsheviks won power, Pan Rosenthal began immediately, not to change Russia, but to stimulate a worldwide revolution. Lenin didn't believe that communism could be built in one country, especially one so backward. The creation of the Comintern was the greatest event in history. The political vacuum created by the collapse of central governments, the rebellion of the fleet in Kiel, revolts in Berlin and other German cities—all were signs that the hour was striking.

Even one day before the Battle of Warsaw the Party had believed that revolution would break out in Poland. Alas, the masses rose in defense of their own class enemy. Poles! . . . Pan Rosenthal waved his hand dismissively. Marchlewski had warned him that it would be like that.

"The peasants shlaughteled the malaudels."

—

With no viable alternative they started building socialism in one country. No one knew how this could be done. Until finally Stalin, "the foulth geniuth!," pointed the way. Industrialization and collectivization moved full steam ahead. A hellish tempo! In order to get it accomplished before any intervention. It's not at all surprising that so many mistakes were made. How many Trotskyites, Zinovievites, Kamenevites, and Bukharinites eluded punishment and are lurking in back alleys even today! Enemies are everywhere. Therefore, the most important thing is vigilance. (He licked his chapped lips.) People should line themselves up against the wall for their political blindness.

I recalled how Pani Rosenthal, taking leave of us after Michał's birthday celebration and already wearing her hat and coat, had patted me on the head and said to her husband, "*Guck mal, sieht er nicht wie junger Bucharin aus?*" (Take a good look. Doesn't he resemble the young Bukharin?)

He'd glared at her.

"Bukharin!" he'd cried in a stifled voice. "*Nel'zia!* Impossible!"

—

A soft groan came from behind the screen. The shadow of a hand appeared on the cloth and disappeared. Pan Rosenthal started pondering what would happen when that man's family came to visit him. Access to the clinic was restricted. Especially now, in a time of war.

"War?" I whispered, but Pan Rosenthal, preoccupied with the question of how and under what rules visiting passes are given out here, didn't hear me. It would be best if they took the man away.

"To a hothpital," he muttered. "To Infant Jesus."

—

I went out to use the bathroom. Was it possible that the sick man hadn't heard anything? Could he be unconscious? But what if he wasn't? Let's hope that he's sleeping, I comforted myself, but instead of returning to the room immediately I started walking up and down the corridor beside the rows of white doors.

Yes, there is no doubt that Pan Rosenthal is an egotist and a boor . . . But really, what does that matter? Character does not encumber logic. One has to master one's irritation and submit subjective thinking to objective thinking. Had the Bolsheviks defeated Europe there would have been no Hitler. And had there been no Hitler my entire family would be alive now.

But was that a certainty? Grandfather couldn't stand the Russkis and called them illiterates. "Thieves!" he'd cried in Borysław after the exchange of Polish money for Russian. "They're giving one ruble for a złoty!" And Father? I didn't know his views, but Mother had told me how he'd stood in the dark bedroom looking out at the police building in which the NKVD was headquartered, listening in horror to the shots muffled by the rumbling of truck motors ready to drive deep into Russia.

Several days later people with axes had come running into our courtyard and grabbed Mother away to wash the corpses they'd found in the cellars. A bucket was smashed over her head and she was ordered to use her blouse as a rag. One woman had spat in her face. "Wash the men you murdered!" she'd screamed.

Grandfather died of dysentery in Flossenburg. Father was killed by a bomb. What would have happened to them if Tukhachevsky had reached the Atlantic? "Whoever didn't please *batiushka,* off with his head!" Mother repeated time and again, and sang menacingly in Russian, "Siberia, Siberia, I'm not afraid of Siberia."

I returned to the room.

"What took you so long?" Pan Rosenthal asked.

"I had an upset stomach," I replied.

He asked for a glass of water.

He drank slowly. Drops trickled down from the corners of his mouth and soaked into the pillow. Then he gave me back the glass with his trembling hand and screwed up his eyes.

What will it be now? I wondered. More about vigilance?

He started in about the Second World War.

A great victory, that's true. Had I seen how the red flag was hung from the Brandenburg Gate? Power. Prestige. But he worries that the revolution will be stalled in just half of Europe. And that's too little; one shouldn't rest on one's laurels! It's necessary to go farther. Continent after continent. The final goal is still before us.

"The whole wolld!" he whispered. "Evelything."

He picked up the thread after a pause: Fortunately, where the Red Army hasn't reached, propaganda has. Neither the Marshall Plan nor atom bombs helped them. The Cominform arose four years after the dissolution of the Comintern. And now it's beginning. The entrance of Chinese volunteers is the start. Socialism grows from blood.

"Wal! Wal!"

That evening, having fallen silent, he looked me in the eyes as if he expected some kind of reaction from me. Silence descended. "What does he want from me?" I bowed my head and what came to mind was the little room in the back of the department store on Wilson Square.

I'm finishing my lecture and beginning to examine the faces of my audience. They either lower their heads or turn away. No one is eager for discussion. I, however, don't give up. I remain seated at the lecturer's table; I look at my notes as if searching for something there or I glance meaningfully at my Omega. We'll see who outlasts whom! Weren't we told at the briefing at regional headquarters that sooner or later someone would raise his hand?

"So that's how it is," I thought, continuing to keep my eyes fixed on the floor. Agitation demands patience.

I pictured to myself a huge map of the Comintern on the sixteenth of August when Piłsudski attacked and the Russians started to flee. The Bolshoi was empty already because the Congress had ended nine days earlier. But let us say that it remained in session. What about the flags? Would they have begun moving them back toward the east? Not likely. So they would have stayed where they'd been planted, as if for the future, in expectation of the next attempt, which . . . succeeded a quarter century later.

Suddenly, it occurred to me that I was sitting just like the jester Stańczyk in *Twenty-Four Scenes from the History of Poland*. The bowed head, supported by the chin on the breast, and the intertwined fingers. Only he had a cap with little bells and was pondering the loss of Smolensk. And I?

"A fool!" Pan Rosenthal would have said.

A fool . . . Well, what of it? Be that as it may, he'd entertained as many as three kings! Not an easy feat! Ah, if only I could achieve as much! That reminded me of a new student who had come from Moscow and who didn't know Polish. I had observed him with interest, imagining what he had seen in that enormous country and its capital. I also heard him conversing with the top students, but I kept quiet because my Russian was hopelessly weak.

"How is it possible!" Pan Rosenthal would have exploded, "How is it possible not to know the language of revolution!"

I gnawed my lips.

"So . . . ," Pan Rosenthal finally spoke again, "cat got youl tongue?"

"No, it's nothing," I blurted out, as if yanked into answering.

"Come tomollow," and he rang for the nurse.

When I left the clinic it started raining. Although the stop was close by and I didn't have to wait long for the streetcar, I was soaked to the skin.

At home, Mother ordered me to put on my pajamas, sit down, and have supper.

"How is he feeling?" she asked once again.

"Bad."

The telephone woke me. Mother was again speaking German. When I looked into the hall she covered the receiver with her hand and shook her head significantly. He'd died. Soon after I left. No one expected it. Not even the doctors.

Practically all our friends appeared at Pan Rosenthal's funeral: Cesia and Józio Barski, Pan Odwak and Pan Drobot, as well as Lusia and Zygmunt Wierusz. The only ones missing were Karola (apparently, she'd had to go to Kraków again) and Jurek Łobzowski (no one knew why).

Many militiamen were milling around in front of the cemetery, shuffling the yellow leaves with their boots. Pan Wierusz whispered that some general was also being buried today.

It was drizzling. The rain drummed on the umbrellas. Water flowed in streams along the curbs.

The great iron gate was locked. We entered the grounds of the cemetery through a smaller side gate that was opened for us by a caretaker in a military overcoat.

The long, broad Avenue of Heroes stretched black before us. The fallen leaves had been raked into great piles. Through the bare branches of the trees crosses were visible, stretching into the far reaches of the cemetery. On an immense tombstone not far from the gate these words were carved in large letters:

ONLY HE WHO SERVES THE INTERESTS
OF THE INTERNATIONAL PROLETARIAT
CAN SERVE THE INTERESTS OF THE POLISH NATION
MARCHLEWSKI

When Marchlewski's ashes were brought from Berlin I had had a cold and, although I didn't have a fever, Mother had kept me at home. She didn't want to even hear about me going to the train station and then to the cemetery, where the most important of the ceremonies was to take place. At first, I accepted this unwillingly, angry that she was treating me like a child. When, however, wearing a warm bathrobe and wrapped up in a camel-hair blanket, I stretched out on the daybed, I thought that in fact it was a good thing. To wait in a crowd at the station for hours and after that to have to drag oneself across the entire city to Powązki Cemetery! That wasn't for me.

"One can't expect a Minister like Hilary Minc to stand in line," Michał said once when Karola was complaining about the stores concealed behind yellow curtains and emphasizing that the people hate them. "Minc is for thinking!"

Wasn't I all mixed up in my head? What would Vladimir say if he knew my thoughts?! "Communists must be as hard as steel."

I recalled Nikolai Ostrovsky's book about the youth from Shepetovka who fought in Budyonny's cavalry and then, paralyzed and blind, dictated his recollections so that young communists would be shaped by them.

I pushed away the blanket and got up. I took out of my briefcase the biographical sketch of Marchlewski that had been handed out to us lecturers at the last briefing and, turning on the radio to listen to the live broadcast of the ceremony, started reading. But I couldn't concentrate. I was repeatedly distracted from my reading by the sounds of the "Internationale," military marches, or the words of the occasional poems that were being recited:

> The returned comrade is welcomed
> Not, as in the past, by gendarme and informer,
> But by the workers' Republic
> Coming out into the streets in huge numbers . . .

My hand holding the brochure fell limply onto the blanket and my eyes were glued shut. Could I have a fever? I touched my forehead. It was cool. The hero of *How the Steel Was Tempered* would not have made such a fuss about himself. I jumped up from the daybed again and with an energetic step went to the kitchen where I ate an apple and made myself some strong tea. Returning to my room, I stopped in front of the bookcase in the living room and took down *The Three Musketeers*.

"To unwind," I thought.

Lying comfortably, I opened the book at random and immediately found myself on a ship, sailing through the strait of La Manche. They were waiting for me in the port with a horse. I leaped into the saddle and, mocking the cardinal and the perfidious Lady de Winter, galloped off to Paris with the diamond hairpins of the Queen of France. My friends Athos, Porthos, and Aramis galloped behind me.

Again, the voice of the declaimer reached me from the speaker:

> . . . and they will notice that this is not a bier,
> But a heart burning in the urn,
> That living thought is aflame in the ash
> —and they will carry him, tomorrow, into socialism.

"It's interfering," I thought, and turned off the radio.

Pan Józio tugged at my sleeve.

"Soldiers from 1920 are over there." He pointed to graves on the other side of the avenue.

I cast my gaze over a field with cement crosses. So many of them, even though Tukhachevsky had been taken by surprise.

"And over there?" Beyond the cement crosses were rows of birch trees.

"Participants in the Uprising. They were dug out of the ruins after the war."

"Why aren't any of us carrying his coffin?" I asked after a while.

"Us?" Pan Józio didn't understand.

"Well . . . Pan Rosenthal . . ." I swallowed my saliva.

"There wasn't anyone . . ." He spread his hands wide.

"What about us?"

"Too heavy." He smiled indulgently. "You wouldn't have managed." He bent his umbrella over me. "They brought him in earlier."

In front of General Karol Świerczewski's sarcophagus, which stood in the center of the Avenue of Heroes, we turned left and soon caught sight of a hole in the ground and a cart with a coffin. Spades stood upright in the fresh clay and beside them were the gravediggers, Pani Rosenthal, and two old men with open umbrellas.

One of them handed his umbrella to the nearest gravedigger and, having made certain that he would shield him properly from the rain, drew out a sheet of paper from his pocket. In a booming voice, he began taking leave of Pan Rosenthal.

The deceased was born into a world in which injustice and class oppression reigned. Already in Gymnasium he formed a self-educating group. Five students, two farmhands, one railway worker's assistant, and three shoemakers' apprentices belonged to it. On Sunday, near the river, they studied the classics of Marxism. The speaker remembered well how the deceased became a communist. Fleeing to the city before an approaching storm, the "young revolutionary" achieved enlightenment and understood the mechanism of history.

"Meshuggener," Mother formed the word with her lips.

"The deceased was a dialectician," the old man continued, "who understood the Party line unerringly. He thought like a Marxist as naturally as other people breathe. Today we are burying an activist with an exceptional intellectual apparatus and practical experience who transported the flame of revolution to Poland and Germany and returned to his homeland after the Second World War, prepared to dedicate everything to socialism."

The gravedigger who was holding the umbrella involuntarily took a step backward. The old man gave him a scorching look and, taking a quick look at the sky, returned to the biography of Pan Rosenthal who had worked part-time during the last few years in the Section of the History of the Central Committee, cleansing the history of the Polish workers' movement from Trotskyite lies.

Even illness had not broken his will. In the clinic he took an interest in the Korean War and amazed those he conversed with with his analyses of the international situation. The Party was the deceased's life and that is why the people's power assigned him an eternal place in the vicinity of the Avenue of Heroes.

"Honor to his memory!"

He took back his umbrella.

The gravediggers lowered the coffin into the grave on belts, and clumps of wet earth fell onto the wooden lid. There was an odor of rotting roots and leaves.

I imagined that my father was standing among those crosses, angry at not having his own grave.

Right after the war someone had told Mother that his body was found in the ruins of Pani Hirniakowa's house. It seems that some Schupo had found it and ordered that it be buried in the Jewish cemetery. Mother took me there.

The alleys were overgrown with grass. Moss covered the stumps of uprooted trees. Not a trace of digging.

A bomb killed him. But was that really how it happened? Perhaps I had invented it?

The gravediggers tamped down the mound and walked off to smoke. We went over to Pani Rosenthal to offer our condolences.

"There's not even a minyan." Mother embraced her.

"Kaddish!" the widow sobbed. "But he wouldn't have allowed it."

On the way back to the cemetery gate Pan Zygmunt hummed something under his breath and Pani Lusia wondered aloud if it was raining in Mokotów, too, because Marysia was supposed to take Haneczka for a walk.

"An excellent maid," Mother said with conviction.

"A member of the family."

Suddenly everyone started talking about the recent currency change. It was prepared in secret. Not a leak or a rumor. And suddenly, bang! Three new złotys for one hundred old ones. And only one for a hundred in coins.

"A market drain," Pan Odwak asserted.

"I've got a small amount of foreign currency that Michał had left over from his trips to England, Switzerland, and Bulgaria. Just pennies, but still! Should I exchange them, too, or not? There's no way to phone him in Peking . . . I asked him (she indicated me by a movement of her head). He said, absolutely, and right away."

"He's a zealous one," Pani Cesia laughed.

"Super!" Mother added bitingly.

"You can land in the clink for possession of hard currency," Pan Drobot asserted.

"The pounds and francs they took," Mother continued. "For the Bulgarian levs they said no thank you."

They all burst out laughing.

⸺

I scowled at them. The coffin with Pan Rosenthal in it had just been lowered into the grave and, as if nothing had happened, they were gossiping with each other, cracking jokes, and even laughing out loud. Had he meant nothing to them? He'd been a good friend, it seemed; they'd visited each other, conversed, and yet they didn't appear to be concerned. And I? Had that death mattered to me? I had an image of Mother bowing her head significantly over the telephone receiver. I'd felt something like relief, but, horrified that that was inhuman, I'd immediately pushed that impression away from me.

In truth, I hadn't liked him from the start, from the time when after our first visit in his apartment Michał told the story about the heretic-priest who had been shot at dawn by Cossacks from among the troop of fifty guarding Pan Rosenthal in 1920. That affair followed me for a long time. I pictured the unfolding of that incident to myself in detail. After all, he was a Jew! . . . True, Pan Rosenthal learned of the murder only after it had been carried out, but from Michał's telling it didn't appear that he'd had any pangs of conscience. The Cossacks did the killing. And that was all.

Why, then, did I hang out with him? Why did I borrow books, listen to his "lectures," and, when he fell ill and landed in the clinic, visit him almost every day? Lack of will? Devotion? No. Fascination, rather. "The mechanism of history," "dialectical thinking," "the transformation of quantity into quality"—much of what he said made an impression on me and stimulated my mind. I closed my eyes to other matters.

What happened in the clinic was the last straw. His inhuman attitude toward what was behind the screen. (I wonder: is he alive?) The hypocritical concern about whether they'd allow the man's family to come inside. After all, the only thing he was concerned about was his own comfort. The crazy dreams about war! Joy because of Korea. And that pressuring of me, clearly felt, that I should declare myself, that . . . I should swear an oath? A shudder ran through me. It's good, then, that he's gone and won't be harassing me any more.

I took a deep breath.

"You'll miss him." Pan Józio handed me a piece of candy.

"Yes," I mumbled, unwrapping the paper. "We all will."

"Not us." He shook his head, smiling. "You."

I felt a wave of heat, but I didn't say anything. I only seemed to hear someone whispering in my ear, "Thith is not yet the end. Come tomollow."

In the meantime, a long procession for the next funeral had begun walking through the wide-open gate. A military band was playing Chopin's *Funeral March*. We started passing them at Marchlewski's tomb. Branches were reflected in the brass of their instruments. Bayonets glittered over the honor guard's rifles. Drops of water splashed against the brims of their round caps. Perfectly erect soldiers carried the coffin, which was draped in a white-and-red flag. Behind it came scouts with his medals on a pillow. Carts with wreaths. Black letters on silver-and-gold sashes. The widow was escorted by a young girl and a general with wavy lines on his shoulder boards. Finally, a crowd: officers, ladies, and gentlemen with flowers.

"Carnations!" Pani Lusia whispered. "They cost a fortune."

"And the roses?" Mother outbid her.

The band was already passing Świerczewski's sarcophagus, but new mourners kept pouring in through the gate. Now our friends were talking about the dead general. Pan Wierusz had read the *Tribune* in the morning. From 1936 to 1941 there was a gap in his biography.

I stopped listening.

The rain stopped. Drops of water dripped from the trees. Birds began stirring on the branches and several of them flew off into the cemetery.

The old men and Pani Rosenthal drove off in a Citroën. We got into our Demokratka. Mother, Pani Lusia, and I in back, Pan Zygmunt in front next to Dziadzio. The car began to move. The Barskis and Pan Odwak and Pan Drobot were waving at us but I lost sight of them right away.

A violent thud reached us on Okopowa Street.

"My God!" Mother almost jumped. "Like during the war!"

"It's a salvo from the cemetery," I said soothingly.

"What kind of a salvo!" Dziadzio laughed. "Someone's exhaust pipe backfired. It's too early for a salvo."

certificate
of **maturity**

Under the Linden Tree

Physics was taught by Pani Bukowiecka, who was short and thin, with reddish-gold hair on top of which her chalk-smeared glasses often sat. Our lessons took place in the laboratory across from the hall with the columns. Here, a long laboratory table with a metal sink and Bunsen burner took the place of a teacher's desk. The class sessions usually resembled deliberations in the House of Lords, which Michał, at least, characterized as a place where everyone does whatever he wants to do. On this day, the teacher, horrified by our ignorance and approaching graduation exams, had organized a review of all the material. It was now the turn of the question of entropy, or disorder, and Pani Bukowiecka drew two arrows pointing in opposite directions on the blackboard, then crossed out one of them with a large X.

I had already encountered the concept of entropy in Eddington's book, *The Expanding Universe,* which Jurek Łobzowski had bought for me in a secondhand bookstore in Kraków. I had read it all night. It turned out that entropy is constantly growing and it's impossible to reverse the process. (That's what the X on the blackboard was supposed to represent.) Matter, emitting energy, is continuously transforming itself and descending into ever lesser degrees of organization. Some configurations will last longer, but in the end everything will dissolve into light. The earth awaits thermodynamic chaos. A cosmic obliteration of differences, or what the Russians refer to disparagingly as *uravnilovka.*

Isn't this equally applicable to societal matters? Perhaps the virus that destroys the existing order acts the same way among people? If mountains disintegrate, what then of the works of human hands and minds? And yet Professor Rybka insists that communism will crown the history of mankind, the final and enduring system. Enduring? Does historical materialism not take the laws of physics into consideration? Why does Rybka say this?

"Because they ordered him to," Karola would say.

I opened my notebook to a new page and extended the point of my Hardtmuth pencil. What should I draw here? Seeking a theme, I started looking around the lab.

On the side wall, in a wooden cupboard with glass doors, was a silver scale. Sometimes we transferred it to the laboratory table, and with the help of brass weights and thin plates with engraved numbers we checked how much the air in an "empty" jar weighed or if a billiard ball immersed in water loses as much weight as Archimedes predicted it would. We also placed on the scale flies, the heaviest of which weighed eighty grams.

Shelves covered the back wall. On the lowest shelf were a heavy copper transformer, an electrostatic machine that shot out blue and white sparks, and a Wheatstone's bridge with which we measured the resistance of hairpins and metal combs. Higher up were wooden straightedges, triangles, and compasses for drawing on the blackboard with chalk. Finally, right beneath the ceiling, among pieces of honey-gold amber, stood a Leyden jar wrapped in chocolate-wrapper foil.

Only once, when the topic was electrostatics, Żuk (the tallest in the class) took the jar down from the shelf and set it beside the burner. Pani Bukowiecka said then that the creator of this device was a Dutchman, Pieter van Müsschenbrock. Evald von Kleist had built a similar device, but he hadn't told anyone about it.

"Was he so timid?" Abramowska opened her eyes wide.

"Could he have been frightened?" The teacher stroked her protruding chin and her thickly rouged cheeks with her fingers. "When he touched the bottle for the first time he got an electric shock and fainted."

Having finished with entropy, Pani Bukowska took up the movement of a particle. She called Łopatka to the blackboard and told him to write out Newton's first law. The boy started scrawling:

IF NO FORCE IS ACTING ON A BODY

IT WILL MOVE AT A CONSTANT VELOCITY . . .

"How can that be?" Ania Wendek asked, astonished. "It will move even if nothing is pushing it?"

"It either moves or its rests," Abramowska explained.

"Who told you 'or'?"

"Newton," Żuk trumpeted from the rear.

Finally, I hit upon what to draw and with my tried-and-true method made a horizontal line in the center of the page. Above this horizon I started sketching hills and clouds that I made misty by rubbing with my thumb. Soon vegetation covered the ground, dots and dashes above, leaves, branches, and trunks below. Water poured down from the hills. Vertical smudges, gaining in thickness, connected with each other and finally flooded the bottom of the page with the foamy current of a river.

On the bank of the river I placed a knight with a sword at his belt, and beside him a girl facing into the depths of the page like those fishermen's wives in the second painting. Wishing to shade her braid, I replaced the hard H5 lead with a soft H2. Or maybe I should draw her again, but turned so that she is looking at the knight? But could I manage to recreate her face from memory?

—

I had noticed her a few days before in the hall with the columns. (I was standing there with Żuk and competing with him as to which one of us was more afraid of the graduation exam.) She had a blonde braid and under her navy-blue pinafore a sailor's jacket and tie. I thought she glanced at me and smiled enigmatically. Had Żuk seen it, too? She walked off in the direction of our classrooms and disappeared around the bend in the corridor. That's where the corridor ended. I decided to wait until she came back. So when Żuk started getting ready to leave, I procrastinated as long as I could. I wasn't mistaken! She soon reappeared. She was walking back rapidly. The sunflowers embroidered on her slippers twinkled across the floor. Without stopping she looked straight at me again. I saw big, blue eyes.

"Who's that?" I asked Żuk.

"You don't know her? That's The Reader. She knows all the books."

"What's her name?"

"Elżbieta. From the ninth . . ."

"A or B?"

"A," Żuk laughed. "Boy, have you been smitten!"

"What do you mean?!" I shrugged my shoulders.

At the next break I went up to the second floor, stood near the wall newspaper for the ninth-grade class, and, pretending I was reading, glanced stealthily at the girls passing by. She wasn't among them. In the newspaper's main picture a May Day procession was marching. It was led by three men: one wearing coveralls, one a trench coat, and one a green shirt with a red tie. Behind them came a crowd carrying images of the leaders, red banners, and the slogan WE SHALL DEFEND PEACE.

I grew impatient. Should I look in on IXa? No, that's too pushy. I looked at the text under the picture. Its caption: "Who desires war?" I started reading:

> Colleagues!
>
> In the press and on the radio there is a lot of talk about peace. That we must fight for it and defend it like the holiest thing. Let us ask: Against whom?
>
> Not long ago there was a war, the most atrocious in history. We were little then, but many of us remember the round-ups, the street

executions, and the buildings burning during the Uprising. The results of that hecatomb are visible to this day. Ruins and graves, a decimated nation.

It would seem that after such a horrible lesson war would never again threaten anyone, for everyone would understand its monstrousness and draw the appropriate conclusions. Alas, that is not so. There are still those in the world who think completely differently from us. Human life has no meaning for them. They worry only about profit—profit and still more profit. They will sacrifice everything for fortune.

They are manufacturers, bankers, and merchants. In America and in England, the bourgeois countries. They want to make a quick fortune. And how best to amass it? With armaments! But in order to sell rifles, cannons, and shells one must have a ready market. And how to achieve this? Through war. They have no scruples about bringing us to that point.

This is against whom we must defend peace. At present it is not some nation or state that is lying in ambush, but an entirely new enemy: imperialism! A worthless system based on capital, profit, and violence.

"A little naive, but not bad," I thought. But I couldn't dawdle any longer. I quickly cut across the corridor and, pretending to be distracted, looked into her classroom. She was standing between two benches, her back turned, talking with her girlfriends. I retreated and walked away.

"What is the second law?" Pani Bukowiecka asked.
Łopatka wrote:

FORCE EQUALS MASS TIMES SPEED

"That law applies even in Einstein," she stated respectfully.
"And the remaining laws?" Ania Wendek asked.
"They turned out to be approximations."
"Aha!" Ania sighed ironically. "Yet everyone thought they were true."
The teacher wagged her finger at Ania and said that Newton's first and third laws require correction only when approaching the speed of light.
"Where?" Ania expressed amazement.
"Not 'where,'" the teacher corrected her, "only, 'under what conditions.' Speed is not a place!"
"What kind of correction is that?" Ania was not concerned about her gaffe.

"Study physics and you'll find out." Pani Bukowiecka pointed her finger at her and made a mysterious face.

"Oh, thank you very much!"

"Thanks from me, too," Anielka Klepacka whispered, lifting her head from her novel.

—

From then on I would see her in various places. Alas, she was never alone. I decided to lie in wait for her in front of the school after our classes were over. If she came out alone I would walk up to her and offer to carry her briefcase. I'd leave mine in my classroom. Why haul two?

This plan didn't have the desired result, however. I didn't give up; although I was afraid that someone would notice, I lay in wait for her every day. "One of these days it will have to succeed," I consoled myself during moments of doubt.

—

"The third law," the teacher's voice proclaimed.

There was the squeal of chalk:

EVERY ACTION IS ACCOMPANIED BY
AN EQUAL AND OPPOSITE REACTION

"Now what's this about a reaction?" Ania Wendek wrung her hands. "I don't understand."

"Just memorize it like a vocabulary list." Abramowska put her arms around her.

"You mustn't be afraid." Żuk rolled his eyes like a clown.

"But it's true that I'm afraid!" Ania sighed.

Żuk thrust out his chest and hummed the fighting song of our organization:

We're the Union of Polish Youth!
We're the Union of Polish Youth!
We are not afraid of reaction!

"Children! Children!" Pani Bukowiecka panicked and raised her hand with its thin fingers.

The giggling died down.

—

After class I went down to the coatroom and, fastening my jacket buttons, headed toward the open door. Why is Newton's first law only an approximation? What complaint can be brought against it? Is an object capable of speeding up or slowing down all by itself, without a stimulus?

I heard an imperious girl's voice behind me: "Without a briefcase?"
I turned around. Unbelievable! And yet it was she! The Reader!

"I didn't take my briefcase today," I started lying as if reading from a script. "The handle broke off and my mother took it to be repaired. I don't have a spare. I can carry yours." I was acting according to my plan even though stage fright was eating at me.

"Thank you. Please do." She smiled and handed me her bag. "It's very heavy. The teacher returned *The Magic Mountain* to me today; she borrowed it from my mother."

"*The Magic Mountain*?" I asked uncertainly.

"Thomas Mann's novel."

"Aha . . . ," I stammered, as if I knew whom she was talking about. "The Englishman," I guessed.

"What kind of an Englishman!" she laughed. "Mann's a German. He received the Nobel Prize in 1929. Then he emigrated."

"A Jew?" I thought and held out my right hand.

"Wilhelm," I introduced myself.

"Elżbieta." She offered me her hand.

"What's it about?" I lifted the bag a little in order to point at the book protruding from it.

The question obviously animated her.

"A young German engineer, Hans Castorp," she began with a smile, "arrives in Davos in order to visit his cousin in a sanatorium for consumptives. It turns out that he, too, has a spot on his lungs. And he remains there for seven years until the outbreak of the First World War."

"Tuberculosis . . . It's a horrible disease," I interjected.

"When the Germans drove us out after the Uprising, my papa contracted tuberculosis. And things would have gone very badly for him were it not for a certain gardener. The children called him 'Cat's Faith.'"

"That's funny!" I thought. "In Trzebinia, on the walls of our gardener's hothouse where he raised lilies with blue and yellow flowers and long, sharp leaves, cats were drawn in chalk."

"That gardener," she continued, "wrote poems, but he didn't have anyone who could evaluate them. When he heard that there was an intellectual from Warsaw in the village, he brought them over immediately. Daddy corrected his rhymes and he healed my father with his 'pear-apples.'"

"Did it help?"

"Of course it did."

"It's hard to believe that fruit . . ."

"That's the way it was." She didn't let me finish.

The approach of the front was announced by the distant thunder of artillery. She saw trucks with fleeing Germans. One, behind a barn, was crying and ripping up photographs.

"They fled from us, too," I said, and recalled how, with my eyes fixed on the sky lighting up with flashes through the slits in the well casing, I had prayed to my father that the earth, shaken by explosions, would not bury us.

At Wilson Square we turned toward the apartment building across from the Universal Department Store. It resembled the prow of a ship with a cut-off beak that had drilled its way into the square. The front wall, with a druggist's shop and grocery store below and a terrace above them that wasn't used by anyone, was like a mighty captain's bridge with rows of small square windows. The side walls, somewhat lower and running alongside Słowacki and Krasiński Streets, which diverged from each other like rays, were the ship's boards. One of them was shorter than the other because a bomb had destroyed the last stairwell.

"I live here," and she pointed out a window on the second floor.

We went to the rear of the building where a luxuriant linden tree grew behind the iron fence connecting the "boards." Its branches touched an open window that appeared to belong to her apartment. There was a bench under the linden tree, probably brought there from a nearby park, and beside it toys lay scattered about in a wooden sandbox.

"What happened to Castorp?" I asked when she reached for her bag.

"A certain Settembrini, an Italian humanist, took him under his wing. He argued that force and prejudice on the one hand, and freedom and knowledge on the other, are battling for the world." She let her hand drop. "The Italian believed in the triumph of reason. But Hans had his doubts."

"And does someone love someone?" I prolonged our conversation.

"Of course," she smiled condescendingly. "Castorp falls in love with Mme Chauchat. An extraordinary woman! Independent. Full of life. She's always late and when she enters the dining room she slams the door. It's described beautifully! Unfortunately, Hans is shy. I've read three hundred pages already, and he hasn't even spoken to her."

"How does it end?" I picked up the bag meaningfully.

"Badly," she said sadly. "Mama says that Mme Chauchat will leave and Hans will go to war. Well, I've got to go. Thanks."

Our hands touched again. Under the linden she flung her bag over her shoulder, looked around, and ran into the entranceway.

At home, no one had heard of *The Magic Mountain*. It turned out, however, that Karola had read *Buddenbrooks* before the war. Also by a Mann. But was he the same one? It's a popular name . . .

"He fled Germany." Karola glanced at Michał.

"Yes, I know," he confirmed it, and added, "an antifascist."

—

E. (that's what I called her in my heart) and I would meet after classes, walk together to Wilson Square, and talk about books. She knew almost every book that I had read, whether Polish, French, or Russian, but she remembered them differently. I noticed it when we talked about *War and Peace*. She was able to quote entire portions of Natasha's conversations with Bolkonsky and Bezukhov, but she knew virtually nothing about the battles of Austerlitz and Borodino. She was suspicious of victories and saw only misfortune in defeats. She didn't like either the hussars or the cavalry.

She was interested in the education of orphans. I told her about Makarenko's *bezprizornye,* the abandoned children in his orphanage, and about Janusz Korczak, who went to his death with the children. Ordinary families also interested her. Once, she confided that she would love to look into windows in order to see how people eat their dinners, help their children do homework, or sew and mend.

"What's unusual about that?" It was hard to conceal my surprise.

After we reached the ship-building we'd walk back to school in order to set out again for Wilson Square.

—

Once, in order to get out from under rain, we sat down on the bench under the linden tree where it was semidark and the air was close. The large leaves didn't let the rain through. From then on we came there often, resting our feet on the wooden frame of the sandbox that was filled with dirty earth. Usually there were no children here and the only trace of their presence was a shovel stuck in the earth and a scratched-up red boat.

A man's cough could be heard through the open window on the second floor. It was gentle and soft. More like clearing his throat. Her father? I looked over at E. several times, but she appeared not to notice anything. The man who coughed said nothing or else spoke so softly that I couldn't hear him.

At times I caught myself looking at myself through her eyes. In her gaze I was different from how I saw myself "from inside." A trace of shame and fear. Decisive, suave, somewhat arrogant. Leaning my head against the trunk of the tree, I observed E. toying with a torn-off leaf. We would philosophize a little. The sense of good and evil—was it innate or acquired?

"Everyone has it from childhood," she said. "That's why we can't deceive ourselves."

"As a rule," I confessed, "I do everything instinctively. Bing! Bang! Sometimes, however, I think things over for a long time and even after I've made a decision I continue vacillating."

"It torments you . . . ," she lowered her voice.

"What?" I was curious about what she'd say.

"Your conscience," she joked.

"So, you know!" I laughed.

One day it was pouring rain. Water started piling up in the sandbox. It quickly covered the low-lying hillocks and soon all that protruded from it was the handle of the shovel, the stern of the boat that was stuck in the dirt, and the peak of the "mountain" that the children had constructed. Surrounded by a milky wall, we sat in silence. Although the rain didn't touch us, the bench was damp. I ran my finger over it, leaving a wet trail. The water level kept rising. Soon the shovel disappeared and the boat bobbed up onto the surface and began sailing freely toward the "mountain." The foamy liquid started flowing onto the glistening grass.

"So it's impossible to fool oneself?" I asked suddenly.

"Yes, impossible," she said with conviction.

The rain stopped. The cough could be heard again. The boat got stuck on the "mountain" and a fly was circling around the receding water.

Several days later we arranged to go to the All-Poland Exhibition of the Plastic Arts.

At first, E. didn't want to go although I urged her to as hard as I could. My stories about Mayakovsky's futurist posters and the battle depictions from the Russian journal *Ogonyok* made things even worse. No and no! She's not interested in this. And suddenly, when I had already lost hope and stopped trying to persuade her, she said she'd go. I wonder what influenced that decision.

Vladimir stopped me as we were leaving school and handed me an issue of some periodical.

"What is it?" I asked.

"*Free Thought.*" The atheists' monthly. A painting of the Virgin Mary had "burst into tears" in the Lublin cathedral. So many peasants poured in that the entire railroad line was off schedule. We have to resist this.

"Headquarters wants you to say something about religion as the opium of the masses. Marx . . . ," he began, but for the first time I interrupted him.

"I can't manage it." I glanced at my Omega. "I'm in a hurry to get to the National Museum."

"And what's there?" He furrowed his brows.

"Socialist realist art."

"Well, that's probably all right." He clapped me on the shoulder and added amicably, "Isn't it miraculous in its own way that miracles always occur during sowing, harvest, or the digging of root crops?"

"Who knows . . ." I shrugged.

In the streetcar I rolled up the journal so the title wasn't visible. I was afraid of people. There was certainly not a single "atheist" in that carriage. Even I, although I had already stopped talking with my father in my soul and suspected that he harbored evil intentions toward me, could not believe that I would never see him again. "What kind of a communist am I?" I thought bitterly. I'm lacking in backbone. I shirk assignments. I zig and zag. I was overcome with fury at Vladimir. I just had to pop up in front of him! How can I come out against religion when my mother lights candles for the dead, Julek goes to synagogue, and Jurek to church? Anyway, Jews shouldn't have to deal with such questions.

The sun was shining above the museum. Soon, E. arrived. She was wearing a white blouse, gray skirt, and sandals. She was holding a fringed kerchief.

In the marble entry hall, in front of the coatroom, there were piles of felt shoe covers with strings for ties. Leaning against the wooden counter and standing first on the left, then on the right foot, we tied them to our shoes and moved smoothly behind a group that was "skating" ahead of us. A bald man was leading it, speaking at length about the "Party-mindedness of art."

"What is this?" he asked his listeners rhetorically. "Nothing other than comprehension of the truth that the Party is the leader of the nation. This fact must be embodied in a painting or a book."

"Whoever doesn't understand stylistic changes," a short woman added, "supports the old aesthetics and, by doing so, imperialism itself."

The man looked at her with respect and, pointing at a bronze Paul Robeson who, with the gesture of a Roman tribune, was "singing" in front of the entrance to the large exhibit hall, unexpectedly broke into English.

"Sixteen tons," he shouted loudly. (Whom was he addressing? Were there foreigners in the group?)

"A symbol of a proletarian," the woman added now.

E.'s face betrayed nothing. Come on! Let's get to the pictures!

The exhibit hall seethed like a beehive. Officials with briefcases, students, soldiers wearing caps—everyone glided forward against a background of unnaturally large figures of our leaders (Bierut on a rostrum, Cyrankiewicz with a pen in his hand, Rokossowski on a horse) and gigantic forms of workers and peasants.

This was not what I had expected. Not a trace of Mayakovsky. Faded colors and heaviness substituted for his intensity. Nor was it the realism from *Ogonyok*. The fairy tale–like colorful battles with the Germans were painted with different paints. It took an effort for me to master my disappointment.

Ah, well . . . Times had changed. Obviously, this was necessary. One must not be a snobbish aesthete. The Party-mindedness of art is the most important thing. I looked at the paintings again and their stern dignity and simplicity slowly began to reach me. A mood that I knew from conferences and meetings came over me.

In the meantime, the bald man's group had stopped in front of a May Day parade, a reproduction of which hung in the wall newspaper on the first floor, while he himself leaned against its wooden frame. E., watching him, started plucking at her fringes.

"What do you like most?" I asked in order to turn her attention away from him.

"I don't know anything about painting." She pouted slightly.

"But what are you feeling?"

"Nothing," she said reluctantly.

Under the influence of her indifference my disappointment returned. The colors faded away entirely and an ugly grimace distorted the faces of leaders and heroes. When we passed the painting in which boys in green shirts, red ties, and shorts were releasing peace doves, it seemed to me that I'd seen that somewhere. But where? Suddenly, I recalled the German art quarterlies from Ligota. The boys with the doves looked like those other boys from the Hitlerjugend. The comparison horrified me, and turning around as if in fear that someone might have caught me in this juxtaposition, I let *Free Thought* drop from my hand. It fell onto the floor, title up.

"The atheists' monthly . . . ," E. laughed mockingly.

"What's the harm in that? Not everyone believes in God."

"Are you one of them?"

"I don't know myself." I picked up the journal. "What about you?"

"I'm a Catholic."

"Do you attend church?"

"I used to. Not anymore."

"And why?"

"Oh, it's not worth talking about . . ."

"Tell me. I'm curious."

"The priest called our school the devil's abode. The atheists' school! Our school!" she repeated angrily. "I couldn't accept that."

"She knows what she wants," I thought with respect. "She has character." And what about me? I have a muddle in my head. Should I give the lecture or not give the lecture? Why even think about this? I'll tell Vladimir that I don't have time before the exam. He should leave me in peace.

We walked in silence through the exhibit hall with the posters. Again workers, many of them with visored caps on their heads. A woman from Kraków and a peasant on a tractor: FOR PROSPERITY! FOR SOCIALISM! A woman reaper handing fresh ears of grain to Marshal Rokossowski. A young soldier with his mother and father: THE JOY AND PRIDE OF HIS PARENTS. A kulak with missing teeth and extended right hand (his left fist behind his back) differed shockingly from these happy people: OLD WISDOM TEACHES: DON'T TRUST A RICH MAN! HE'LL GIVE TO YOU WITH ONE HAND, AND GRAB WITH THE OTHER! In the middle of the floor the main poster was stretched out on an easel: Stalin in a white uniform with gold buttons and Bierut in a suit. The Polish leader, though smaller, for some reason had bigger ears.

"Someone's going to pay for that," I thought, amused. "Although . . . since it was in the National Museum? Maybe that's how it should be?"

After we left the museum we didn't talk about the paintings. E. said that although the war ended six years ago it was still hard to believe it had. She's always "hearing" the Germans in the Gdańsk Station winding up their mortars that sounded like mooing cows. Everyone in the neighboring cellar died then.

"Mama was crying that we'll never see Father again. He wasn't with us," she sighed. "But I comforted her by saying that we'd meet Daddy in heaven." She tied her kerchief around her neck. "And where did you survive?"

"In Borysław," I replied. "Near Lwów."

"That's why you drawl," she smiled.

"I'm a Jew," I shot back, not exactly apropos, and looked at her seriously.

"Were you in the ghetto?" she asked.

"I was in hiding. By myself or with my mother. Sometimes with my father."

"Did they survive?"

"My mother did."

"And your father?"

"A bomb killed him," I said uncertainly.

"A bomb?!" She expressed surprise.

"A Russian airplane . . ."

"You and your mother?"

"We hid in a well."

"Where?" she shrieked, taken aback.

"Not *where,* but *under what conditions.*" Pani Bukowiecka's voice echoed inside me and I said calmly, "There was a hiding place behind the well casing."

"Do you have a photograph of your father?" she asked after a while.

I shook my head. Once, Mother had taken his photograph out of her pocketbook and, looking me in the eye, had asked if I remembered him. Where was that? In Warsaw? No. Not in Trzebinia either. So, in Ligota. Ever since, I'd avoided that pocketbook. Even when it stood on the credenza I was afraid that it would fall over and its contents would scatter over the floor.

"Do you look like him?"

"I don't think so," I said. "He was tall and blond. But I draw like he did."

"The Polish teacher said that she has a student in the eleventh grade who draws pictures during class. She showed us your little people."

"Do you draw?" I asked.

"Only little houses. Two windows, a door, and a chimney on the roof."

—

I turned the key silently and entered our apartment. In the kitchen, Mother and Pani Krzakowa were talking about the painting of the Virgin Mary.

"A miracle!"

Pani Krzakowa unwrapped the *Tribune* from around the calves' feet she'd brought.

"Apparently, she was also crying in the chapel on Puławski Street."

Mother sniffed the meat.

"Out of grief for us." The merchant wiped her eyes.

"I'll take them," Mother decided. "He adores cold feet."

"Do you add parsnip?" the merchant asked out of curiosity.

"Parsnip, boiled beets, and hard-boiled eggs. Aha!" she reminded herself. "I also need kielbasa to dry."

"A kilo?"

"That would be fine."

"I'll bring it when I come back."

"And where are you going?" Mother asked.

"What do you mean, where!" Pani Krzakowa was taken aback. "To Lublin."

I went into the living room and slipped *Free Thought* into the book by Stalin that already held my notebook with "A Ship in the City." Then I sat down in the armchair and picked up from the carpet the last volume of *The Magic Mountain,* which I'd borrowed from E. Weighing it in my hand, I thought that Michał, like Settembrini, believes in the triumph of reason. Hadn't he declared immediately after the war that history had begun once again? A new concept. The end of social injustice and obscurantism. What did it matter that the country was in ruins and there was resistance and ignorance all around? There would be changes. In socialism, everything is only a question of time. Universities for the gifted. Glass houses for workers.

Karola mocked his naïveté, Julek advised his brother to be careful, Jurek Łobzowski didn't believe that Michał is a true communist because he has a good heart, and Mother was waiting for her husband to wise up so we could leave the country.

Under the linden tree, it was different.

Graduation

Michał was in China.

In the meantime, his secretary, returning ahead of him, brought a silver-gray chinchilla fur coat from him. It was squeezed into a rather small valise. Mother removed it carefully, lifted it by the collar, and shook it gently. It unwrinkled and fluffed out. No sign of being crushed! A fairy tale! Only a little too big. There's always something not quite right. But why? After all, Chinese women are so small.

"Do you remember?" She looked at me.

Yes, I remembered. She'd had a chinchilla coat before the war, too. When she opened the wardrobe I would stand near her, prepared to touch it. "You may stroke it," she'd say. "It's beautiful, right?"

"You have a kind husband!" the secretary sighed and recalled with a laugh how the Director threatened the members of the delegation that he wouldn't pay them their stipend if they bought presents for themselves and not for their wives.

"That's Michał to a T!" Karola laughed afterward.

A few days later, the telephone rang.

"Answer it," Mother said. She was mixing dough for crescent rolls at that moment.

I lifted the receiver.

"An international call," the operator announced. "Please wait. I'm connecting you with China."

"Michał!" I yelled, and Mother started scraping the dough from her hands with the dull edge of a knife.

"Peking on the line," I heard now. "Please speak."

"Hello! Speaking," I said nervously.

"I can hear that," Michał's voice reached me. "Are you studying for your graduation exam?"

Always the same thing. Even from China!

"Of course," I said. "And how are things with you?"

"Did the fur coat arrive?"

"Yes. It's beautiful."

"Does Mother like it?"

"It's just a little too big."

"That's nothing; it can be shortened. For you I have a fountain pen with a gold nib."

"Green? Like a Pelikan?"

"Ruby. For your exam. So you can write nicely."

"No need to worry."

"Well, put Mommy on."

—

A week later the Ministry phoned to say that Michał would return the next day. Mother started thinking about what to prepare to welcome him home. There's no carp in the spring, so fish wasn't an option because he didn't like other kinds. Pani Krzakowa wouldn't be bringing veal for a few more days. The only beef in the stores was intestines. So what other choices were there? Chicken and chicken soup. She'd seen chickens at the market that weren't at all bad.

She had scarcely made up her mind, however, when the phone rang again; this time, it was the secretary. She had just spoken with the Director on a high-frequency line. They were stuck in Sverdlovsk. They'd had an accident with a wheel and were waiting for a new plane from Moscow. There would be a delay. It was unlikely that they'd arrive tomorrow. Maybe the day after. But there was no cause for worry. They're in good hands. We just have to wait patiently.

"The devil take them!" Mother slammed down the receiver. "In good hands! Wait patiently! What else have I been doing my whole life long?"

She grabbed the receiver again and dialed Karola's number.

"Can you imagine?" she began. "Another accident! This is beyond human understanding! No more airplanes. From now on he's going to travel by train."

"Even to China?" I interjected.

She waved her hand at me impatiently.

"The last time it was a wing. Now it's a wheel. I'm not going to let him go anywhere anymore in that damned Russian crap."

—

Dziadzio drove Michał home from Okęcie Airport. Despite his long trip and adventure in Sverdlovsk, Michał did not appear to be tired and was in a great mood. The negotiations had gone well. That they took so long? What of it; the Chinese check every word. They are responsible people and honest. Even the rickshaw drivers to whom he'd given his purchases to transport them to the embassy never stole a thing.

While Mother unpacked colorful towels and lacquer figurines he told us about the enormous receptions at which he'd seen Mao Zedong and Zhou Enlai.

They'd been served various worms and hundred-year-old eggs with green yolks. No wonder he taught their Chinese cook how to make Russian pierogi.

At the opera he was seated in the first row. But they played so loudly it was hard to endure it. Finally, the ambassador advised him to give his invitations to other people.

"Do you know what is the worst curse you can hurl at a European?"

"No, what?" Mother smiled at him.

"May the Chinese invite you to the theater!"

I listened to this while playing with my pen. Some kind of Chinese letter was engraved on the broad nib. I dipped it into an inkwell and sucked the ink inside it with the help of a metal lever. Then I drew swirls on a sheet of Chinese stationery. The pen glided across the paper like a thin brush.

In school, the principal summoned me and asked if I remembered that I needed the Minister's permission to be admitted to the graduation exam. Father was supposed to have arranged it.

"He was in China," I said uncertainly.

"Yes, but he's back now."

"Yes," I stammered softly.

"Remind him. It's in your own interest."

The next day, Karola wrote the petition, Dziadzio drove it over to the Ministry of Education, and Michał made a phone call to wherever it was required. Three days later, with permission now, I knocked on the principal's door again.

She was surprised by such a speedy resolution of the matter.

"What, already?" she asked, mockingly. "That was quick!"

"As you wished," and I gave a little restrained smile.

"Well, yes." She looked over the letter from the Ministry attentively. "Now, let us hope from now on everything will depend only on you."

As I left her office I encountered Vladimir.

"You put me in some fix with this religion!" He shook his head. "I don't have a single lecturer."

"What about yourself? Can't you give the talk?"

"What are you saying! I've got the exam on my mind."

"And I don't?" I shrugged.

"Well, yes," he growled reluctantly.

"Besides which," I added, "is it worth fighting against religion?"

"Religion is the opium of the masses," he recited coldly. "It is ignorance and superstitions. You don't want to defend reason? Are you capitulating? Where's your scientific worldview?"

"Here!" I pointed to my forehead. "But reason has its limits."

"What are you talking about?" He raised his eyebrows.

"We don't know everything," I said. "And the world is infinite."

"So what do you propose? What should we rely on?"

"On reason, of course, but in certain matters let everyone do what he wants to."

"In what matters?"

"Conscience."

"That's just it!" he bridled.

"A fundamental principle: live and let live."

"Even class enemies?"

"What enemies? Churchgoers."

He shook his head.

"People have to believe in reason!"

"By being forced to?"

"Who's talking about forcing anyone? Am I?" He pointed at himself and added after a moment, "By force of arguments."

"What kind?" I asked soberly.

"In general: science. Physics, evolution, and, especially, astronomy."

"Today's laws will turn out to be errors or approximations tomorrow. Like Newton's laws."

"Marxism, too?" He changed his tone abruptly.

"Marxism?" I repeated and looked away.

"Have you fallen asleep, or what?" he grumbled.

"No, what gave you that idea . . ." I lifted my head.

"You've changed lately." He looked me in the eyes.

I was overcome with anxiety.

⌁

The graduation exam was approaching.

For a couple of days now Żuk and I had been quizzing each other on history. He lived near E. His room was small and narrow, a tiny den in comparison with the living room in which I lounged in my armchair. Except that the living room belonged to everyone while this "hole" was his exclusively.

Żuk stretched out on his daybed and I sat on a chair next to his desk.

We mainly hammered dates into our heads, especially the dates of wars and battles. As if everything else was less important.

"Wars and wars," Żuk sighed. "They couldn't think up anything better."

"Do you think a new one will break out?" I asked gloomily.

"It'll be the next date . . ."

Once, Łopatka came and we started discussing who would receive the title of top student after the exam.

"Weissówna," Żuk wagered.

"Abramowska," Łopatka countered.

"But do you know," I asked unexpectedly, "who would definitely have gotten it?"

"Who?" they asked, curious.

"Suchocki," I said smiling, thinking that if he hadn't left school we would certainly have studied together and maybe we would both have gotten it.

"You're wrong," Żuk insisted.

"He wouldn't have had a chance," Łopatka seconded him.

"Why?" I asked, surprised.

"He didn't belong to the Union of Polish Youth."

The day before the written exams I got together with E. She was leaving the next day for a school trip to Czechoslovakia.

"Before the graduation exam," she said, "they get the younger classes out of the way."

"Call me after you return. Classes will be over then."

"Fine."

"Do you have my number?" I asked, surprised that she didn't ask me to give it to her.

"No," she replied calmly.

"Then how do you expect to get it?"

"In the usual way. From the post office. There's a telephone book there."

"And what if my number is restricted?" I made a secretive face.

"I doubt it is."

"On what grounds?"

"On the grounds of . . . intuition." She chuckled.

I tore a page out of my notebook, took out my Chinese pen, and wrote down the number.

"Tomorrow's the Polish exam . . . ," I mumbled, handing her the folded slip of paper.

"What will you write about?"

"How should I know?" I said, taken aback. "After all, I don't know the topic."

"You can write independently of topics."

"How's that?"

"If you have some idea in your head. When one really has something to say."

"I have various things to say."

"Well, at least, what would you like to write about?"

"About *The Magic Mountain* . . . ," I laughed.

"Did you finish it?" She was pleased.

"The first volume."

"Oh, then you'd better not." She quickly lost her enthusiasm.

"Of course I won't. I was only joking."

"Then what?"

I thought about it.

"There's something, but I don't know how to tell you."

"Tell me at least what it's about."

There was a moment of silence. I thought about the notebook tucked into Stalin's book.

"I'll write it and then I'll show it to you. Or I'll read it out loud."

"I'm going to hold you to it."

On the written exam I chose to write about the poetry of Broniewski and I took the approach that I knew was required. Revolutionary-patriotic contents. Revolutionary romanticism. The myth of Promethean sacrifice. Valor and dedication. Waryński the proletarian leader. The Dąbrowski coal fields. The giant furnaces of Magnitogorsk. I could go on like that for pages on end. In conclusion, I adorned it all with a quote from Bierut, who said that socialism does everything for the development of man while imperialism disdains man and is intoxicated with the cult of the dollar.

I handed in my work with the conviction that I would get a good grade. If only I hadn't tripped myself up on spelling.

Now mathematics.

We were allowed into the gym at 8:45. The exercise equipment had been removed. Only the ladders that were fixed to the walls remained. There were three rows of desks, separated equally from each other to make cheating impossible. On each desk were a couple of pieces of paper, writing implements, and a ruler and compass. Facing the desks, behind a table covered with a green cloth, sat Pani Bukowiecka, some man from the central school administration, and Professor Rybka, who checked the roll.

At nine o'clock the principal and the math teacher, Pan Błoński, who taught only astronomy for our grade, entered.

"It's time," Pani Pawelcowa signaled by nodding her head.

Pan Błoński cut open a white envelope with his penknife, removed a sheet of paper from it, and walked over to the blackboard. We followed

every movement of his hand. Three problems: one in algebra, one in trigonometry, and one in geometry.

"You have five hours," said Pani Pawelcowa. "You do not have to do
them in order. Solutions must be written in ink. You may use pencil only
for your rough calculations, but you must also hand in your scratch paper.
Are there any questions?" She looked around.

"May we go to the bathroom?" Łopatko's voice was heard.

Someone laughed uncertainly.

"One at a time," Pani Bukowiecka smiled.

"And report your name before you go out," added the principal. Then
she looked at her watch and said, "The time is measured from right now."

And she left together with Pan Błoński.

I took out my ruby pen, copied the problems, and looked at them
closely once more. The algebra question demanded knowledge of equa-
tions with two unknowns; for the trigonometry question, the law of sines;
and for the geometry question, Tales's theorem. I knew it well.

I removed my Omega, placed it on the desk, and got down to work. Because I had difficulty with multiplication and division, I solved and checked
the first two problems with letters so as not to make a mistake in this area
at least. Only then did I insert numbers and check the results separately.
Then, with the help of ruler and compass, I did the geometry. Four hours
had passed. Weissówna and Abramowska were still writing. I was first!

Pani Bukowiecka, walking back and forth among the desks, stopped
beside me several times. Finally, after one of those times, she pulled over a
chair, sat down, and looking sideways ostentatiously, started fanning herself with a brochure of some sort.

"Have you finished?" she asked softly.

"Yes," I whispered.

"Did you check your answers?" She barely moved her lips.

"Yes."

"Well then, show me what you've cranked out," she said through her
teeth.

I pushed the paper over toward her.

She scanned the lines and then started writing down some fragments
on the back of the brochure.

"Is something wrong?" I couldn't restrain myself.

"You'll find out at the oral exam." She stood up, smiling, and again
started walking around between the rows of desks.

She'd spoiled my good mood. What was she really concerned about?
Had she wanted to warn me about something in this way? Had I made a
mistake somewhere? Did she want me to check everything again?

I looked at my Omega! Half an hour left! I began from the beginning. Step after step. But I couldn't find a mistake. I lifted my head from the page and sought my teacher's eye.

She was sitting beside Ania Wendek and fanning herself with a folded *People's Tribune.*

The brochure was lying on the desk.

When I got home, Mother and Karola were in the dining room.

"Well, how did it go?" they both screamed almost simultaneously.

"Very well. I finished first."

"That doesn't mean anything," Mother bristled. "You could have made mistakes."

"I don't think so." I chuckled mysteriously.

"What makes you so sure?" asked Karola.

"One knows certain things." I couldn't stop bantering. "Besides which, the teacher saw."

"And?"

"She wrote down my results and walked away . . ." Still, I bit my tongue. "No, it's nothing . . ." I waved my hand dismissively.

"That's some proof!" Mother jeered.

"You'll see and you'll be convinced."

"I believe him." Karola squeezed my hand.

Mother cheered up, too.

"Well, in that case . . . ," she interjected, "it's the polytechnic, right?"

"I don't want to be an engineer."

"What then?" asked Karola.

"I don't know yet. I'd like to study history."

"Some profession!" Mother made a pained face.

"In that case, economics."

"Professor Schaff once told Michał . . ."

"Who is Schaff?" I interrupted her, pretending that I didn't know whom she was referring to.

"Don't joke," Karola interjected. "The greatest Polish Marxist."

"He told Michał," Mother continued, "that you should knock that out of your head."

"Why?"

"There's no reason to ask. He knows."

"Now that's an argument for me!" I declared ironically. "In that case," I poured oil on the fire, "I'll go study in Moscow."

"What?!" Mother almost leaped up.

"Since everything here is bad . . ."

"Don't be a fool!"

"I'm speaking seriously. After all, courses of study are better there."

"You've lost your mind! Anyway, I won't let you."

"I'll have a talk with Michał."

"Be my guest."

"Why are you so against it?" I looked her in the eye.

"We didn't run away from there in '44 so that you could return now."

"On a Polish passport? That's different, I should think."

"Russia is Russia!" Mother said. "Anyway," she changed the topic, "Julek has applied for a passport to Israel. I hope that won't hurt Michał." She stood up heavily. "I'll make you something to eat. I've got compote. Would you like some?"

"Yes."

"And find Andersen's *Fairy Tales,* because Lusia needs it for Haneczka."

Julek's decision threw me off balance. So he'd done it! And I'd thought he was only engaging in idle talk. What would happen now? Would Michał not be made a Vice Minister? Or maybe they'd throw him out of work completely?

I took out the *Fairy Tales* and sat down in the armchair. Once, I had dreamed that a sorceror in a sleigh kidnapped Kay. I'd even sketched it. Yes, I'd definitely sketched it. What did he look like? Where are those sketches? I probably threw them out. I started leafing through the pages. I recalled how Gerda found Kay in the palace of the Snow Queen. He was sitting in the middle of an empty hall whose floor was formed by a frozen lake. Its surface was cracked into millions of little pieces and Kay was assembling numbers and words from the sharp fragments.

I curled up in the chair.

I dreamed that I was in the well. The large stone with which we concealed the entrance was pushed aside into the interior of the hiding place and in the bright light everything could be seen clearly. We were huddling together like rats.

"Murderers!" our landlord yelled from above. "The police are looking for you! They found him hanging by his tie."

"Max, calm down!" Kopcio crawled out of the well to mollify the landlord.

What had happened began to sink in. A bomb had struck Pani Hirniakowa's house and exposed the attic. Father was hanging there on a tie attached to the rafter. It was determined that he was a Jew. The Schupo decided that he was killed by other Jews who had fled. By us, apparently.

"Right after I left with Moszek . . . ," Mother whispered.

"He didn't want you to come back." Nusia put her arms around her.

"I can't live like this," Mother said.

"He knew he was dying. What would you have done with the body?"

"Oh, stop it . . . ," Mother burst out sobbing.

"Think about him," and Nusia nodded in my direction.

They started crawling toward the opening.

"Where are you going?" I screamed.

"Quiet!" They both put their hands over their mouths at the same time. "We have to slide the stone back in place."

I was afraid that they would run away!

"Don't leave me!" I screamed as loudly as I could, and overturned the bucket. Horrified that I had dumped out our excrement, I woke up with a start.

"You were tossing around so violently that you spilled the compote," I heard Mother's voice from somewhere below. She picked up the glass from the carpet.

Karola came in, intrigued by the racket.

"What happened?" she asked.

"He had a dream about something," Mother said. "It's all because of that exam. I still have a dream in which I forget to appear for the French exam and they are going to have to take back my diploma."

So, it was only a dream! Fortunately! I picked a piece of cooked apple off my cheek and settled in more comfortably. Again, I remembered nothing.

"Eat your sandwich." Mother handed me the plate.

"My throat hurts."

She touched her lips to my forehead.

"Is it cool?" Karola asked.

"Yes."

"I wouldn't mind drinking some compote," I said.

In the morning, before the oral exams, I realized that I didn't have my Omega. What could have happened? I'd fastened the strap insecurely and it had fallen off somewhere without my noticing it. That would be disastrous. Or maybe I'd simply left it on the desk in the gym?

If that's what happened, there was a chance that I'd get it back. Unless someone stole it . . .

An unpleasant shiver ran through me. Why do things like this always have to happen to me? What will Mother say? And Michał! Old Pan Akerman appeared before my eyes, the one who in Trzebinia, shortly before his death, had studied the Omega's works through his loupe. Those damned dead objects! I completely lost all desire for breakfast.

"You're going to the exams without eating?" Mother bristled. "You've lost your mind."

"I'll think better," I grumbled, carefully pulling down my shirt sleeves.

"More likely, you'll faint," she fired back, and persuaded me to eat a cheese sandwich.

In school I started searching right away. First, I approached the janitor, Pan Stolarczuk, and asked if he'd happened to find a watch. No, he hadn't found one, nor had anyone reported finding one to him. Then I headed for the teachers' room and asked for Pani Bukowiecka to come out.

"I lost my watch. A commemorative Omega . . . Could you please ask if anyone has found it?"

"Are you sure it happened in school?"

"When I was working on the mathematics exam it was still lying on the desk. That's the last time I saw it."

She promised that she'd find out.

Then I confided in Żuk.

"Try to find out something. You can't imagine how important this is to me."

He nodded sadly.

The oral exams in Polish, mathematics, and especially history went smoothly for me. All that remained was physics. I wouldn't have been at all anxious if it weren't for the fact that Pan Błoński was one of the examiners.

Before he started teaching us astronomy I had known him only from stories. Fame surrounded him. An exceptional mind. A splendid mathematician. A tongue like a razor. So I was very happy that he was going to come to us. The more so since I already knew Jeans's and Eddington's books and was passionate about them.

Pan Błoński, however, turned out to be a strange pedagogue. He made jokes, indulged in long digressions ("general education," he called them) in which his coolness, even loathing, for the new system could be felt. He bantered with the girls. For astronomy, however, or at least its students, he had no respect. "It's too hard for you," he repeated. Or, "Who cares about astronomy today?"

"What do you mean, who?" I rebelled internally. I do, for example. And I raised my hand to ask a question that was supposed to dazzle him with my knowledge. The teacher didn't let me speak, however. And he never questioned me about anything.

"Why doesn't he call on me?" I asked Żuk once during a break.

"Why does it upset you?" He shrugged. "It should make you happy. You're left in peace."

But I didn't have peace. "He's deliberately ignoring me," I told myself. "What's it about?"

Finally, during one of our lessons, when the occasion arose I jumped up without being called on, to speak about the theory of relativity. Pan Błoński didn't interrupt me; he listened to everything I had to say, after which he said drily, "Did someone ask you to speak?"

"No." I bowed my head.

"Well then?" He pulled a haughty face. "We don't need your two cents here. We can manage without you." And he started ostentatiously spouting some kind of drivel.

I sat down heavily. Well then, everything was clear. He couldn't stand me because I am . . . I didn't finish the thought, however, because another voice immediately rose up in me saying that I am oversensitive and am always nitpicking. "Here, in this school?!" I shouted inside myself. "In this 'drop of socialism'? A teacher is an antisemite? No, that's impossible!"

But yes . . . Too often in his "general education" digressions allusions appeared to "foreigners," to "those who once were this and today are that," to "big-mouthed smart-alecks." I had no doubt whom he was alluding to, though he did it cautiously and never overstepped a delicate line. I couldn't accuse him of anything. True, he disparaged me, and in a particular way, but at the end of the year he gave me a grade of B, which was a real distinction because he often joked that only he was capable of earning an A.

For this reason, too, walking around among the columns now and waiting to be called, I was thinking about Pan Błoński. If only he doesn't play some trick on me. After all, this is his last chance.

The door to the physics lab opened every so often and Pani Bukowiecka invited in the next poor soul. We followed him with our eyes without interrupting our nervous pacing. Only when he appeared again, pale and perspiring, did we run over to greet him.

"Well?" we all shouted. "How did it go?"

He waved his hand resignedly.

"What about Błoński? Does he also ask questions?" I interrogated him.

"Does he ever!" Żuk teased me, although he hadn't been examined yet. "And he has especially sharp teeth for you."

"Stupid jokes," I muttered.

"You won't come out of there alive," Łopatka gigled. "He'll shred you into a pulp. Like a Baltic jellyfish!"

Finally, my hour struck.

Pan Błoński was seated behind the laboratory table. At the sight of me he unfolded a newspaper and started reading ostentatiously.

"It's the end." A shudder came over me. "He's going to finish me off."

In the meantime, Pani Bukowiecka signaled to me that I should go over to the blackboard, and she leaned against a desk.

"How does the emission or absorption of light take place?" she asked.

"In quanta."

"Who discovered this?"

"Max Planck."

"When?"

"In 1900."

"What is a quantum?"

"A portion of light whose energy is equal to the product of Planck's constant and the frequency of a light wave."

"How much does Planck's constant equal?"

I wrote that h with a stick drawn through it equals 1.05438 times ten to the minus thirty-fourth power and, I added, it is one of the fundamental constants in the cosmos.

"A true constant, my dear," Pan Błoński spoke up from behind the newspaper, "is only the result of a mathematical proof. The square of the hypotenuse is equal to the sum of the squares of the sides, and twenty-six is the only integer found between the square and the cube of two other integers. Those are constants. Everything else changes."

I listened to this in terror, but at the same time, with admiration. He had suddenly shown his lion's paw. But what was he aiming at? Could this be the prelude to a frontal attack?

But no attack followed. Despite this, I couldn't restrain myself from somehow parrying Pan Błoński's thrust.

"That's true, I agree, but . . . ," I began, but Pani Bukowiecka nervously interrupted me and said sharply, "This is not a scientific discussion; it's just a graduation exam in physics. So, tell me, please, what is a perfectly black body?"

"A perfectly black body completely absorbs the rays that are falling on it."

"And what does it emit?"

"Nothing."

"I have no more questions."

"That's all?" I asked hesitantly.

"Yes, thank you."

Pan Błoński laid down his paper. A pale, contemptuous smile flickered across his face.

The day before the examination grades were to be announced the principal summoned me.

"Bravo, my boy!" she began. "You passed with all A's. Congratulations. To tell the truth, I didn't expect this. In principle, you deserve the title of top student. You cannot receive it, however, because you loafed around for two years and rode along only on what you were good at. We have to consider the entirety: industriousness, meticulousness, and so forth. Several girls deserve this title more than you do. True, it guarantees acceptance without an exam to a higher institution of learning, but you'll do fine anyway."

"Did everyone pass?" I asked.

"Everyone," she replied. "But I have a 'consolation prize' for you." She opened a desk drawer and extracted my Omega.

A hot wave came over me.

"Isn't this yours?" she asked with a mocking smile.

"Yes!" I almost shouted.

"It would be better if you didn't bring such expensive objects to school. It's your father's, isn't it?"

"It was . . . once upon a time . . . ," I stammered. "He gave it to me."

She shook her head indulgently and handed me the watch.

"Thank you! Thank you very much!" And I kissed her hand.

I returned home with a light heart. I opened the door and fell into the apartment, wanting to tell Mother as quickly as possible about the principal's congratulations. But no one was home. I made myself a slice of bread and dry kielbasa and went into the living room.

On the canvas of *The Future* the paint had flaked off in many places and the sails looked as if they had holes. Perhaps Józio could fix it?

So, the graduation exam was behind me! The end of school. Freedom! What was E. doing? Surely, she'll call soon.

I took out Stalin's book and with it the notebook with "The Ship" and started reading it, imagining how I would read it to E.

"Why did I say as soon as I finish writing when I had already finished it?" I lifted my head from the text. "I lied to her again."

"Doesn't your conscience bother you?" It was as if I heard her voice.

I reached for the Chinese pen, took another look at *The Future,* and started writing a poem on a new page:

> *Paper boats sail on a springtime puddle,*
> *Their mud-coated boards soak up the water.*
> *The boats grow ever heavier and will never see the shore,*
> *They will sink on the wrinkled surface.*

Parade

We waited for our turn.

In our tri-cornered caps made from flyers, amid a forest of flagpoles, we sat in the roadway, eyes fixed on the end of the lane. Behind a line of security personnel wearing red armbands, their hands joined to prevent anyone entering the roadway, marched rows of people with flags and medals. Occasionally they stopped to let in groups from the cross streets. At those times they propped up the staffs of their flags on the pavement and the rods on which mock-ups of tractors, houses, and factories rested, and let their heads droop. Then, as if on command, the security men blew their whistles again and the parade moved on.

"It's already after noon," Łopatka complained, "and we had to assemble at seven."

"What would you have preferred?" Żuk drawled. "It's always the same."

"It's not easy to coordinate a mass demonstration," Vladimir informed us, and pointed to my tie. I lifted my hands to my neck. The tie was loose. I tightened the knot and put my hands in my pockets.

A chess piece! A knight! How come I have it with me? I pulled it out slowly and looked discreetly at my slightly opened hand. It leered at me with its eye. Yes, of course! Jurek Łobzowski . . . yesterday . . . and the others . . . the farewell! They had come to say goodbye to me as if I were going away somewhere. "It's only a parade," I said, but they kept insisting, "Take care of yourself! Be well!" Pan Józio and Pani Cesia. Karola and Julek with a valise. They gave me presents for the road. "Leave me in peace," I said. "I don't need anything. I'll be back in the afternoon."

"It just begins in the afternoon," said Karola. "Here, take along these pears. They'll certainly come in handy."

"And take this," Julek whispered, thrusting tefillin into my hand.

And finally Jurek . . . with this knight: "Remember, that's the most important thing."

Suddenly the prow of a ship appeared at the end of the lane. It was decorated with the figure of a woman with outstretched arm. The ship moved slowly until the hull, supported on rods carried by sportsmen, occupied my entire field of vision and blocked out the buildings on the other side of the street. At that moment a whistle sounded and the mock-up fell down. Only the masts and the wooden arm of the woman protruded above the heads of the security personnel.

"Stand!" Vladimir bellowed. "That's our ship."

Throwing off our tri-cornered hats, we started running in that direction.

"Onto the deck!" Vladimir pushed us from the rear.

"Me, too?" Żuk asked in surprise.

"We undeserving ones," Łopatka bowed and scraped like a gentrified peasant.

"Faster!" Vladimir urged us on. "Just watch out for the deck! Don't stamp on it! So as not to break it!"

We clambered up. A persistent whistle—and the ship rose up, sailing above the crowds on the sidewalks.

Passing alongside the lines of security personnel and militiamen we approached the dais. Who was standing there? I couldn't see. We stopped again in order to let another group in until finally we went all the way.

"Lengthen your stride!" the security men shouted.

"Left!" Vladimir commanded. "Left! . . . Left! . . . Left! . . ."

A military band was standing in front of a café. From above I saw their green caps, the golden interiors of the trumpets, and the white skin of the drums. The conductor raised his arms. The instruments flashed. The roar of trumpets! The crash of cymbals! The "Red Banner" resounded. Vladimir started conducting and soon the words of the marching people reached us:

> The executioners have long poured out our blood,
> The people's bitter tears still flow,
> However, the day of reckoning will come,
> Then we will be the judges!

But what is this? Are my eyes deceiving me? Mother and Pani Lusia are drinking coffee at a little table. The café is open! On such a day? Mother points me out feverishly to Pani Lusia, who is looking in her pocketbook for her glasses. She can't find them.

> So onward, onward, let's raise up our song!
> Our banner floats above the thrones,
> It carries the thunder of vengeance,
> The anger of the people,
> Sowing the seeds of the future.

Suddenly Żuk and Łopatka leaned over to me from both sides and, screaming out the chorus, started singing at the top of their lungs:

We, the First Brigade,
The rifle-bearing group,
Have flung our life's fate
Onto the pyre,
The pyre, the pyre!

"Have you gone mad?" I hissed.

From behind the wooden arm the beams of the dais loomed up.

The deck rocked and lowered violently. I almost fell down. At the last minute I grabbed hold of a mast. In the meantime, Żuk and Łopatka had jumped down and disappeared in the crowd. I raised my head slowly. On the dais, surrounded by secretaries and generals, stood Pan Rosenthal with his finger pointing at me.

"Well, at last!" he shouted. "You've come! I've been waiting for you for so long."

"What do you mean, long? After all, I came to see you every day . . ."

"But you had your head in the clouds. You spent time sitting in the bathroom. Other people spoke . . . they whispered: 'He's an arrogant aesthete. There'll be no use from him.'"

"I passed with all A's."

"The graduation exam!" he bristled. "The only important things are dialectics and the mechanism of history. Don't be so worried! I didn't believe that you are lazy and a maneuverer. That you eavesdrop in the streetcar to hear what people are saying about the Uprising. I believed in you and I was not mistaken."

"What do you mean by that, sir?"

"You came! That's the most important thing. For me, that's a declaration."

"I'm not declaring anything."

Pan Rosenthal held out his hand as if he wanted to restrain me, then turned around to the people gathered on the dais:

"Honored comrades! This young man is giving me back my life! Thanks to him I exist. Thanks to him and within him. I name him my successor."

"Long live!" someone cried from the crowd.

"Long live! Long live! Long live!" the megaphones roared.

I felt weak. I started to descend from the deck.

"Where to?" shouts resounded.

"Seasickness," I mumbled. "I'm nauseated."

"Help him! Take him under the arms!" Pan Rosenthal shouted. "His place is here. He'll recover in just a minute."

Vladimir and the security personnel grabbed me under the arms and carried me up onto the dais as if I weighed nothing.

"Welcome, comrade . . . ," a general said to me. "What is your Party pseudonym?"

"Horse . . . Horse . . . ," the word twisted in my head, but I didn't say anything.

"Come on, say it, don't be ashamed!"

I reached into my pocket, but instead of the chess piece I touched the tefillin. I slid my hand nervously into my other trouser pocket. There it is! I pulled out the horse. But before I could begin speaking Vladimir grabbed it from me and cried out joyfully:

"His pseudonym is Jumper! Because he's able to jump! Very high. To the stars!"

Loud bravos resounded and Vladimir added, "And he says that up there . . . there is no God!"

"Give it back!" I screamed in a rage and woke up.

Did I wake up? Was it all a dream? Or, rather, a fantasy? Or maybe I was still dreaming? In my hand I held the notebook with the notation, "Ship in the City," that I wanted to read to E. She had just returned from Prague and phoned me. Now I am waiting under the linden tree for her to come downstairs. Not trusting myself and thinking I was still asleep, I looked around. The bench and the sandbox. The familiar courtyard. The linden tree. And the window from which a soft cough could be heard every so often.

Yes, I knew where I was.